Satoshi Yamamoto

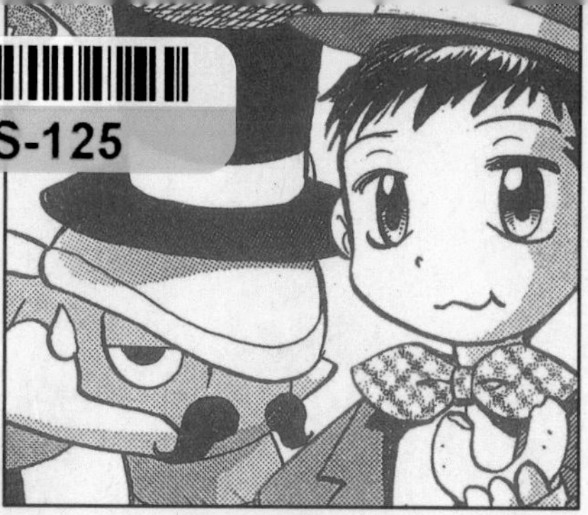

Pokémon™ Adventures Diamond and Pearl Platinum

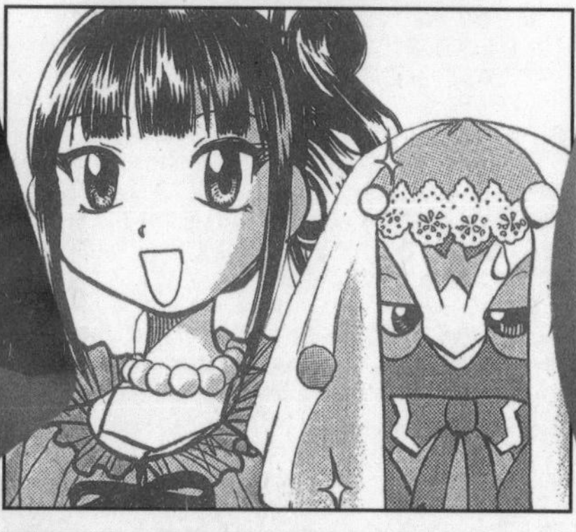

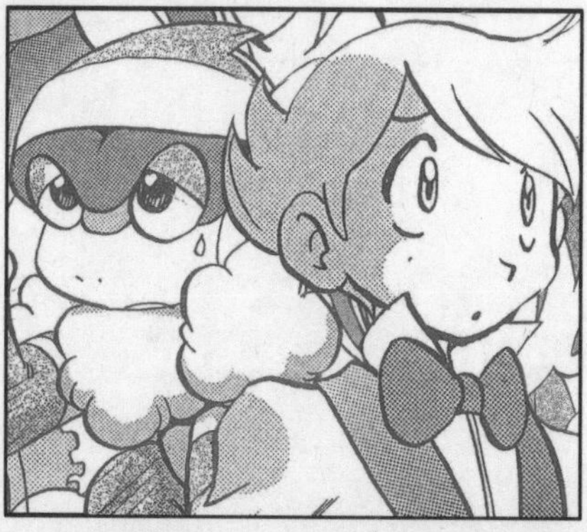

Story

Hidenori Kusaka

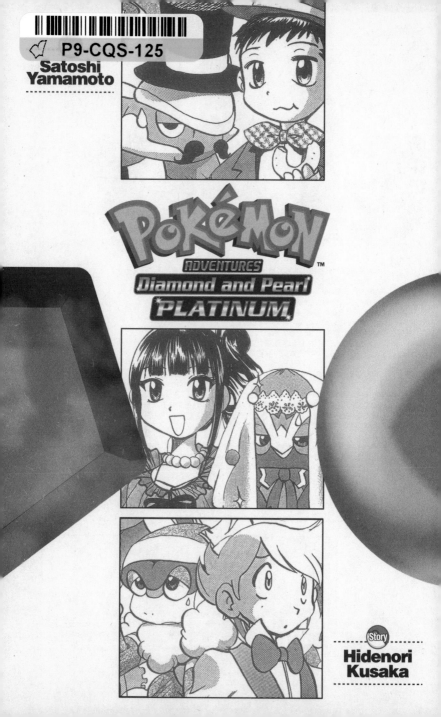

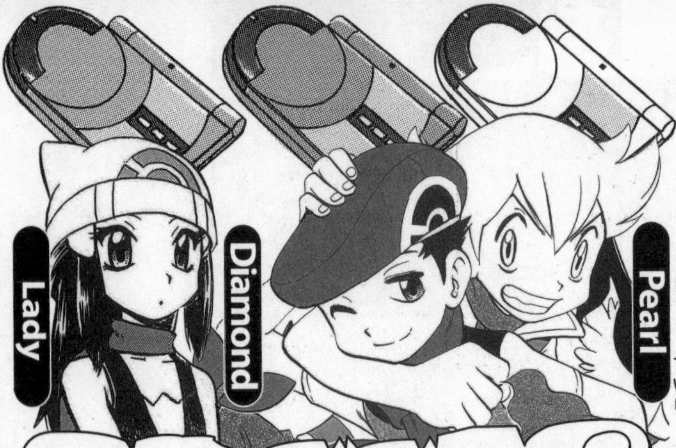
Lady
Diamond
Pearl

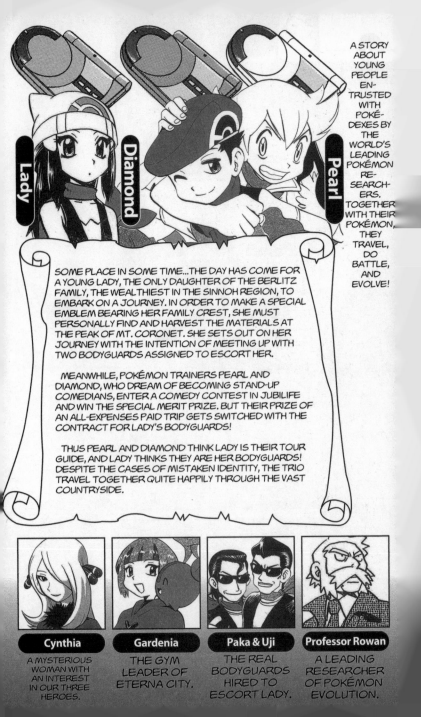

A STORY ABOUT YOUNG PEOPLE EN-TRUSTED WITH POKÉ-DEXES BY THE WORLD'S LEADING POKÉMON RE-SEARCH-ERS. TOGETHER WITH THEIR POKÉMON, THEY TRAVEL, DO BATTLE, AND EVOLVE!

SOME PLACE IN SOME TIME...THE DAY HAS COME FOR A YOUNG LADY, THE ONLY DAUGHTER OF THE BERLITZ FAMILY, THE WEALTHIEST IN THE SINNOH REGION, TO EMBARK ON A JOURNEY. IN ORDER TO MAKE A SPECIAL EMBLEM BEARING HER FAMILY CREST, SHE MUST PERSONALLY FIND AND HARVEST THE MATERIALS AT THE PEAK OF MT. CORONET. SHE SETS OUT ON HER JOURNEY WITH THE INTENTION OF MEETING UP WITH TWO BODYGUARDS ASSIGNED TO ESCORT HER.

MEANWHILE, POKÉMON TRAINERS PEARL AND DIAMOND, WHO DREAM OF BECOMING STAND-UP COMEDIANS, ENTER A COMEDY CONTEST IN JUBILIFE AND WIN THE SPECIAL MERIT PRIZE. BUT THEIR PRIZE OF AN ALL-EXPENSES PAID TRIP GETS SWITCHED WITH THE CONTRACT FOR LADY'S BODYGUARDS!

THUS PEARL AND DIAMOND THINK LADY IS THEIR TOUR GUIDE, AND LADY THINKS THEY ARE HER BODYGUARDS! DESPITE THE CASES OF MISTAKEN IDENTITY, THE TRIO TRAVEL TOGETHER QUITE HAPPILY THROUGH THE VAST COUNTRYSIDE.

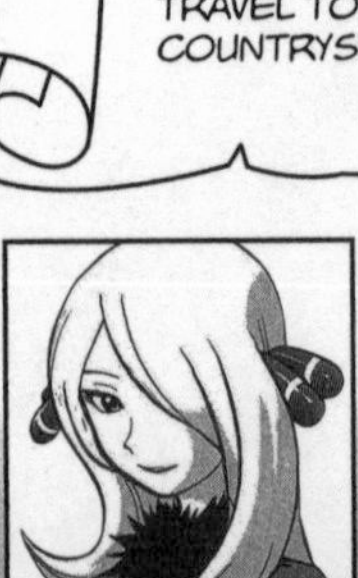

Cynthia

A MYSTERIOUS WOMAN WITH AN INTEREST IN OUR THREE HEROES.

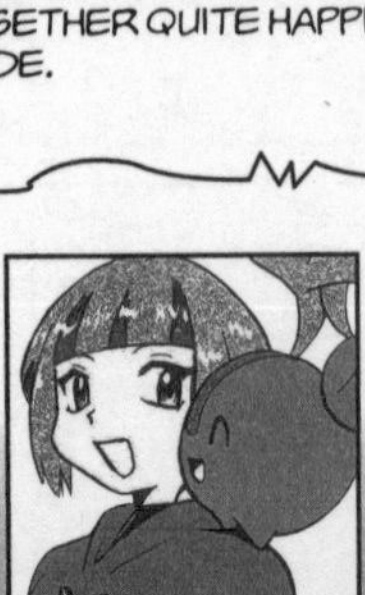

Gardenia

THE GYM LEADER OF ETERNA CITY.

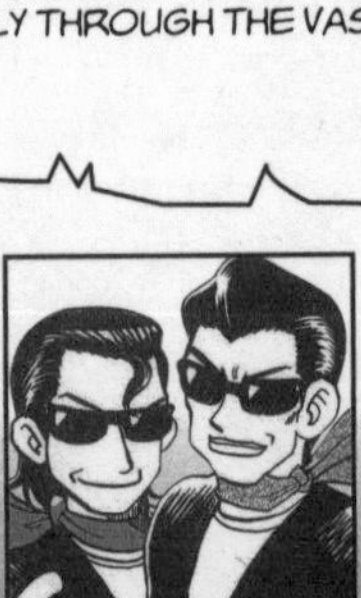

Paka & Uji

THE REAL BODYGUARDS HIRED TO ESCORT LADY.

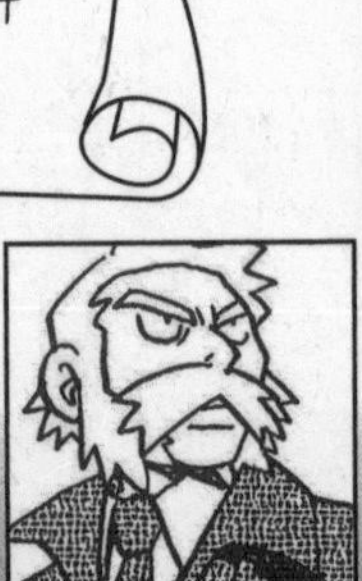

Professor Rowan

A LEADING RESEARCHER OF POKÉMON EVOLUTION.

POKÉMON ADVENTURES™

Diamond and Pearl

PLATINUM

2

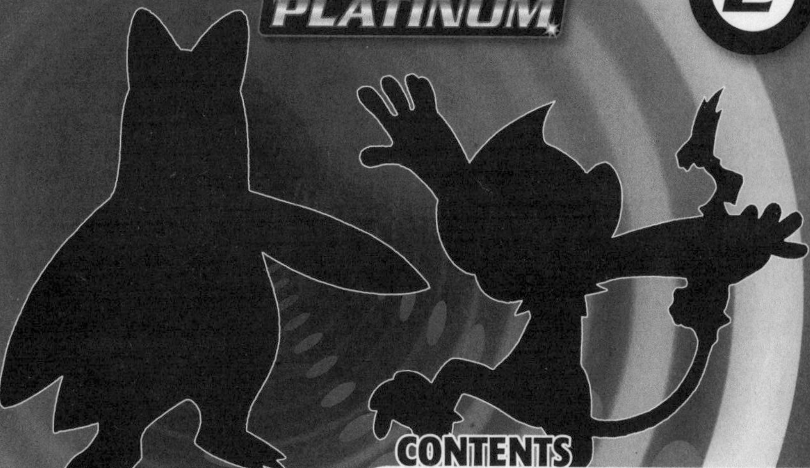

CONTENTS

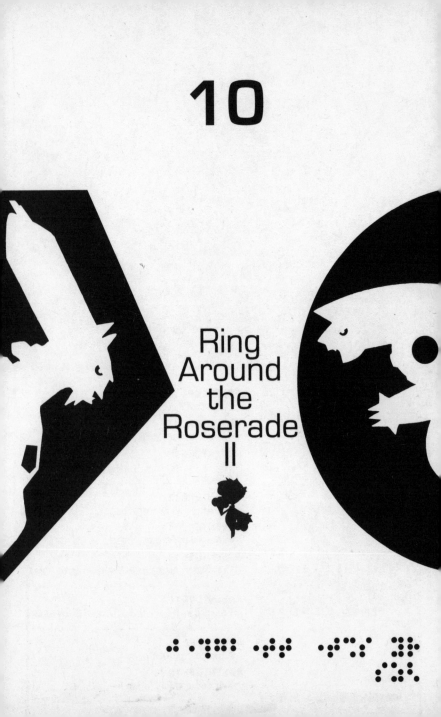

10

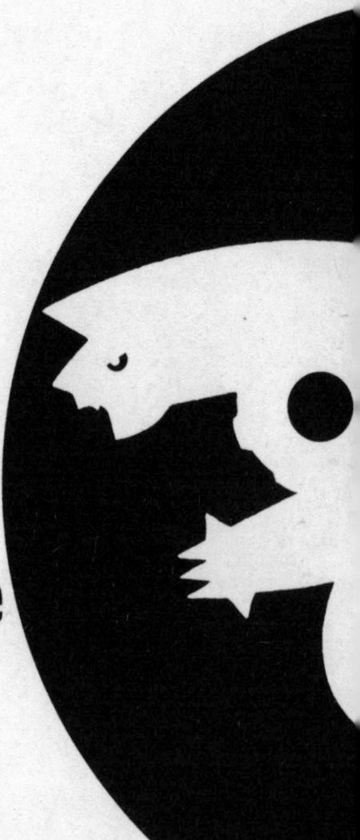

Ring Around the Roserade II

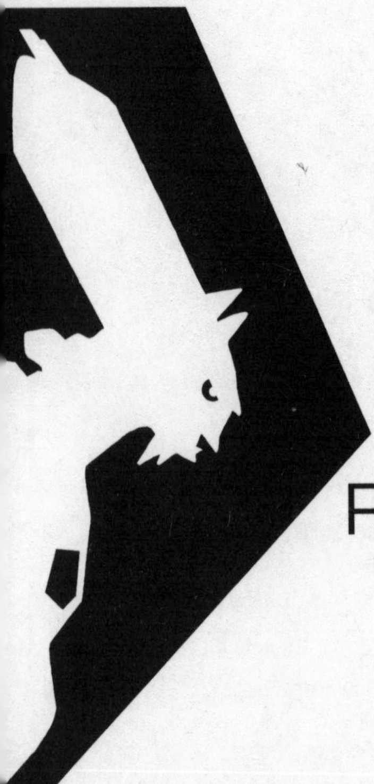

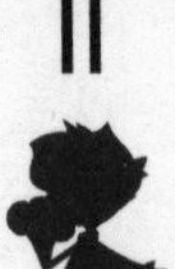

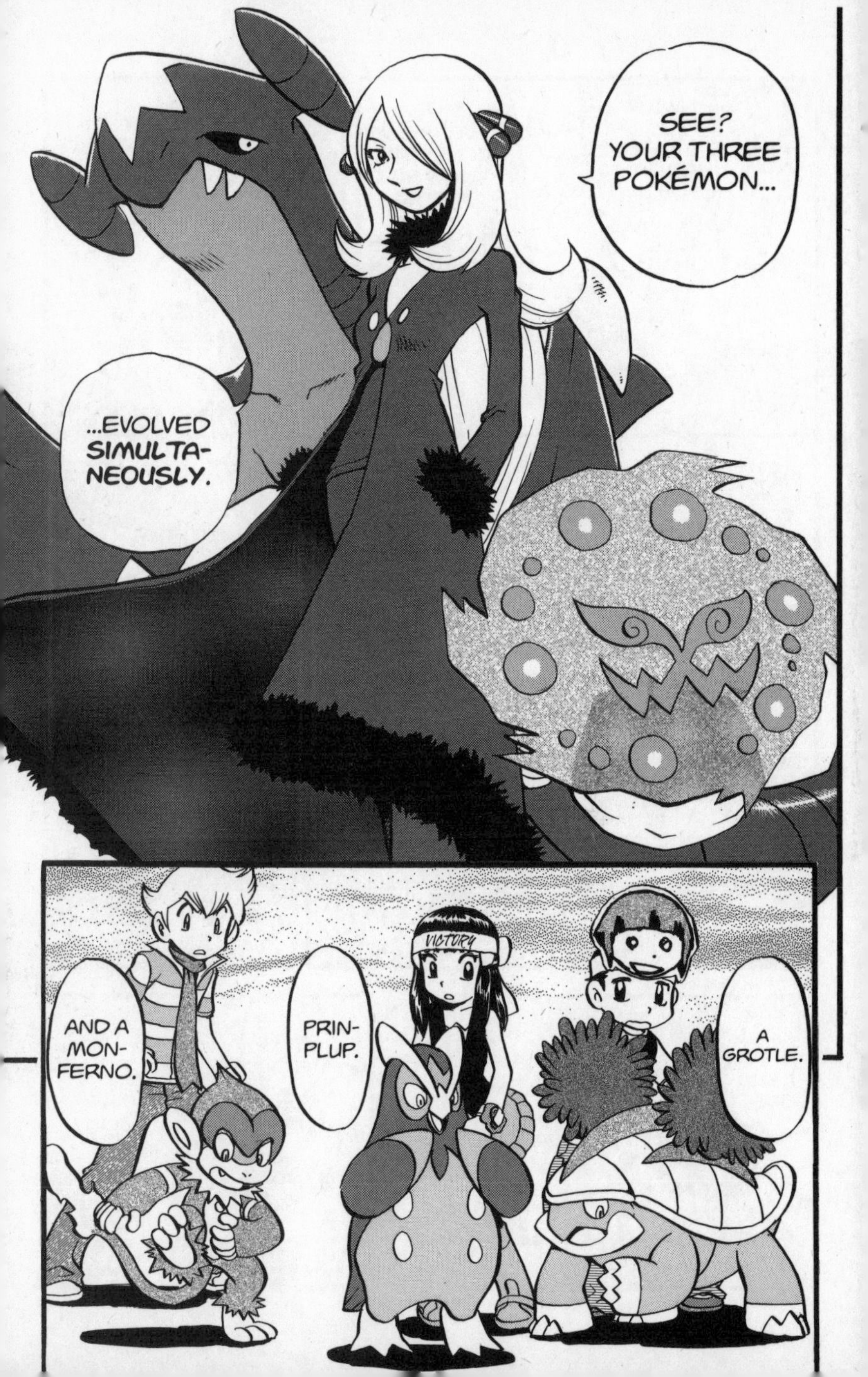
SEE? YOUR THREE POKÉMON...
...EVOLVED SIMULTA-NEOUSLY.
VICTORY
A GROTLE.
PRIN-PLUP.
AND A MON-FERNO.

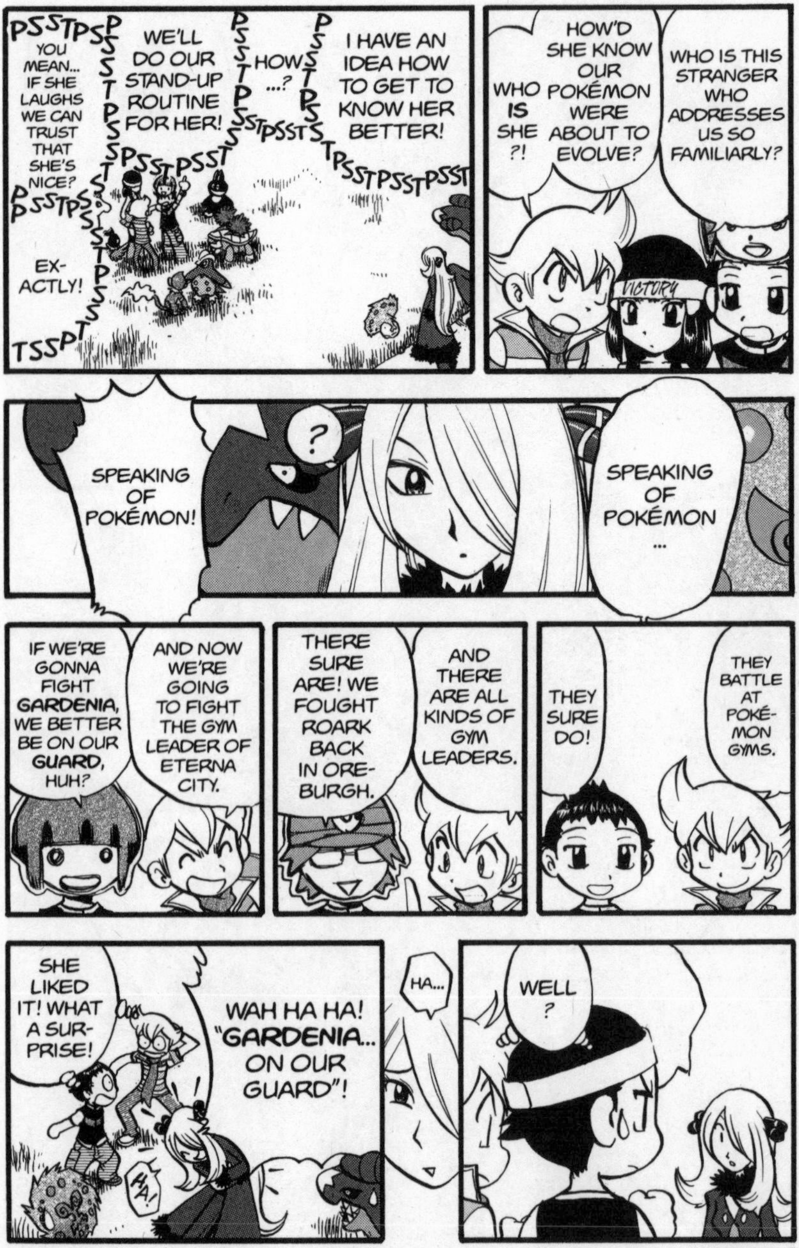
WHO IS THIS STRANGER WHO ADDRESSES US SO FAMILIARLY?
HOW'D SHE KNOW OUR POKÉMON WERE ABOUT TO EVOLVE?
WHO IS SHE ?!
I HAVE AN IDEA HOW TO GET TO KNOW HER BETTER!
HOW ...?
WE'LL DO OUR STAND-UP ROUTINE FOR HER!
YOU MEAN... IF SHE LAUGHS WE CAN TRUST THAT SHE'S NICE?
EX-ACTLY!
PSSTPSSTPSSTPSST
SPEAKING OF POKÉMON ...
SPEAKING OF POKÉMON!
THEY BATTLE AT POKÉ-MON GYMS.
THEY SURE DO!
AND THERE ARE ALL KINDS OF GYM LEADERS.
THERE SURE ARE! WE FOUGHT ROARK BACK IN ORE-BURGH.
AND NOW WE'RE GOING TO FIGHT THE GYM LEADER OF ETERNA CITY.
IF WE'RE GONNA FIGHT GARDENIA, WE BETTER BE ON OUR GUARD, HUH?
WELL ?
HA...
WAH HA HA! "GARDENIA... ON OUR GUARD"!
SHE LIKED IT! WHAT A SUR-PRISE!
HA HA!

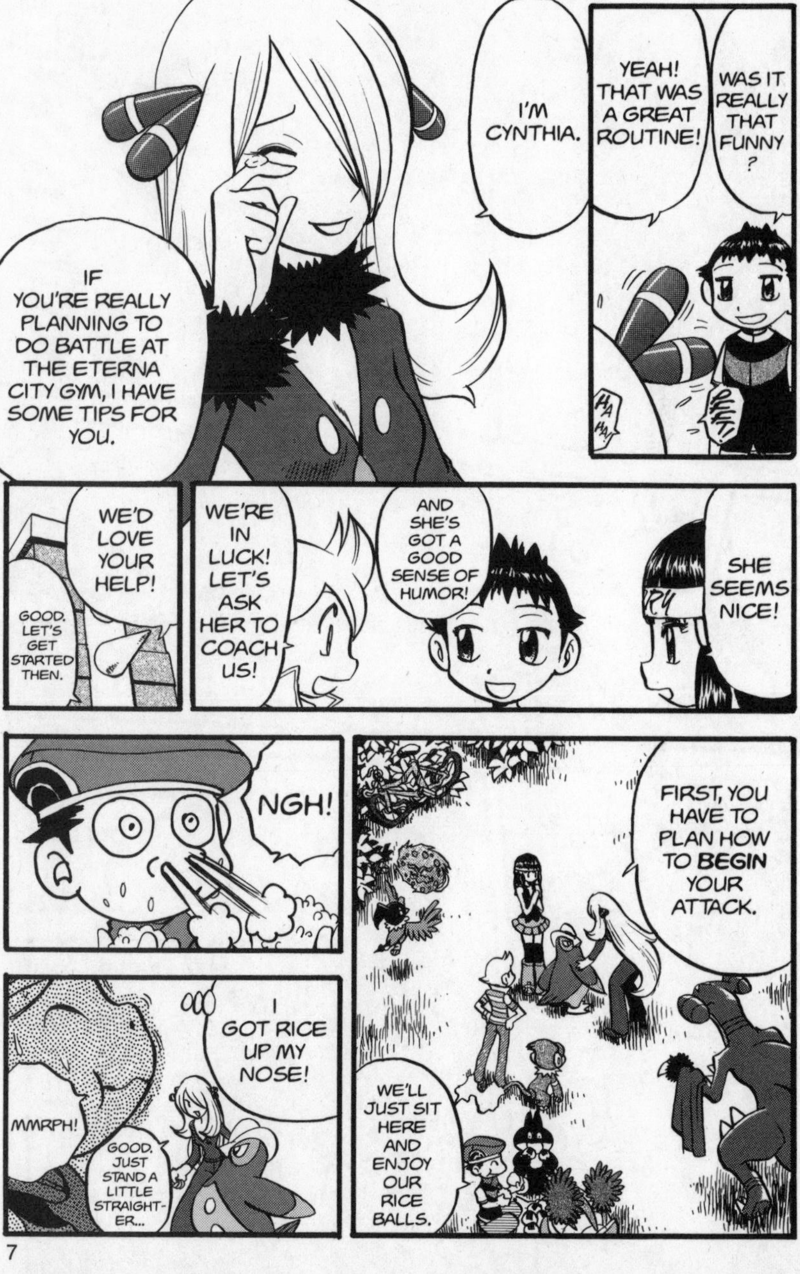
WAS IT REALLY THAT FUNNY?
YEAH! THAT WAS A GREAT ROUTINE!
I'M CYNTHIA.
IF YOU'RE REALLY PLANNING TO DO BATTLE AT THE ETERNA CITY GYM, I HAVE SOME TIPS FOR YOU.
SHE SEEMS NICE!
AND SHE'S GOT A GOOD SENSE OF HUMOR!
WE'RE IN LUCK! LET'S ASK HER TO COACH US!
WE'D LOVE YOUR HELP!
GOOD. LET'S GET STARTED THEN.
FIRST, YOU HAVE TO PLAN HOW TO **BEGIN** YOUR ATTACK.
WE'LL JUST SIT HERE AND ENJOY OUR RICE BALLS.
NGH!
I GOT RICE UP MY NOSE!
MMRPH!
GOOD. JUST STAND A LITTLE STRAIGHTER...

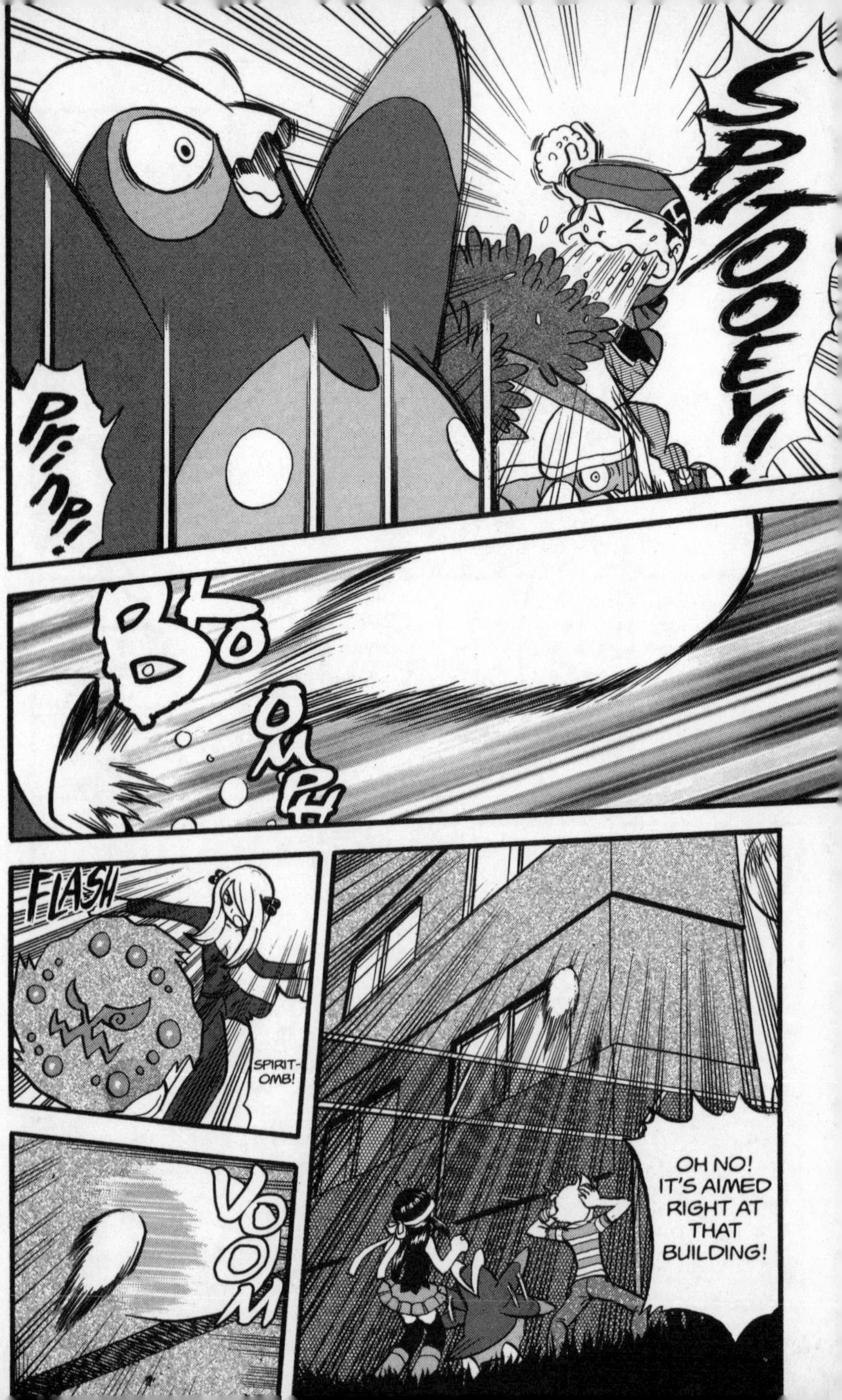

SPITOOOEY!
PRINP!
BLOOMPH
OH NO! IT'S AIMED RIGHT AT THAT BUILDING!
FLASH
SPIRIT-OMB!
VOOOM

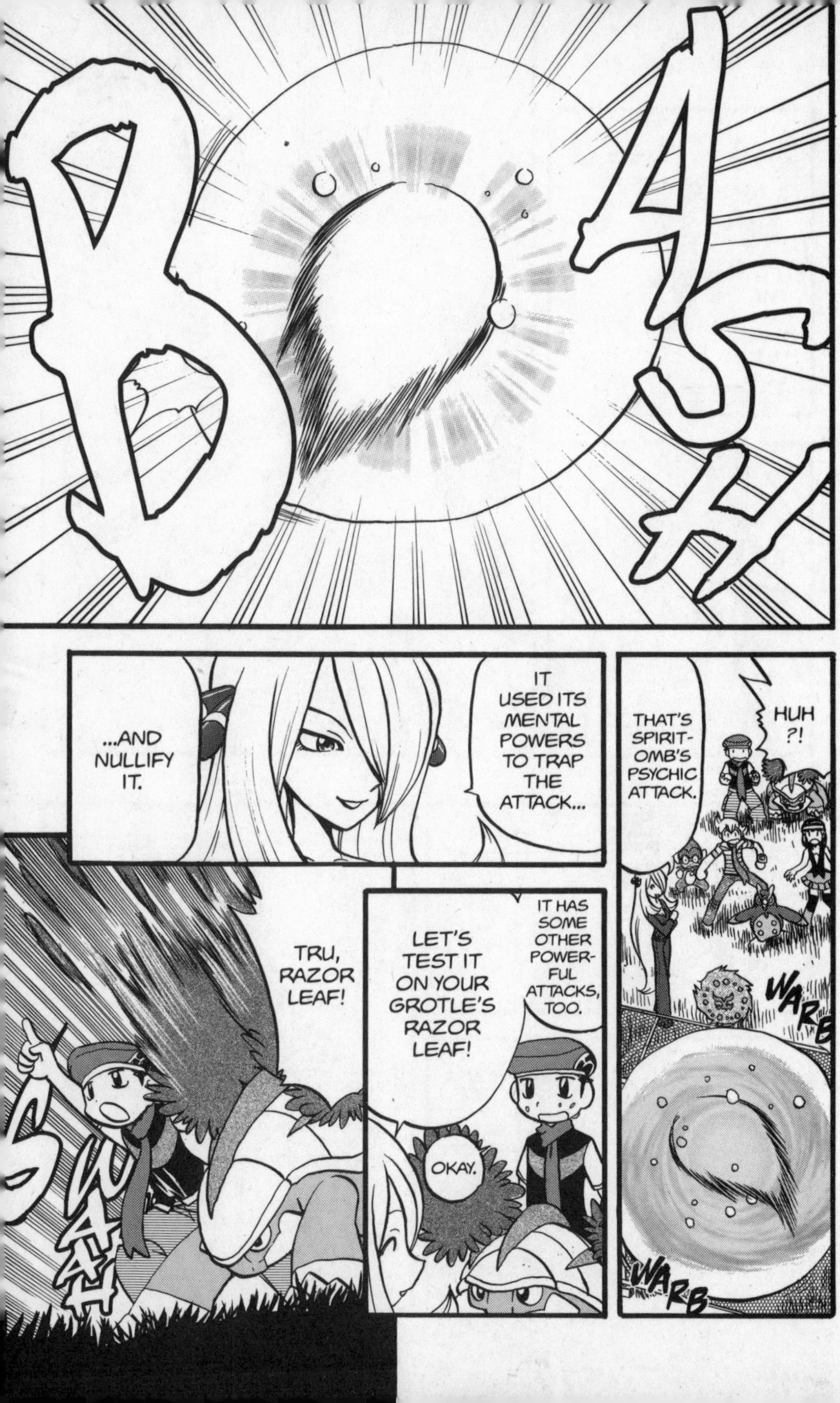
BASH
HUH ?!
THAT'S SPIRIT-OMB'S PSYCHIC ATTACK.
WARB
WARB
IT USED ITS MENTAL POWERS TO TRAP THE ATTACK...
...AND NULLIFY IT.
IT HAS SOME OTHER POWER-FUL ATTACKS, TOO.
LET'S TEST IT ON YOUR GROTLE'S RAZOR LEAF!
OKAY.
TRU, RAZOR LEAF!
SWAAH

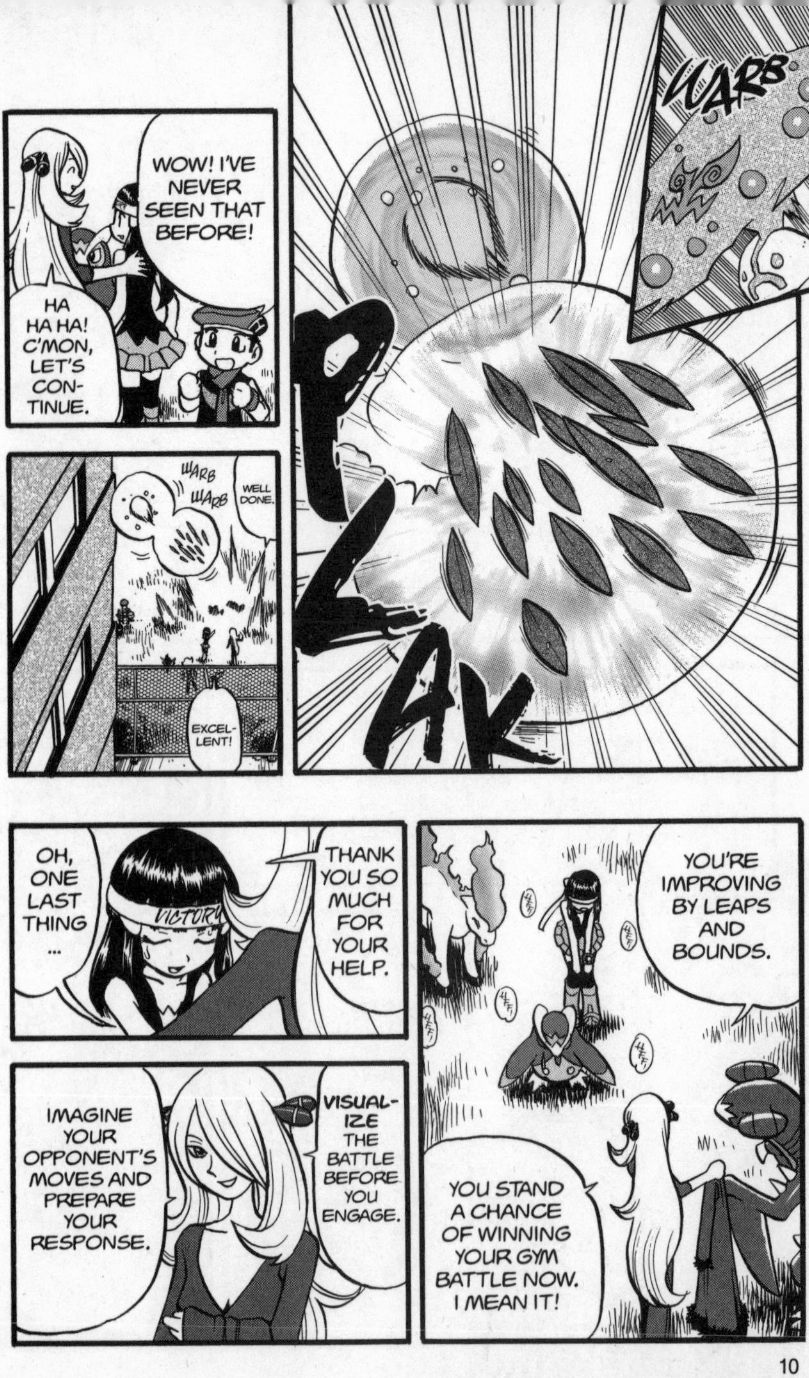

WARB
WOW! I'VE NEVER SEEN THAT BEFORE!
HA HA HA! C'MON, LET'S CON-TINUE.
WELL DONE.
WARB
WARB
EXCEL-LENT!
YOU'RE IMPROVING BY LEAPS AND BOUNDS.
YOU STAND A CHANCE OF WINNING YOUR GYM BATTLE NOW. I MEAN IT!
THANK YOU SO MUCH FOR YOUR HELP.
VICTORY
OH, ONE LAST THING ...
VISUAL-IZE THE BATTLE BEFORE YOU ENGAGE.
IMAGINE YOUR OPPONENT'S MOVES AND PREPARE YOUR RESPONSE.

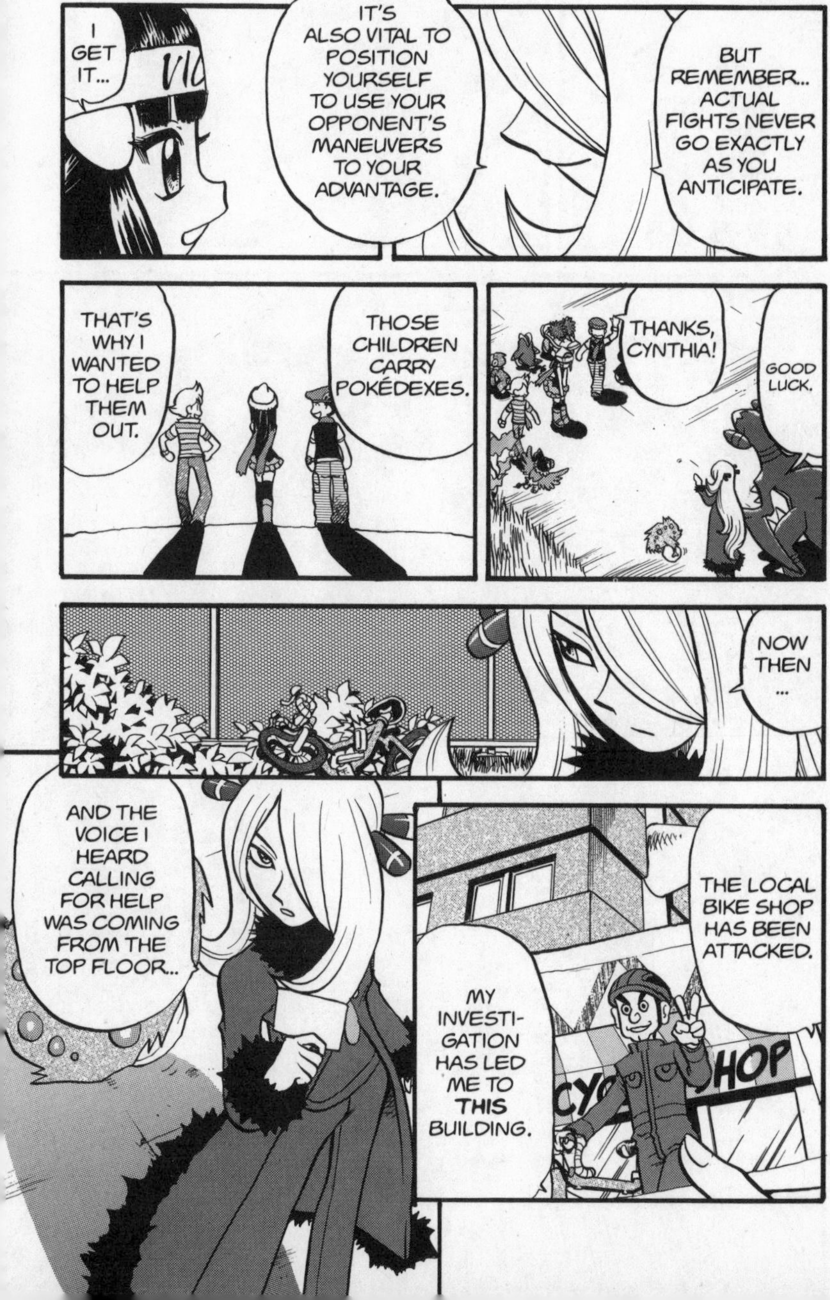
BUT REMEMBER... ACTUAL FIGHTS NEVER GO EXACTLY AS YOU ANTICIPATE.
IT'S ALSO VITAL TO POSITION YOURSELF TO USE YOUR OPPONENT'S MANEUVERS TO YOUR ADVANTAGE.
I GET IT...
GOOD LUCK.
THANKS, CYNTHIA!
THOSE CHILDREN CARRY POKÉDEXES.
THAT'S WHY I WANTED TO HELP THEM OUT.
NOW THEN ...
THE LOCAL BIKE SHOP HAS BEEN ATTACKED.
MY INVESTI-GATION HAS LED ME TO **THIS** BUILDING.
AND THE VOICE I HEARD CALLING FOR HELP WAS COMING FROM THE TOP FLOOR...

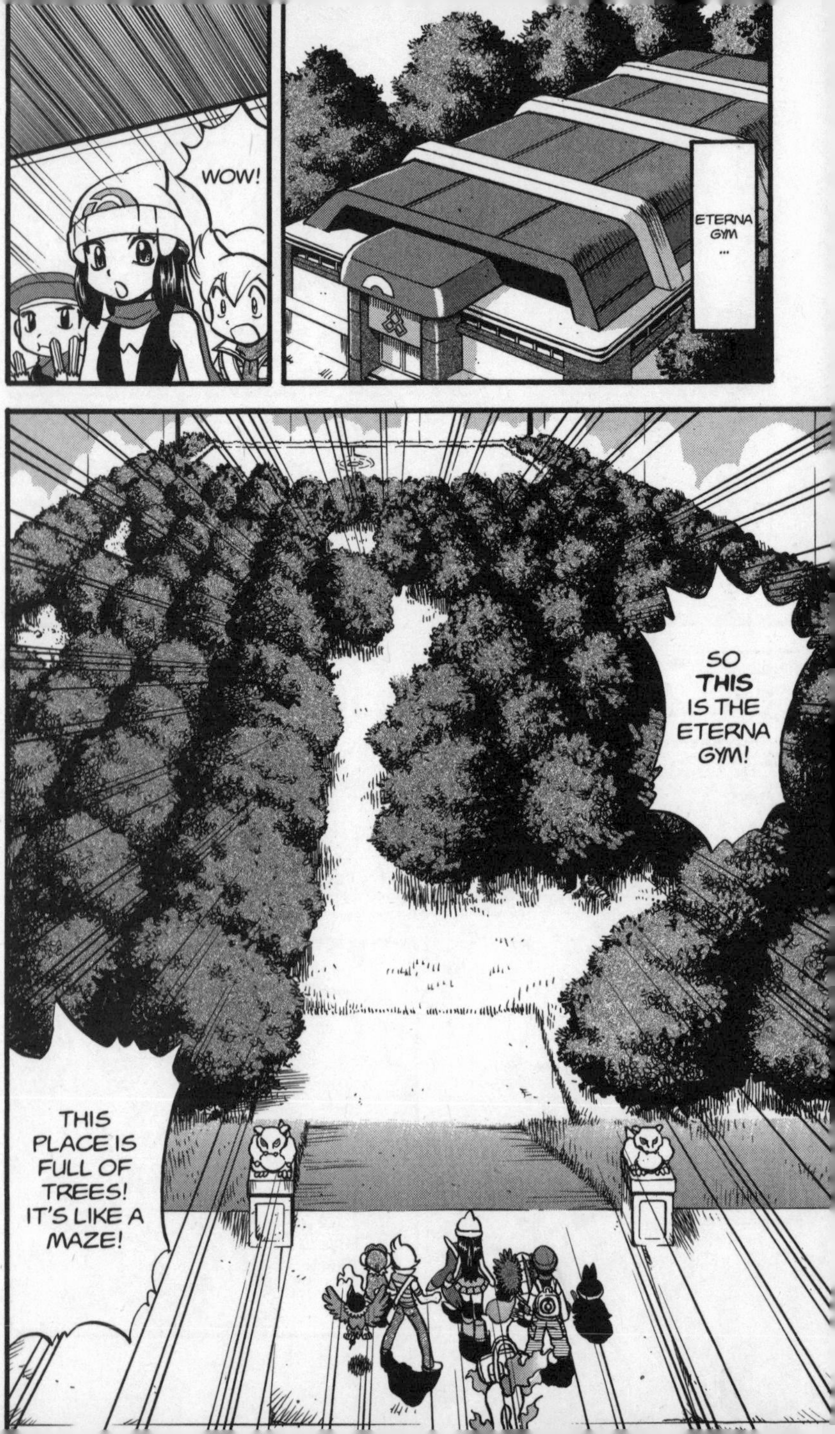
ETERNA GYM ...
WOW!
SO THIS IS THE ETERNA GYM!
THIS PLACE IS FULL OF TREES! IT'S LIKE A MAZE!

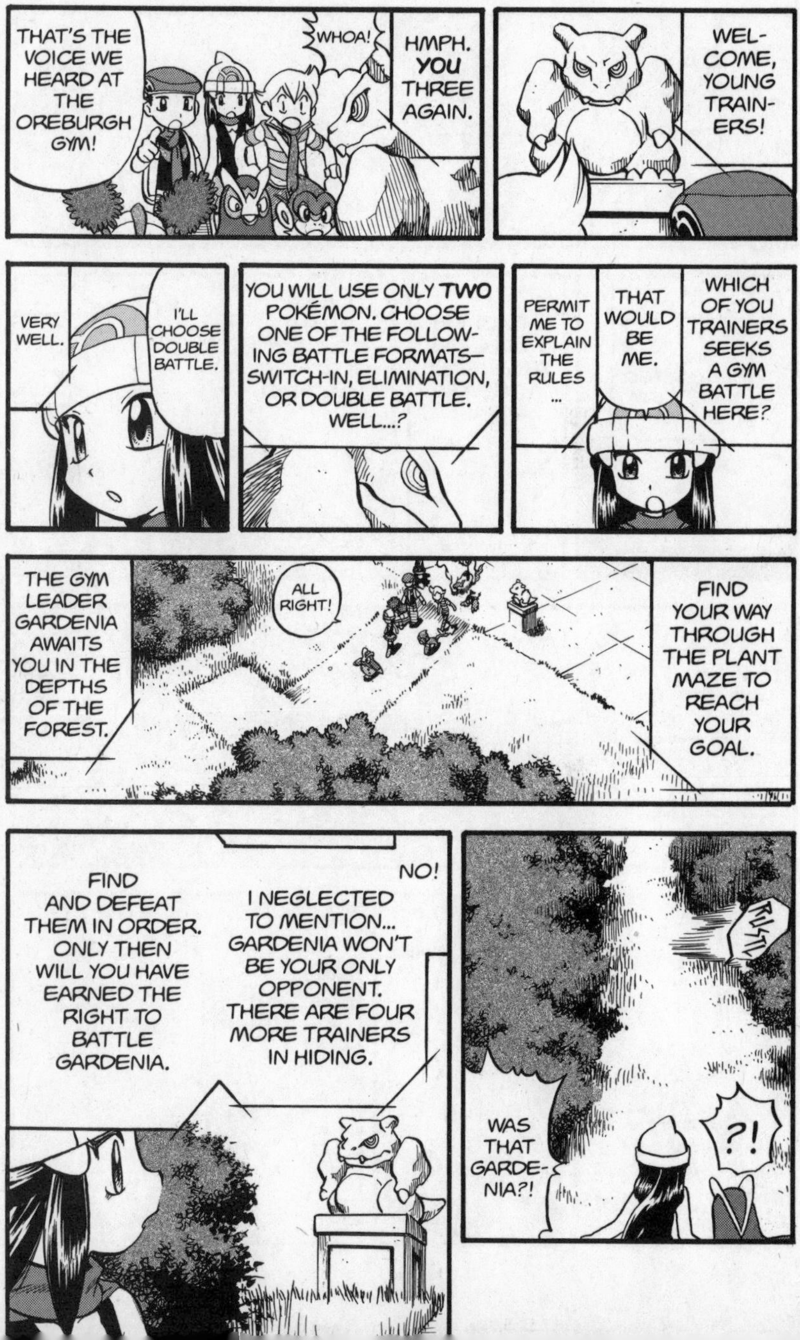
WEL-COME, YOUNG TRAIN-ERS!
HMPH. YOU THREE AGAIN.
WHOA!
THAT'S THE VOICE WE HEARD AT THE OREBURGH GYM!
WHICH OF YOU TRAINERS SEEKS A GYM BATTLE HERE?
THAT WOULD BE ME.
PERMIT ME TO EXPLAIN THE RULES ...
YOU WILL USE ONLY TWO POKÉMON. CHOOSE ONE OF THE FOLLOWING BATTLE FORMATS—SWITCH-IN, ELIMINATION, OR DOUBLE BATTLE. WELL...?
I'LL CHOOSE DOUBLE BATTLE.
VERY WELL.
FIND YOUR WAY THROUGH THE PLANT MAZE TO REACH YOUR GOAL.
ALL RIGHT!
THE GYM LEADER GARDENIA AWAITS YOU IN THE DEPTHS OF THE FOREST.
?!
WAS THAT GARDE-NIA?!
NO!
I NEGLECTED TO MENTION... GARDENIA WON'T BE YOUR ONLY OPPONENT. THERE ARE FOUR MORE TRAINERS IN HIDING.
FIND AND DEFEAT THEM IN ORDER. ONLY THEN WILL YOU HAVE EARNED THE RIGHT TO BATTLE GARDENIA.

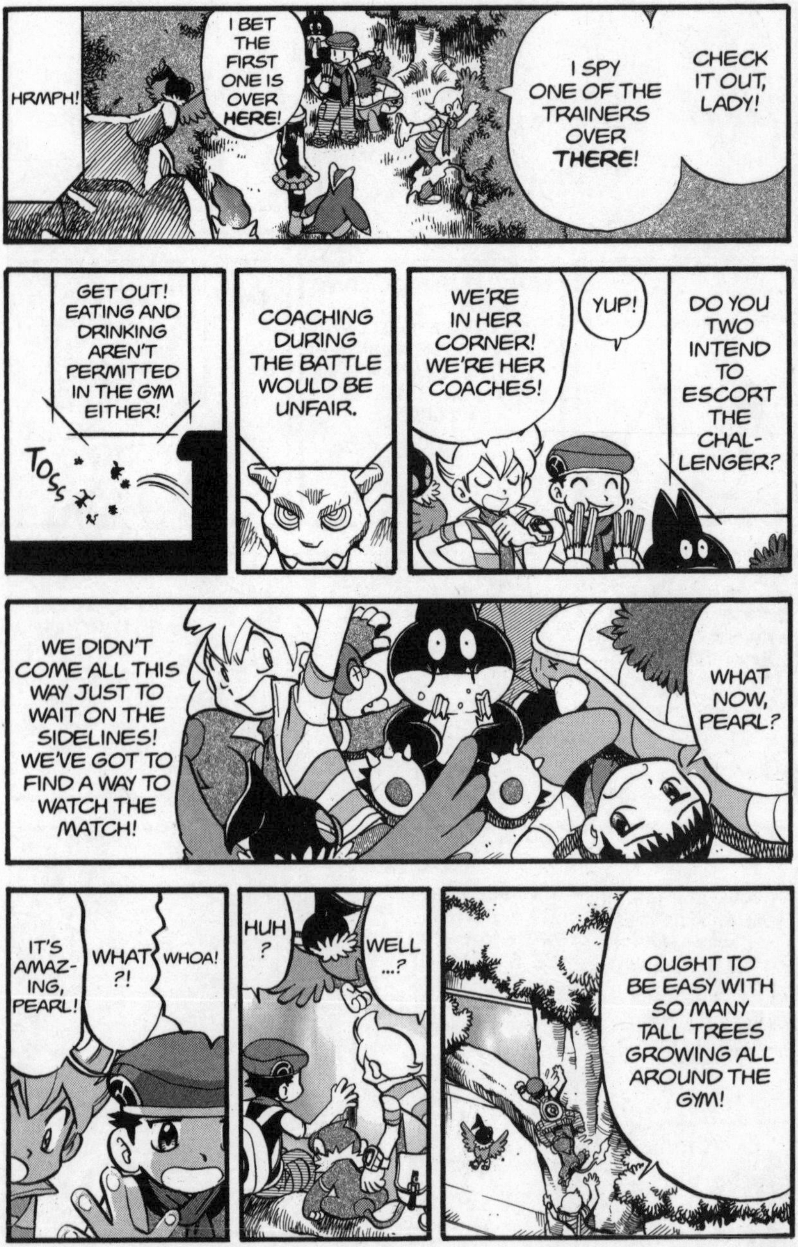
CHECK IT OUT, LADY!
I SPY ONE OF THE TRAINERS OVER THERE!
I BET THE FIRST ONE IS OVER HERE!
HRMPH!
DO YOU TWO INTEND TO ESCORT THE CHALLENGER?
YUP!
WE'RE IN HER CORNER! WE'RE HER COACHES!
COACHING DURING THE BATTLE WOULD BE UNFAIR.
GET OUT! EATING AND DRINKING AREN'T PERMITTED IN THE GYM EITHER!
TOSS
WHAT NOW, PEARL?
WE DIDN'T COME ALL THIS WAY JUST TO WAIT ON THE SIDELINES! WE'VE GOT TO FIND A WAY TO WATCH THE MATCH!
OUGHT TO BE EASY WITH SO MANY TALL TREES GROWING ALL AROUND THE GYM!
WELL ...?
HUH ?
WHOA!
WHAT ?!
IT'S AMAZ-ING, PEARL!

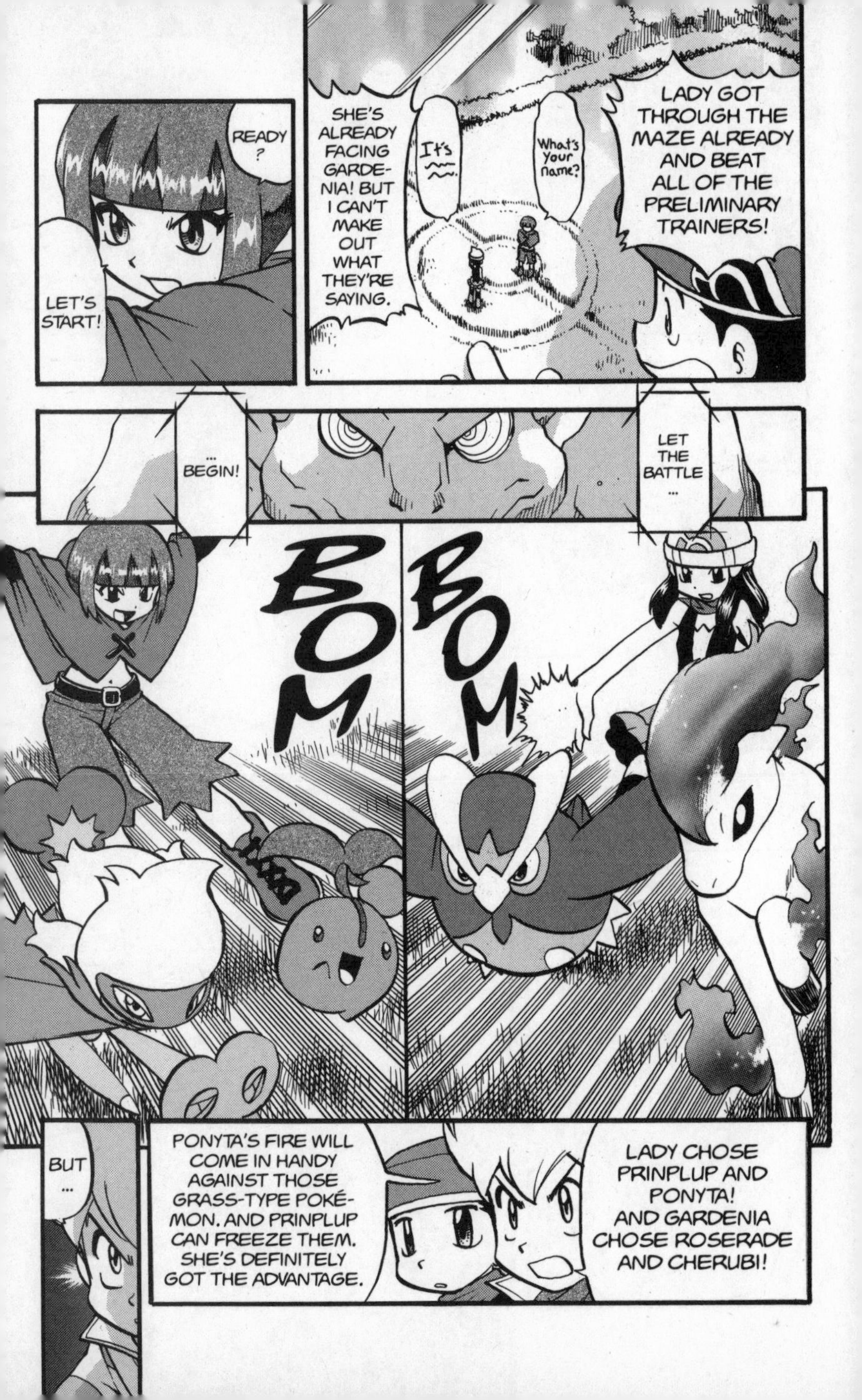
LADY GOT THROUGH THE MAZE ALREADY AND BEAT ALL OF THE PRELIMINARY TRAINERS!
What's your name?
It's
SHE'S ALREADY FACING GARDE-NIA! BUT I CAN'T MAKE OUT WHAT THEY'RE SAYING.
READY?
LET'S START!
LET THE BATTLE ...
... BEGIN!
BOM
BOM
LADY CHOSE PRINPLUP AND PONYTA! AND GARDENIA CHOSE ROSERADE AND CHERUBI!
PONYTA'S FIRE WILL COME IN HANDY AGAINST THOSE GRASS-TYPE POKÉ-MON. AND PRINPLUP CAN FREEZE THEM. SHE'S DEFINITELY GOT THE ADVANTAGE.
BUT ...

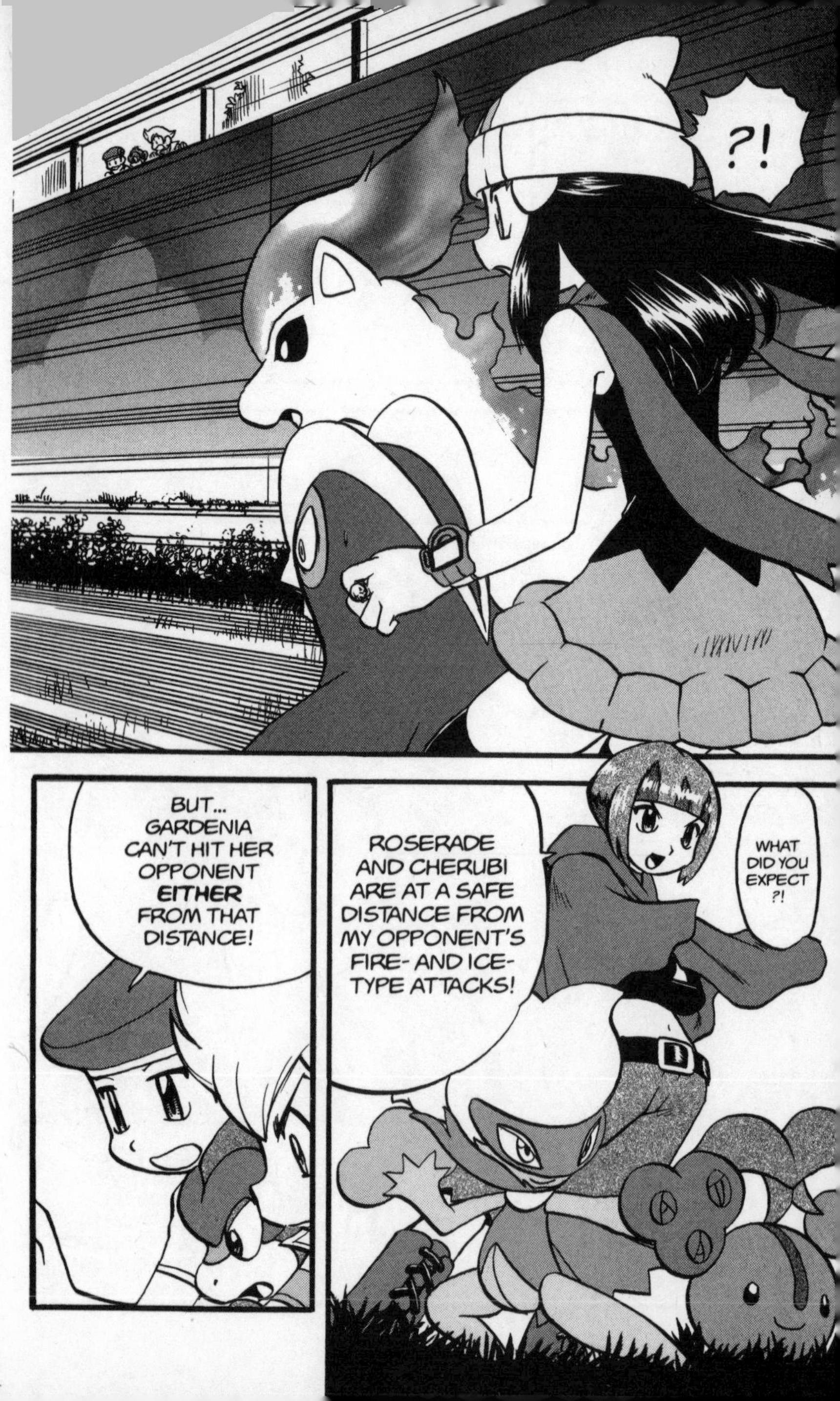
?!
WHAT DID YOU EXPECT ?!
ROSERADE AND CHERUBI ARE AT A SAFE DISTANCE FROM MY OPPONENT'S FIRE- AND ICE-TYPE ATTACKS!
BUT... GARDENIA CAN'T HIT HER OPPONENT **EITHER** FROM THAT DISTANCE!

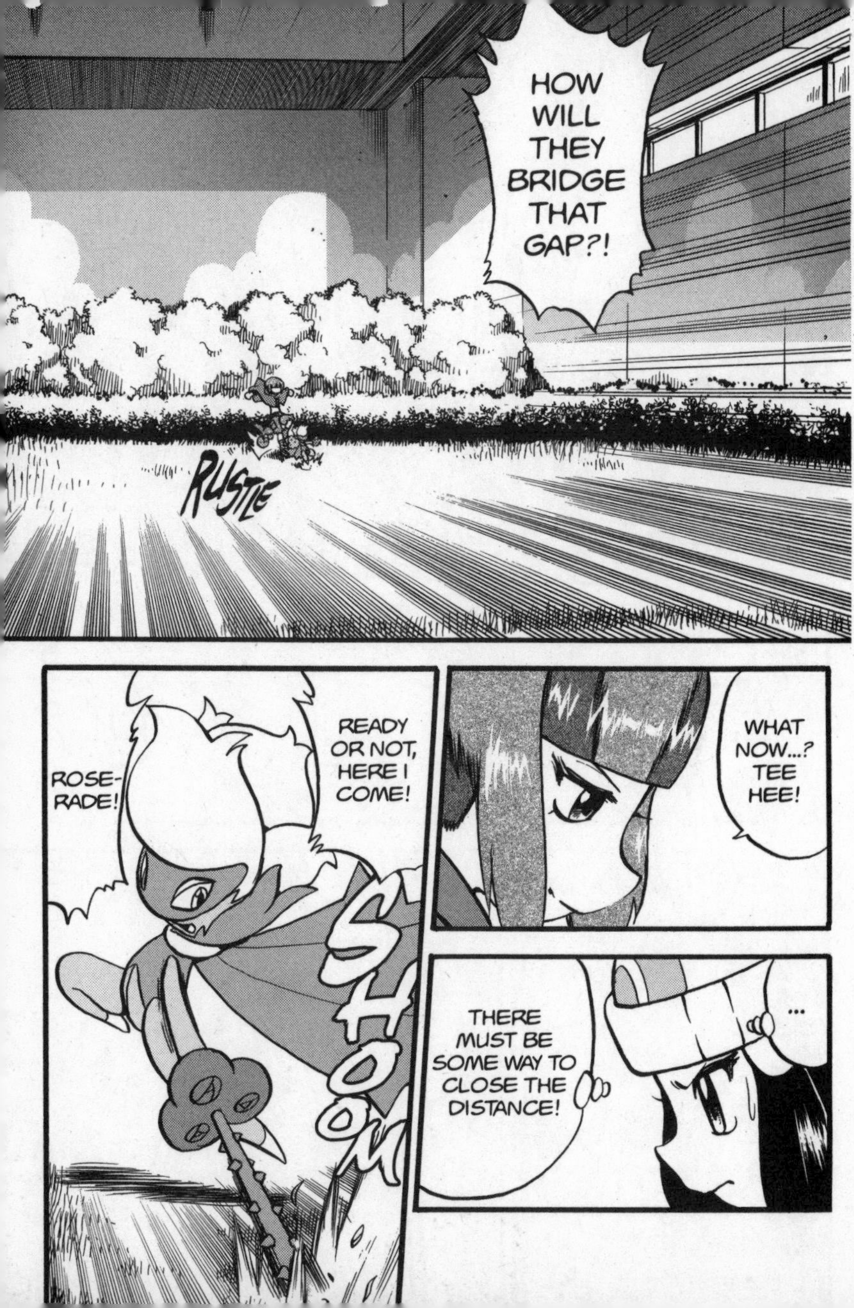
HOW WILL THEY BRIDGE THAT GAP?!
RUSTLE
WHAT NOW...? TEE HEE!
...
THERE MUST BE SOME WAY TO CLOSE THE DISTANCE!
READY OR NOT, HERE I COME!
ROSE-RADE!
SHOOM

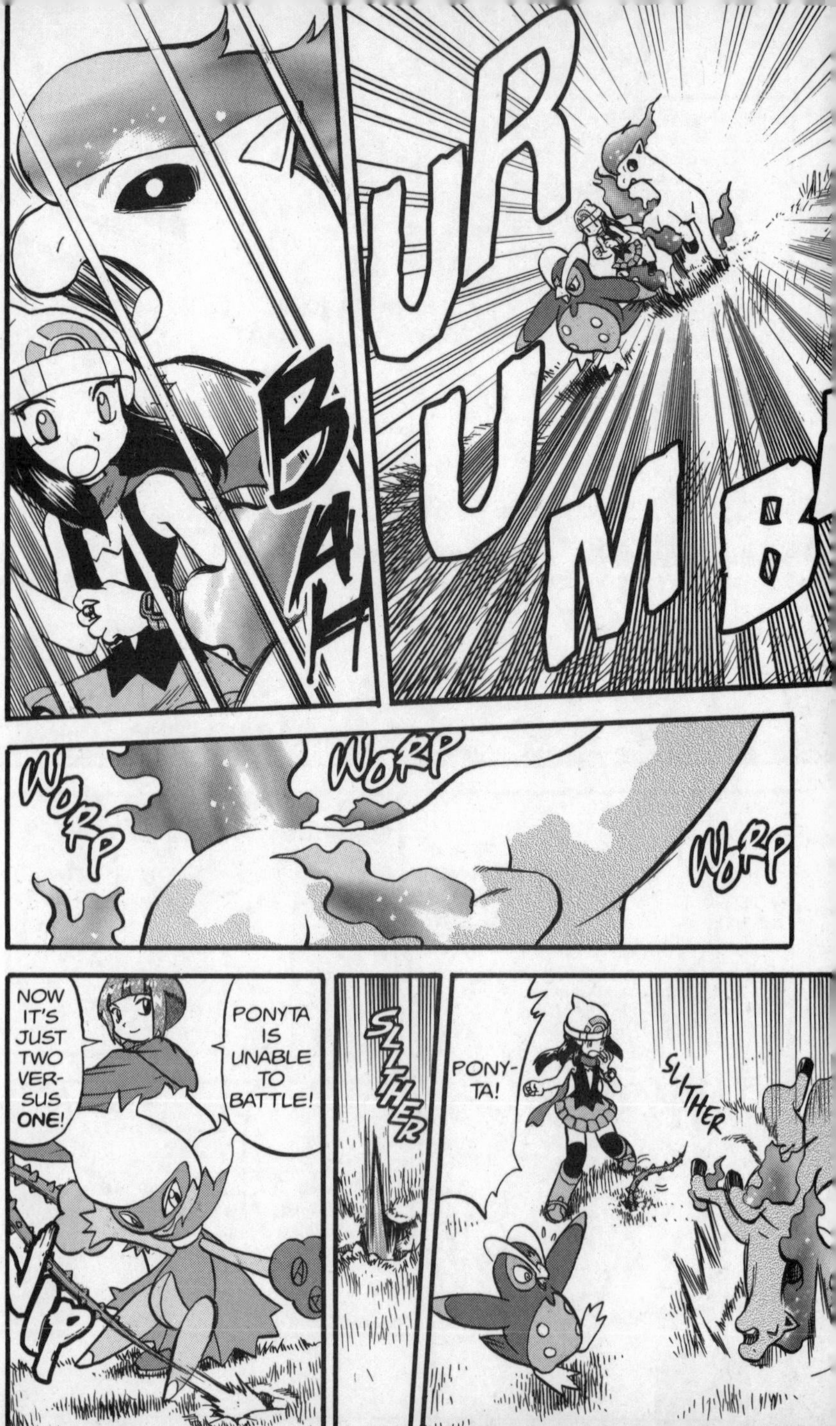

UR
UMB
BA
WORP
WORP
WORP
SLITHER
PONY-TA!
SLITHER
PONYTA IS UNABLE TO BATTLE!
NOW IT'S JUST TWO VERSUS ONE!

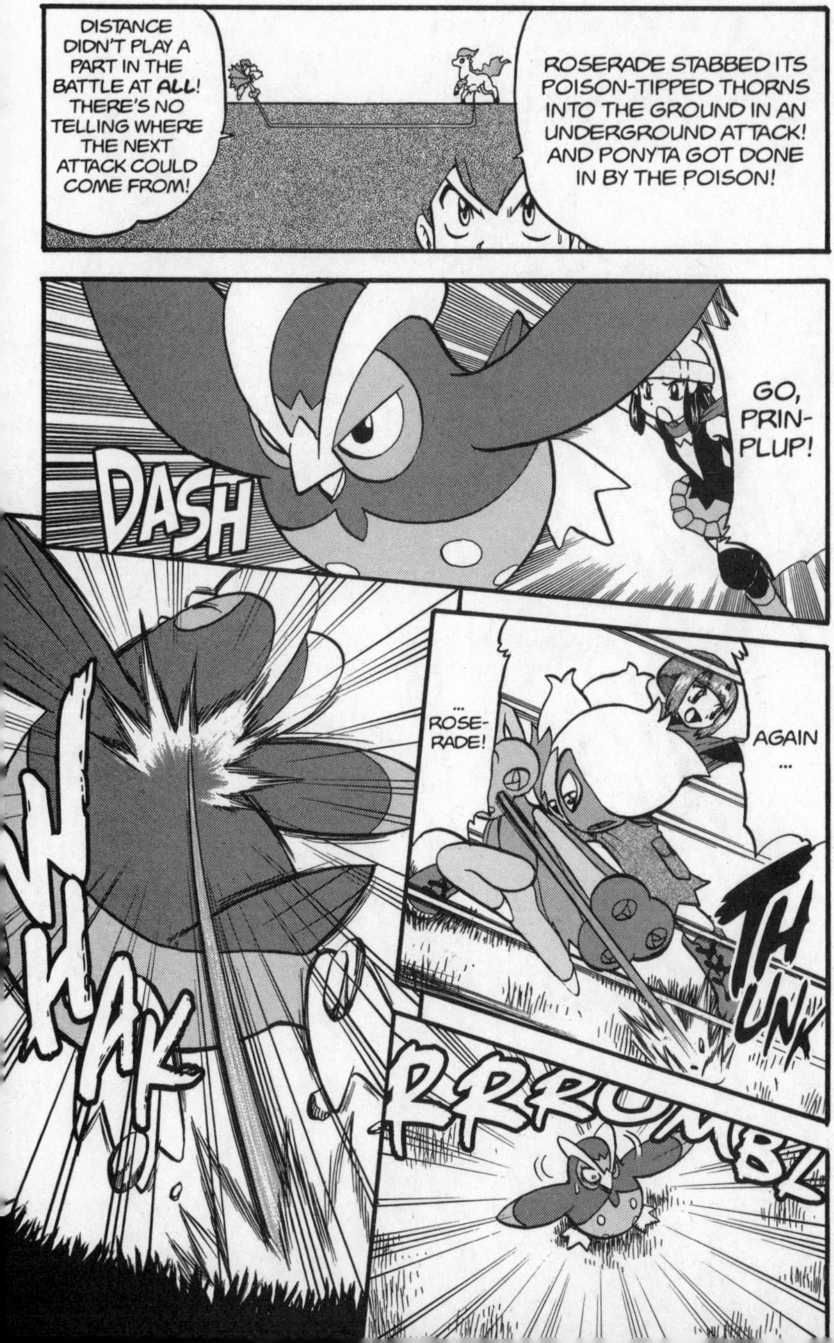
ROSERADE STABBED ITS POISON-TIPPED THORNS INTO THE GROUND IN AN UNDERGROUND ATTACK! AND PONYTA GOT DONE IN BY THE POISON!
DISTANCE DIDN'T PLAY A PART IN THE BATTLE AT **ALL**! THERE'S NO TELLING WHERE THE NEXT ATTACK COULD COME FROM!
GO, PRIN-PLUP!
DASH
AGAIN ...
... ROSE-RADE!
THUNK
RRRUMBL
WHAK

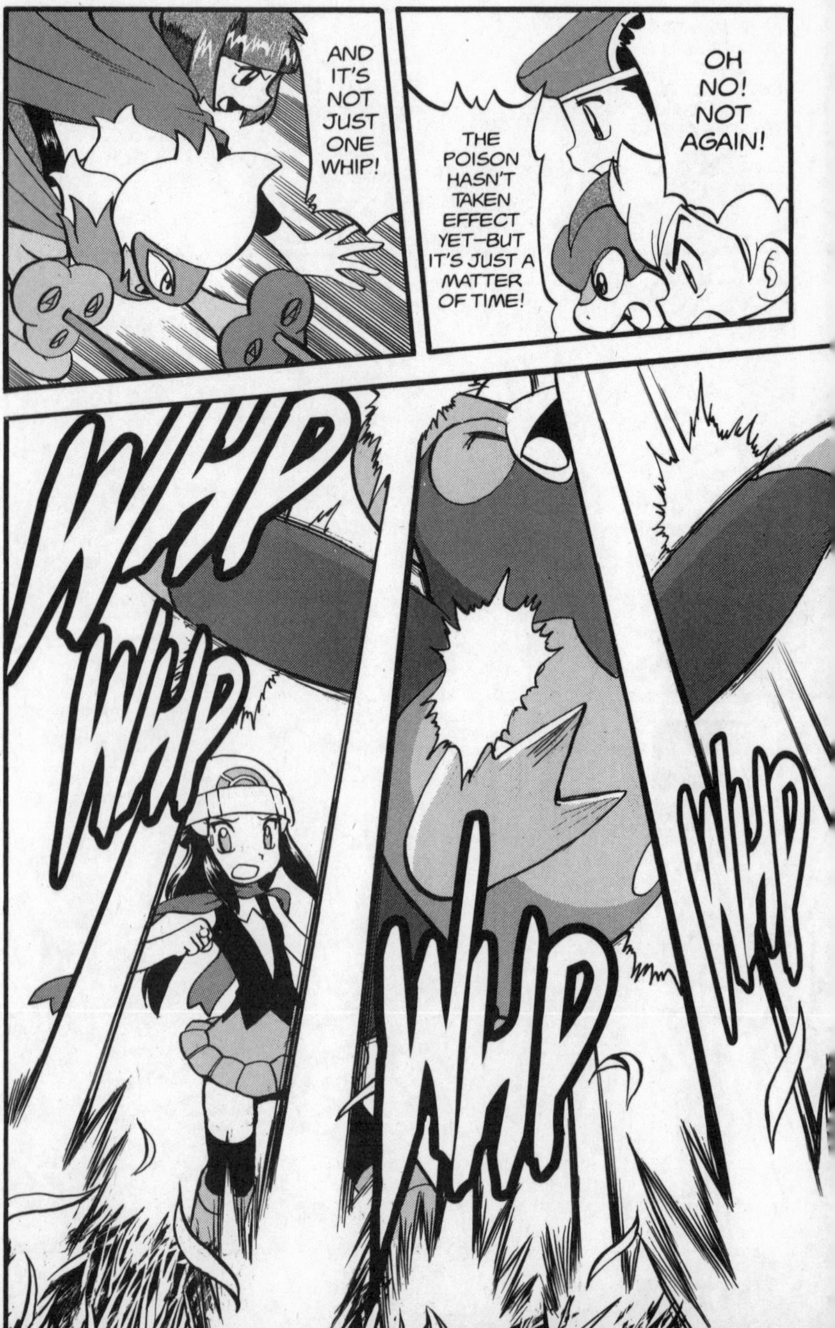
OH NO! NOT AGAIN!
THE POISON HASN'T TAKEN EFFECT YET—BUT IT'S JUST A MATTER OF TIME!
AND IT'S NOT JUST ONE WHIP!
WHIP
WHIP
WHIP
WHIP

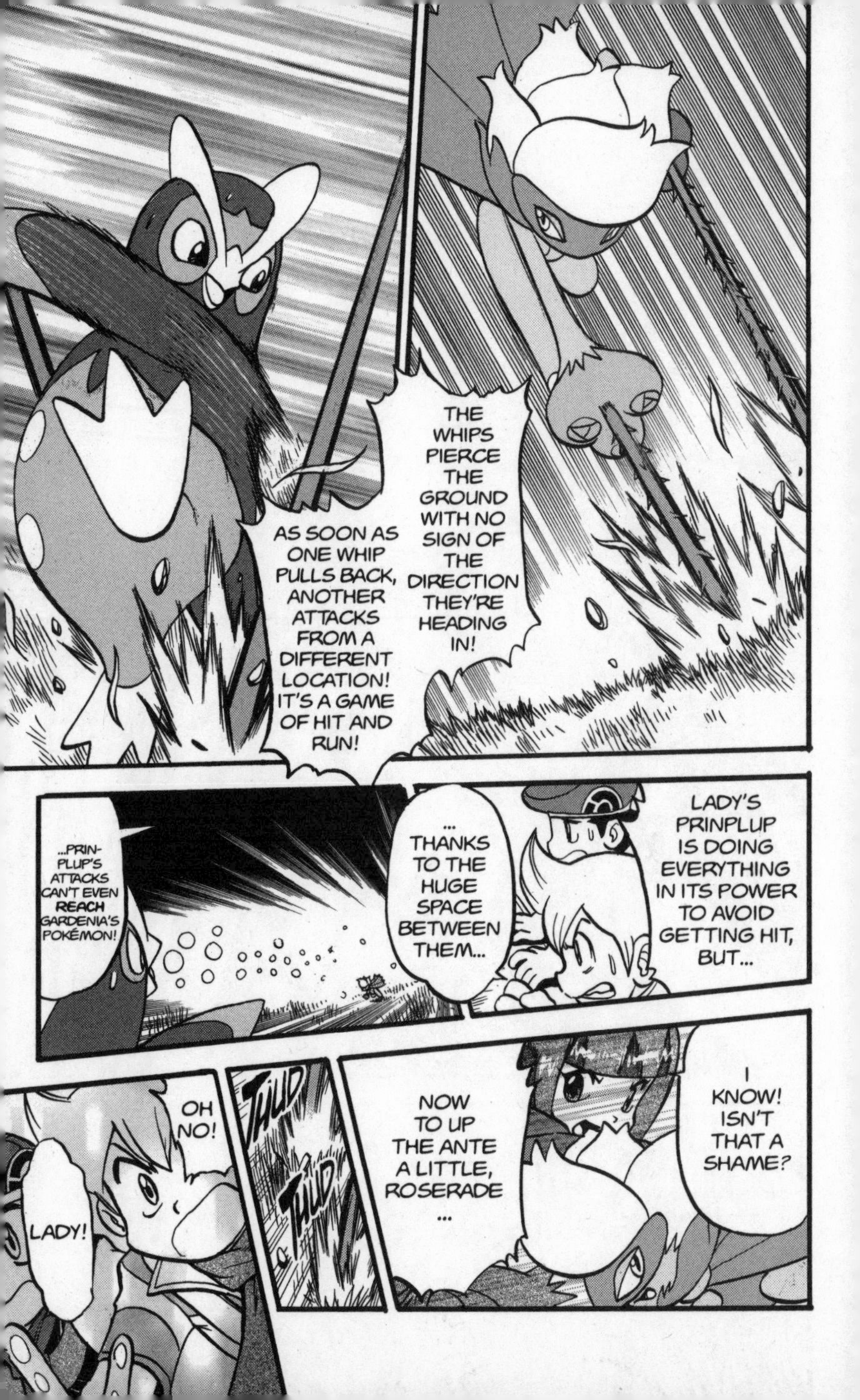
THE WHIPS PIERCE THE GROUND WITH NO SIGN OF THE DIRECTION THEY'RE HEADING IN!
AS SOON AS ONE WHIP PULLS BACK, ANOTHER ATTACKS FROM A DIFFERENT LOCATION! IT'S A GAME OF HIT AND RUN!
LADY'S PRINPLUP IS DOING EVERYTHING IN ITS POWER TO AVOID GETTING HIT, BUT...
... THANKS TO THE HUGE SPACE BETWEEN THEM...
...PRIN-PLUP'S ATTACKS CAN'T EVEN **REACH** GARDENIA'S POKÉMON!
I KNOW! ISN'T THAT A SHAME?
NOW TO UP THE ANTE A LITTLE, ROSERADE ...
THUD
THUD
OH NO!
LADY!

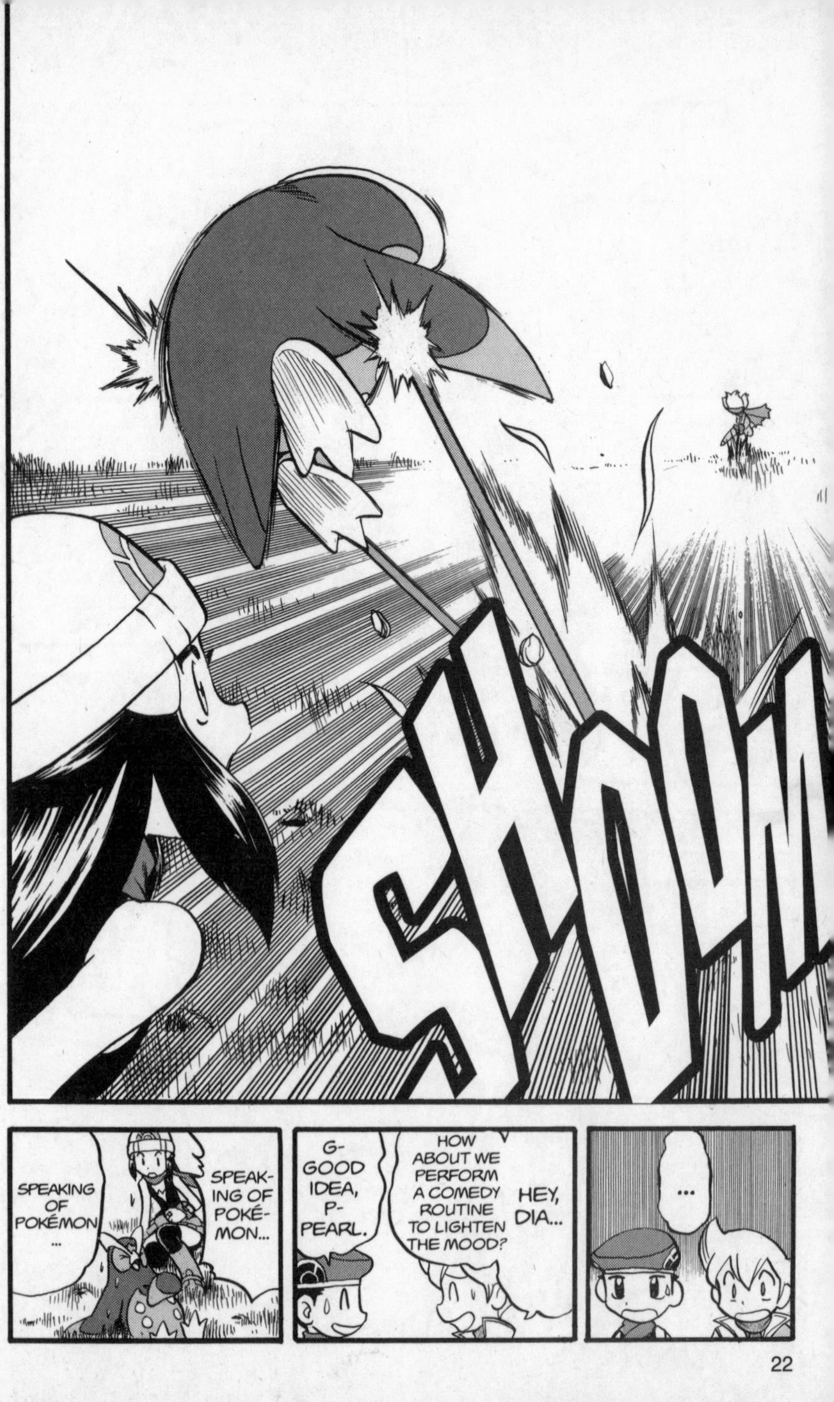
SHOOM
...
HEY, DIA...
HOW ABOUT WE PERFORM A COMEDY ROUTINE TO LIGHTEN THE MOOD?
G-GOOD IDEA, P-PEARL.
SPEAK-ING OF POKÉ-MON...
SPEAKING OF POKÉMON...

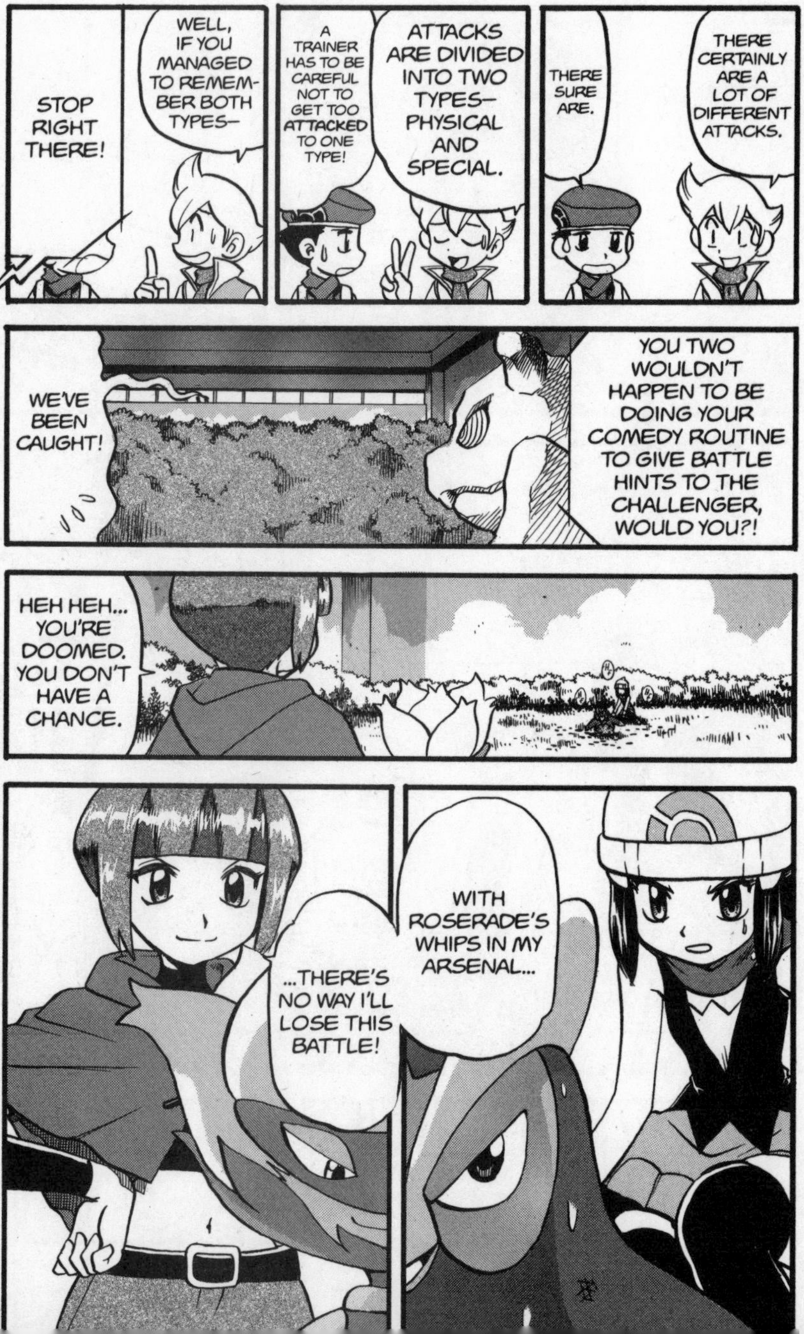
THERE CERTAINLY ARE A LOT OF DIFFERENT ATTACKS.
THERE SURE ARE.
ATTACKS ARE DIVIDED INTO TWO TYPES— PHYSICAL AND SPECIAL.
A TRAINER HAS TO BE CAREFUL NOT TO GET TOO ATTACKED TO ONE TYPE!
WELL, IF YOU MANAGED TO REMEM-BER BOTH TYPES—
STOP RIGHT THERE!
YOU TWO WOULDN'T HAPPEN TO BE DOING YOUR COMEDY ROUTINE TO GIVE BATTLE HINTS TO THE CHALLENGER, WOULD YOU?!
WE'VE BEEN CAUGHT!
HEH HEH... YOU'RE DOOMED. YOU DON'T HAVE A CHANCE.
WITH ROSERADE'S WHIPS IN MY ARSENAL...
...THERE'S NO WAY I'LL LOSE THIS BATTLE!

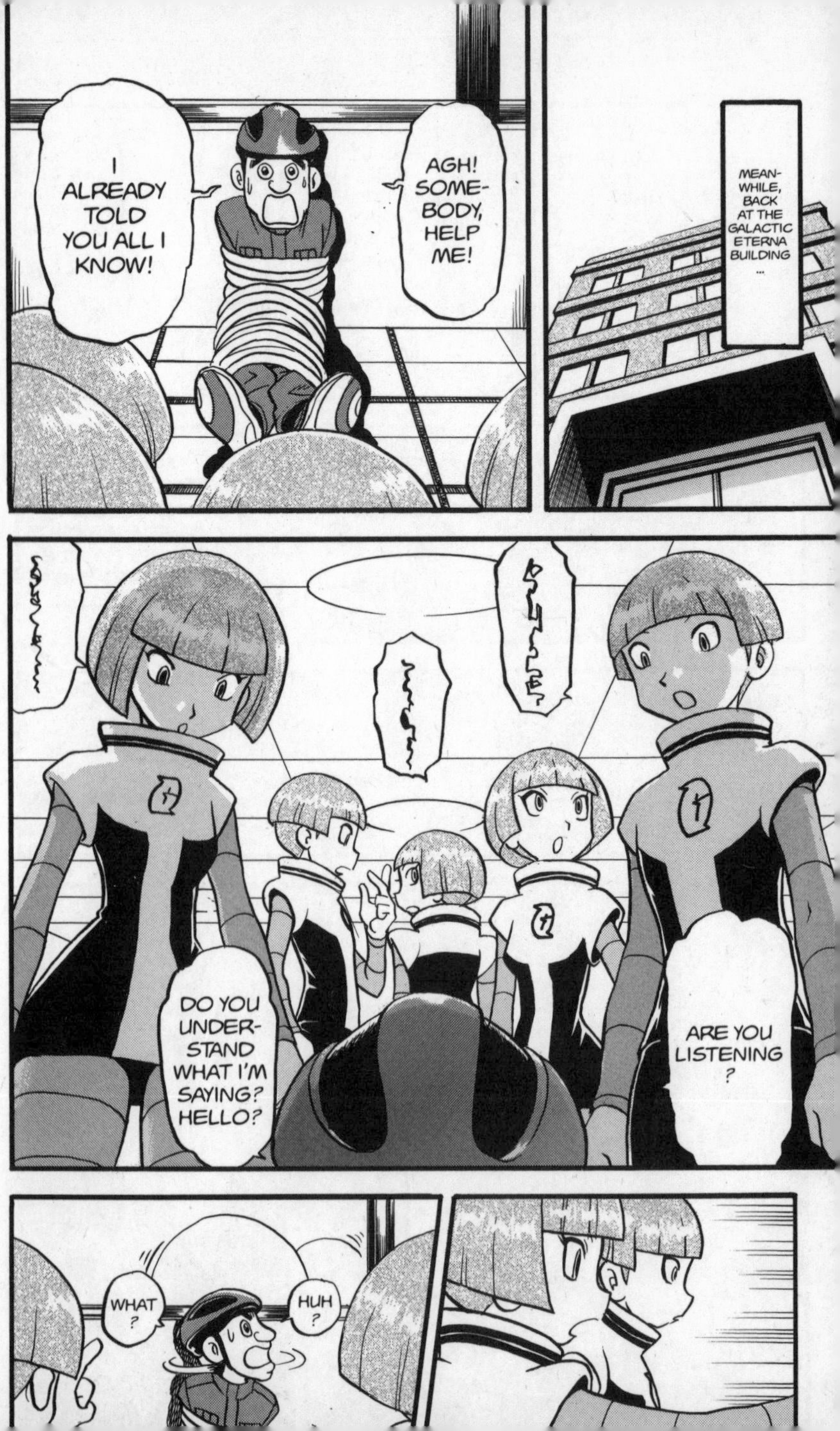
MEAN-WHILE, BACK AT THE GALACTIC ETERNA BUILDING ...
AGH! SOME-BODY, HELP ME!
I ALREADY TOLD YOU ALL I KNOW!
ARE YOU LISTENING?
DO YOU UNDER-STAND WHAT I'M SAYING? HELLO?
HUH?
WHAT?

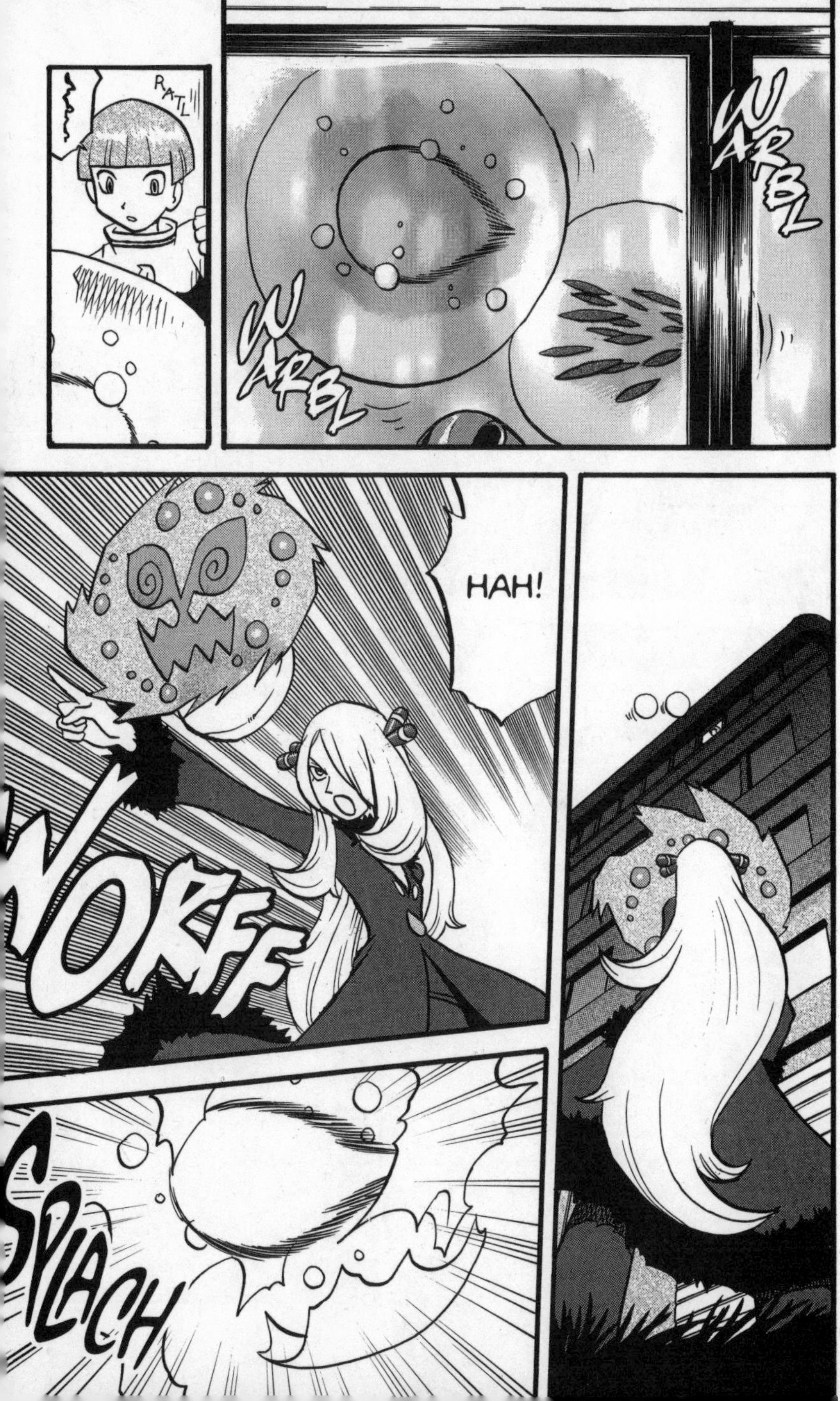
WARBL
WARBL
RATL
HAH!
WORFF
SPLACH

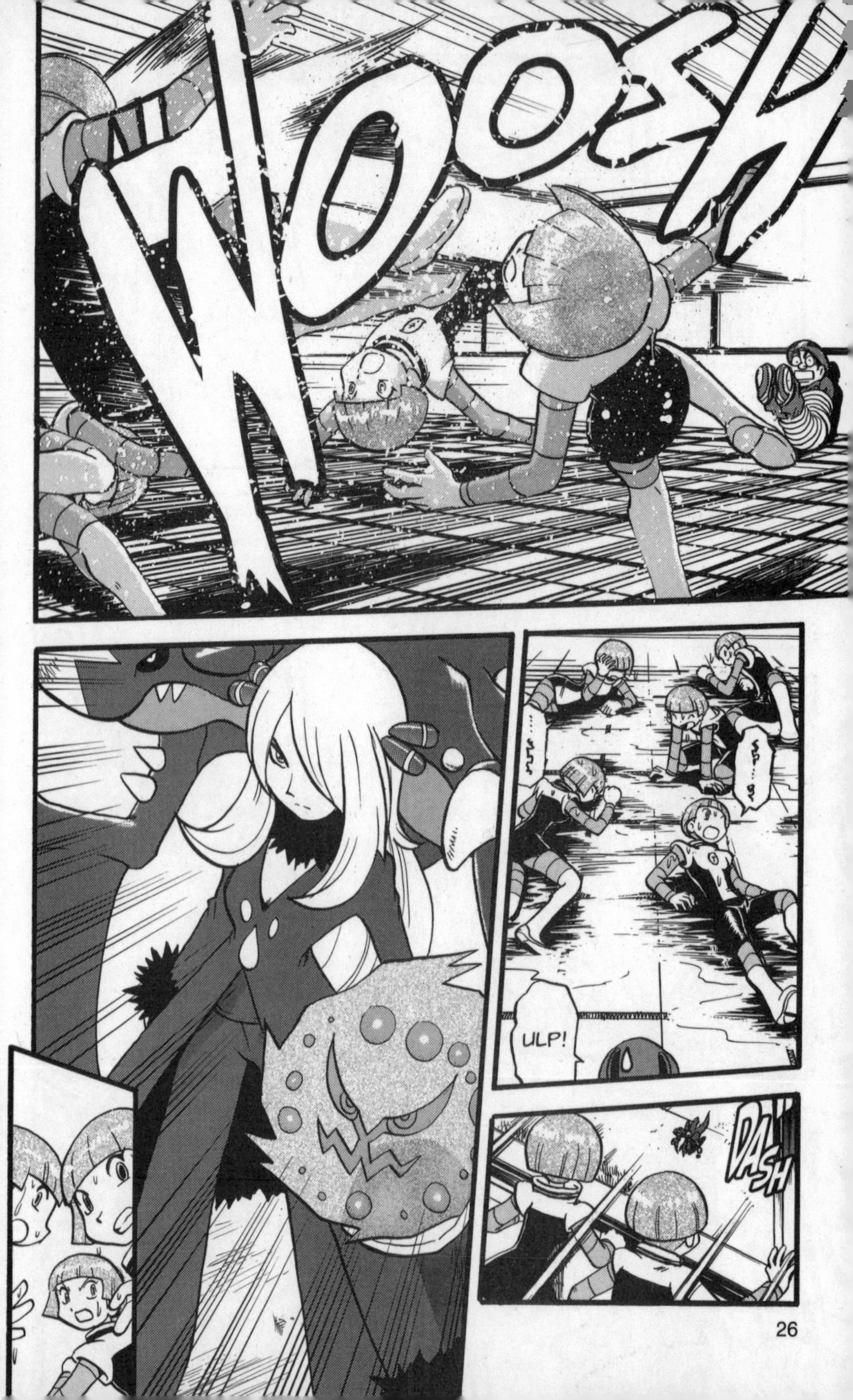
WOOSH
ULP!
DASH

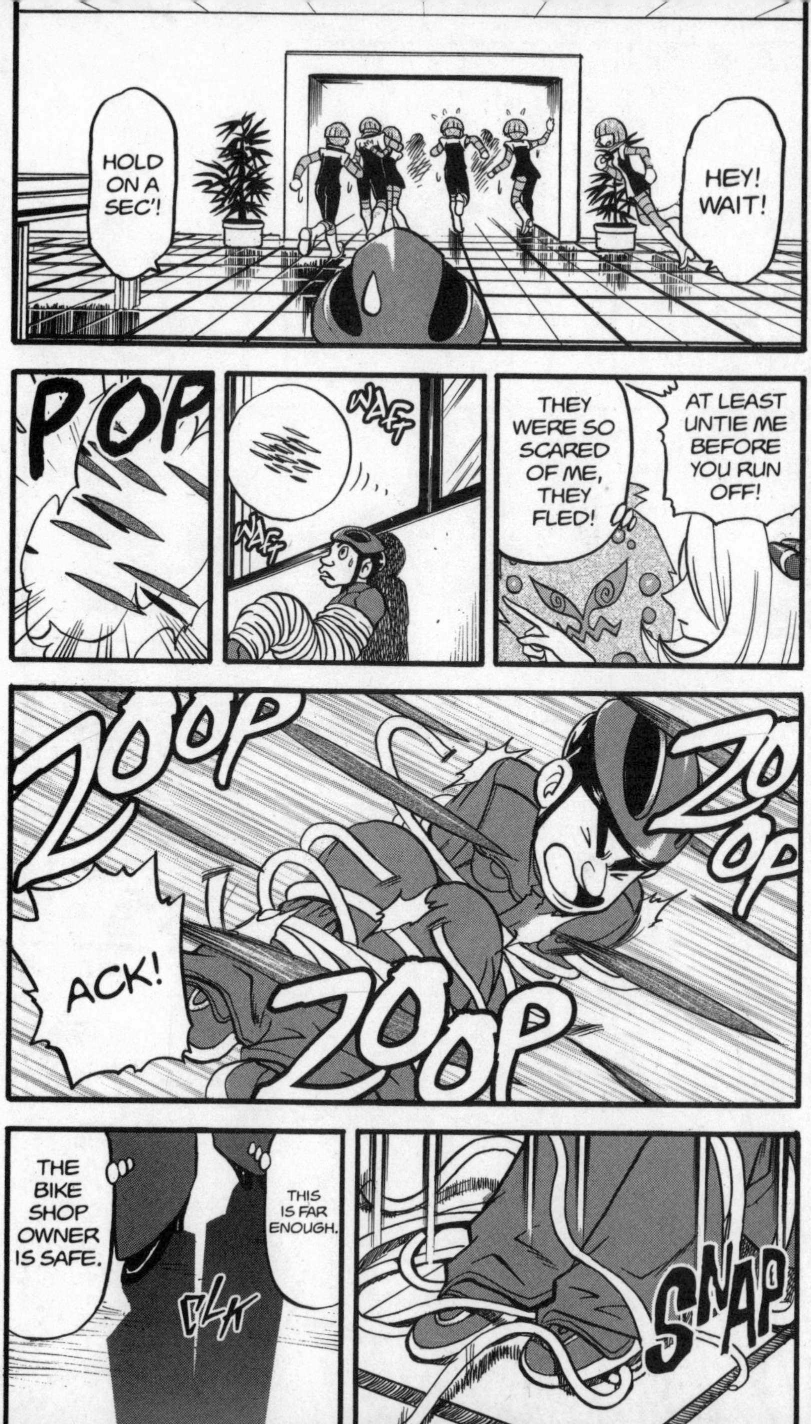
HEY! WAIT!
HOLD ON A SEC'!
AT LEAST UNTIE ME BEFORE YOU RUN OFF!
THEY WERE SO SCARED OF ME, THEY FLED!
WAFF
WAFF
POP
ZOOP
ZOOP
ZOOP
ACK!
SNAP
THIS IS FAR ENOUGH.
THE BIKE SHOP OWNER IS SAFE.
CLK

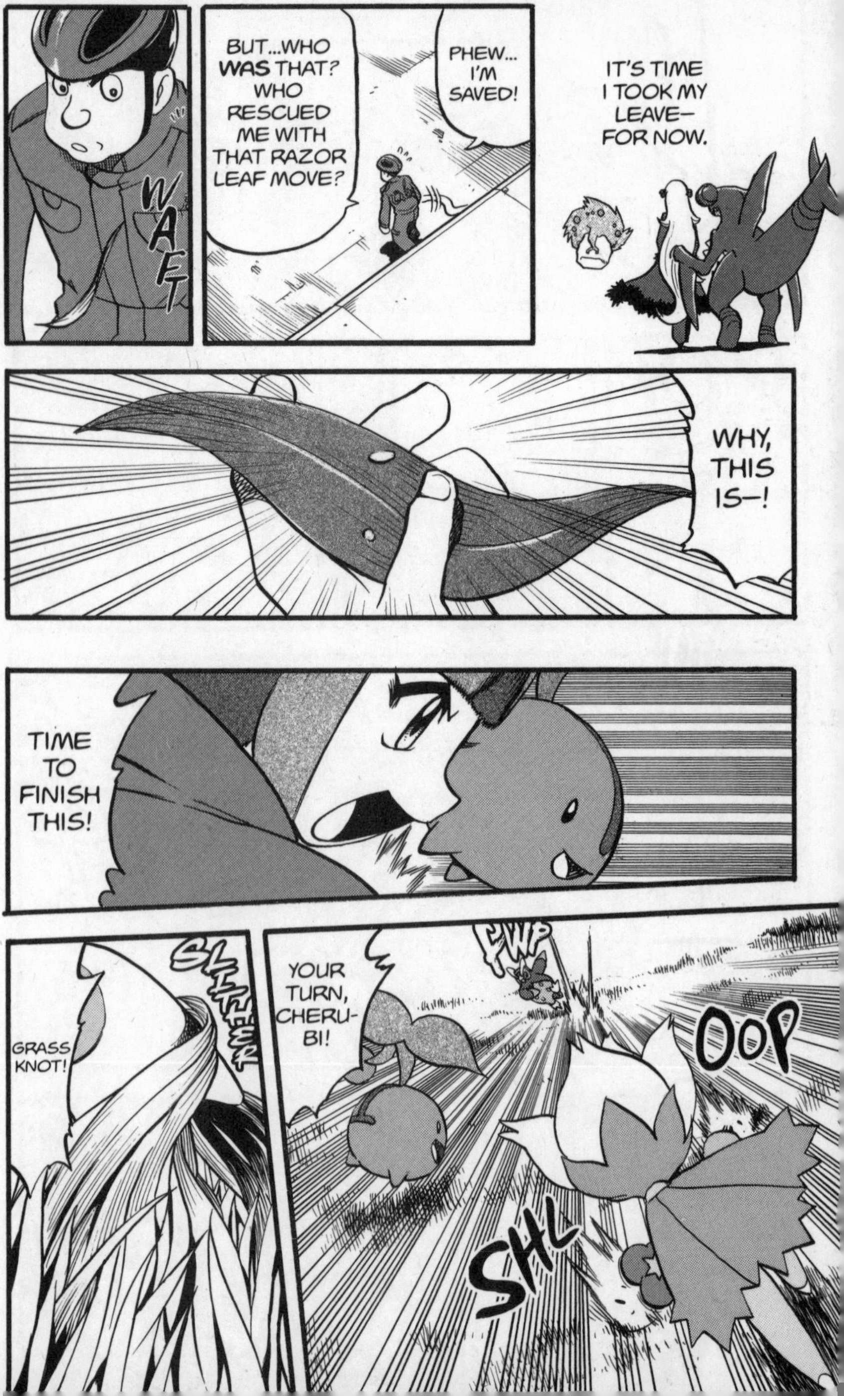
IT'S TIME I TOOK MY LEAVE— FOR NOW.
PHEW... I'M SAVED!
BUT...WHO WAS THAT? WHO RESCUED ME WITH THAT RAZOR LEAF MOVE?
WAFT
WHY, THIS IS—!
TIME TO FINISH THIS!
OOP
YOUR TURN, CHERUBI!
SHL
SLITHER
GRASS KNOT!

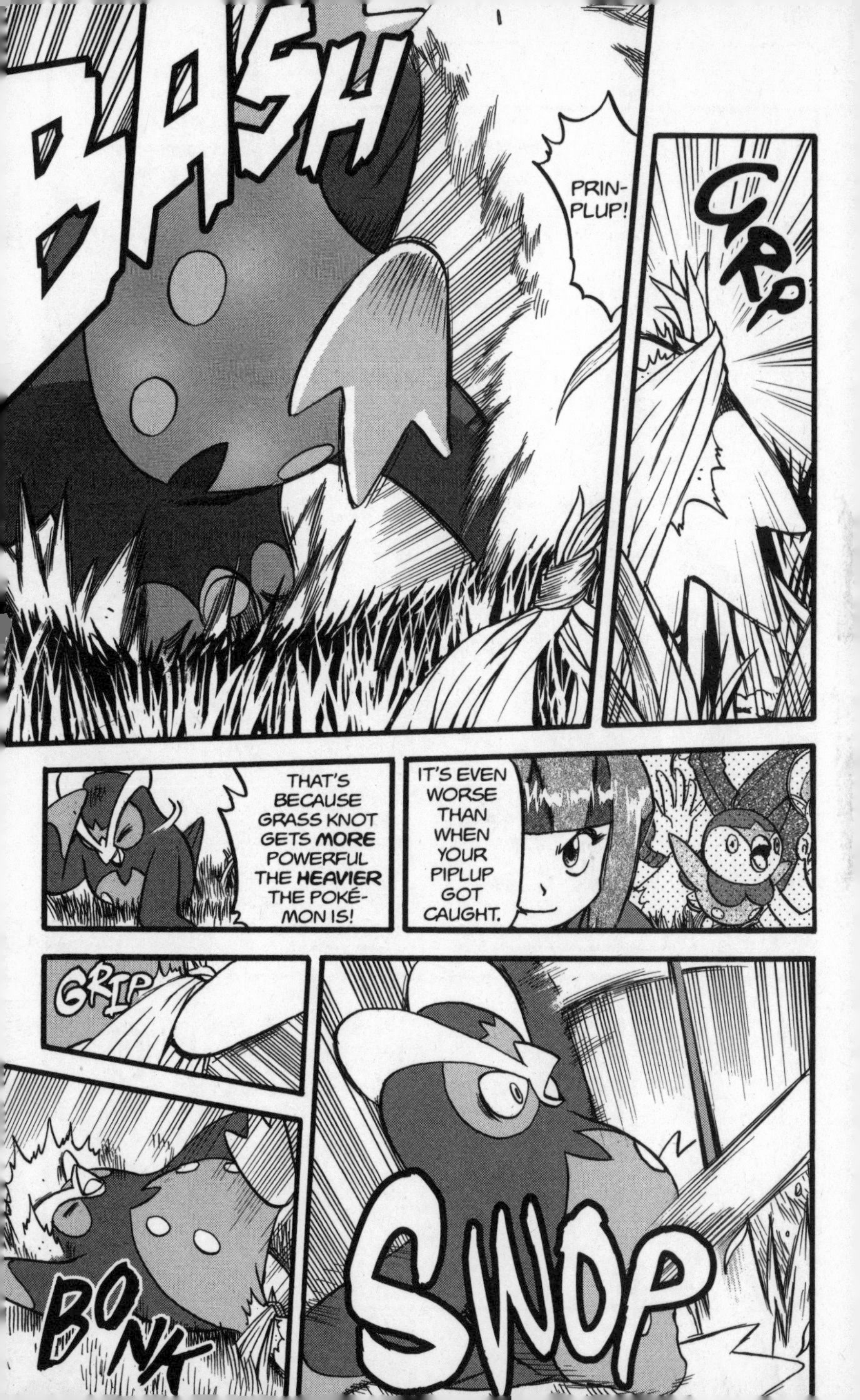
GRP
PRIN-PLUP!
BASH
IT'S EVEN WORSE THAN WHEN YOUR PIPLUP GOT CAUGHT.
THAT'S BECAUSE GRASS KNOT GETS **MORE** POWERFUL THE **HEAVIER** THE POKÉ-MON IS!
SNOP
GRIP
BONK

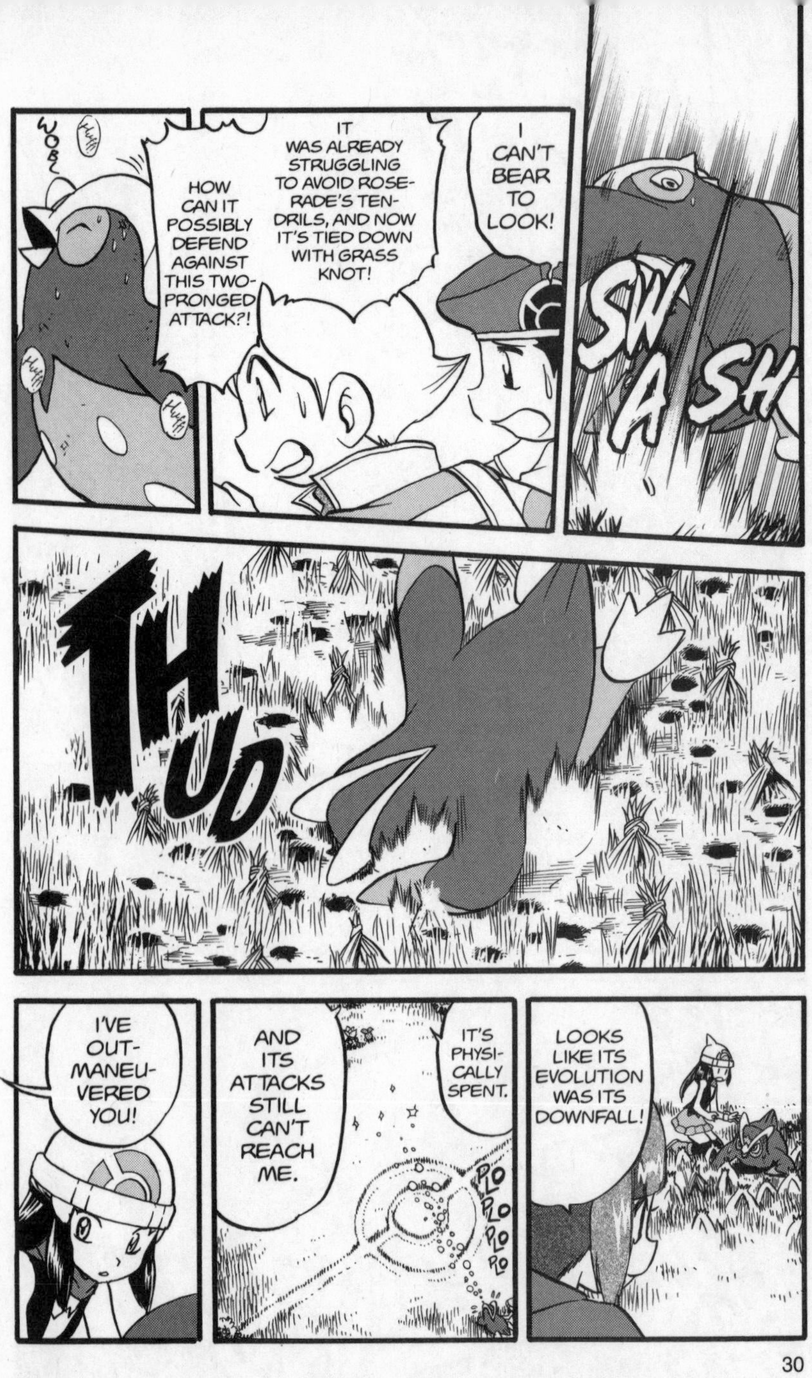
SWASH
I CAN'T BEAR TO LOOK!
IT WAS ALREADY STRUGGLING TO AVOID ROSERADE'S TENDRILS, AND NOW IT'S TIED DOWN WITH GRASS KNOT!
HOW CAN IT POSSIBLY DEFEND AGAINST THIS TWO-PRONGED ATTACK?!
WOBL
Huff
Huff
Huff
THUD
LOOKS LIKE ITS EVOLUTION WAS ITS DOWNFALL!
IT'S PHYSICALLY SPENT.
AND ITS ATTACKS STILL CAN'T REACH ME.
PLO PLO PLO PLO PLO
I'VE OUTMANEUVERED YOU!

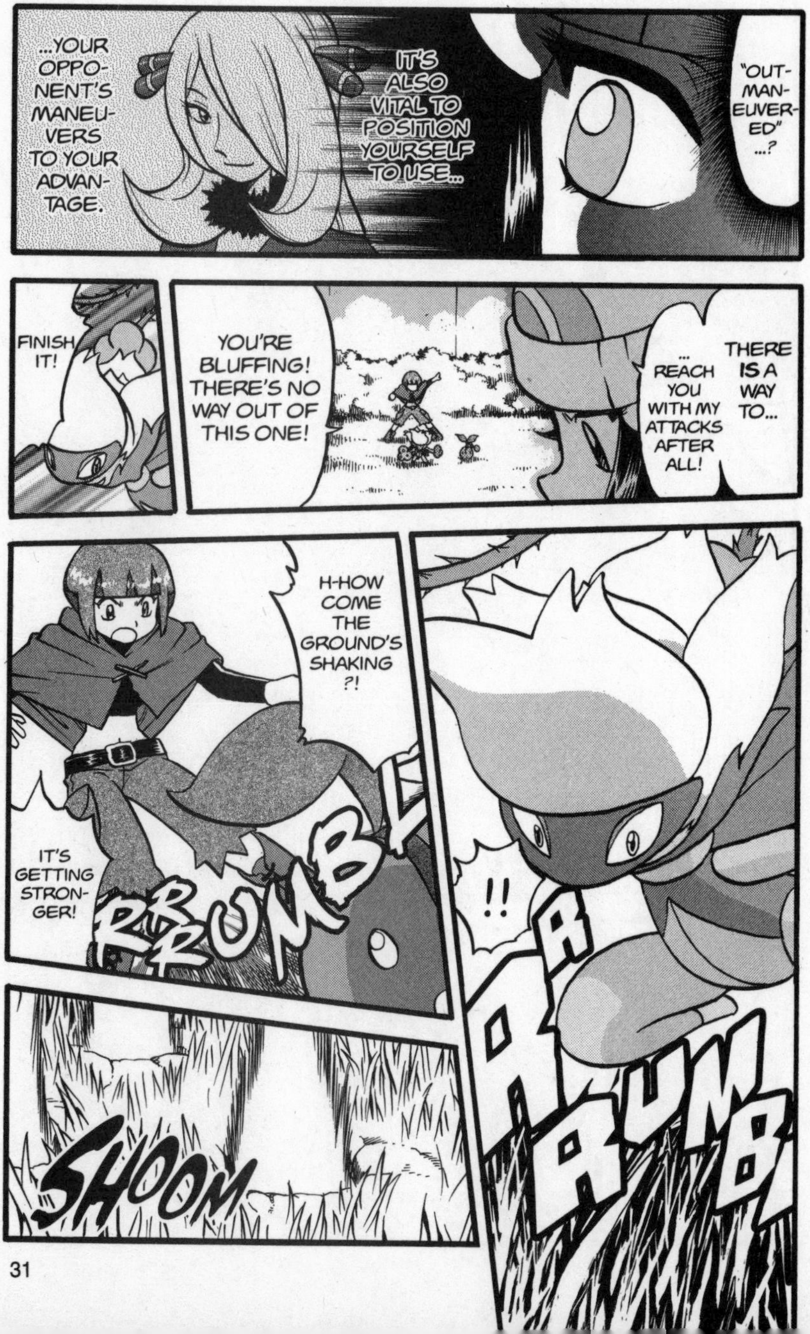
"OUT-MANEUVERED" ...?
IT'S ALSO VITAL TO POSITION YOURSELF TO USE...
...YOUR OPPONENT'S MANEUVERS TO YOUR ADVANTAGE.
THERE IS A WAY TO...
...REACH YOU WITH MY ATTACKS AFTER ALL!
YOU'RE BLUFFING! THERE'S NO WAY OUT OF THIS ONE!
FINISH IT!
!!
RRUMB
H-HOW COME THE GROUND'S SHAKING?!
IT'S GETTING STRONGER!
RRRUMBL
SHOOM

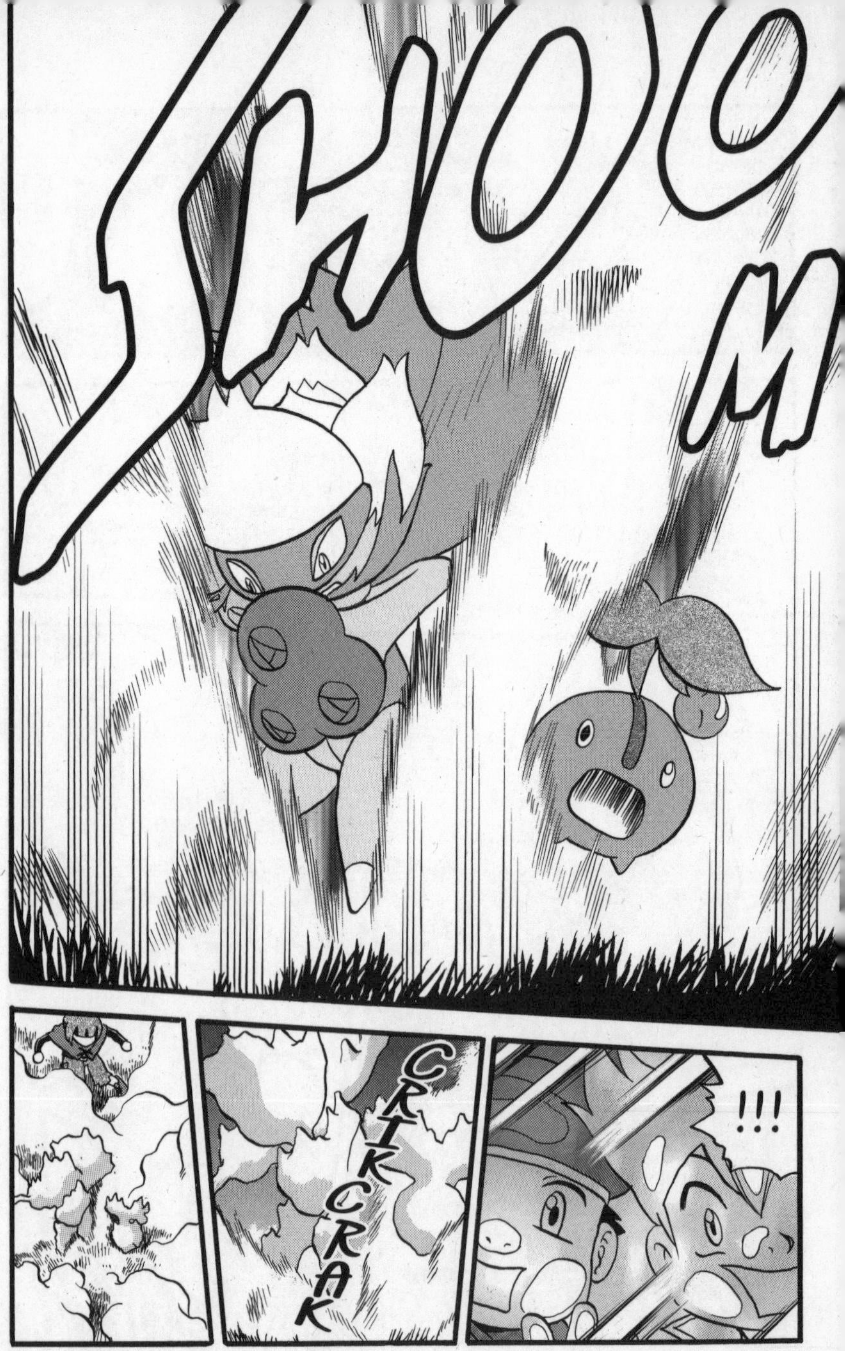
SHOOM
!!!
CRIK CRAK

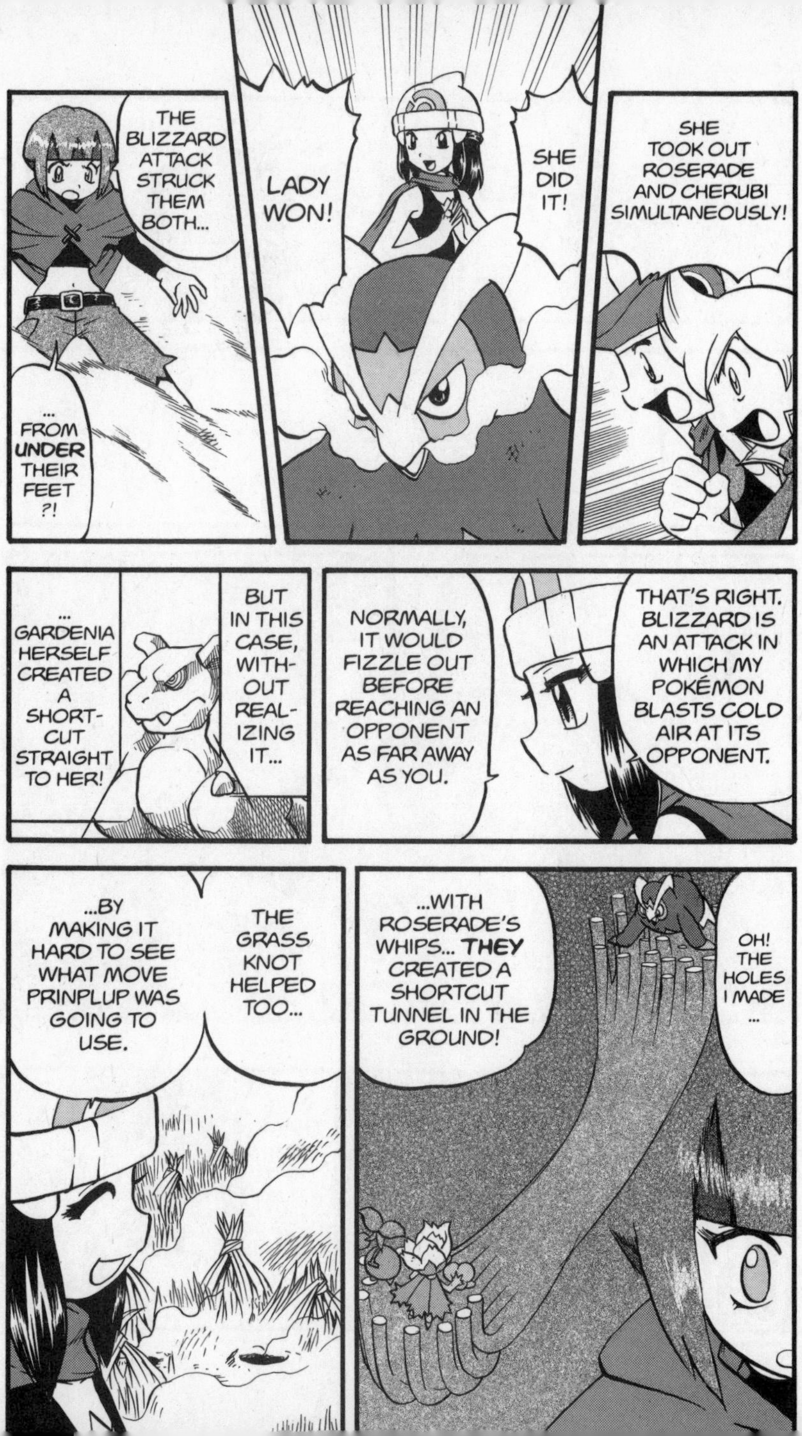
SHE TOOK OUT ROSERADE AND CHERUBI SIMULTANEOUSLY!
SHE DID IT!
LADY WON!
THE BLIZZARD ATTACK STRUCK THEM BOTH...
...FROM UNDER THEIR FEET?!
THAT'S RIGHT. BLIZZARD IS AN ATTACK IN WHICH MY POKÉMON BLASTS COLD AIR AT ITS OPPONENT.
NORMALLY, IT WOULD FIZZLE OUT BEFORE REACHING AN OPPONENT AS FAR AWAY AS YOU.
BUT IN THIS CASE, WITH-OUT REAL-IZING IT...
...GARDENIA HERSELF CREATED A SHORT-CUT STRAIGHT TO HER!
OH! THE HOLES I MADE...
...WITH ROSERADE'S WHIPS... **THEY** CREATED A SHORTCUT TUNNEL IN THE GROUND!
THE GRASS KNOT HELPED TOO...
...BY MAKING IT HARD TO SEE WHAT MOVE PRINPLUP WAS GOING TO USE.

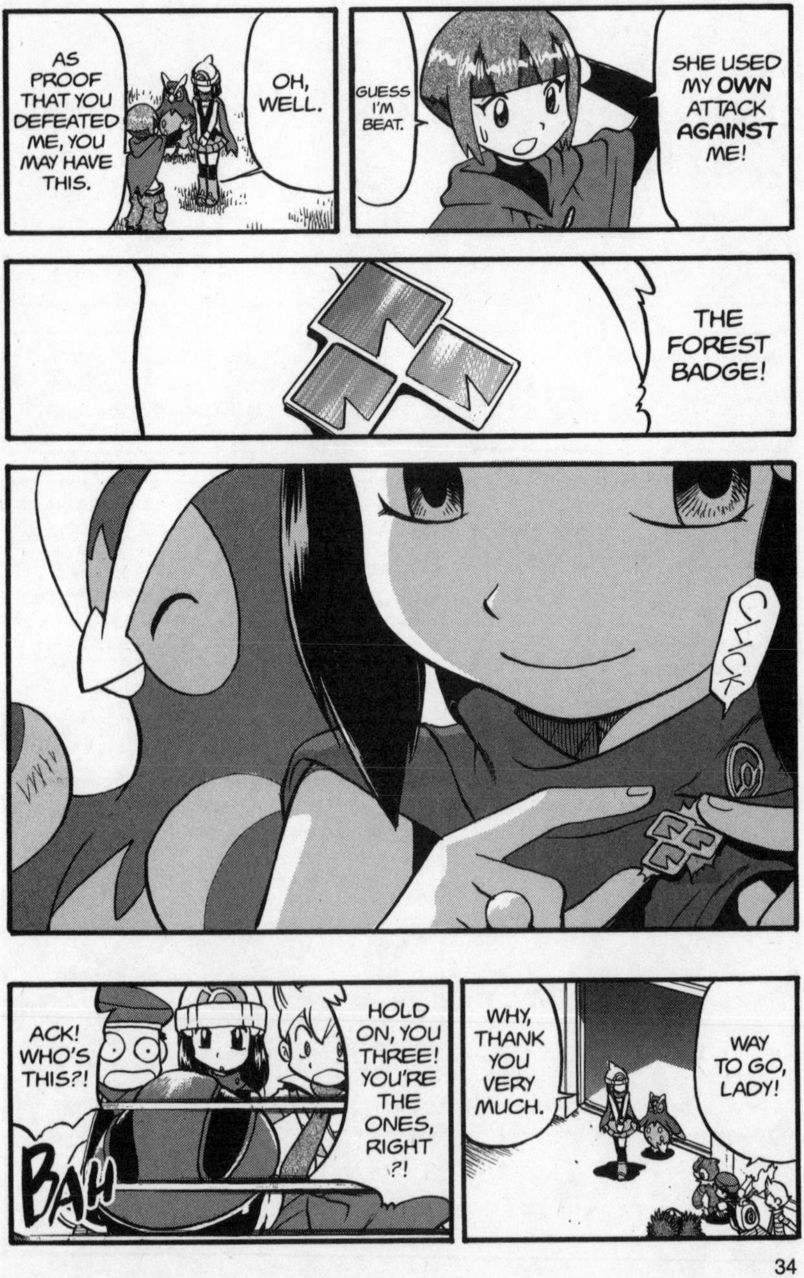
SHE USED MY OWN ATTACK AGAINST ME!
GUESS I'M BEAT.
OH, WELL.
AS PROOF THAT YOU DEFEATED ME, YOU MAY HAVE THIS.
THE FOREST BADGE!
CLICK
WAY TO GO, LADY!
WHY, THANK YOU VERY MUCH.
HOLD ON, YOU THREE! YOU'RE THE ONES, RIGHT?!
ACK! WHO'S THIS?!
BAH

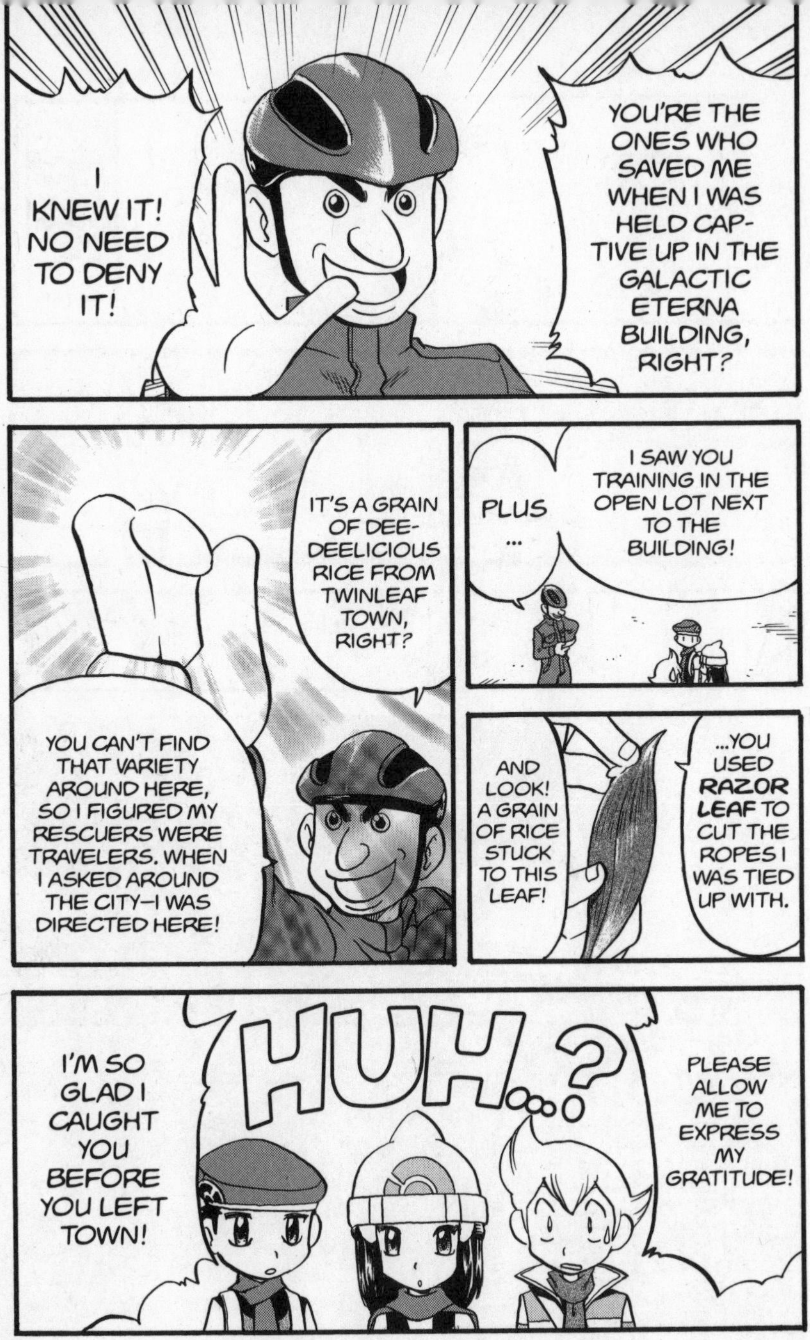
YOU'RE THE ONES WHO SAVED ME WHEN I WAS HELD CAP-TIVE UP IN THE GALACTIC ETERNA BUILDING, RIGHT?
I KNEW IT! NO NEED TO DENY IT!
I SAW YOU TRAINING IN THE OPEN LOT NEXT TO THE BUILDING!
PLUS ...
...YOU USED **RAZOR LEAF** TO CUT THE ROPES I WAS TIED UP WITH.
AND LOOK! A GRAIN OF RICE STUCK TO THIS LEAF!
IT'S A GRAIN OF DEE-DEELICIOUS RICE FROM TWINLEAF TOWN, RIGHT?
YOU CAN'T FIND THAT VARIETY AROUND HERE, SO I FIGURED MY RESCUERS WERE TRAVELERS. WHEN I ASKED AROUND THE CITY—I WAS DIRECTED HERE!
PLEASE ALLOW ME TO EXPRESS MY GRATITUDE!
HUH...?
I'M SO GLAD I CAUGHT YOU BEFORE YOU LEFT TOWN!

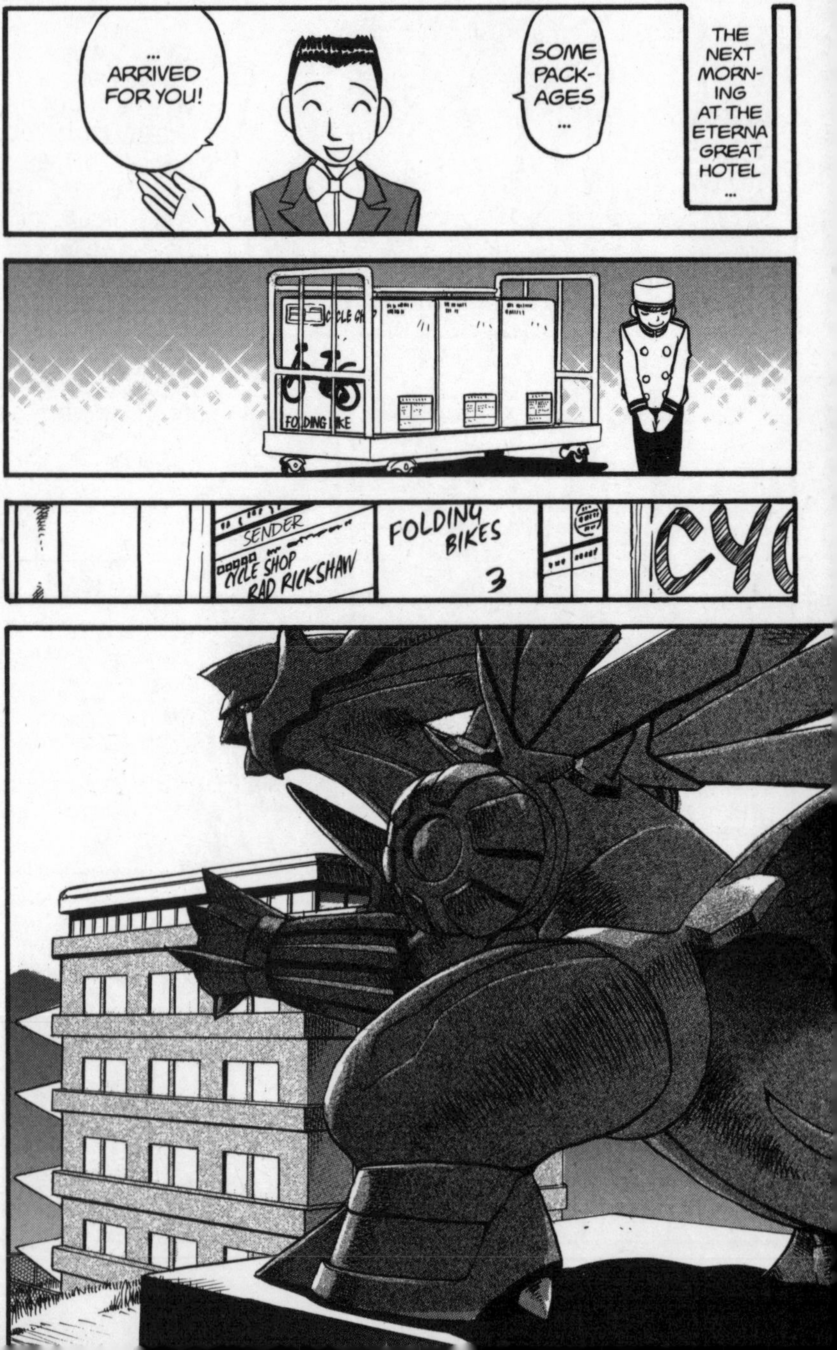
THE NEXT MORNING AT THE ETERNA GREAT HOTEL ...
SOME PACKAGES ...
... ARRIVED FOR YOU!
FOLDING BIKE
CYC
FOLDING BIKES 3
SENDER
CYCLE SHOP RAD RICKSHAW

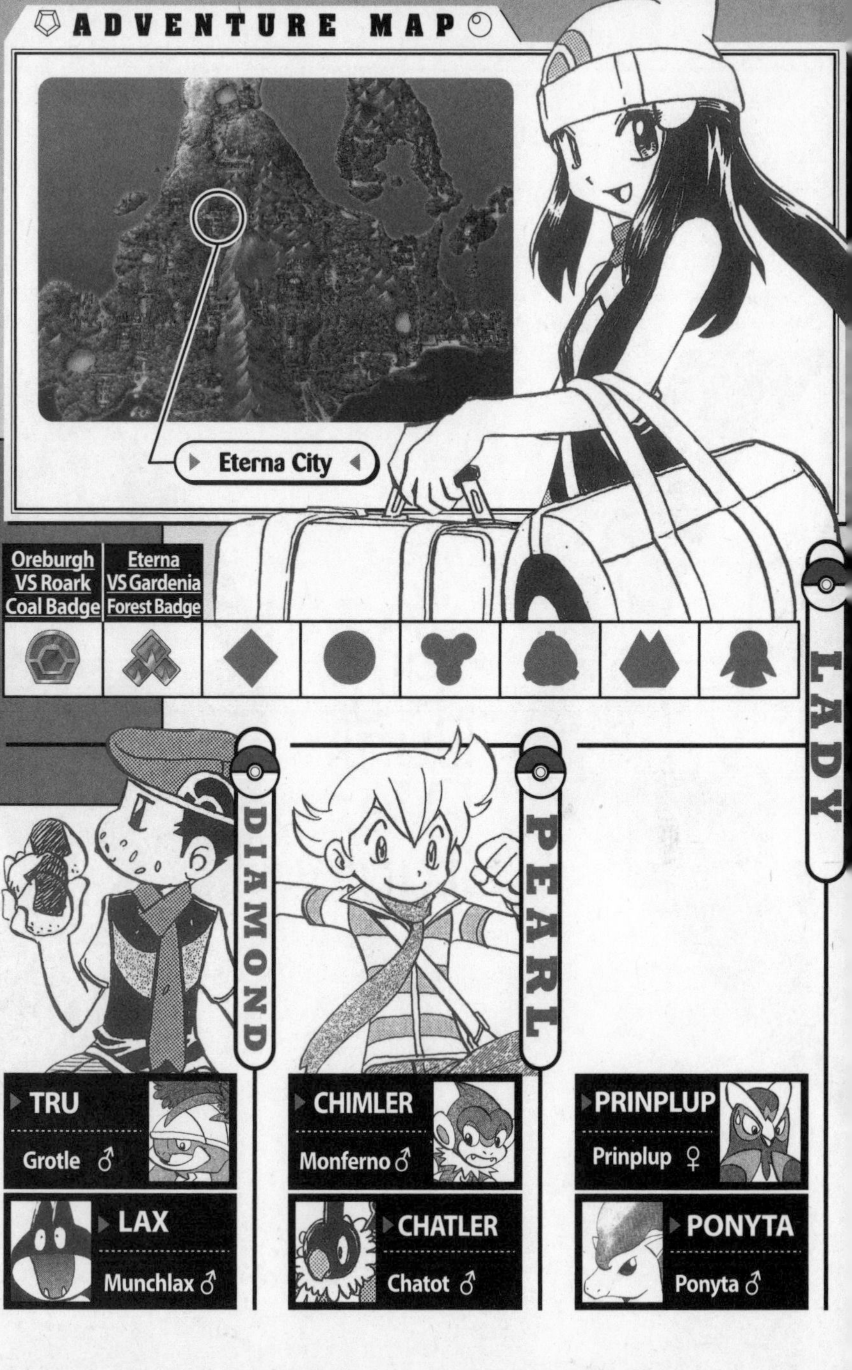
ADVENTURE MAP
Eterna City
Oreburgh
VS Roark
Coal Badge
Eterna
VS Gardenia
Forest Badge
LADY
DIAMOND
PEARL
TRU
Grotle ♂
LAX
Munchlax ♂
CHIMLER
Monferno ♂
CHATLER
Chatot ♂
PRINPLUP
Prinplup ♀
PONYTA
Ponyta ♂

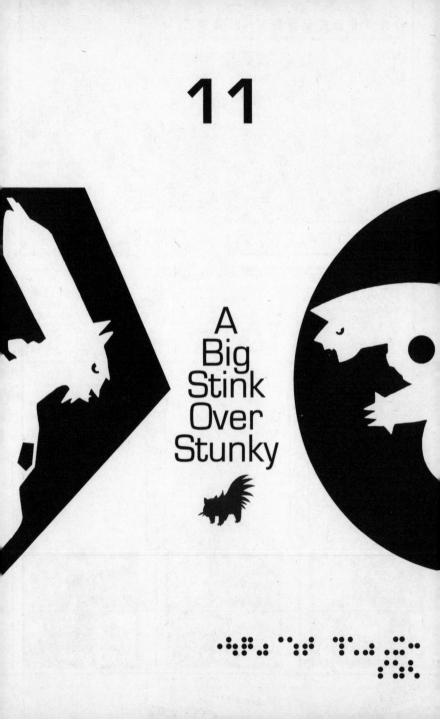

11

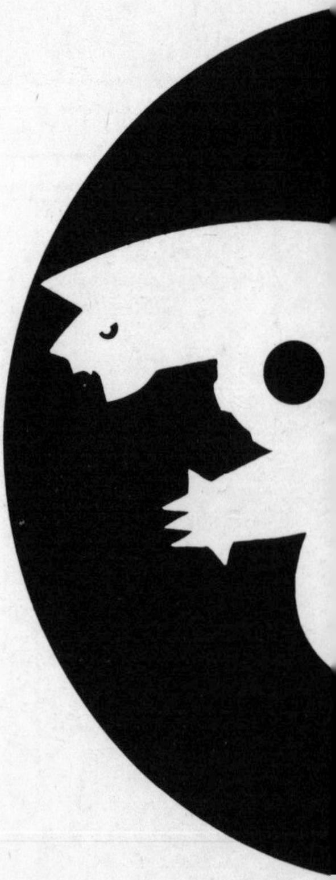

A Big Stink Over Stunky

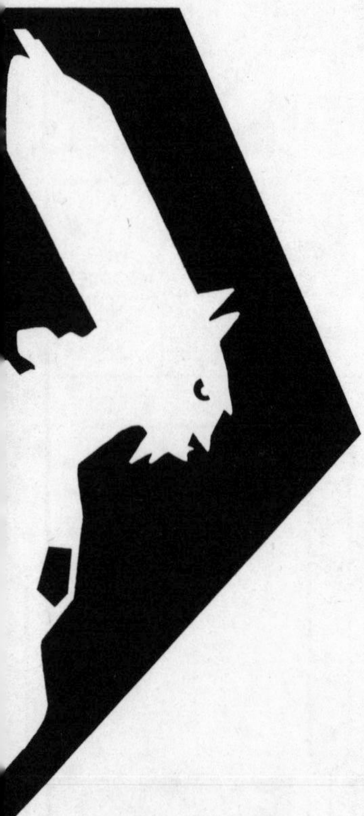

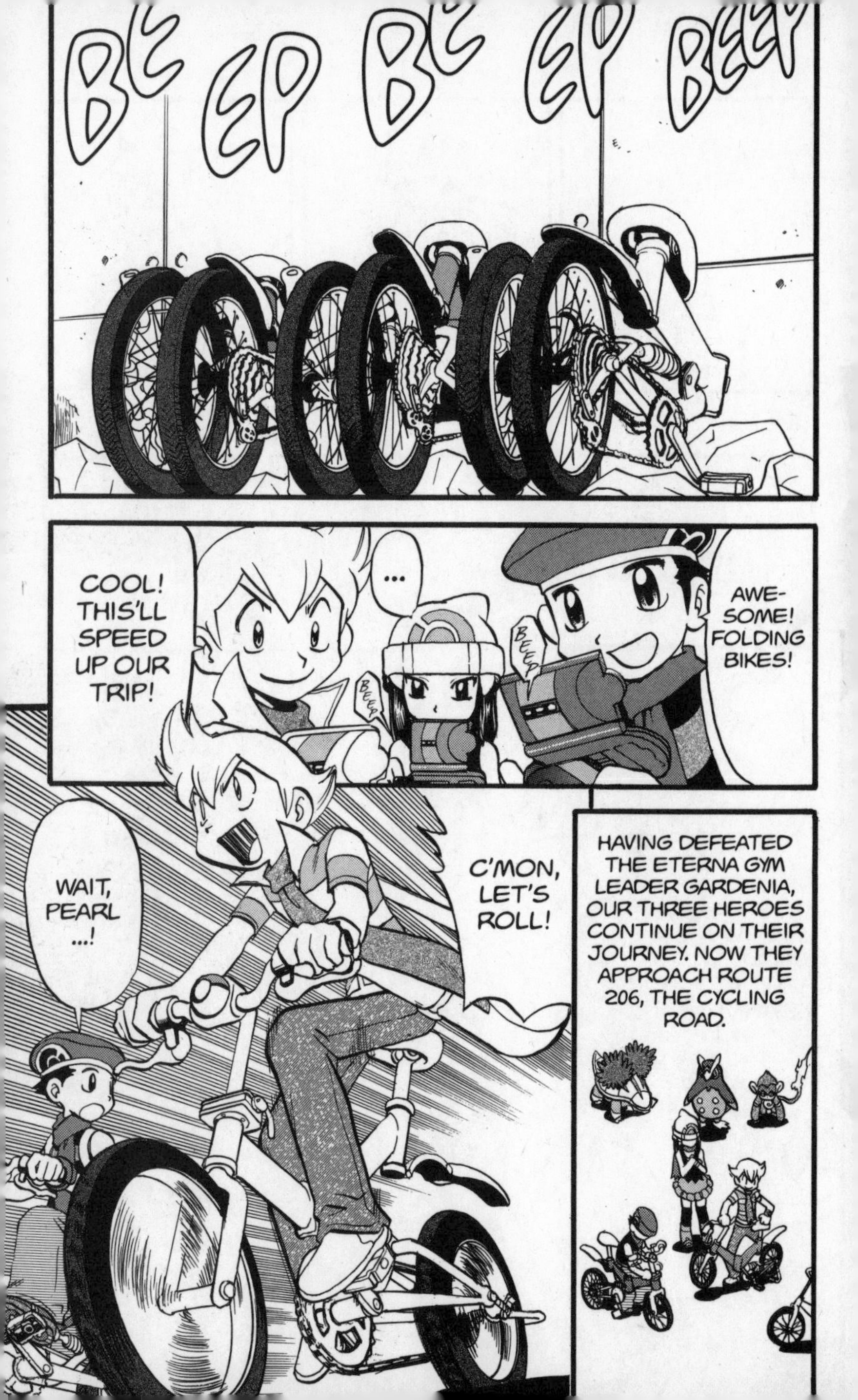

BEEP BEEP BEEP
AWE-SOME! FOLDING BIKES!
BEEP
BEEP
...
COOL! THIS'LL SPEED UP OUR TRIP!
HAVING DEFEATED THE ETERNA GYM LEADER GARDENIA, OUR THREE HEROES CONTINUE ON THEIR JOURNEY. NOW THEY APPROACH ROUTE 206, THE CYCLING ROAD.
C'MON, LET'S ROLL!
WAIT, PEARL ...!

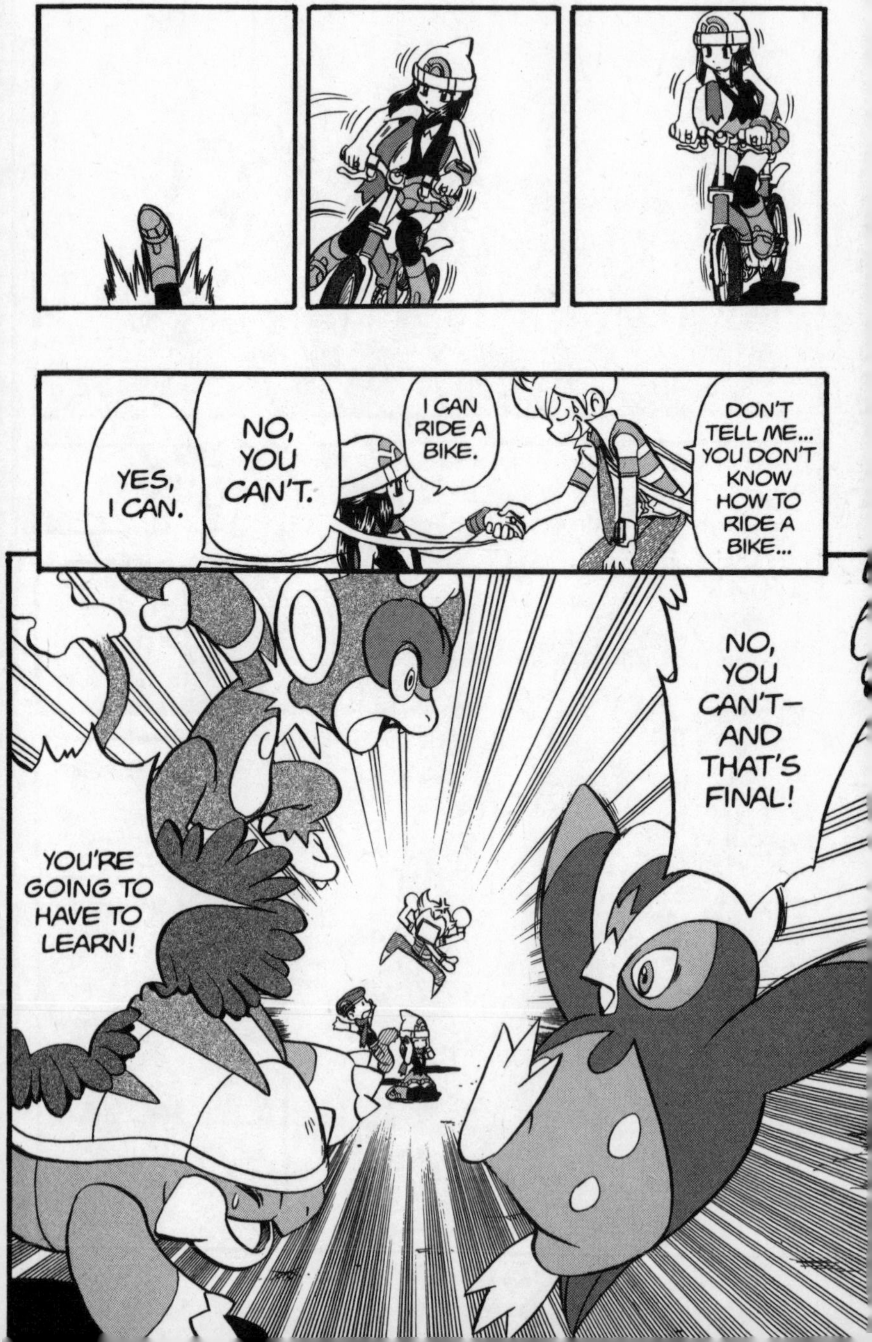
DON'T TELL ME... YOU DON'T KNOW HOW TO RIDE A BIKE...
I CAN RIDE A BIKE.
NO, YOU CAN'T.
YES, I CAN.
NO, YOU CAN'T— AND THAT'S FINAL!
YOU'RE GOING TO HAVE TO LEARN!

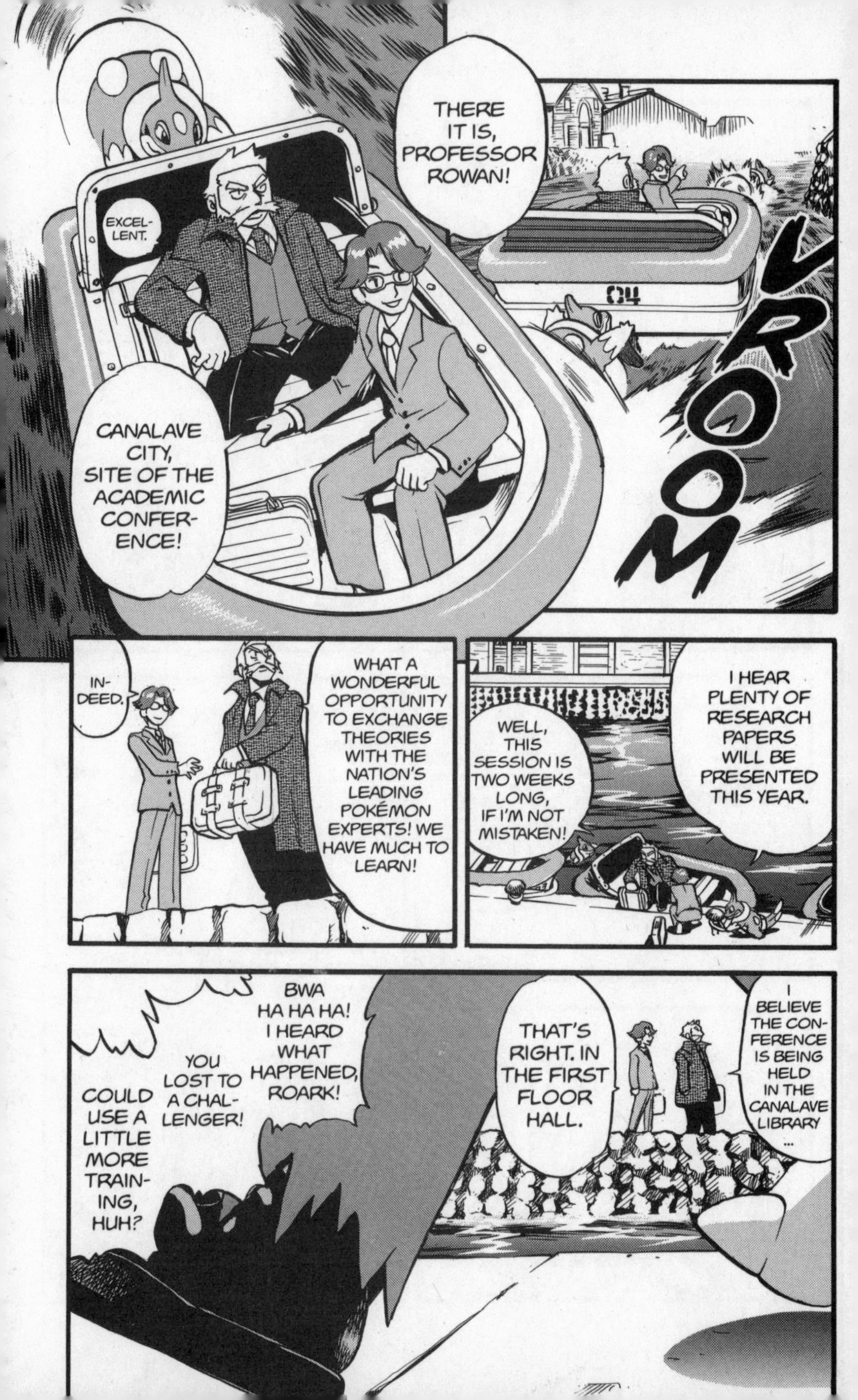

THERE IT IS, PROFESSOR ROWAN!
VROOM
EXCEL-LENT.
CANALAVE CITY, SITE OF THE ACADEMIC CONFER-ENCE!
I HEAR PLENTY OF RESEARCH PAPERS WILL BE PRESENTED THIS YEAR.
WELL, THIS SESSION IS TWO WEEKS LONG, IF I'M NOT MISTAKEN!
WHAT A WONDERFUL OPPORTUNITY TO EXCHANGE THEORIES WITH THE NATION'S LEADING POKÉMON EXPERTS! WE HAVE MUCH TO LEARN!
IN-DEED.
I BELIEVE THE CON-FERENCE IS BEING HELD IN THE CANALAVE LIBRARY ...
THAT'S RIGHT. IN THE FIRST FLOOR HALL.
BWA HA HA HA! I HEARD WHAT HAPPENED, ROARK!
YOU LOST TO A CHAL-LENGER!
COULD USE A LITTLE MORE TRAIN-ING, HUH?

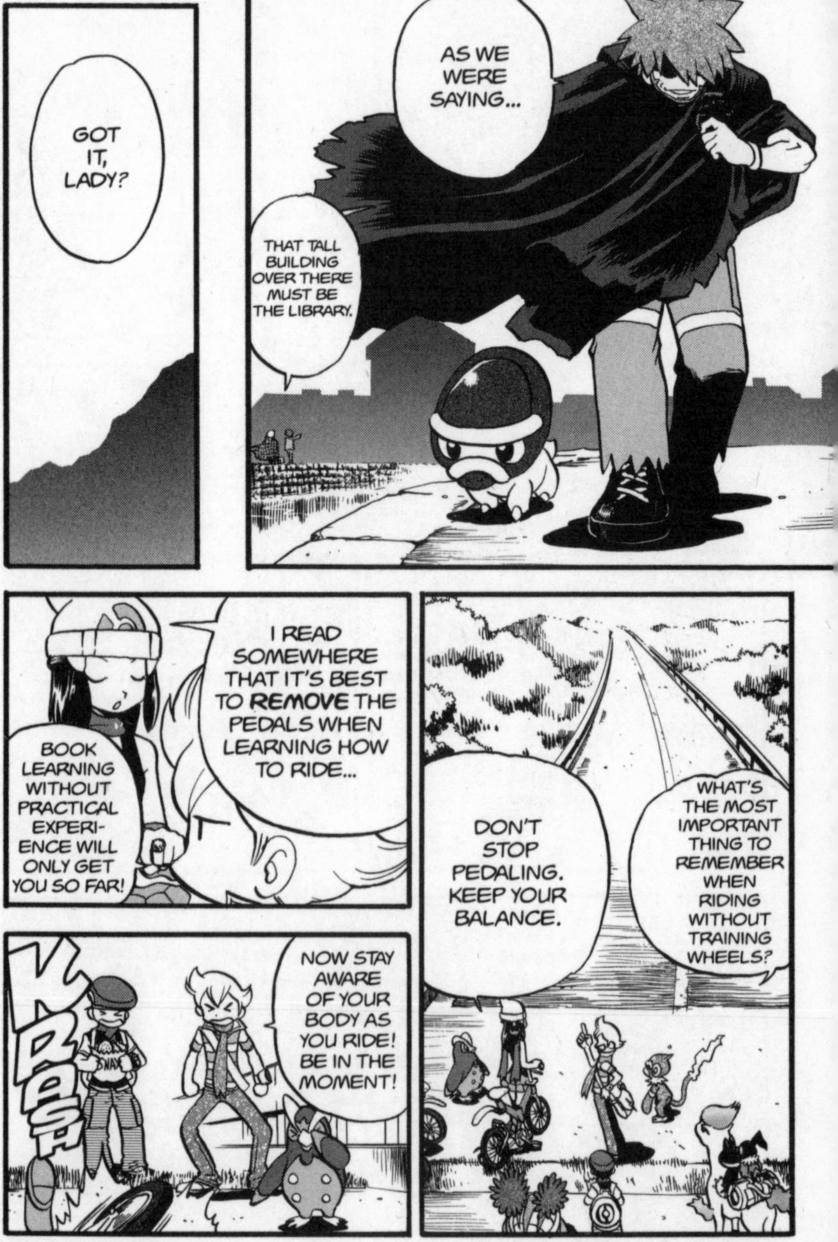
AS WE WERE SAYING...
THAT TALL BUILDING OVER THERE MUST BE THE LIBRARY.
GOT IT, LADY?
WHAT'S THE MOST IMPORTANT THING TO REMEMBER WHEN RIDING WITHOUT TRAINING WHEELS?
DON'T STOP PEDALING. KEEP YOUR BALANCE.
I READ SOMEWHERE THAT IT'S BEST TO **REMOVE** THE PEDALS WHEN LEARNING HOW TO RIDE...
BOOK LEARNING WITHOUT PRACTICAL EXPERIENCE WILL ONLY GET YOU SO FAR!
NOW STAY AWARE OF YOUR BODY AS YOU RIDE! BE IN THE MOMENT!
KRASH

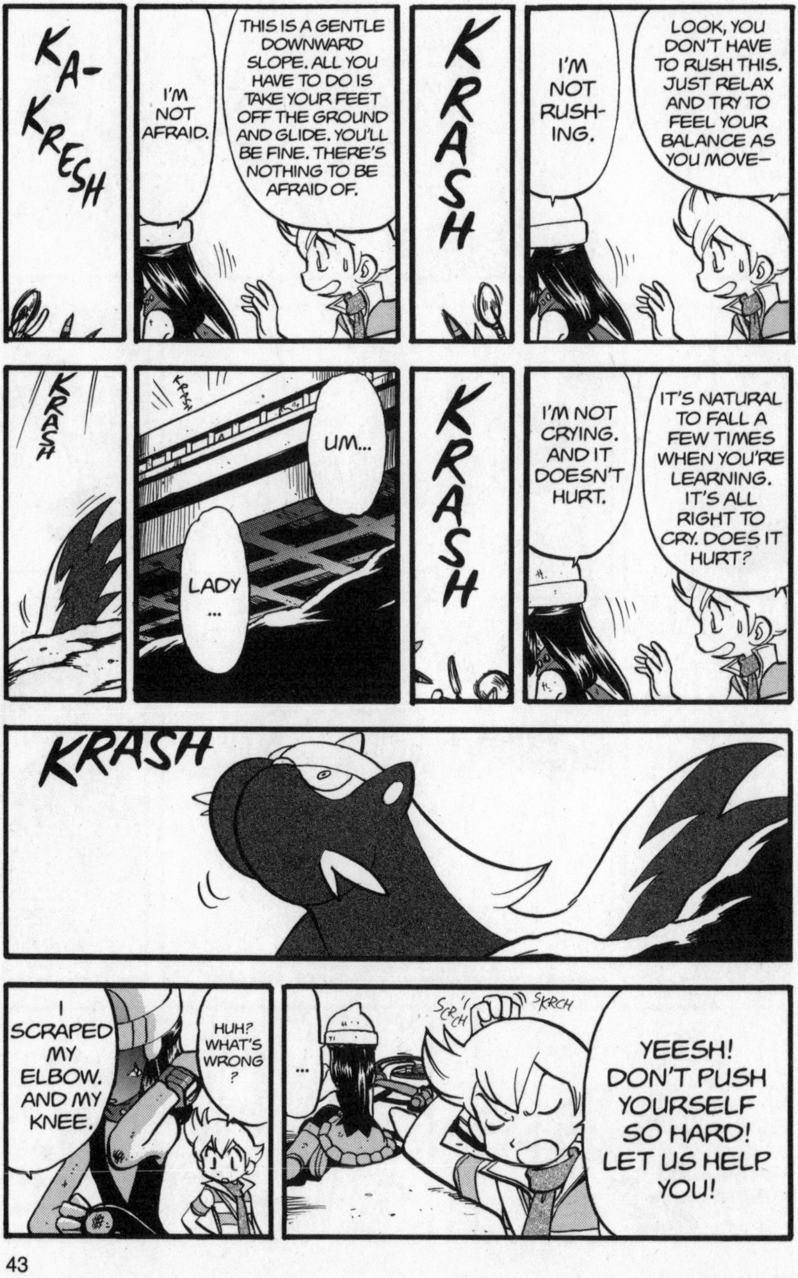
LOOK, YOU DON'T HAVE TO RUSH THIS. JUST RELAX AND TRY TO FEEL YOUR BALANCE AS YOU MOVE—
I'M NOT RUSH-ING.
KRASH
THIS IS A GENTLE DOWNWARD SLOPE. ALL YOU HAVE TO DO IS TAKE YOUR FEET OFF THE GROUND AND GLIDE. YOU'LL BE FINE. THERE'S NOTHING TO BE AFRAID OF.
I'M NOT AFRAID.
KA-KRESH
IT'S NATURAL TO FALL A FEW TIMES WHEN YOU'RE LEARNING. IT'S ALL RIGHT TO CRY. DOES IT HURT?
I'M NOT CRYING. AND IT DOESN'T HURT.
KRASH
UM...
LADY...
KRASH
KRASH
YEESH! DON'T PUSH YOURSELF SO HARD! LET US HELP YOU!
SKRCH
SCRCH
...
HUH? WHAT'S WRONG?
I SCRAPED MY ELBOW. AND MY KNEE.

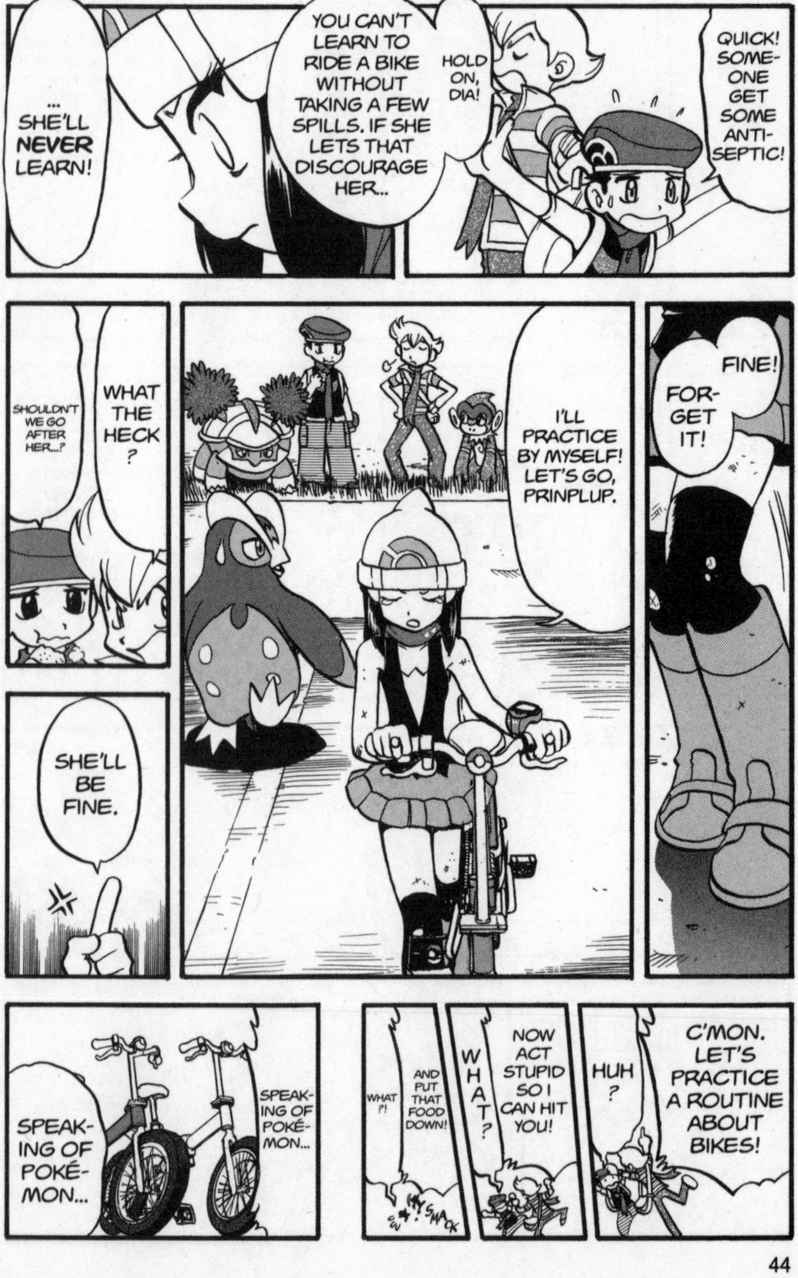
QUICK! SOME-ONE GET SOME ANTI-SEPTIC!
HOLD ON, DIA!
YOU CAN'T LEARN TO RIDE A BIKE WITHOUT TAKING A FEW SPILLS. IF SHE LETS THAT DISCOURAGE HER...
... SHE'LL **NEVER** LEARN!
FINE!
FOR-GET IT!
I'LL PRACTICE BY MYSELF! LET'S GO, PRINPLUP.
WHAT THE HECK?
SHOULDN'T WE GO AFTER HER...?
SHE'LL BE FINE.
C'MON. LET'S PRACTICE A ROUTINE ABOUT BIKES!
HUH?
NOW ACT STUPID SO I CAN HIT YOU!
WHAT?
AND PUT THAT FOOD DOWN!
WHAT?!
SMACK
SPEAK-ING OF POKÉ-MON...
SPEAK-ING OF POKÉ-MON...

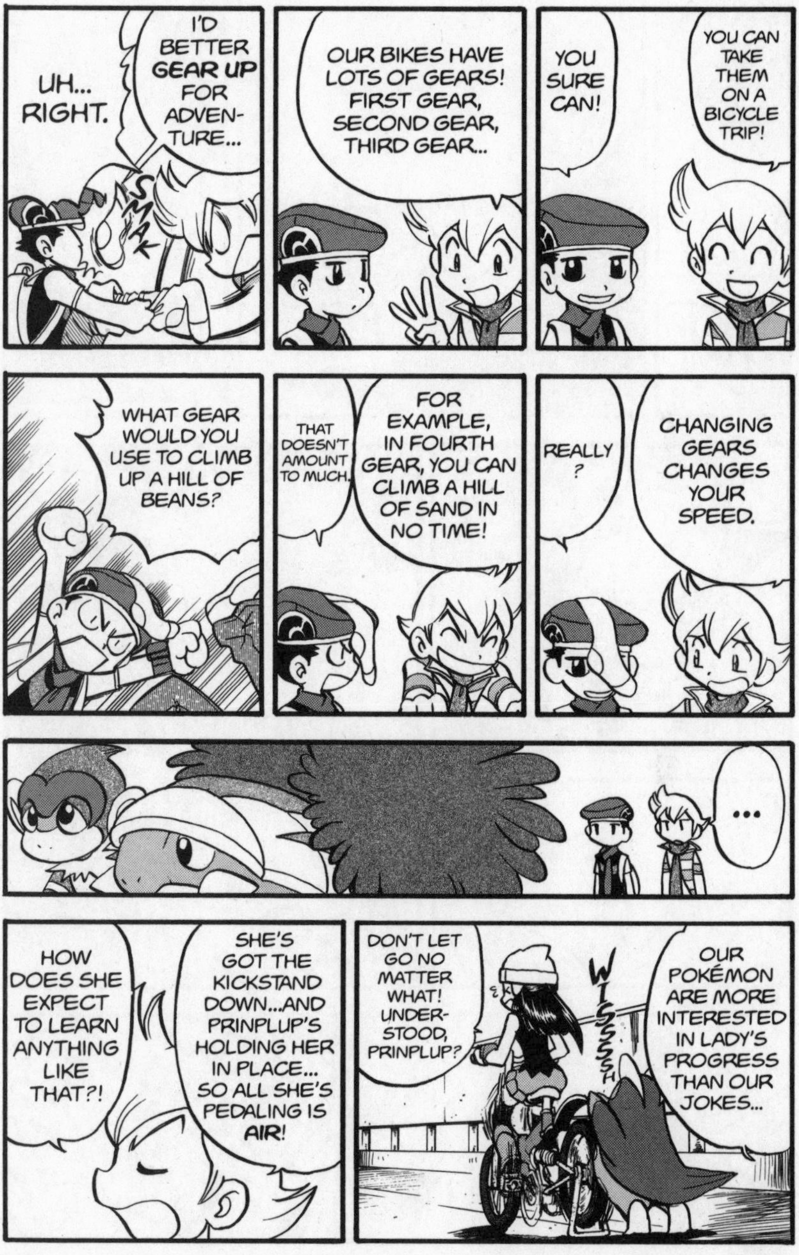
YOU CAN TAKE THEM ON A BICYCLE TRIP!
YOU SURE CAN!
OUR BIKES HAVE LOTS OF GEARS! FIRST GEAR, SECOND GEAR, THIRD GEAR...
I'D BETTER **GEAR UP** FOR ADVEN-TURE...
SMAK
UH... RIGHT.
CHANGING GEARS CHANGES YOUR SPEED.
REALLY?
FOR EXAMPLE, IN FOURTH GEAR, YOU CAN CLIMB A HILL OF SAND IN NO TIME!
THAT DOESN'T AMOUNT TO MUCH.
WHAT GEAR WOULD YOU USE TO CLIMB UP A HILL OF BEANS?
...
OUR POKÉMON ARE MORE INTERESTED IN LADY'S PROGRESS THAN OUR JOKES...
WISSSSH
DON'T LET GO NO MATTER WHAT! UNDER-STOOD, PRINPLUP?
SHE'S GOT THE KICKSTAND DOWN...AND PRINPLUP'S HOLDING HER IN PLACE... SO ALL SHE'S PEDALING IS **AIR**!
HOW DOES SHE EXPECT TO LEARN ANYTHING LIKE THAT?!

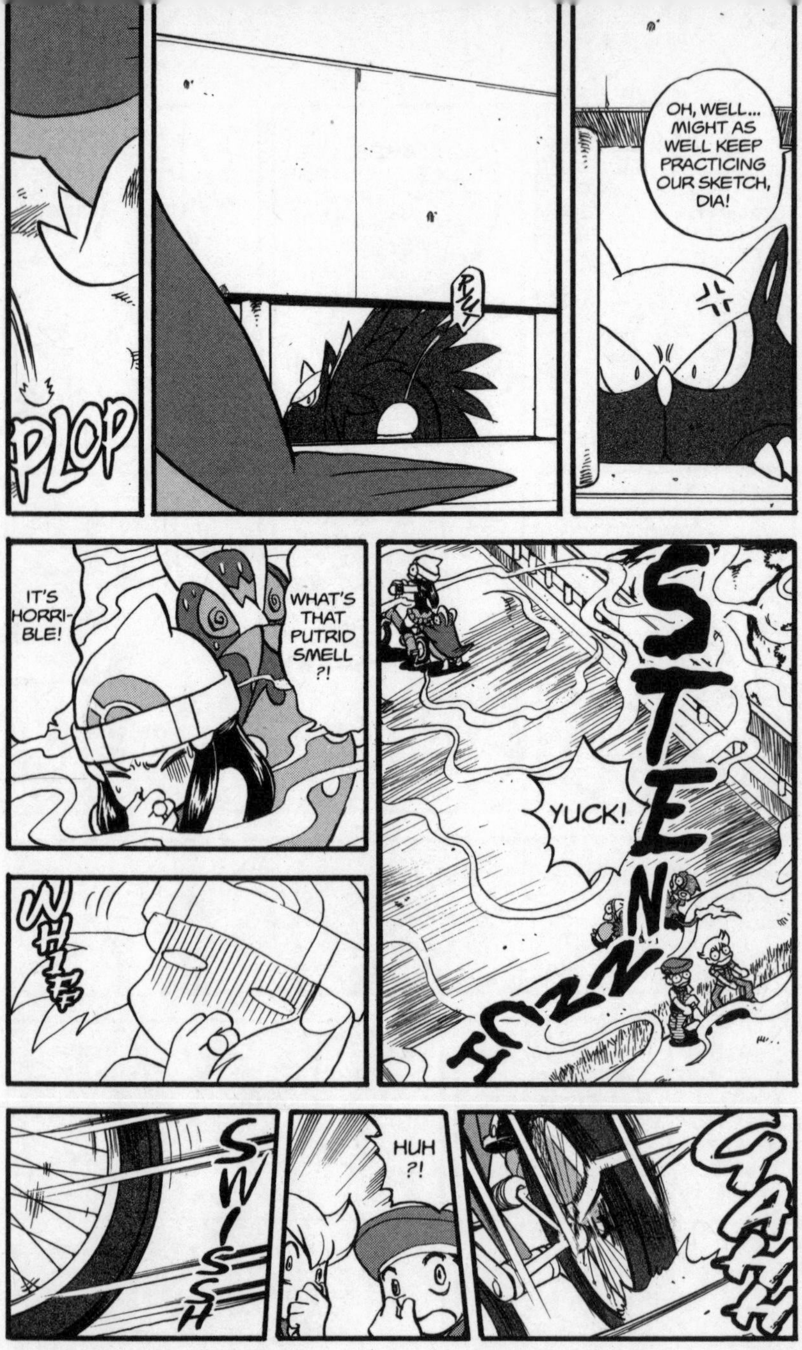
OH, WELL... MIGHT AS WELL KEEP PRACTICING OUR SKETCH, DIA!
PLOP
YUCK!
WHAT'S THAT PUTRID SMELL ?!
IT'S HORRI-BLE!
WHIFF
HUH ?!
SWISSH

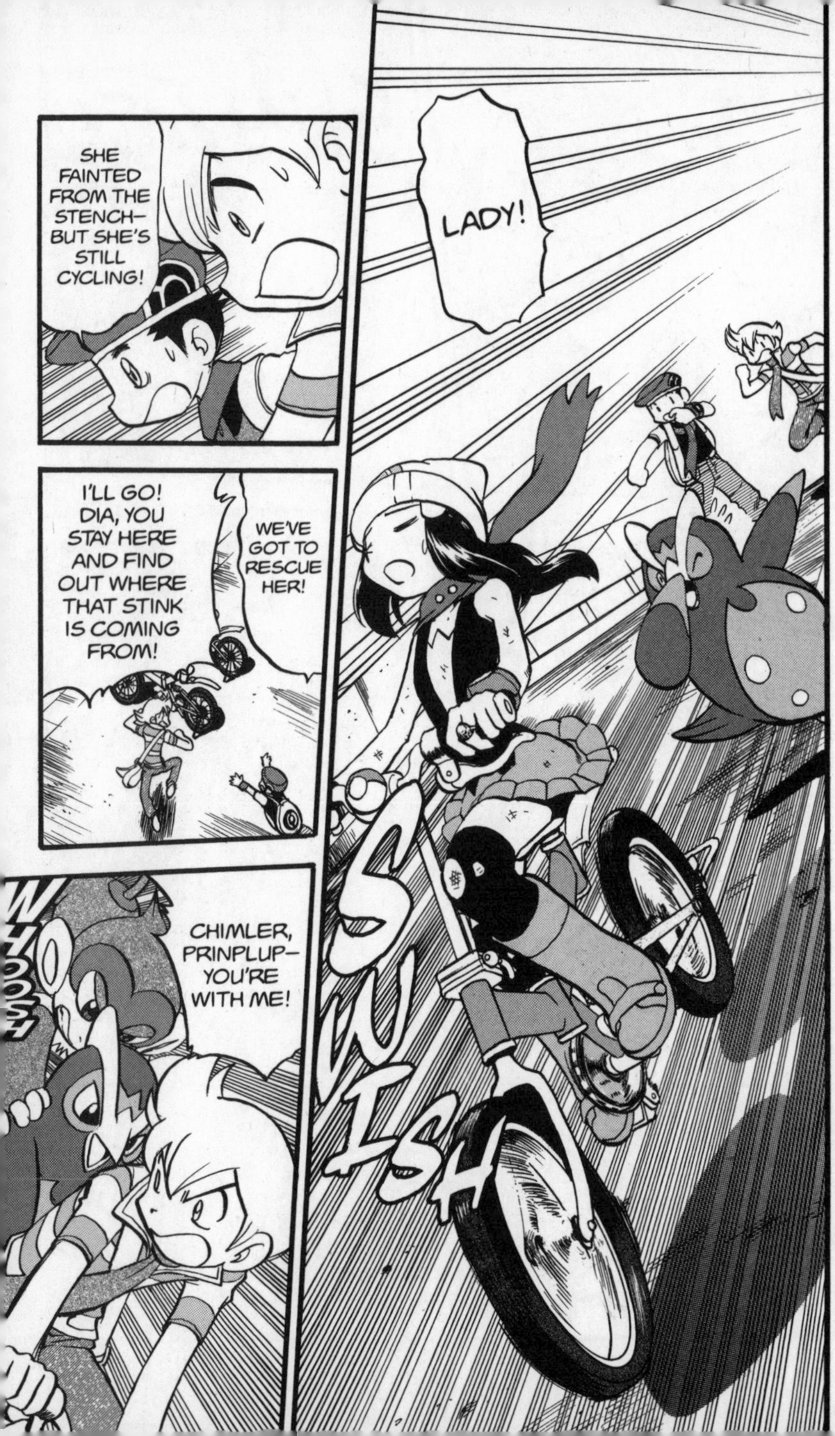
LADY!
SWISH
SHE FAINTED FROM THE STENCH—BUT SHE'S STILL CYCLING!
WE'VE GOT TO RESCUE HER!
I'LL GO! DIA, YOU STAY HERE AND FIND OUT WHERE THAT STINK IS COMING FROM!
CHIMLER, PRINPLUP—YOU'RE WITH ME!
WHOOSH

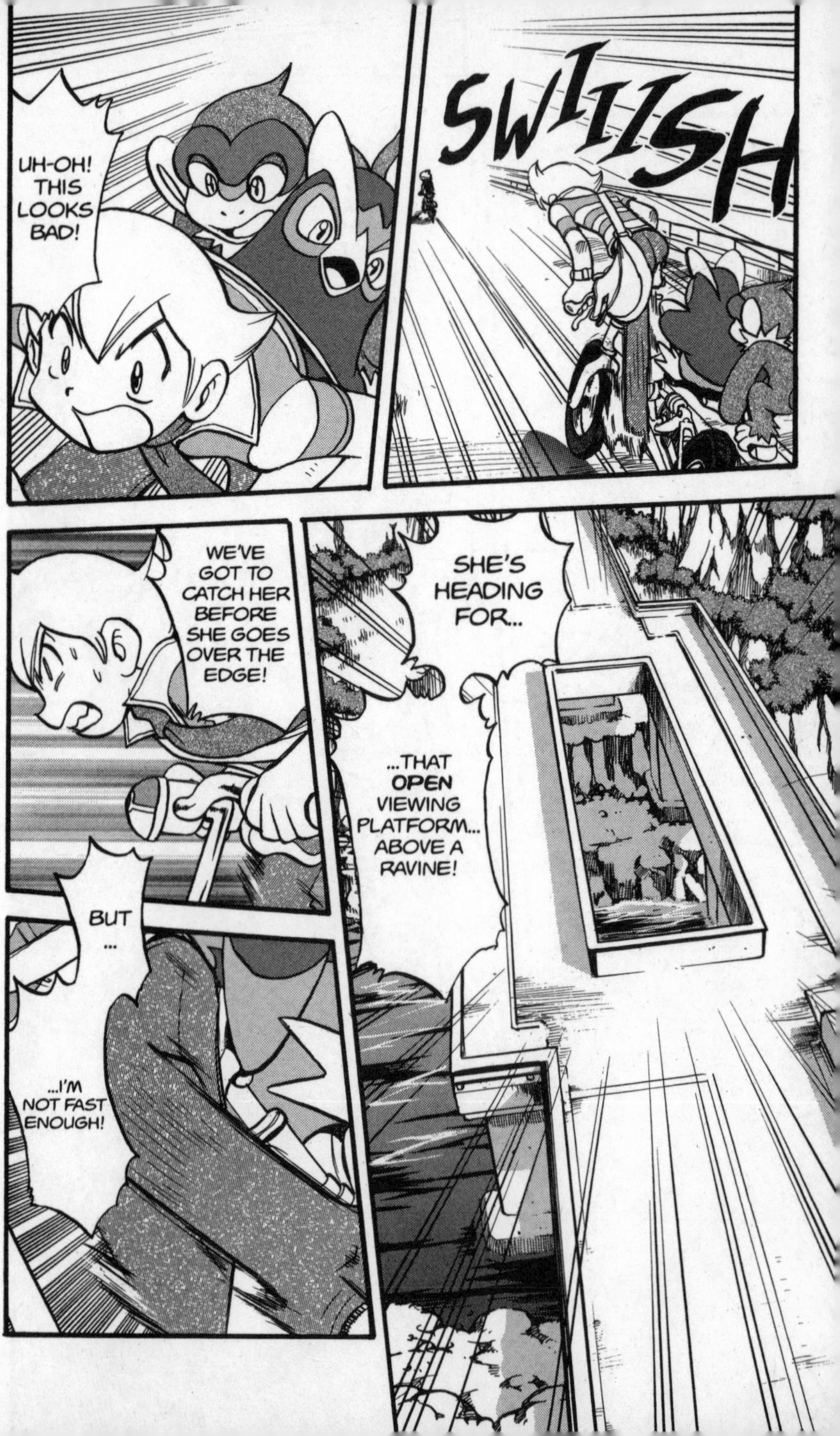
SWIIISH
UH-OH! THIS LOOKS BAD!
SHE'S HEADING FOR...
...THAT **OPEN** VIEWING PLATFORM... ABOVE A RAVINE!
WE'VE GOT TO CATCH HER BEFORE SHE GOES OVER THE EDGE!
BUT ...
...I'M NOT FAST ENOUGH!

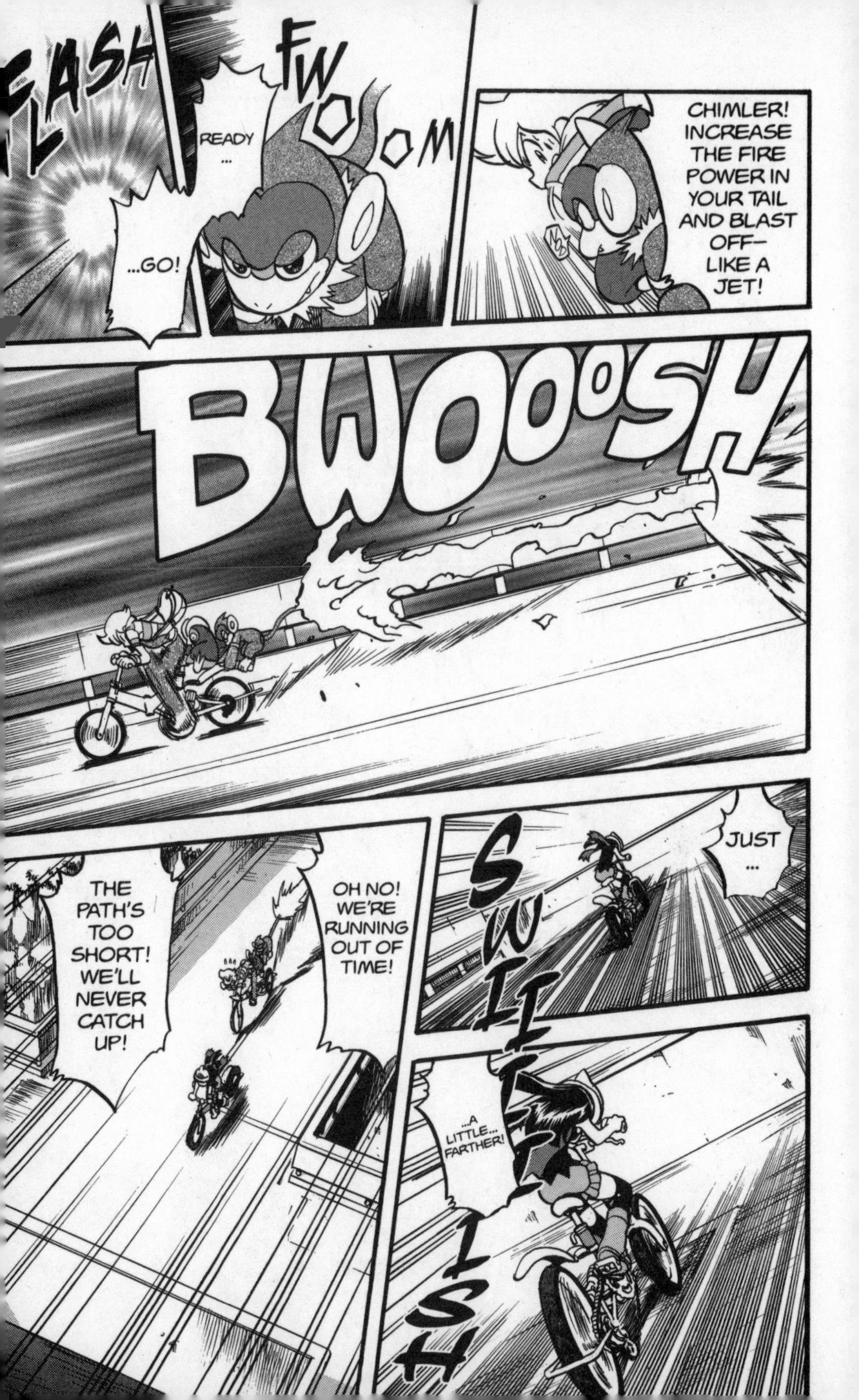
CHIMLER! INCREASE THE FIRE POWER IN YOUR TAIL AND BLAST OFF— LIKE A JET!
FWOOOM
READY ...
...GO!
FLASH
BWOOoSH
JUST ...
SWIIIISH
...A LITTLE... FARTHER!
OH NO! WE'RE RUNNING OUT OF TIME!
THE PATH'S TOO SHORT! WE'LL NEVER CATCH UP!

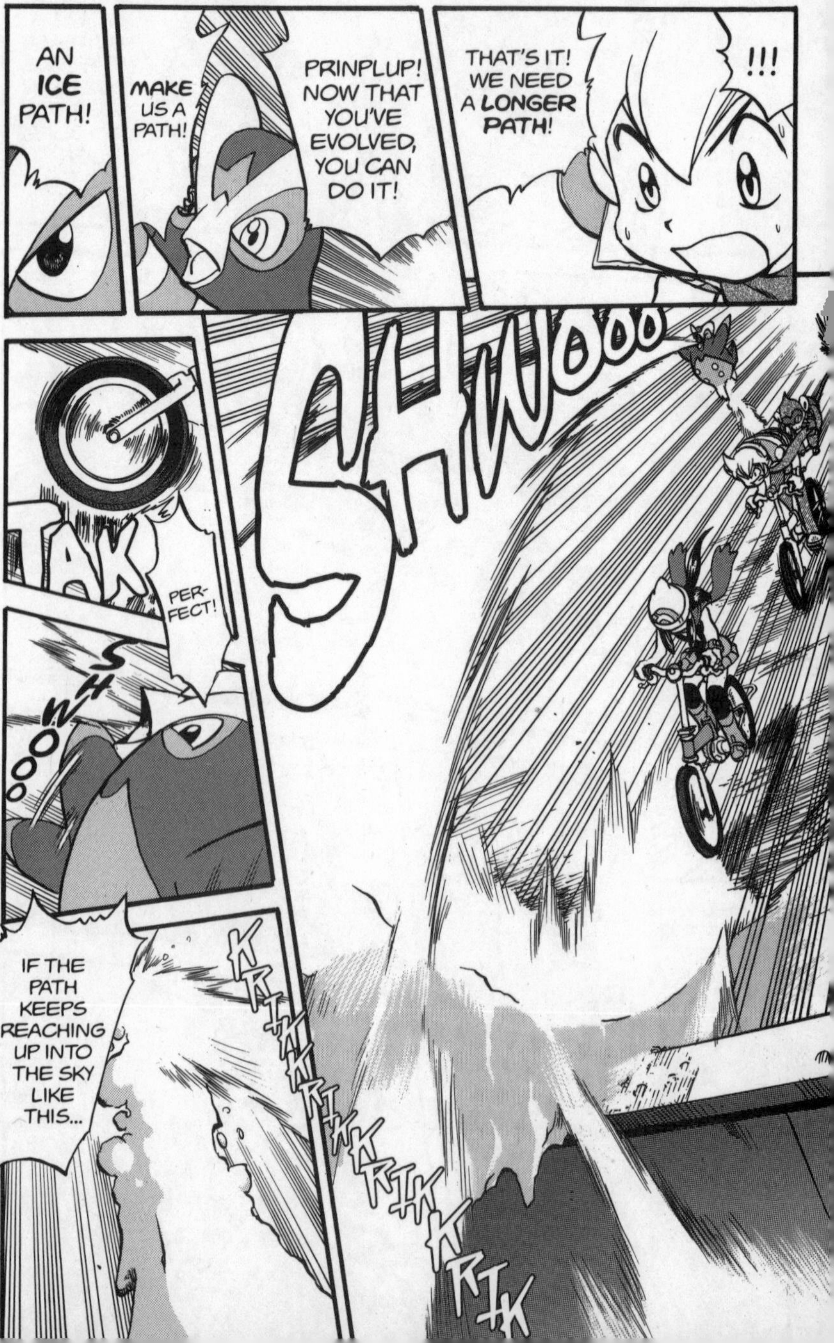
!!!
THAT'S IT! WE NEED A LONGER PATH!
PRINPLUP! NOW THAT YOU'VE EVOLVED, YOU CAN DO IT!
MAKE US A PATH!
AN ICE PATH!
SHWOOO
TAK
PERFECT!
SHWOOO
IF THE PATH KEEPS REACHING UP INTO THE SKY LIKE THIS...
KRIK KRIK KRIK KRIK

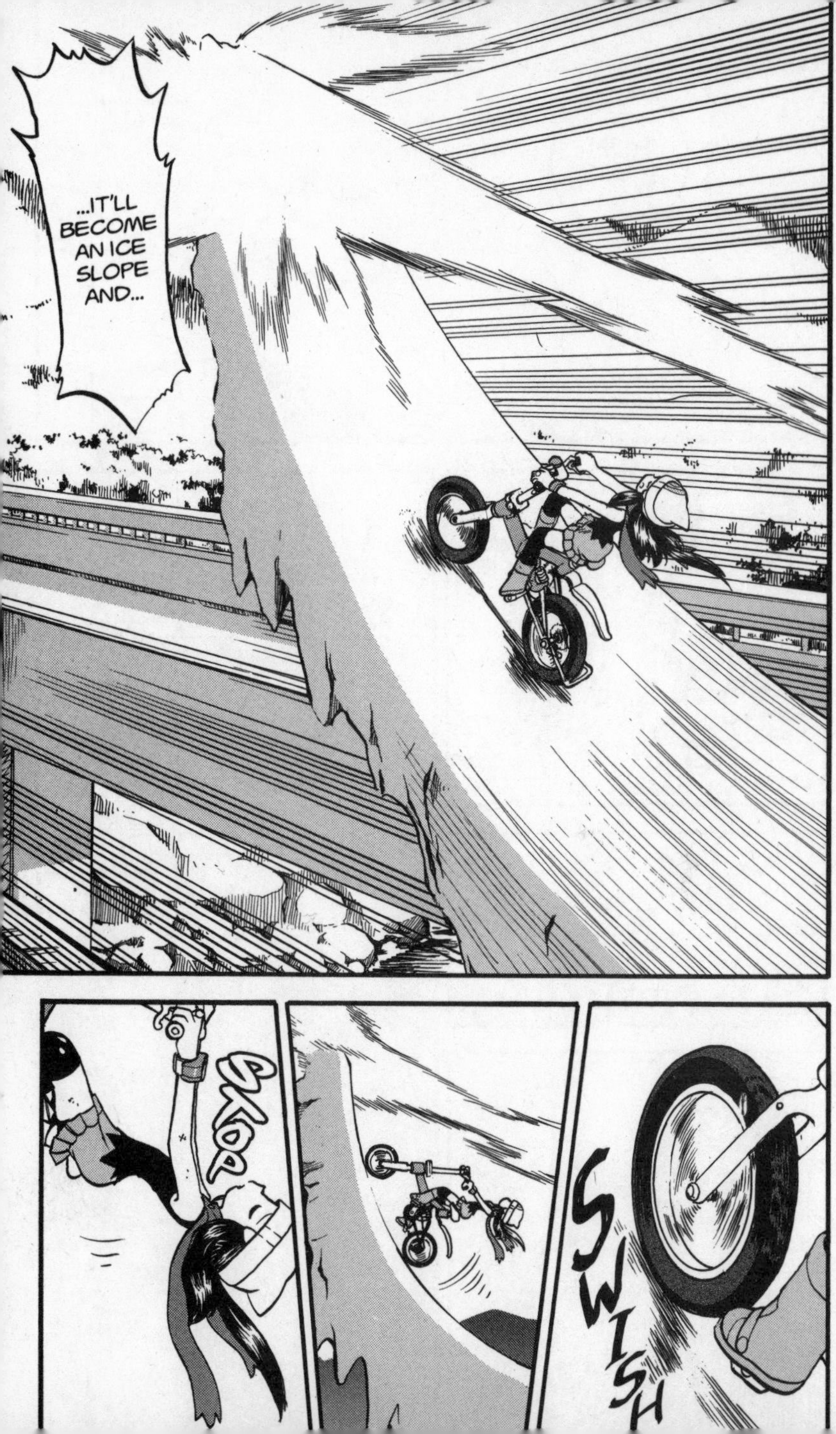
...IT'LL BECOME AN ICE SLOPE AND...
SWISH
SKOP

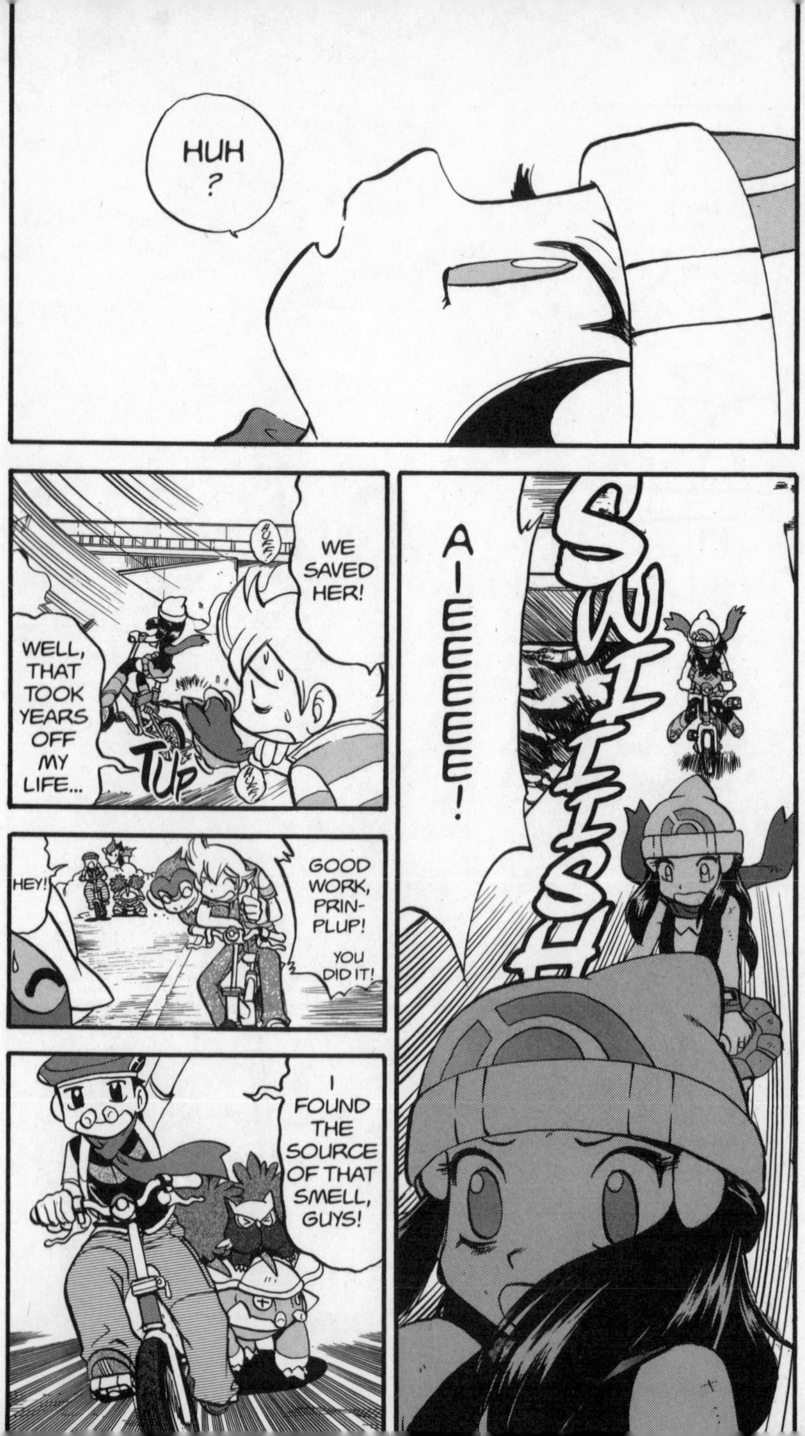
HUH ?
SWIIISH
AIEEEEEE!
WE SAVED HER!
WELL, THAT TOOK YEARS OFF MY LIFE...
TUP
GOOD WORK, PRIN-PLUP!
YOU DID IT!
HEY!
I FOUND THE SOURCE OF THAT SMELL, GUYS!

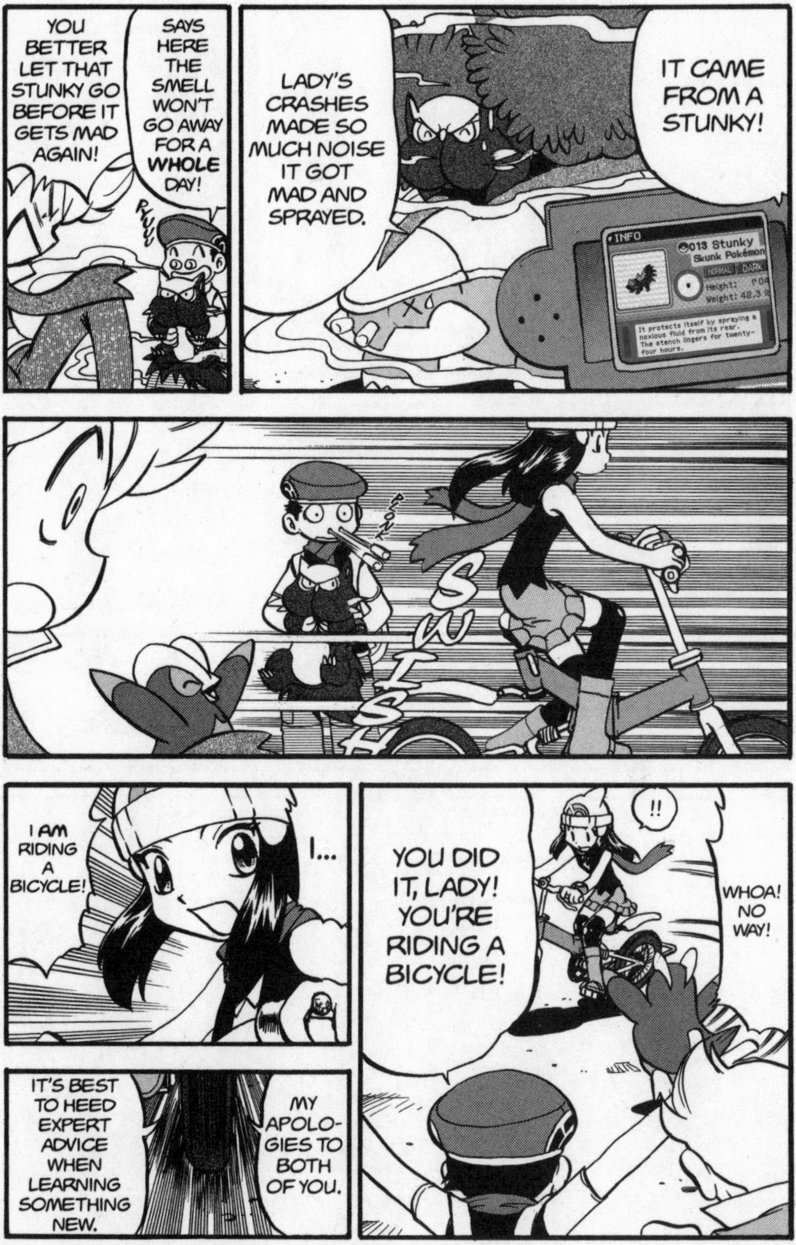
IT CAME FROM A STUNKY!
LADY'S CRASHES MADE SO MUCH NOISE IT GOT MAD AND SPRAYED.
INFO
013 Stunky
Skunk Pokémon
NORMAL
DARK
It protects itself by spraying a noxious fluid from its rear. The stench lingers for twenty-four hours.
SAYS HERE THE SMELL WON'T GO AWAY FOR A WHOLE DAY!
YOU BETTER LET THAT STUNKY GO BEFORE IT GETS MAD AGAIN!
BLONK
SWISH
!!
WHOA! NO WAY!
YOU DID IT, LADY! YOU'RE RIDING A BICYCLE!
I...
I AM RIDING A BICYCLE!
MY APOLOGIES TO BOTH OF YOU.
IT'S BEST TO HEED EXPERT ADVICE WHEN LEARNING SOMETHING NEW.

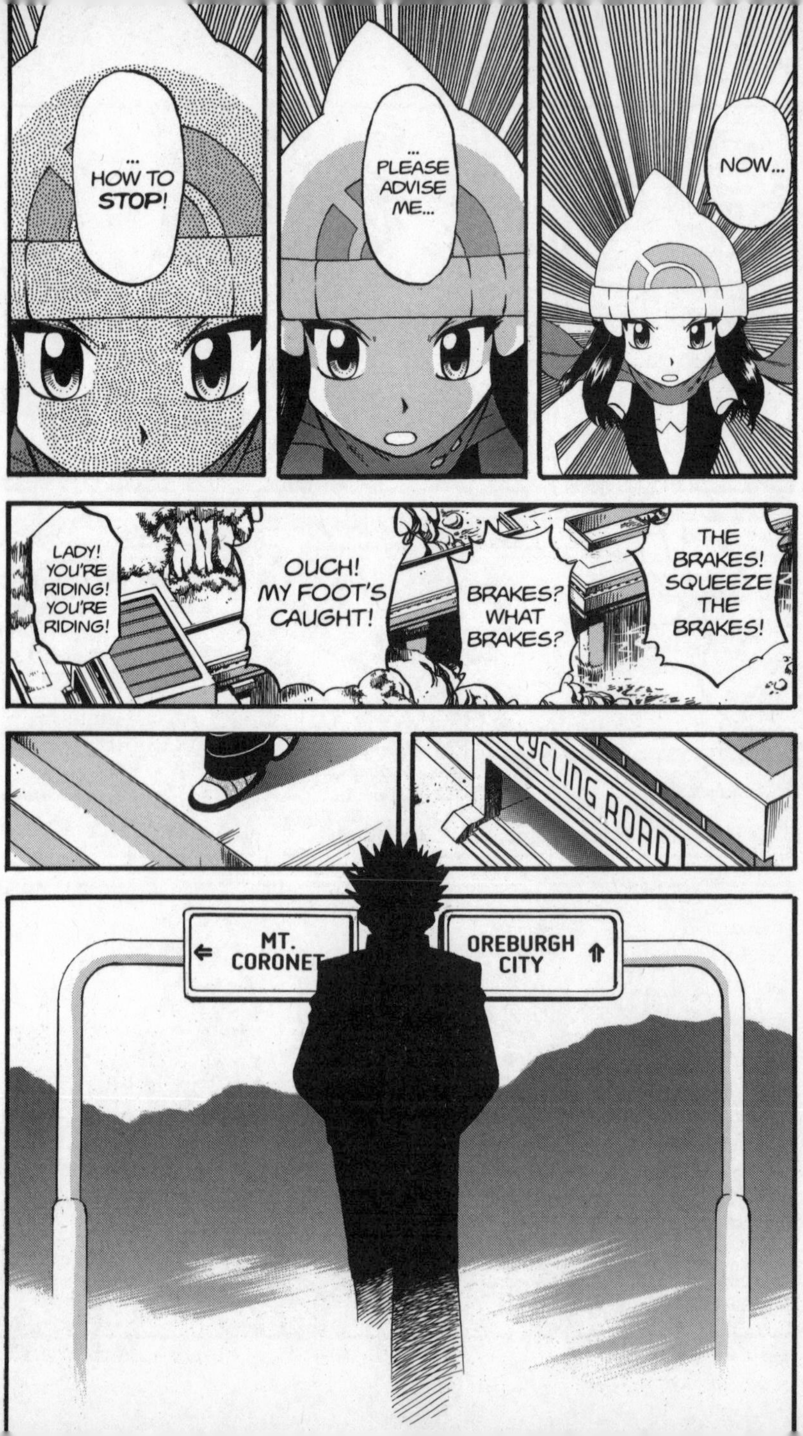
NOW...
...PLEASE ADVISE ME...
...HOW TO STOP!
THE BRAKES! SQUEEZE THE BRAKES!
BRAKES? WHAT BRAKES?
OUCH! MY FOOT'S CAUGHT!
LADY! YOU'RE RIDING! YOU'RE RIDING!
CYCLING ROAD
MT. CORONET ⇐
OREBURGH CITY ⇑

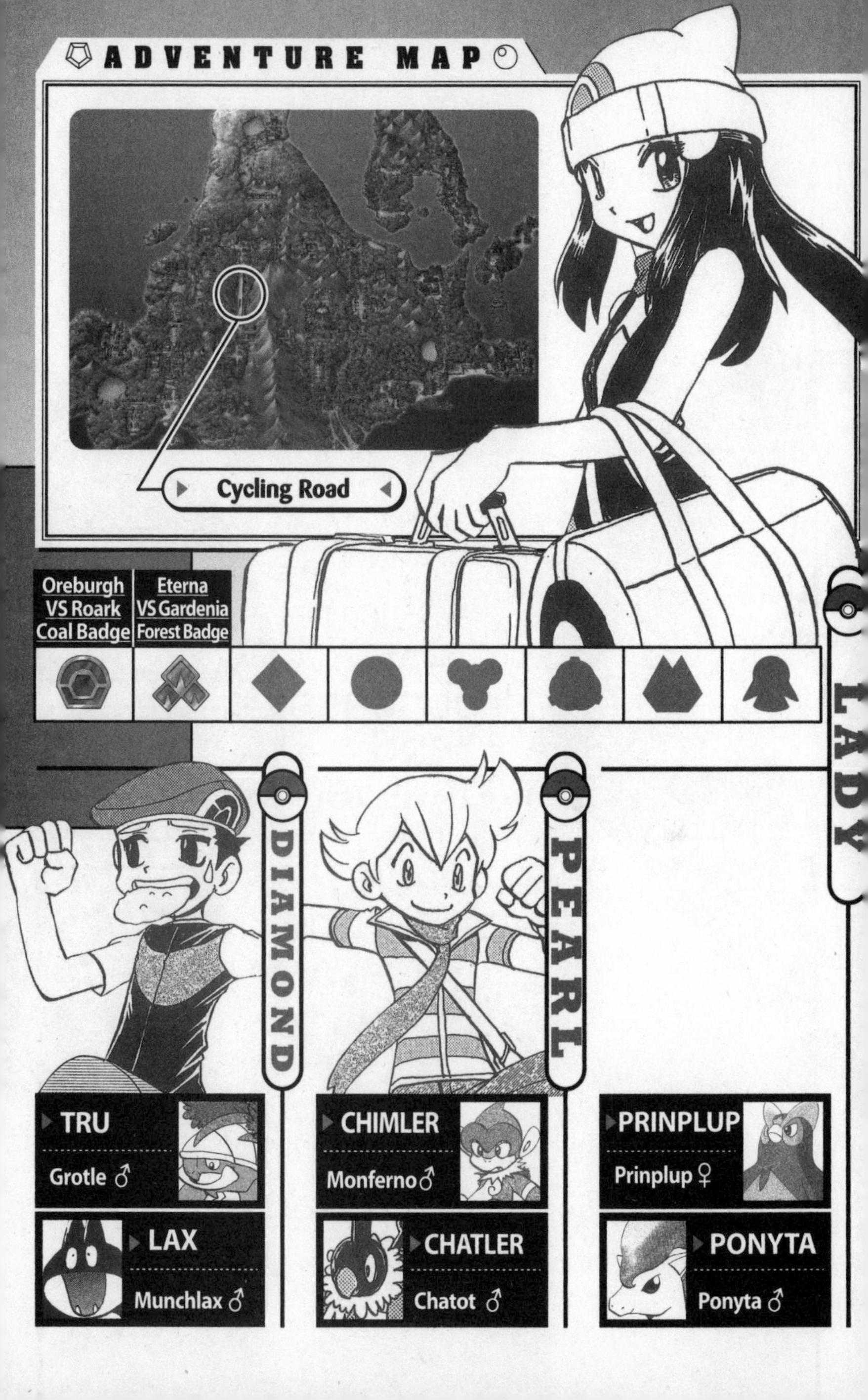
ADVENTURE MAP
Cycling Road
Oreburgh
VS Roark
Coal Badge
Eterna
VS Gardenia
Forest Badge
LADY
DIAMOND
PEARL
TRU
Grotle ♂
LAX
Munchlax ♂
CHIMLER
Monferno ♂
CHATLER
Chatot ♂
PRINPLUP
Prinplup ♀
PONYTA
Ponyta ♂

12

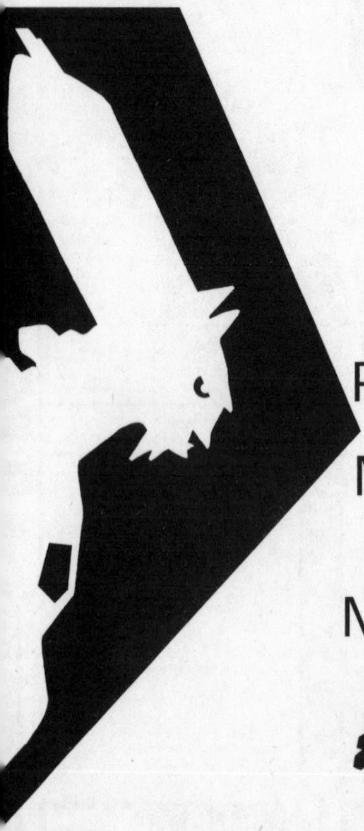

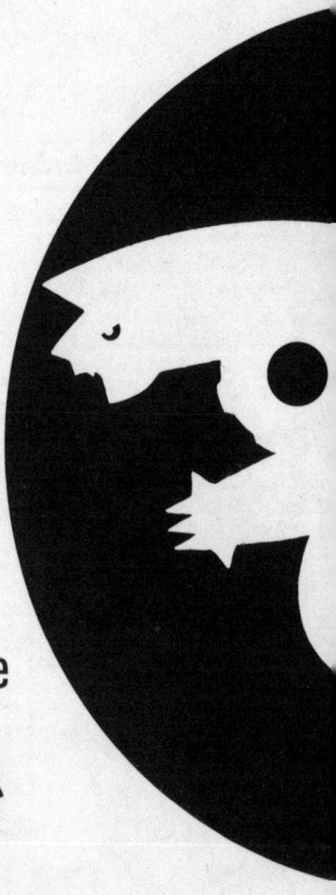

Passing by Probopass and Maneuvering Around Magnezone

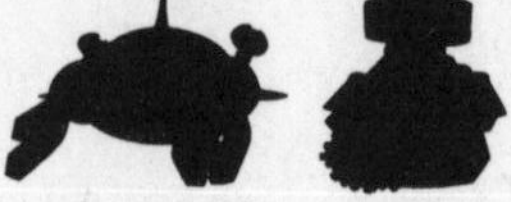

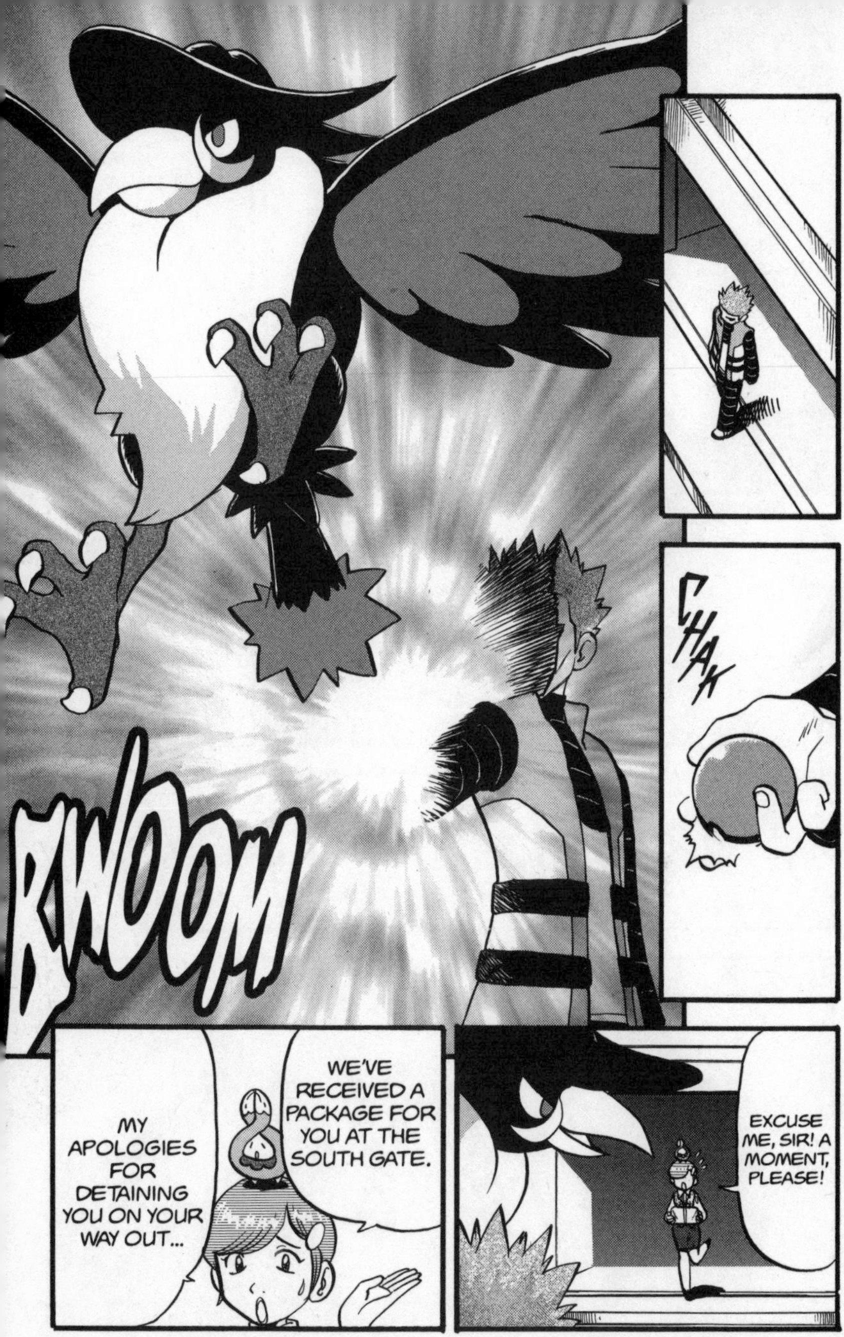
CHAK
BWOOM
EXCUSE ME, SIR! A MOMENT, PLEASE!
WE'VE RECEIVED A PACKAGE FOR YOU AT THE SOUTH GATE.
MY APOLOGIES FOR DETAINING YOU ON YOUR WAY OUT...

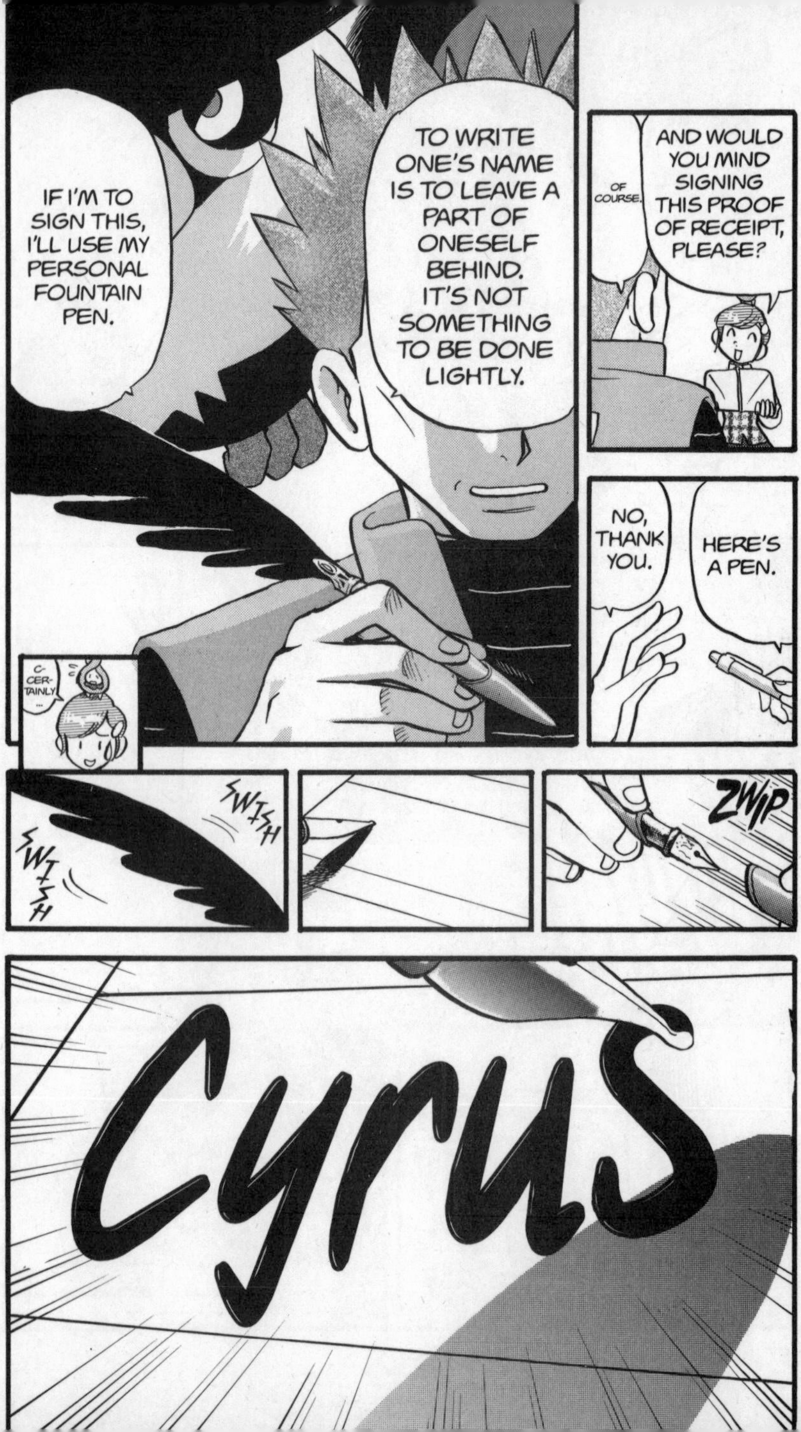
AND WOULD YOU MIND SIGNING THIS PROOF OF RECEIPT, PLEASE?
OF COURSE.
HERE'S A PEN.
NO, THANK YOU.
TO WRITE ONE'S NAME IS TO LEAVE A PART OF ONESELF BEHIND. IT'S NOT SOMETHING TO BE DONE LIGHTLY.
IF I'M TO SIGN THIS, I'LL USE MY PERSONAL FOUNTAIN PEN.
C-CERTAINLY...
ZWIP
SWISH
SWISH
Cyrus

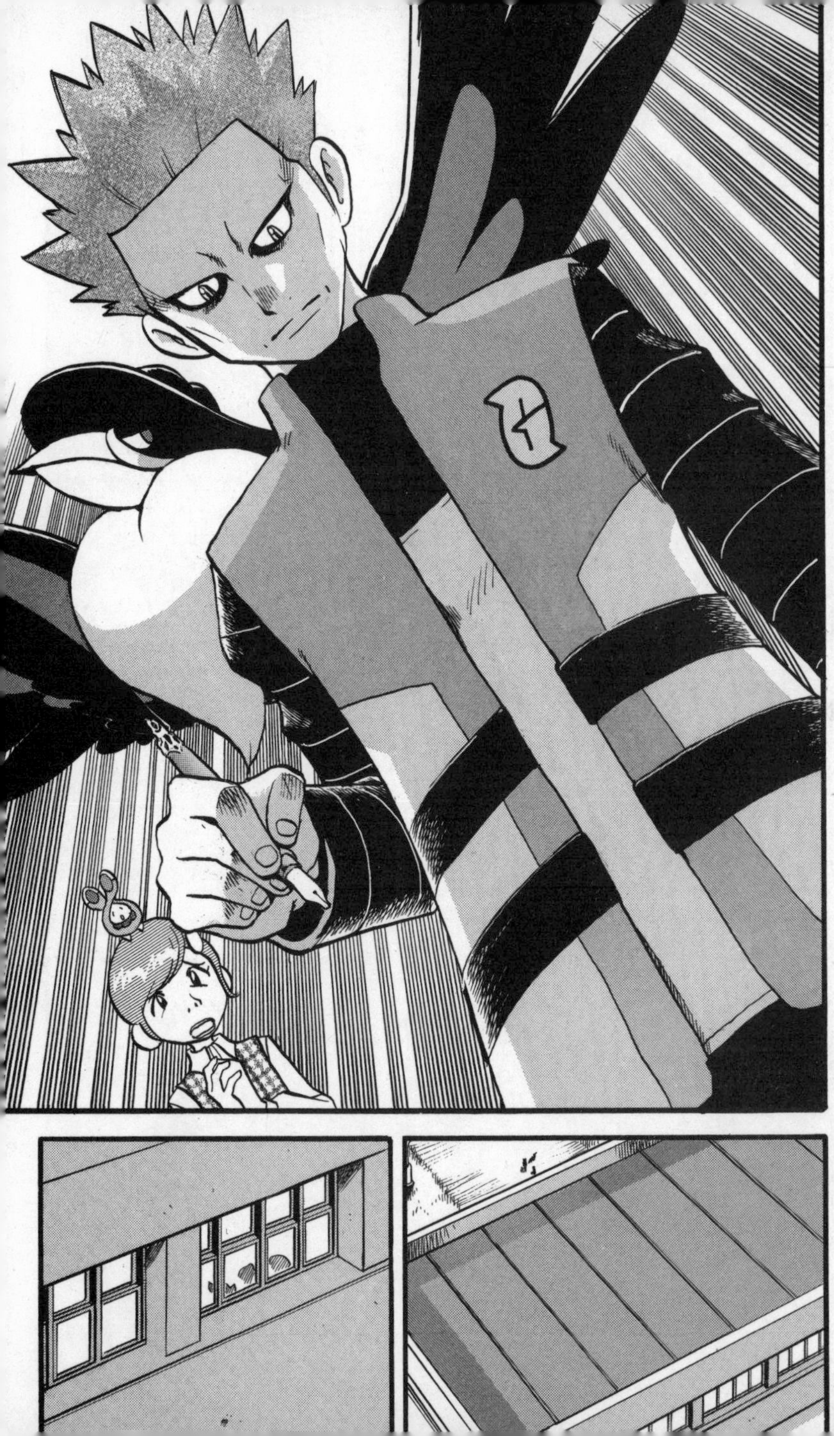

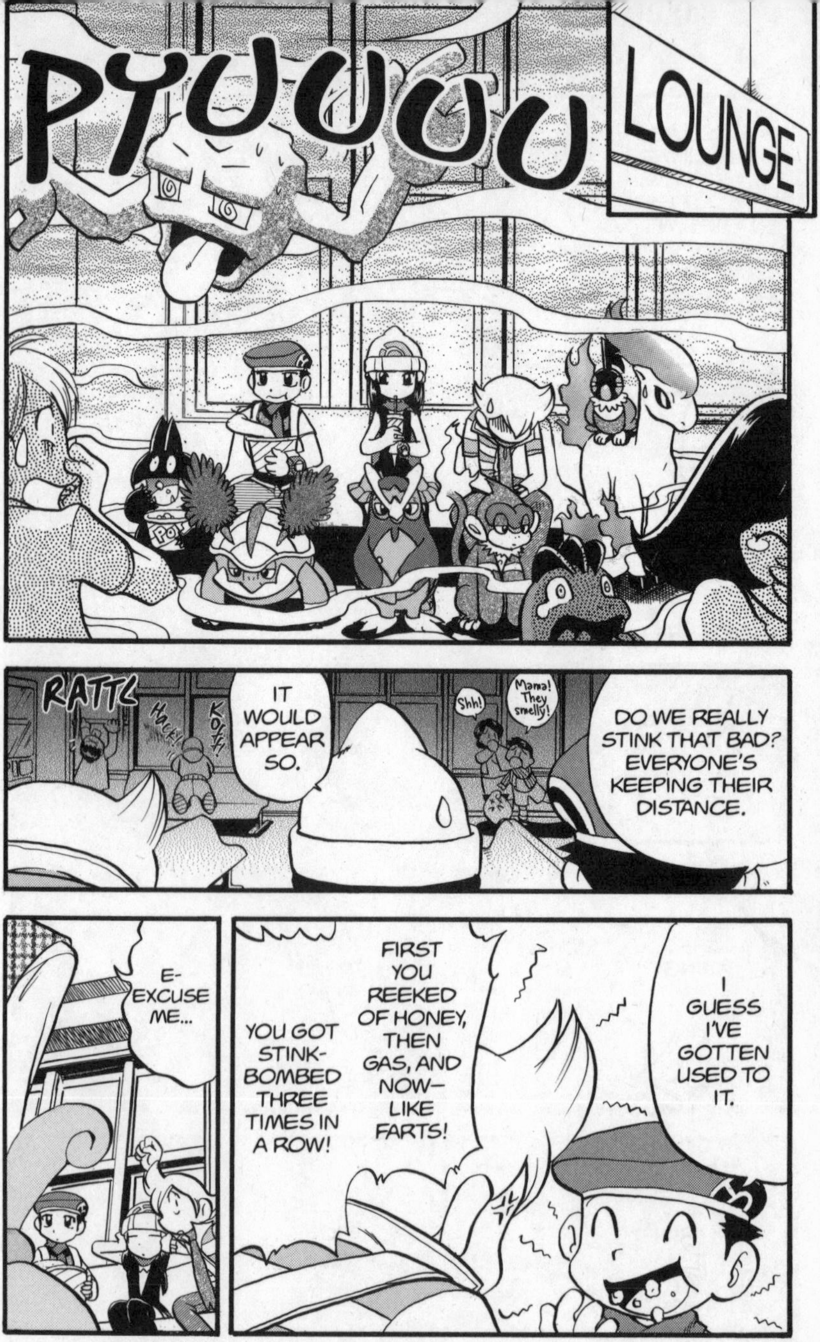
LOUNGE
PYUUUUU
DO WE REALLY STINK THAT BAD? EVERYONE'S KEEPING THEIR DISTANCE.
Mama! They smelly!
Shh!
IT WOULD APPEAR SO.
KOFF!
HACK!
RATTL
I GUESS I'VE GOTTEN USED TO IT.
FIRST YOU REEKED OF HONEY, THEN GAS, AND NOW—LIKE FARTS!
YOU GOT STINK-BOMBED THREE TIMES IN A ROW!
E-EXCUSE ME...

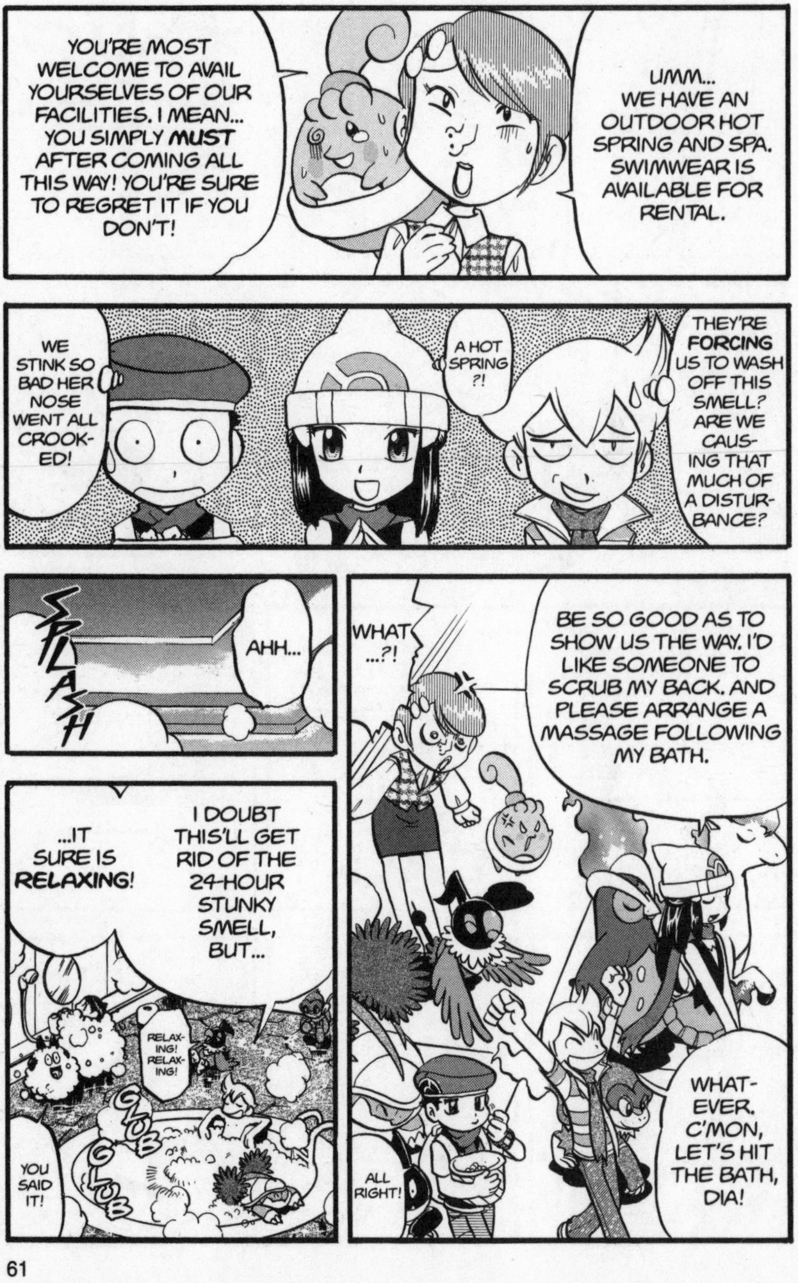
UMM... WE HAVE AN OUTDOOR HOT SPRING AND SPA. SWIMWEAR IS AVAILABLE FOR RENTAL.
YOU'RE MOST WELCOME TO AVAIL YOURSELVES OF OUR FACILITIES. I MEAN... YOU SIMPLY **MUST** AFTER COMING ALL THIS WAY! YOU'RE SURE TO REGRET IT IF YOU DON'T!
THEY'RE **FORCING** US TO WASH OFF THIS SMELL? ARE WE CAUSING THAT MUCH OF A DISTURBANCE?
A HOT SPRING?!
WE STINK SO BAD HER NOSE WENT ALL CROOKED!
BE SO GOOD AS TO SHOW US THE WAY. I'D LIKE SOMEONE TO SCRUB MY BACK. AND PLEASE ARRANGE A MASSAGE FOLLOWING MY BATH.
WHAT...?!
WHATEVER. C'MON, LET'S HIT THE BATH, DIA!
ALL RIGHT!
SPLASH
AHH...
I DOUBT THIS'LL GET RID OF THE 24-HOUR STUNKY SMELL, BUT...
...IT SURE IS **RELAXING**!
RELAXING! RELAXING!
GLOB GLOB
YOU SAID IT!

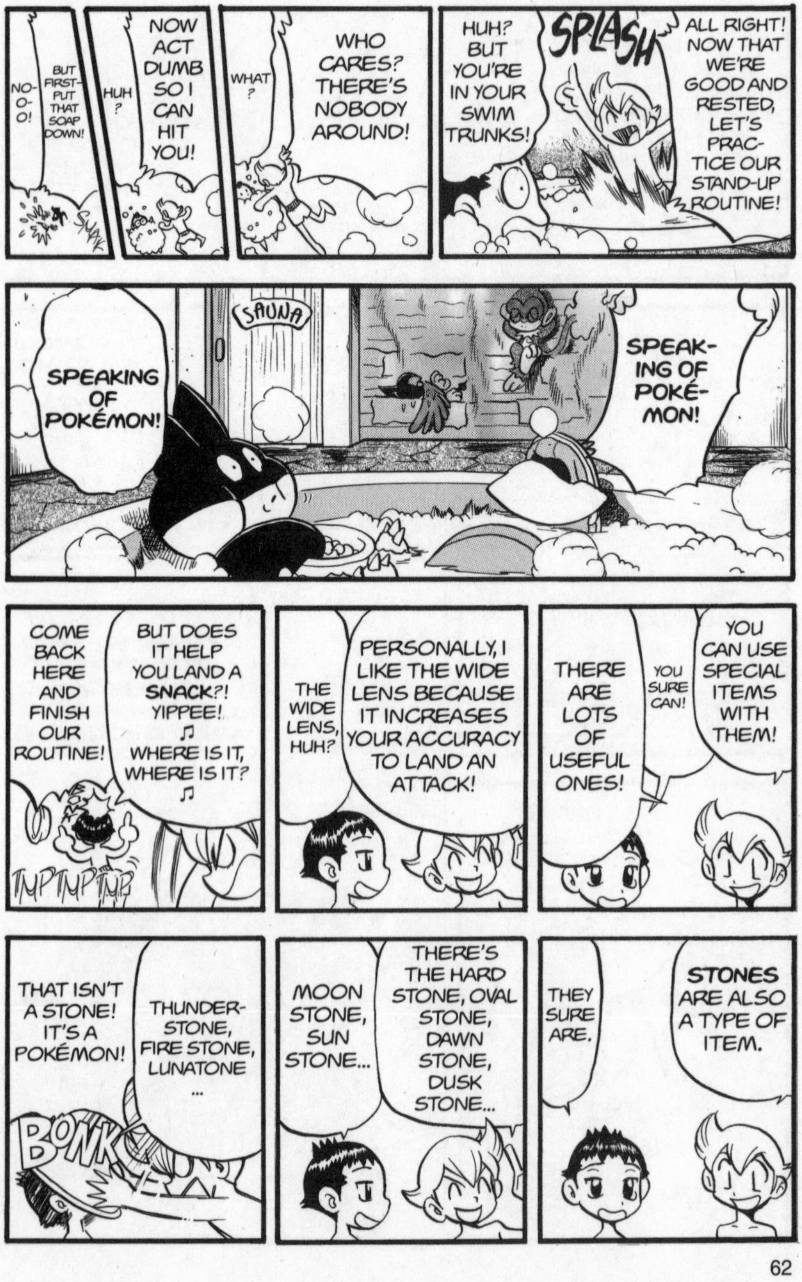
ALL RIGHT! NOW THAT WE'RE GOOD AND RESTED, LET'S PRACTICE OUR STAND-UP ROUTINE!
SPLASH
HUH? BUT YOU'RE IN YOUR SWIM TRUNKS!
WHO CARES? THERE'S NOBODY AROUND!
WHAT?
NOW ACT DUMB SO I CAN HIT YOU!
HUH?
BUT FIRST-PUT THAT SOAP DOWN!
NO-O-O!
SAUNA
SPEAKING OF POKÉMON!
SPEAKING OF POKÉMON!
YOU CAN USE SPECIAL ITEMS WITH THEM!
YOU SURE CAN!
THERE ARE LOTS OF USEFUL ONES!
PERSONALLY, I LIKE THE WIDE LENS BECAUSE IT INCREASES YOUR ACCURACY TO LAND AN ATTACK!
THE WIDE LENS, HUH?
BUT DOES IT HELP YOU LAND A **SNACK**?! YIPPEE! ♫ WHERE IS IT, WHERE IS IT? ♫
COME BACK HERE AND FINISH OUR ROUTINE!
TMP TMP TMP
STONES ARE ALSO A TYPE OF ITEM.
THEY SURE ARE.
THERE'S THE HARD STONE, OVAL STONE, DAWN STONE, DUSK STONE...
MOON STONE, SUN STONE...
THUNDERSTONE, FIRE STONE, LUNATONE ...
THAT ISN'T A STONE! IT'S A POKÉMON!
BONK

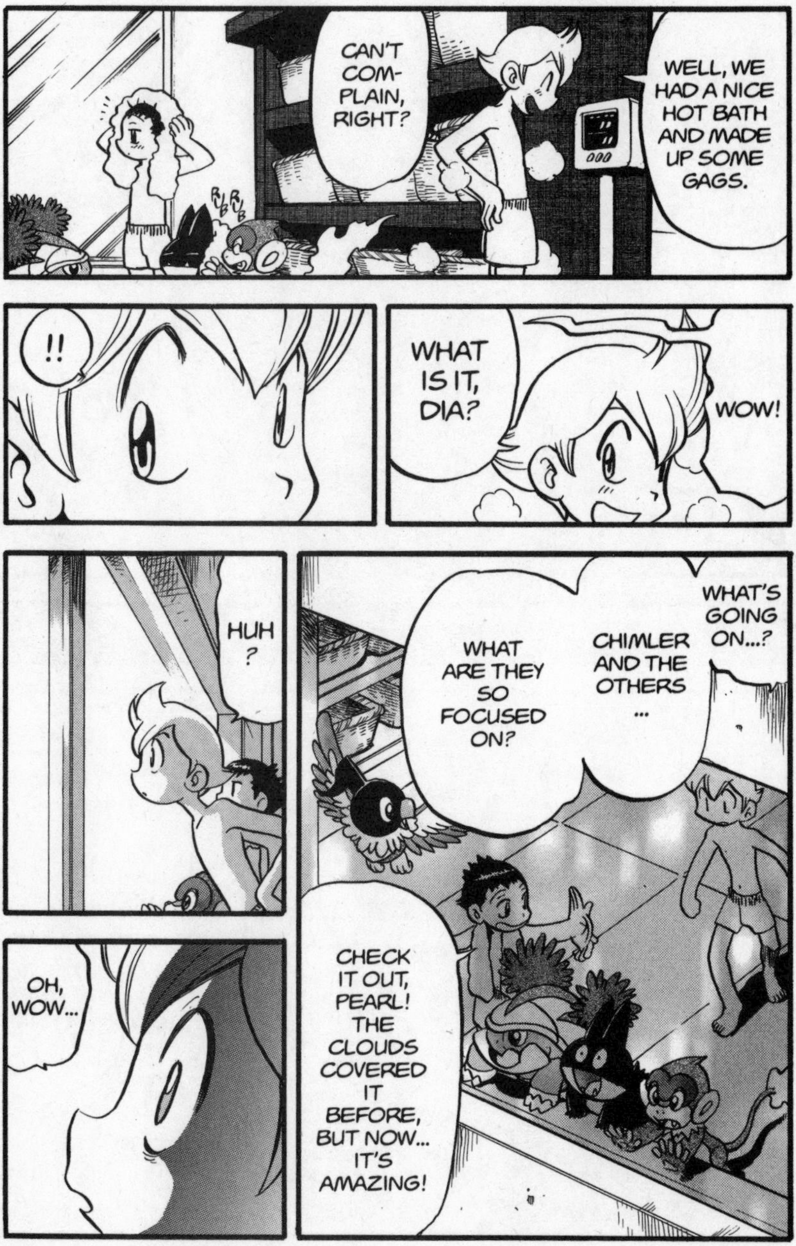
WELL, WE HAD A NICE HOT BATH AND MADE UP SOME GAGS.
CAN'T COMPLAIN, RIGHT?
RUB RUB
WOW!
WHAT IS IT, DIA?
!!
WHAT'S GOING ON...?
CHIMLER AND THE OTHERS...
WHAT ARE THEY SO FOCUSED ON?
CHECK IT OUT, PEARL! THE CLOUDS COVERED IT BEFORE, BUT NOW... IT'S AMAZING!
HUH?
OH, WOW...

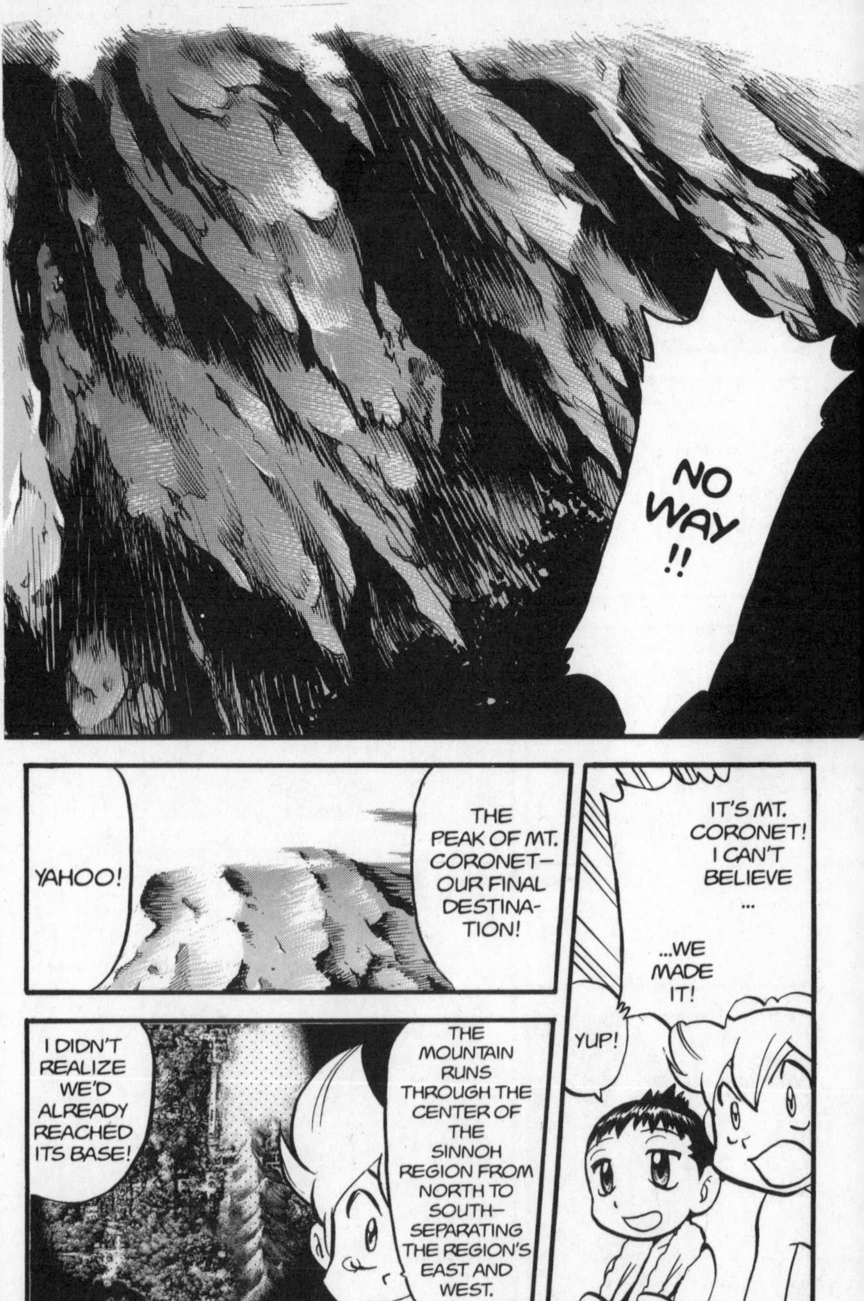
NO WAY!!
IT'S MT. CORONET! I CAN'T BELIEVE ...
...WE MADE IT!
YUP!
THE PEAK OF MT. CORONET— OUR FINAL DESTINATION!
YAHOO!
THE MOUNTAIN RUNS THROUGH THE CENTER OF THE SINNOH REGION FROM NORTH TO SOUTH— SEPARATING THE REGION'S EAST AND WEST.
I DIDN'T REALIZE WE'D ALREADY REACHED ITS BASE!

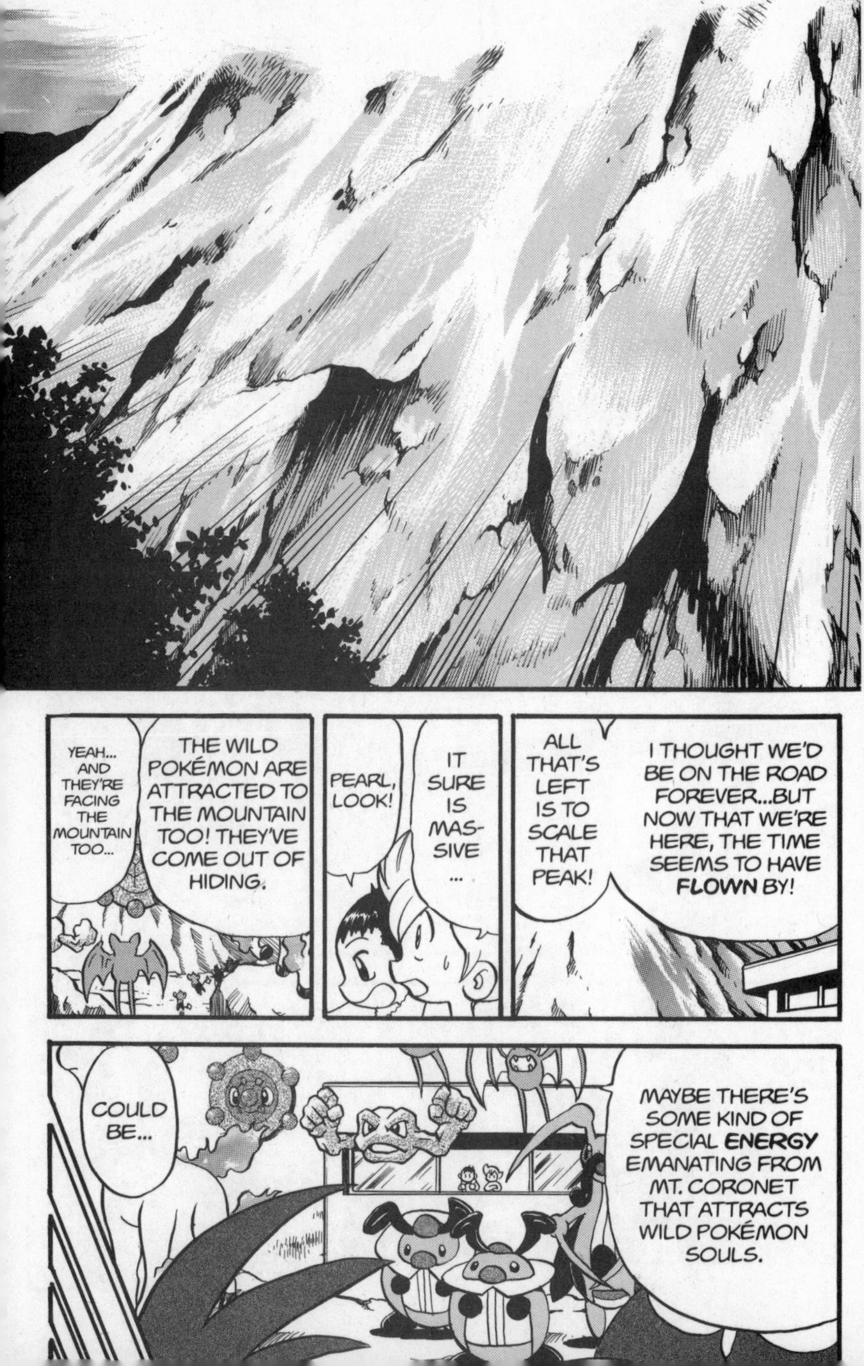
I THOUGHT WE'D BE ON THE ROAD FOREVER...BUT NOW THAT WE'RE HERE, THE TIME SEEMS TO HAVE **FLOWN** BY!
ALL THAT'S LEFT IS TO SCALE THAT PEAK!
IT SURE IS MAS-SIVE ...
PEARL, LOOK!
THE WILD POKÉMON ARE ATTRACTED TO THE MOUNTAIN TOO! THEY'VE COME OUT OF HIDING.
YEAH... AND THEY'RE FACING THE MOUNTAIN TOO...
MAYBE THERE'S SOME KIND OF SPECIAL **ENERGY** EMANATING FROM MT. CORONET THAT ATTRACTS WILD POKÉMON SOULS.
COULD BE...

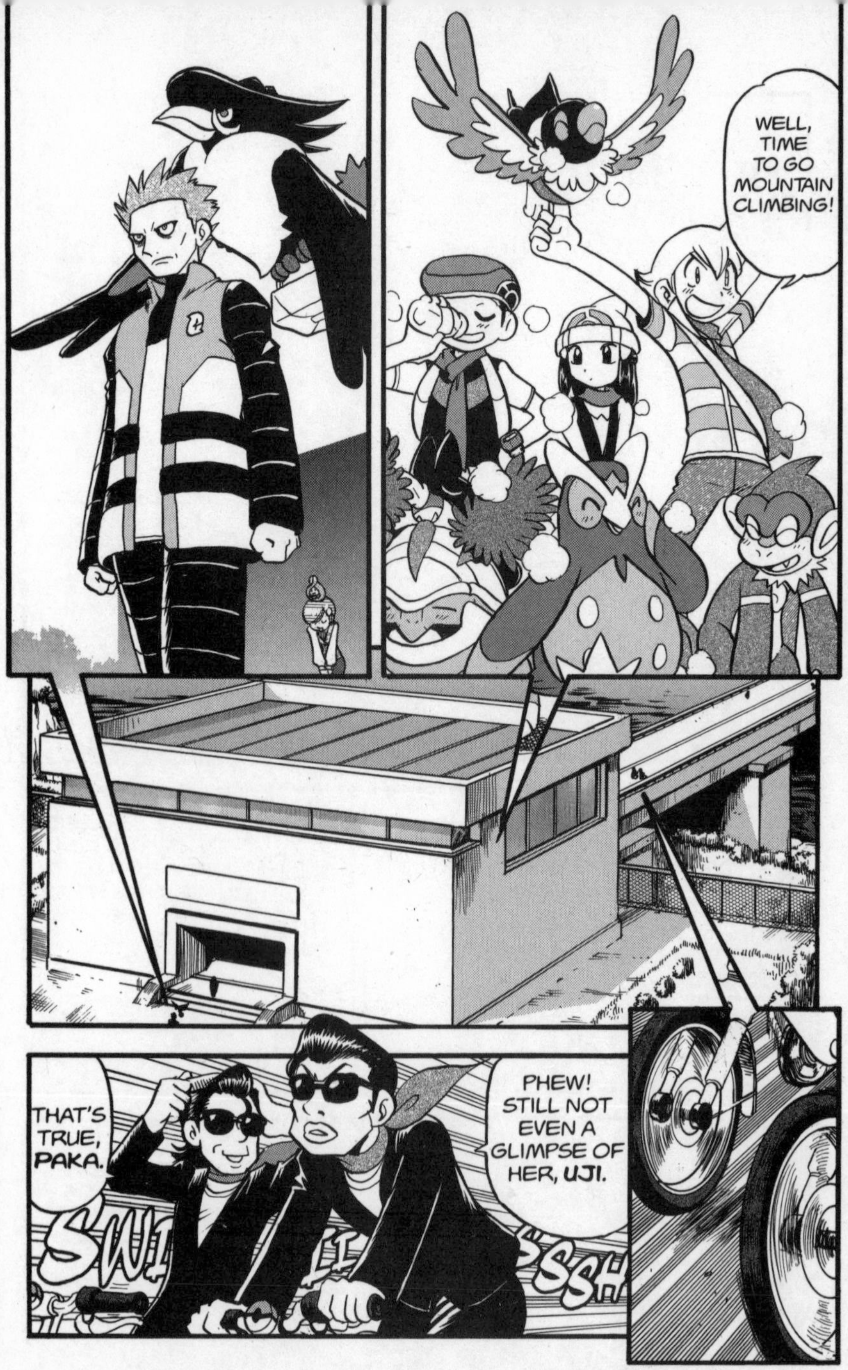
WELL, TIME TO GO MOUNTAIN CLIMBING!
PHEW! STILL NOT EVEN A GLIMPSE OF HER, UJI.
THAT'S TRUE, PAKA.

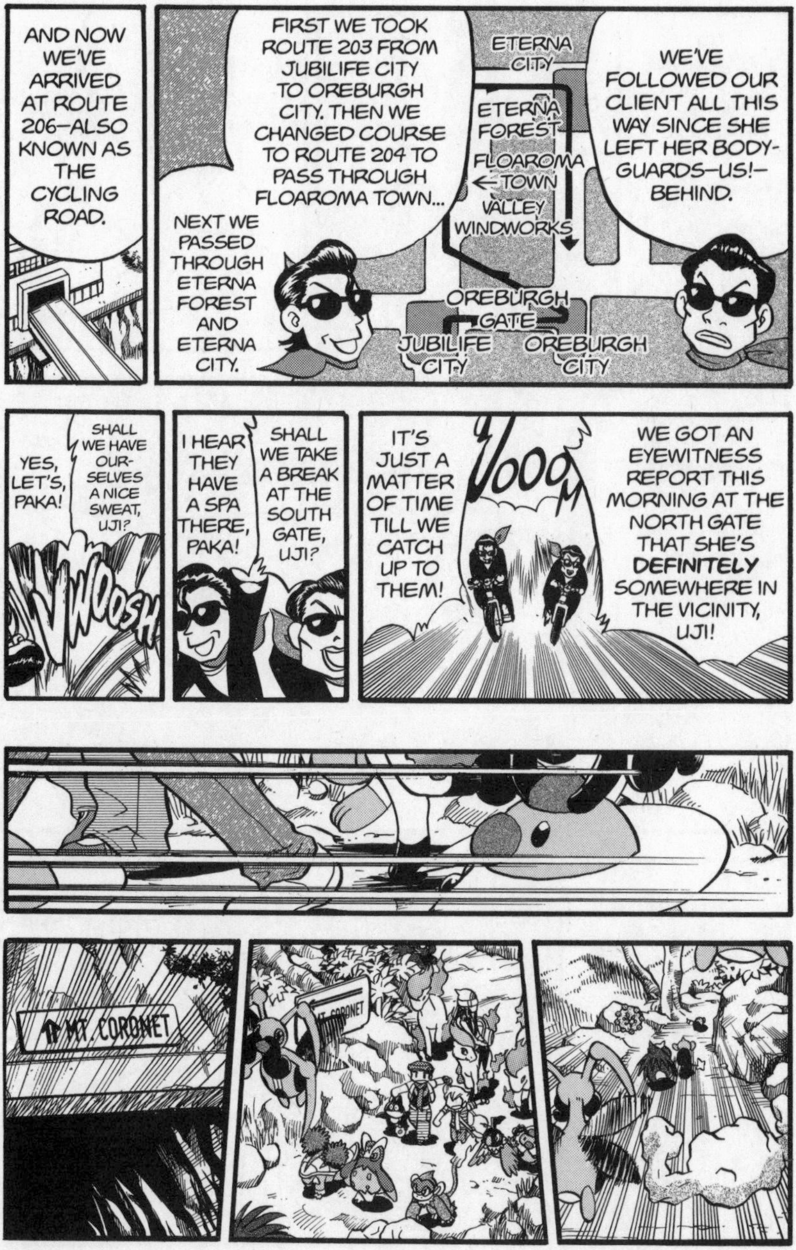
WE'VE FOLLOWED OUR CLIENT ALL THIS WAY SINCE SHE LEFT HER BODY-GUARDS—US!—BEHIND.
ETERNA CITY
ETERNA FOREST
FLOAROMA TOWN
VALLEY WINDWORKS
OREBURGH GATE
OREBURGH CITY
JUBILIFE CITY
FIRST WE TOOK ROUTE 203 FROM JUBILIFE CITY TO OREBURGH CITY. THEN WE CHANGED COURSE TO ROUTE 204 TO PASS THROUGH FLOAROMA TOWN...
NEXT WE PASSED THROUGH ETERNA FOREST AND ETERNA CITY.
AND NOW WE'VE ARRIVED AT ROUTE 206—ALSO KNOWN AS THE CYCLING ROAD.
WE GOT AN EYEWITNESS REPORT THIS MORNING AT THE NORTH GATE THAT SHE'S **DEFINITELY** SOMEWHERE IN THE VICINITY, UJI!
VOOOM
IT'S JUST A MATTER OF TIME TILL WE CATCH UP TO THEM!
SHALL WE TAKE A BREAK AT THE SOUTH GATE, UJI?
I HEAR THEY HAVE A SPA THERE, PAKA!
SHALL WE HAVE OURSELVES A NICE SWEAT, UJI?
YES, LET'S, PAKA!
WOOSH
MT. CORONET

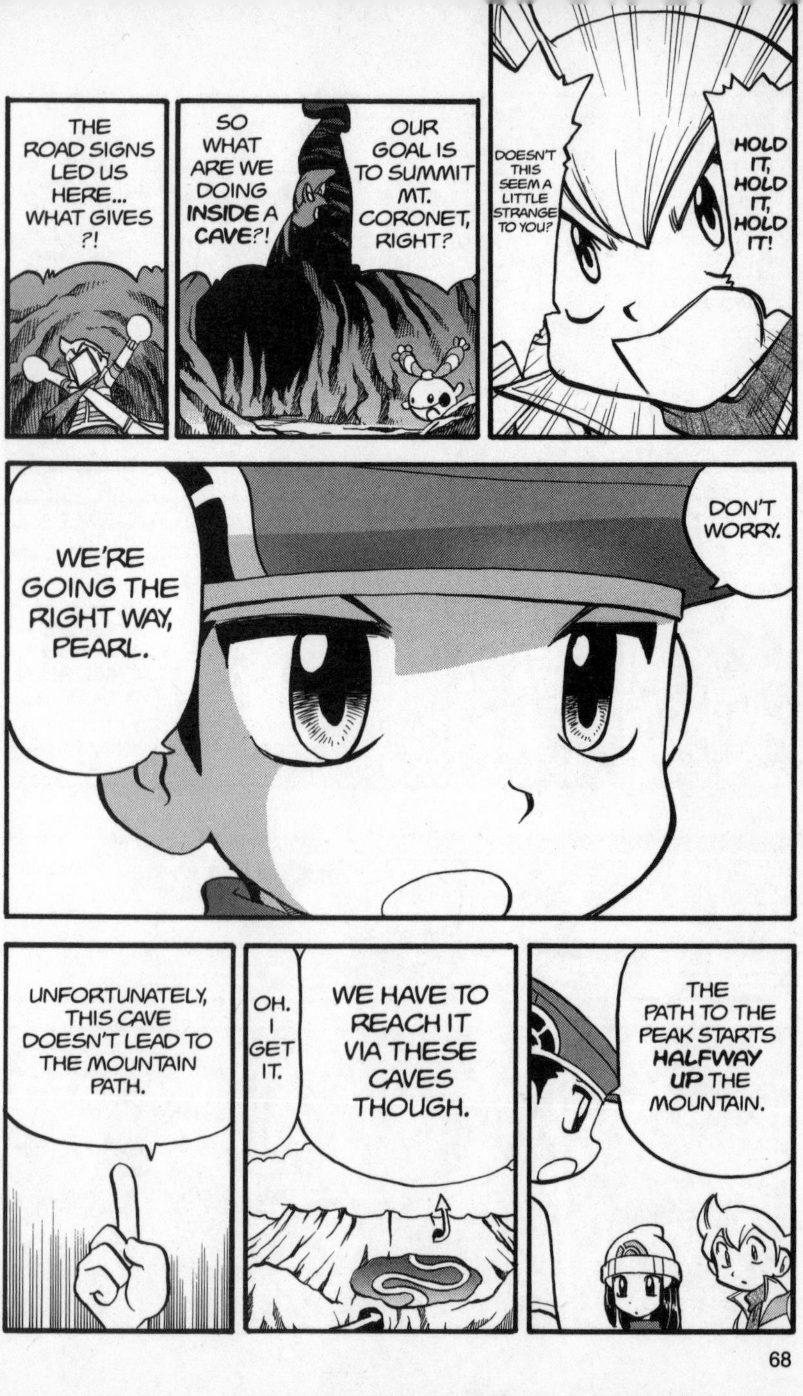
HOLD IT, HOLD IT, HOLD IT!
DOESN'T THIS SEEM A LITTLE STRANGE TO YOU?
OUR GOAL IS TO SUMMIT MT. CORONET, RIGHT?
SO WHAT ARE WE DOING INSIDE A CAVE?!
THE ROAD SIGNS LED US HERE... WHAT GIVES ?!
DON'T WORRY.
WE'RE GOING THE RIGHT WAY, PEARL.
THE PATH TO THE PEAK STARTS HALFWAY UP THE MOUNTAIN.
WE HAVE TO REACH IT VIA THESE CAVES THOUGH.
OH. I GET IT.
UNFORTUNATELY, THIS CAVE DOESN'T LEAD TO THE MOUNTAIN PATH.

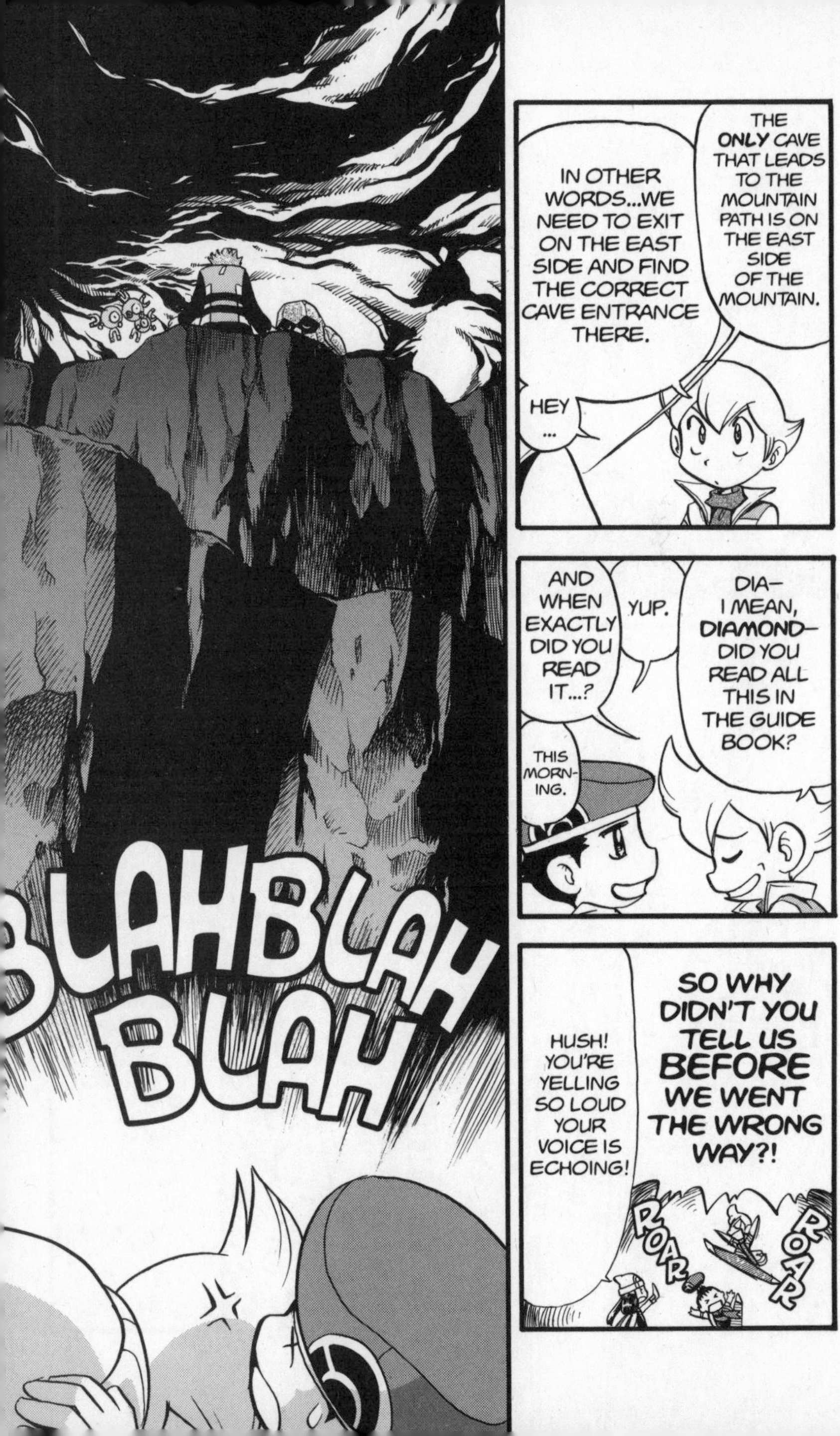
THE ONLY CAVE THAT LEADS TO THE MOUNTAIN PATH IS ON THE EAST SIDE OF THE MOUNTAIN.
IN OTHER WORDS...WE NEED TO EXIT ON THE EAST SIDE AND FIND THE CORRECT CAVE ENTRANCE THERE.
HEY ...
DIA— I MEAN, DIAMOND— DID YOU READ ALL THIS IN THE GUIDE BOOK?
YUP.
AND WHEN EXACTLY DID YOU READ IT...?
THIS MORN-ING.
SO WHY DIDN'T YOU TELL US BEFORE WE WENT THE WRONG WAY?!
HUSH! YOU'RE YELLING SO LOUD YOUR VOICE IS ECHOING!
ROAR
ROAR
BLAHBLAH BLAH

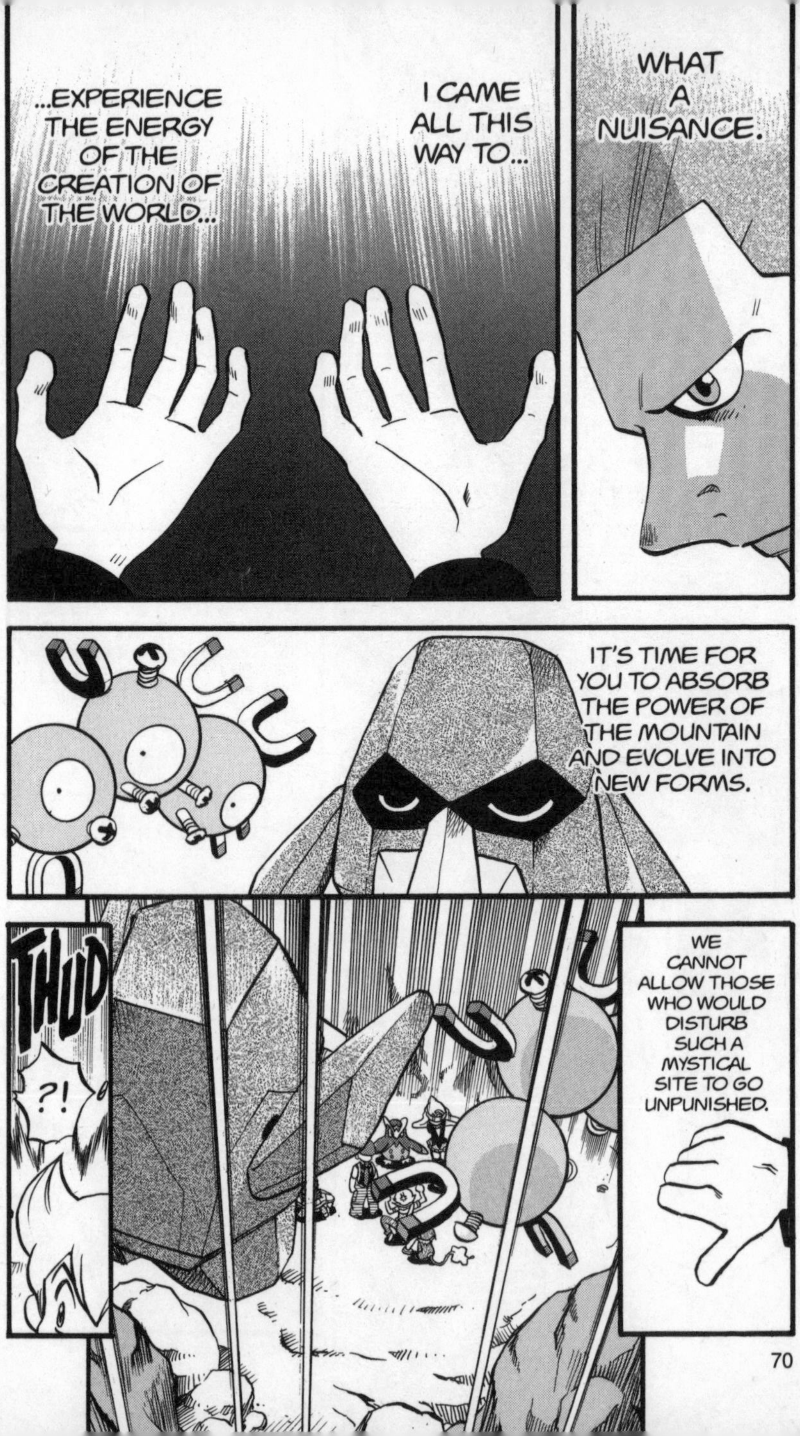
WHAT A NUISANCE.
I CAME ALL THIS WAY TO...
...EXPERIENCE THE ENERGY OF THE CREATION OF THE WORLD...
IT'S TIME FOR YOU TO ABSORB THE POWER OF THE MOUNTAIN AND EVOLVE INTO NEW FORMS.
WE CANNOT ALLOW THOSE WHO WOULD DISTURB SUCH A MYSTICAL SITE TO GO UNPUNISHED.
THUD
?!

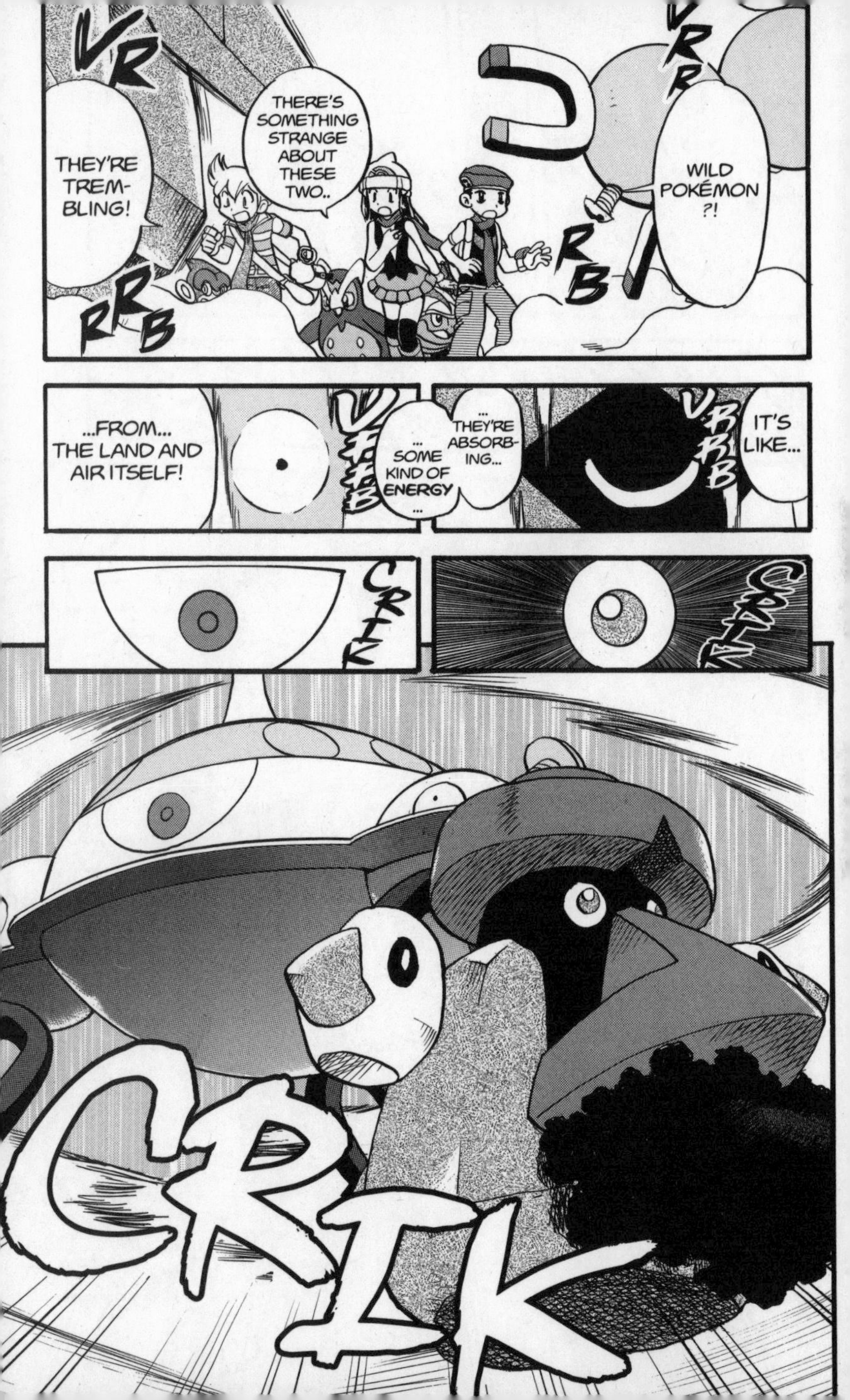
VRR
WILD POKÉMON ?!
RB
THERE'S SOMETHING STRANGE ABOUT THESE TWO..
VR
THEY'RE TREM-BLING!
RRB
IT'S LIKE...
VRRB
...THEY'RE ABSORB-ING...
...SOME KIND OF ENERGY...
...FROM... THE LAND AND AIR ITSELF!
CRIK
CRIK
CRIK

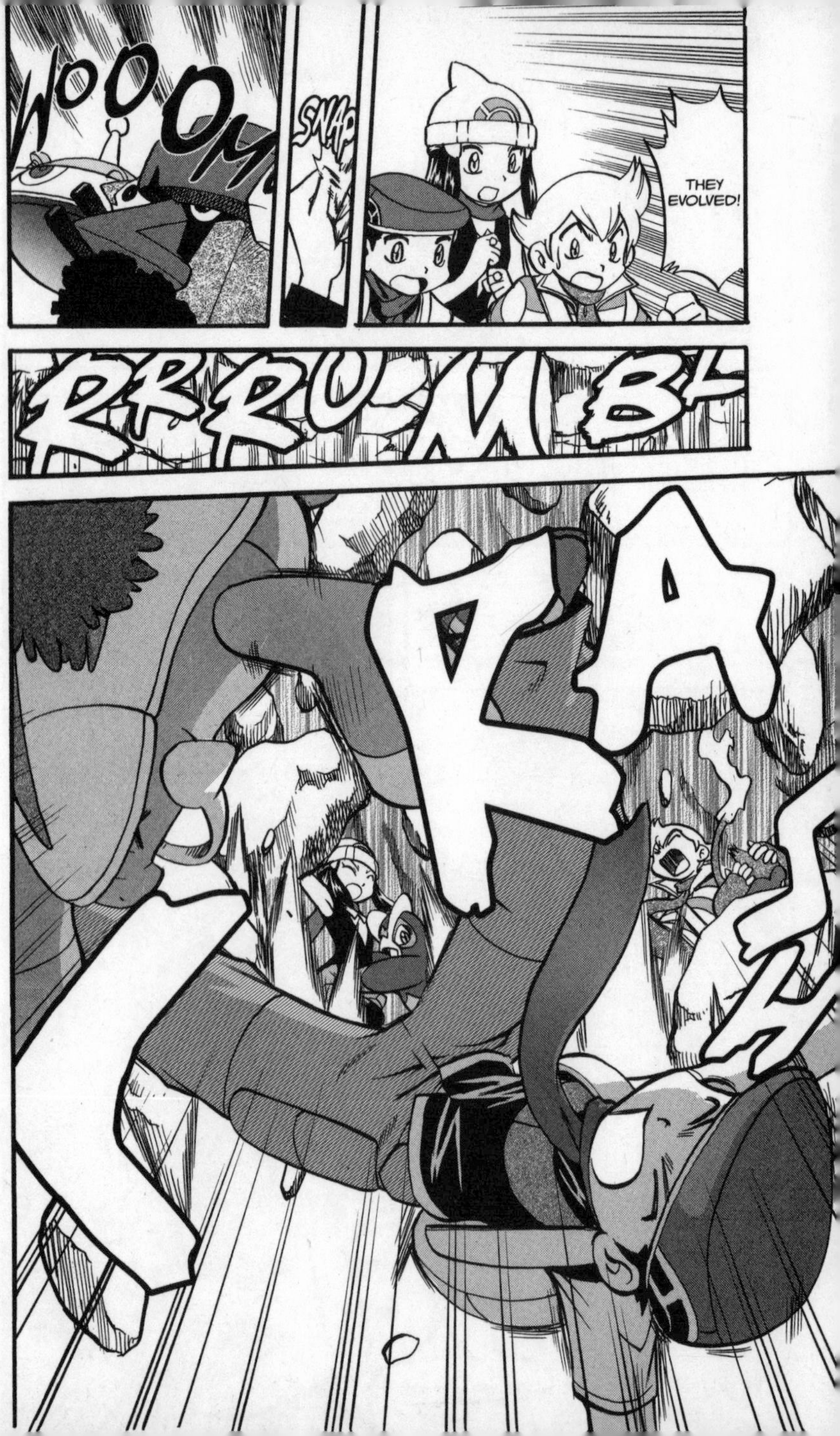
THEY EVOLVED!
SNAP
WOOOOM

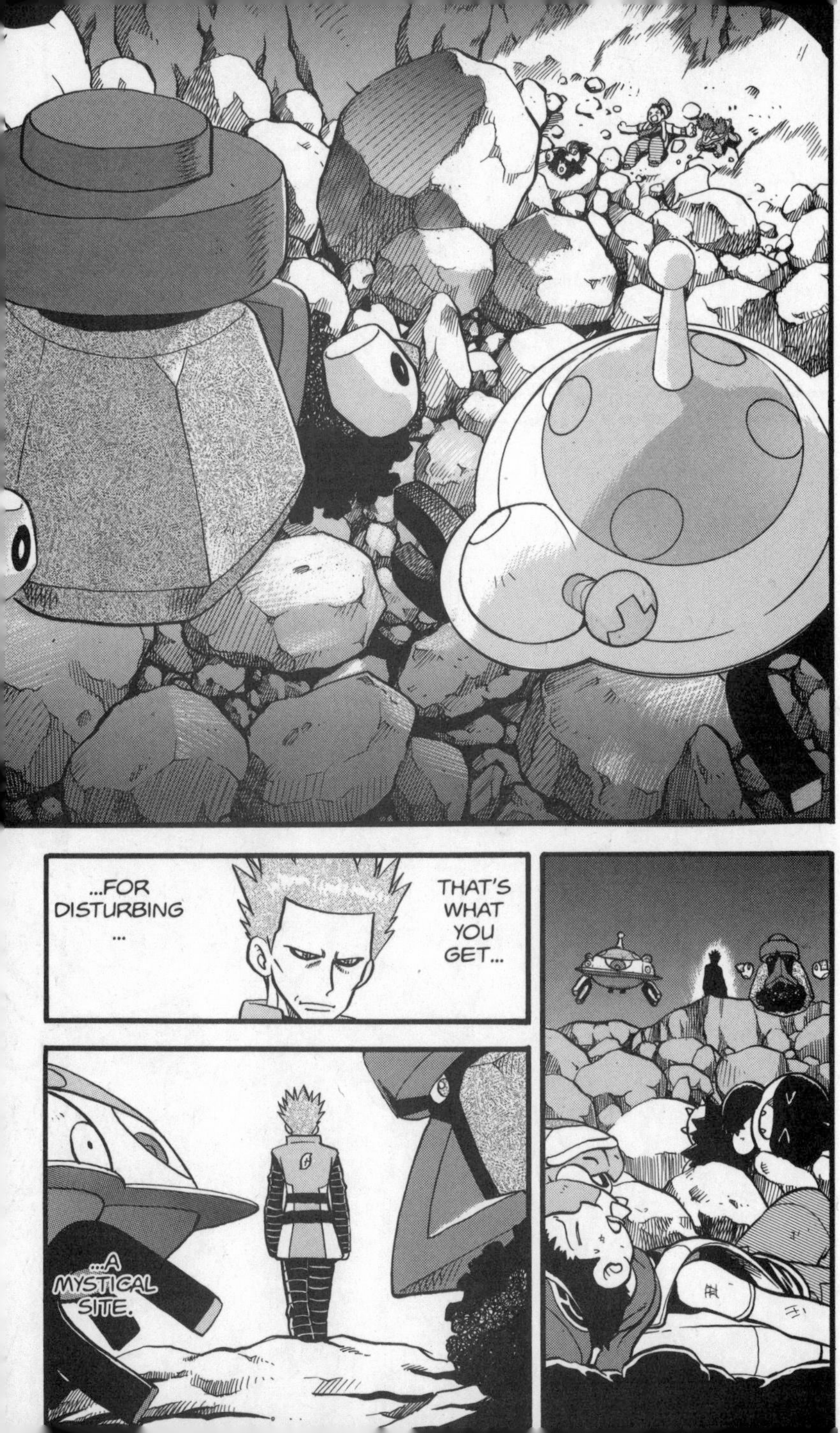
THAT'S WHAT YOU GET...
...FOR DISTURBING ...
...A MYSTICAL SITE.

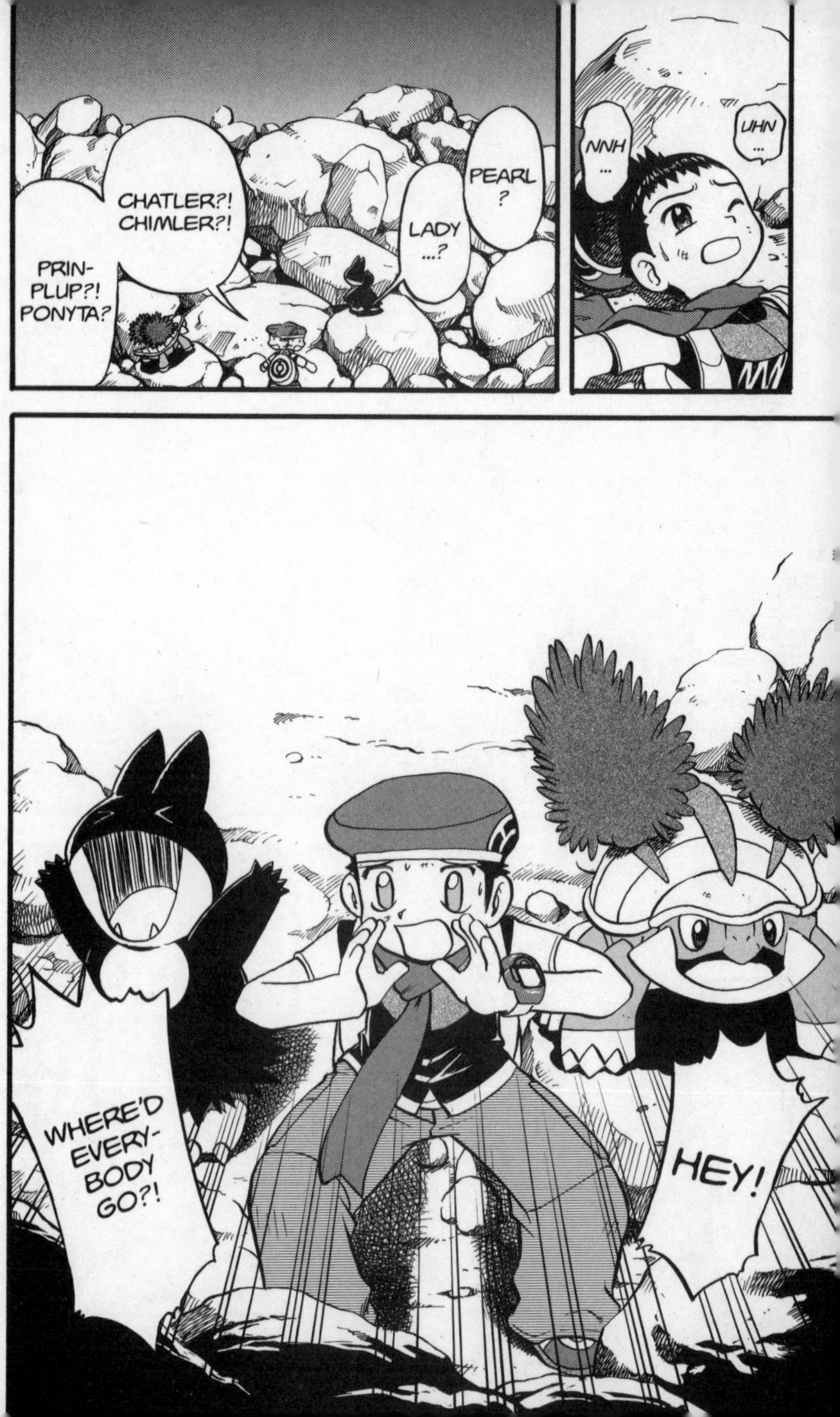
UHN ...
NNH ...
PEARL ?
LADY ...?
CHATLER?! CHIMLER?!
PRIN-PLUP?! PONYTA?
HEY!
WHERE'D EVERY-BODY GO?!

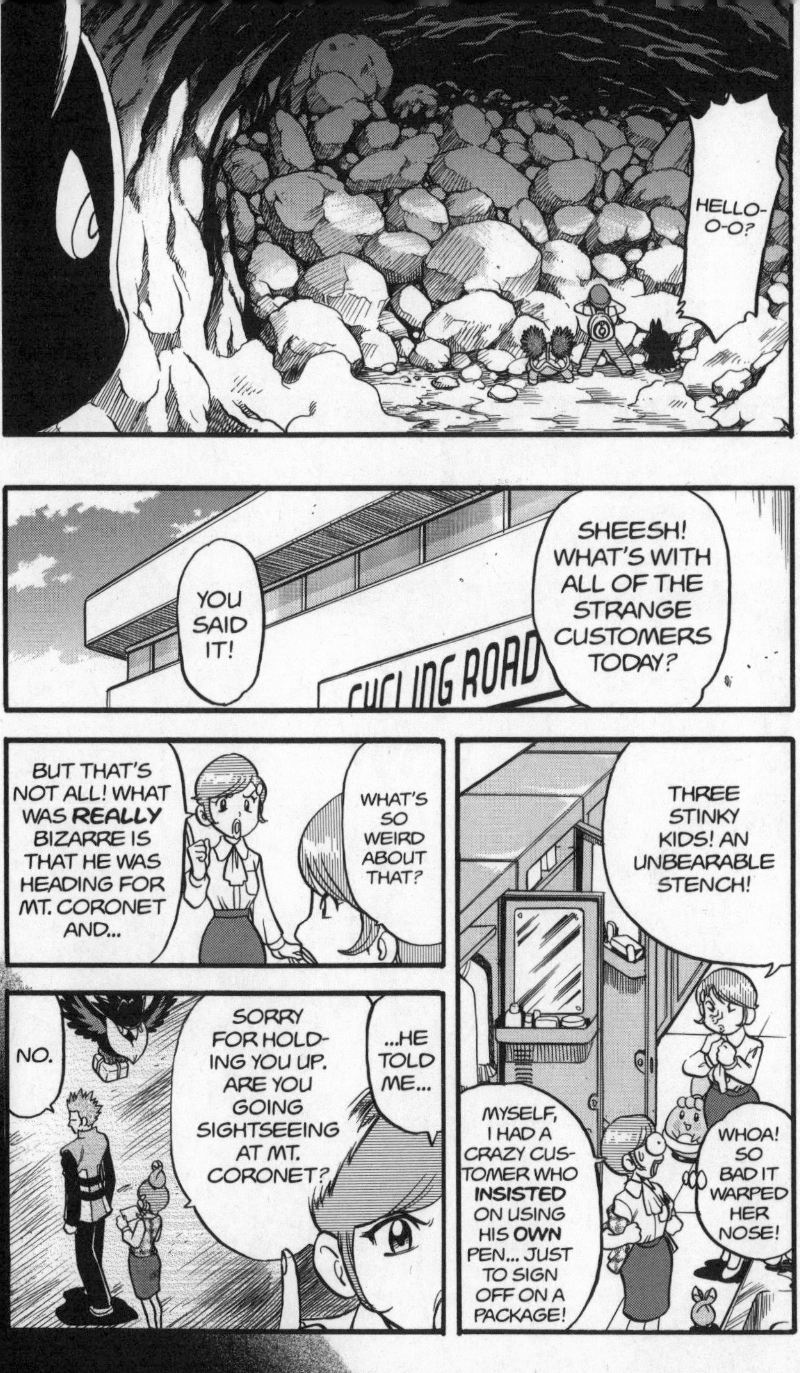
HELLO-O-O?
SHEESH! WHAT'S WITH ALL OF THE STRANGE CUSTOMERS TODAY?
YOU SAID IT!
CYCLING ROAD
THREE STINKY KIDS! AN UNBEARABLE STENCH!
WHOA! SO BAD IT WARPED HER NOSE!
MYSELF, I HAD A CRAZY CUSTOMER WHO INSISTED ON USING HIS OWN PEN... JUST TO SIGN OFF ON A PACKAGE!
WHAT'S SO WEIRD ABOUT THAT?
BUT THAT'S NOT ALL! WHAT WAS REALLY BIZARRE IS THAT HE WAS HEADING FOR MT. CORONET AND...
...HE TOLD ME...
SORRY FOR HOLDING YOU UP. ARE YOU GOING SIGHTSEEING AT MT. CORONET?
NO.

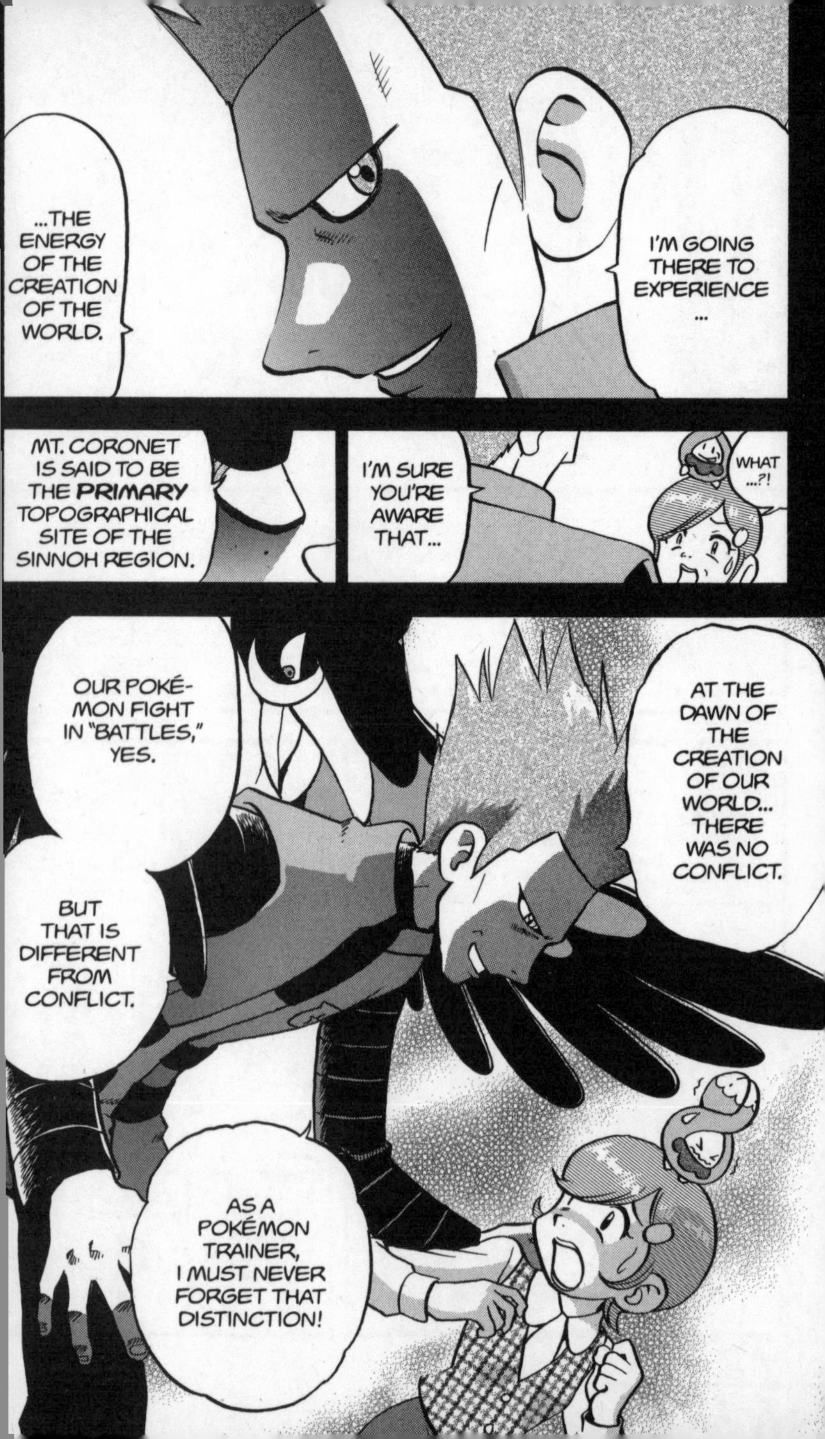
I'M GOING THERE TO EXPERIENCE ...
...THE ENERGY OF THE CREATION OF THE WORLD.
WHAT ...?!
I'M SURE YOU'RE AWARE THAT...
MT. CORONET IS SAID TO BE THE **PRIMARY** TOPOGRAPHICAL SITE OF THE SINNOH REGION.
AT THE DAWN OF THE CREATION OF OUR WORLD... THERE WAS NO CONFLICT.
OUR POKÉMON FIGHT IN "BATTLES," YES.
BUT THAT IS DIFFERENT FROM CONFLICT.
AS A POKÉMON TRAINER, I MUST NEVER FORGET THAT DISTINCTION!

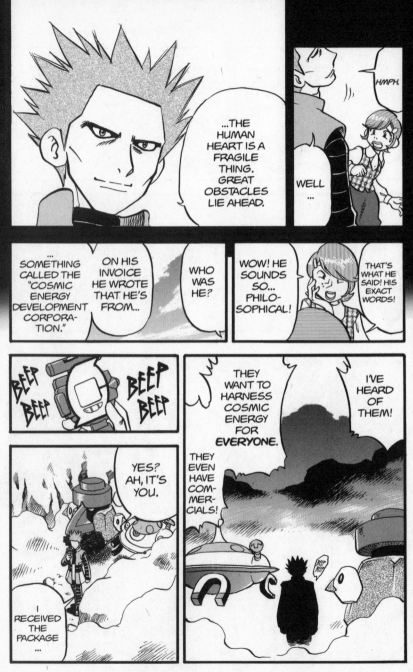

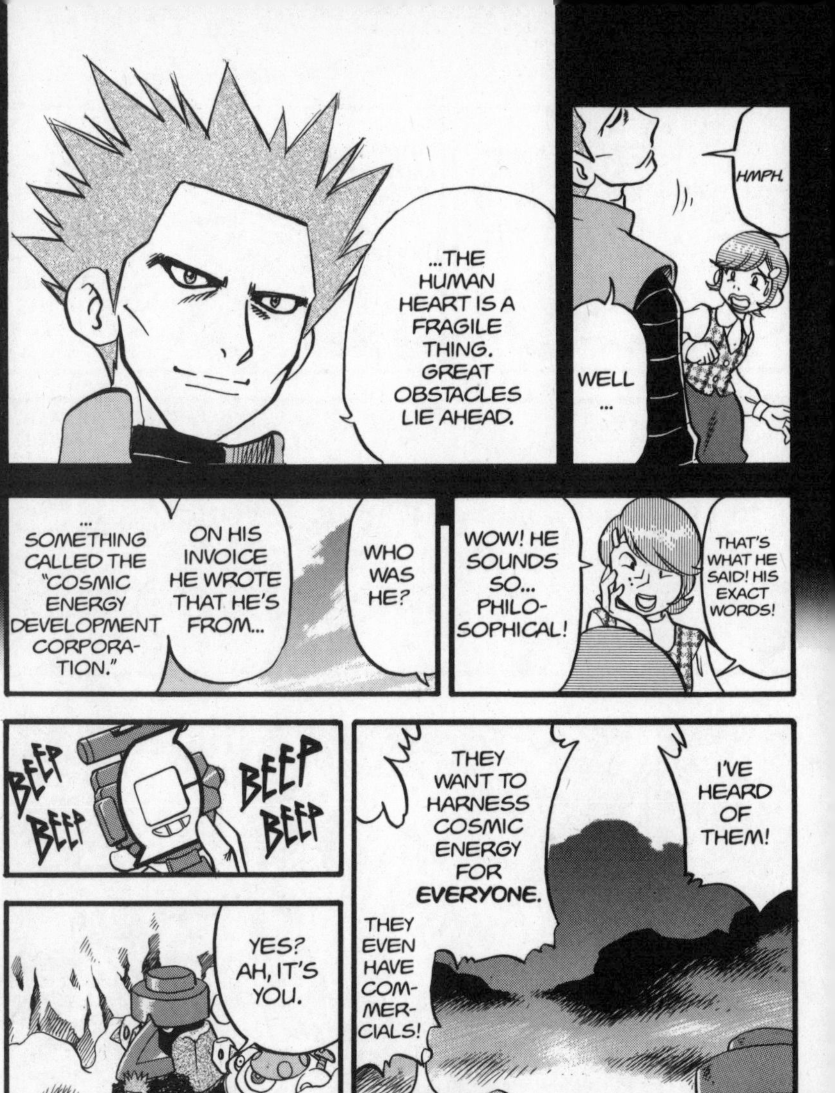
HMPH.
WELL ...
...THE HUMAN HEART IS A FRAGILE THING. GREAT OBSTACLES LIE AHEAD.
THAT'S WHAT HE SAID! HIS EXACT WORDS!
WOW! HE SOUNDS SO... PHILOSOPHICAL!
WHO WAS HE?
ON HIS INVOICE HE WROTE THAT HE'S FROM...
... SOMETHING CALLED THE "COSMIC ENERGY DEVELOPMENT CORPORATION."
I'VE HEARD OF THEM!
THEY WANT TO HARNESS COSMIC ENERGY FOR **EVERYONE**.
THEY EVEN HAVE COMMERCIALS!
BEEP BEEP
BEEP BEEP
BEEP BEEP
YES? AH, IT'S YOU.
I RECEIVED THE PACKAGE ...

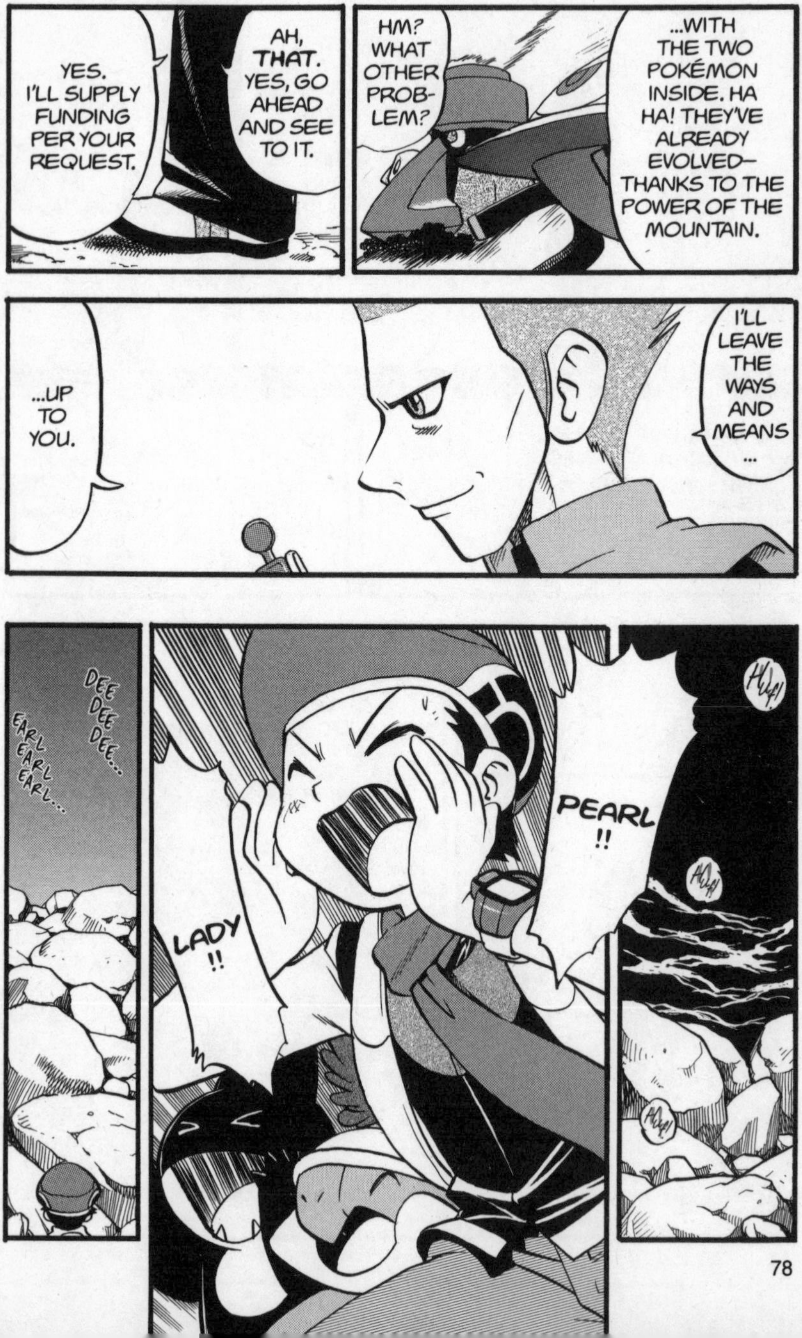
...WITH THE TWO POKÉMON INSIDE. HA HA! THEY'VE ALREADY EVOLVED—THANKS TO THE POWER OF THE MOUNTAIN.
HM? WHAT OTHER PROB-LEM?
AH, THAT. YES, GO AHEAD AND SEE TO IT.
YES. I'LL SUPPLY FUNDING PER YOUR REQUEST.
I'LL LEAVE THE WAYS AND MEANS...
...UP TO YOU.
PEARL!!
LADY!!
DEE DEE DEE...
EARL EARL EARL...

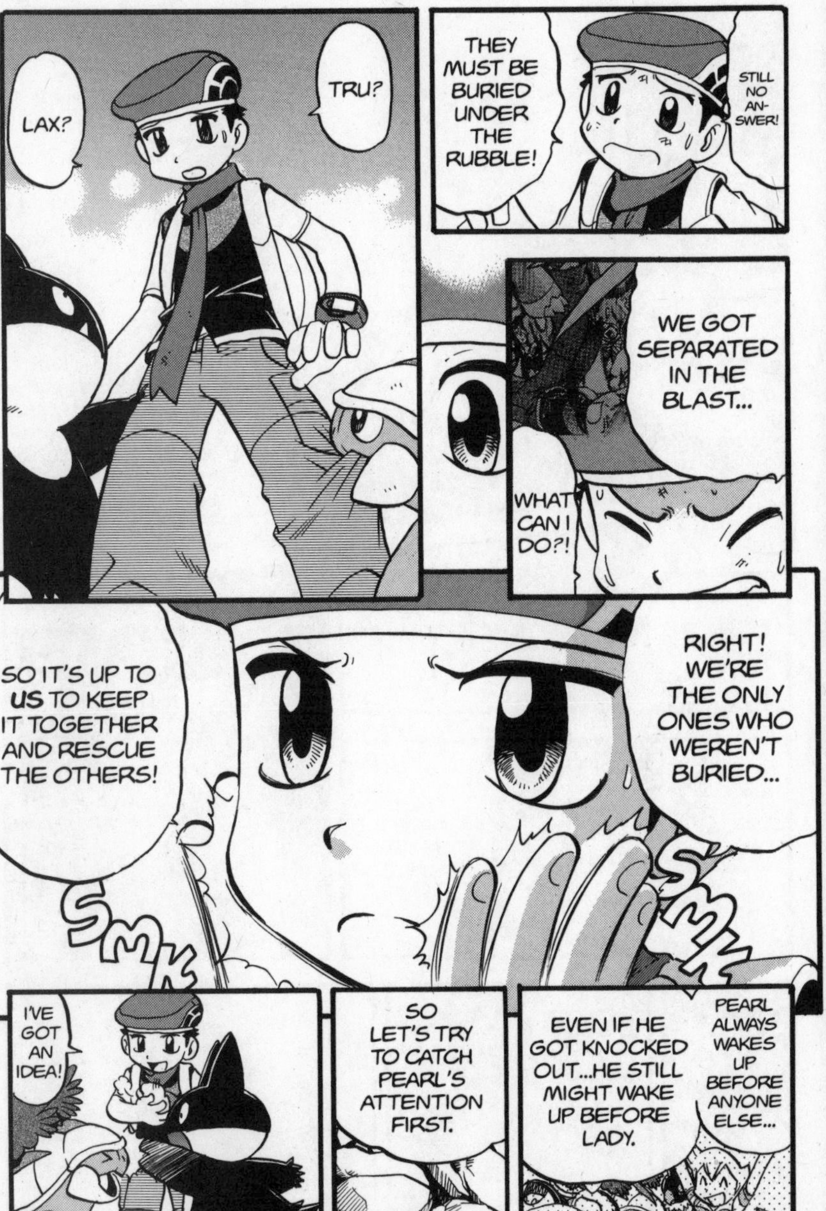
STILL NO AN-SWER!
THEY MUST BE BURIED UNDER THE RUBBLE!
WE GOT SEPARATED IN THE BLAST...
WHAT CAN I DO?!
TRU?
LAX?
RIGHT! WE'RE THE ONLY ONES WHO WEREN'T BURIED...
SO IT'S UP TO **US** TO KEEP IT TOGETHER AND RESCUE THE OTHERS!
SMK
SMK
PEARL ALWAYS WAKES UP BEFORE ANYONE ELSE...
EVEN IF HE GOT KNOCKED OUT...HE STILL MIGHT WAKE UP BEFORE LADY.
SO LET'S TRY TO CATCH PEARL'S ATTENTION FIRST.
I'VE GOT AN IDEA!

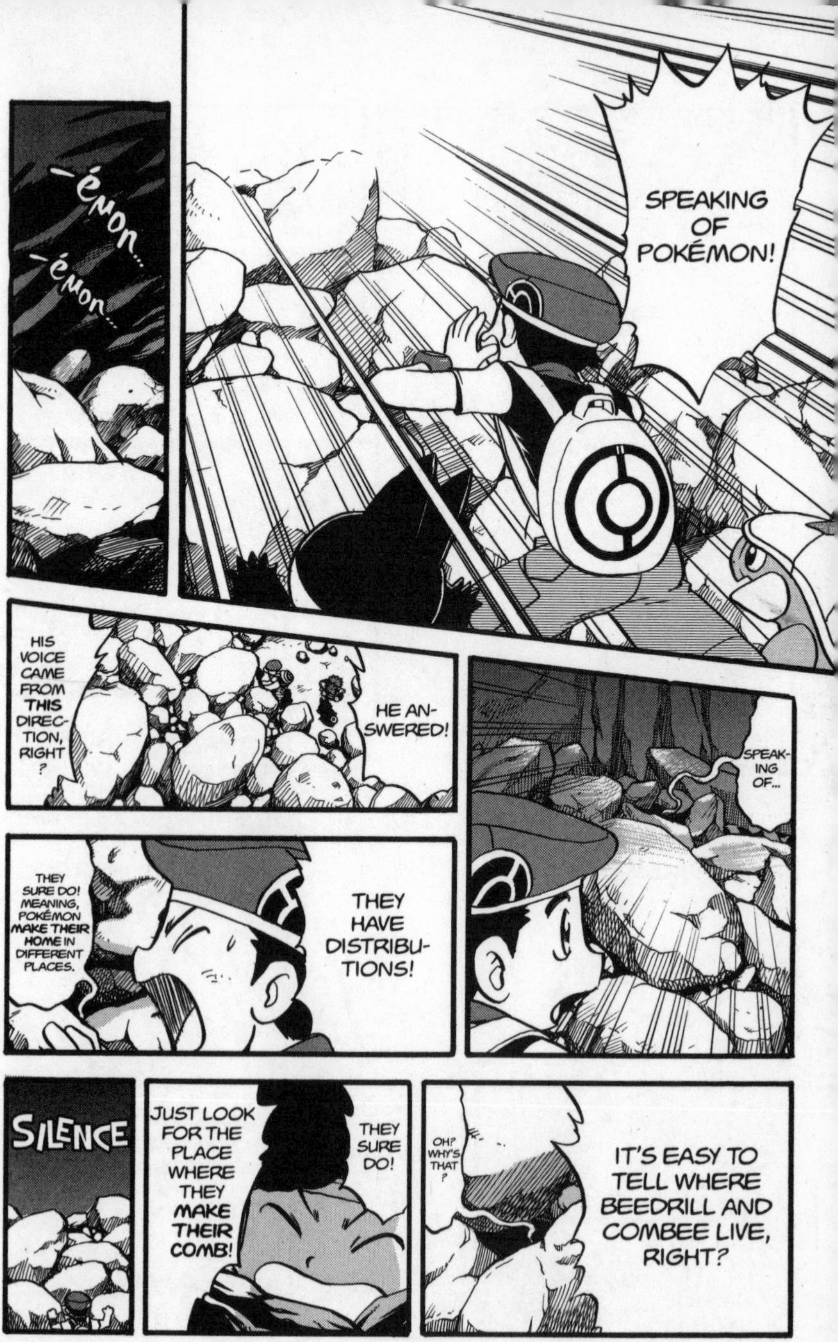
SPEAKING OF POKÉMON!
-émon... -émon...
SPEAK-ING OF...
HE AN-SWERED!
HIS VOICE CAME FROM THIS DIRECTION, RIGHT?
THEY HAVE DISTRIBU-TIONS!
THEY SURE DO! MEANING, POKÉMON MAKE THEIR HOME IN DIFFERENT PLACES.
IT'S EASY TO TELL WHERE BEEDRILL AND COMBEE LIVE, RIGHT?
OH? WHY'S THAT?
THEY SURE DO!
JUST LOOK FOR THE PLACE WHERE THEY MAKE THEIR COMB!
SILENCE

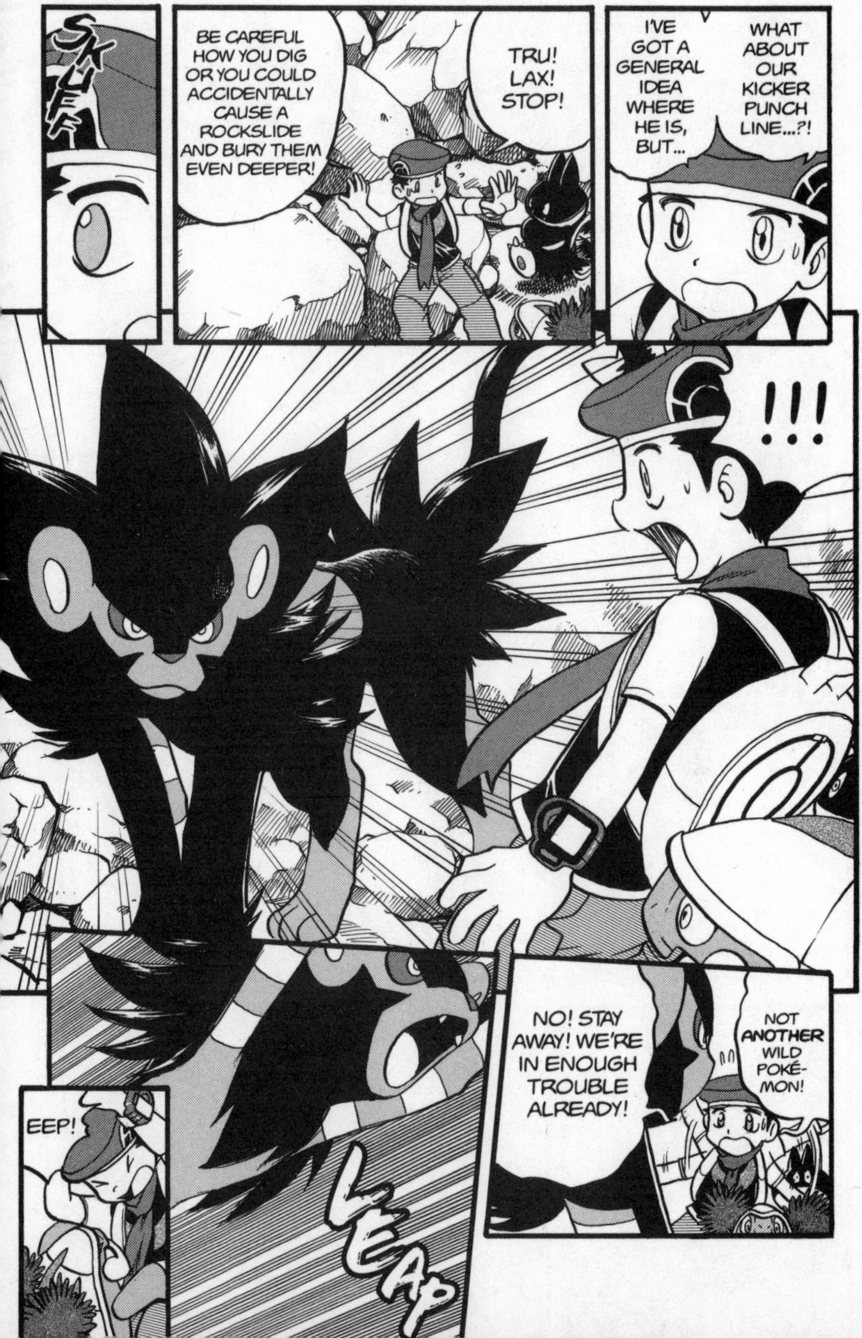
WHAT ABOUT OUR KICKER PUNCH LINE...?!
I'VE GOT A GENERAL IDEA WHERE HE IS, BUT...
TRU! LAX! STOP!
BE CAREFUL HOW YOU DIG OR YOU COULD ACCIDENTALLY CAUSE A ROCKSLIDE AND BURY THEM EVEN DEEPER!
SKUFF
!!!
NOT ANOTHER WILD POKÉ-MON!
NO! STAY AWAY! WE'RE IN ENOUGH TROUBLE ALREADY!
LEAP
EEP!

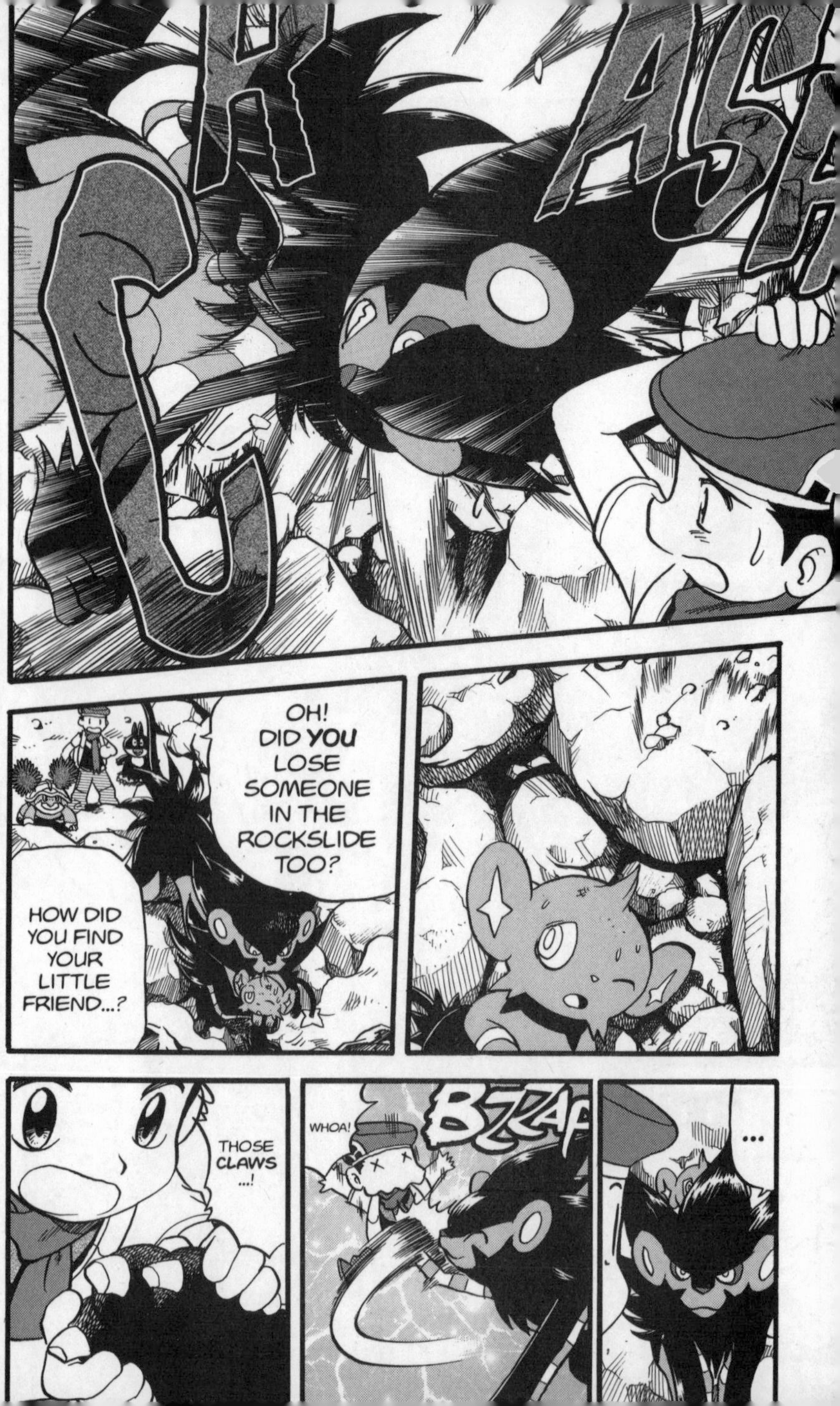
OH! DID YOU LOSE SOMEONE IN THE ROCKSLIDE TOO?
HOW DID YOU FIND YOUR LITTLE FRIEND...?
...
WHOA!
THOSE CLAWS ...!

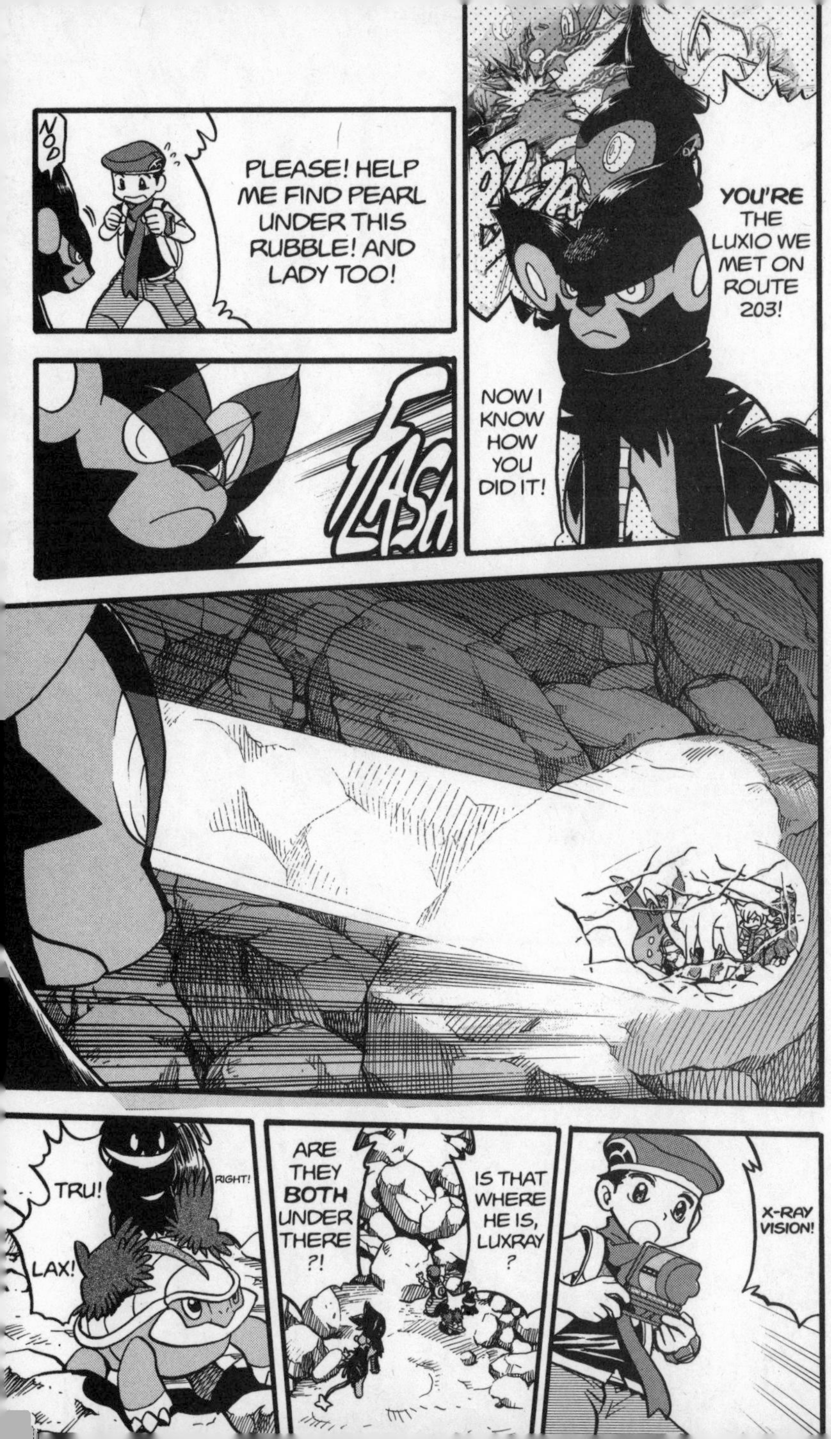
YOU'RE THE LUXIO WE MET ON ROUTE 203!
NOW I KNOW HOW YOU DID IT!
NOD
PLEASE! HELP ME FIND PEARL UNDER THIS RUBBLE! AND LADY TOO!
FLASH
X-RAY VISION!
IS THAT WHERE HE IS, LUXRAY?
ARE THEY BOTH UNDER THERE?!
RIGHT!
TRU!
LAX!

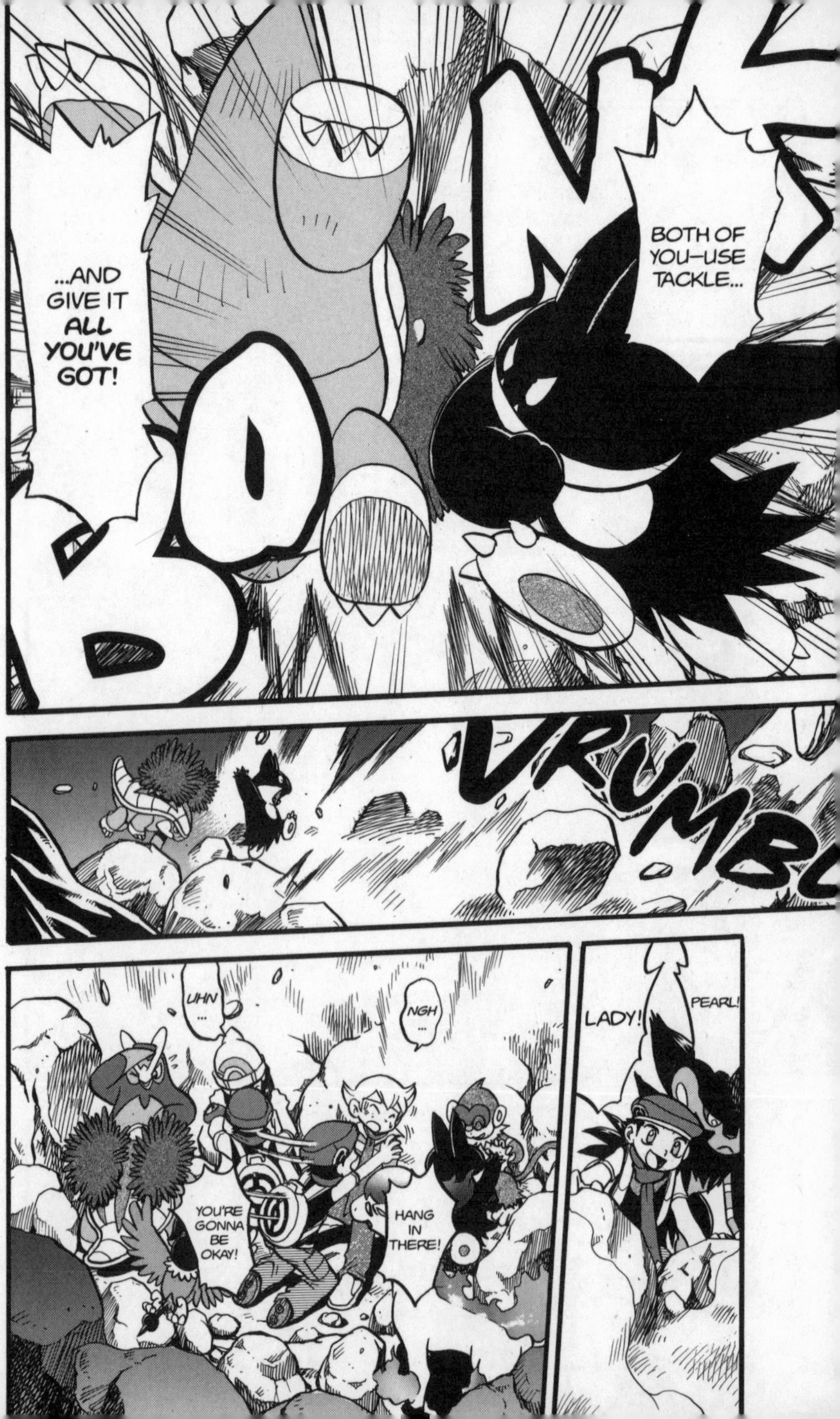
BOTH OF YOU—USE TACKLE...
...AND GIVE IT ALL YOU'VE GOT!
PEARL!
LADY!
NGH...
UHN...
HANG IN THERE!
YOU'RE GONNA BE OKAY!

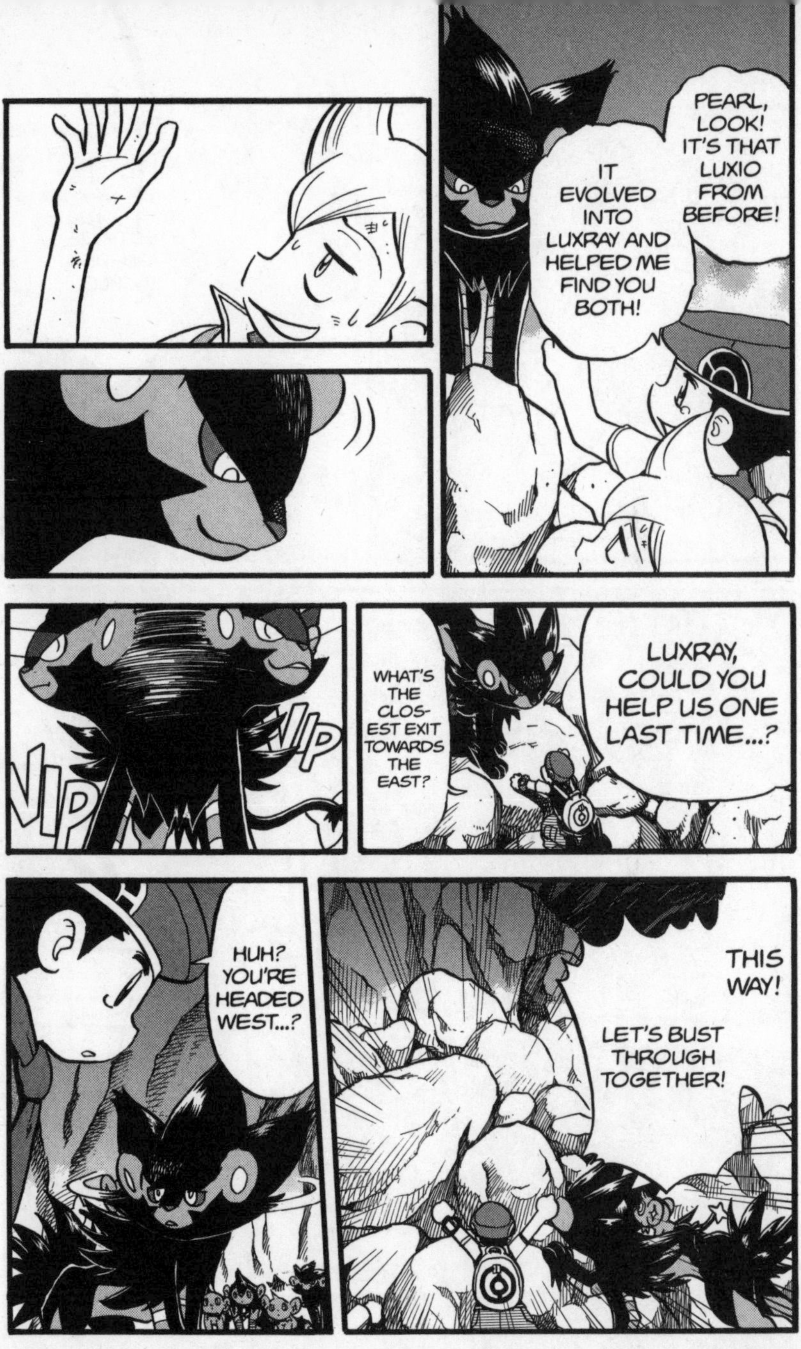
PEARL, LOOK! IT'S THAT LUXIO FROM BEFORE!
IT EVOLVED INTO LUXRAY AND HELPED ME FIND YOU BOTH!
LUXRAY, COULD YOU HELP US ONE LAST TIME...?
WHAT'S THE CLOS-EST EXIT TOWARDS THE EAST?
VIP
VIP
THIS WAY!
LET'S BUST THROUGH TOGETHER!
HUH? YOU'RE HEADED WEST...?

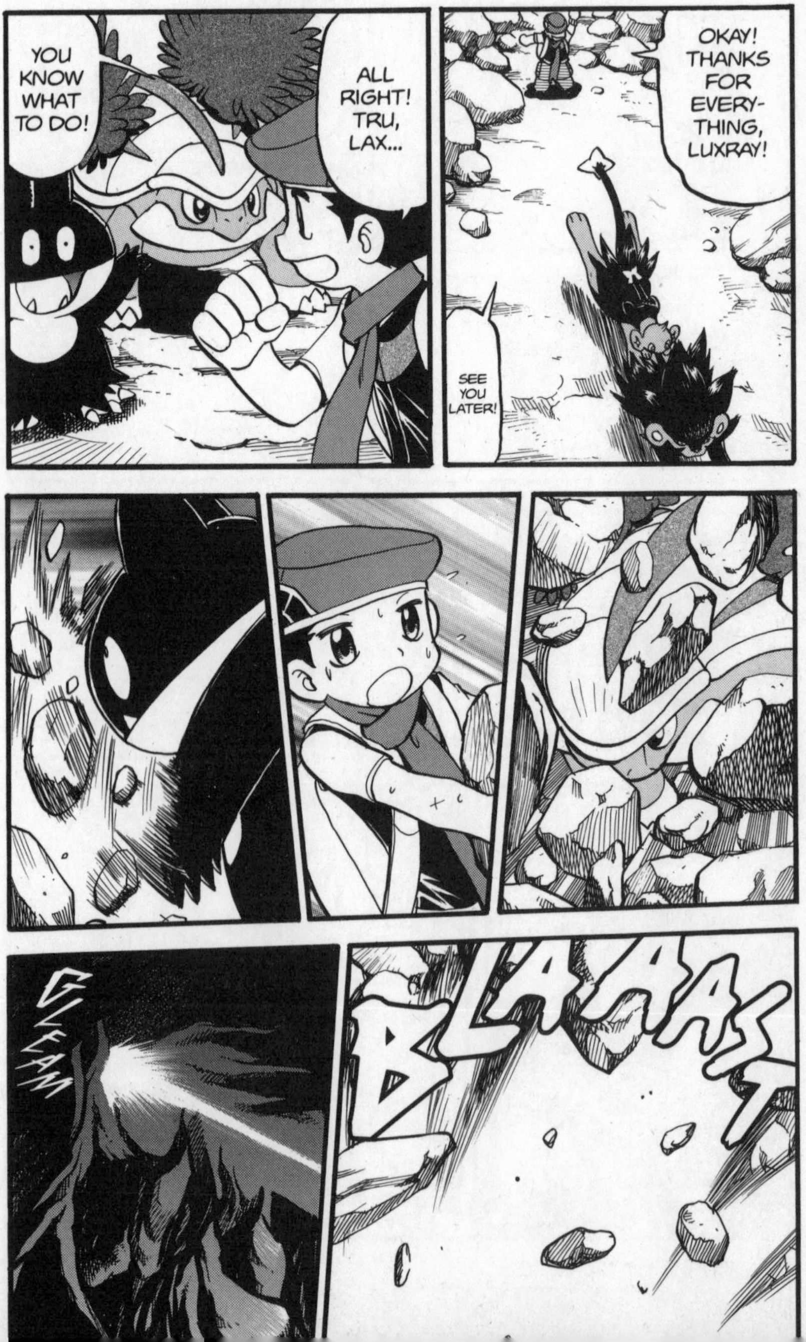
OKAY! THANKS FOR EVERY-THING, LUXRAY!
SEE YOU LATER!
ALL RIGHT! TRU, LAX...
YOU KNOW WHAT TO DO!
BLAAAST
GLEAM

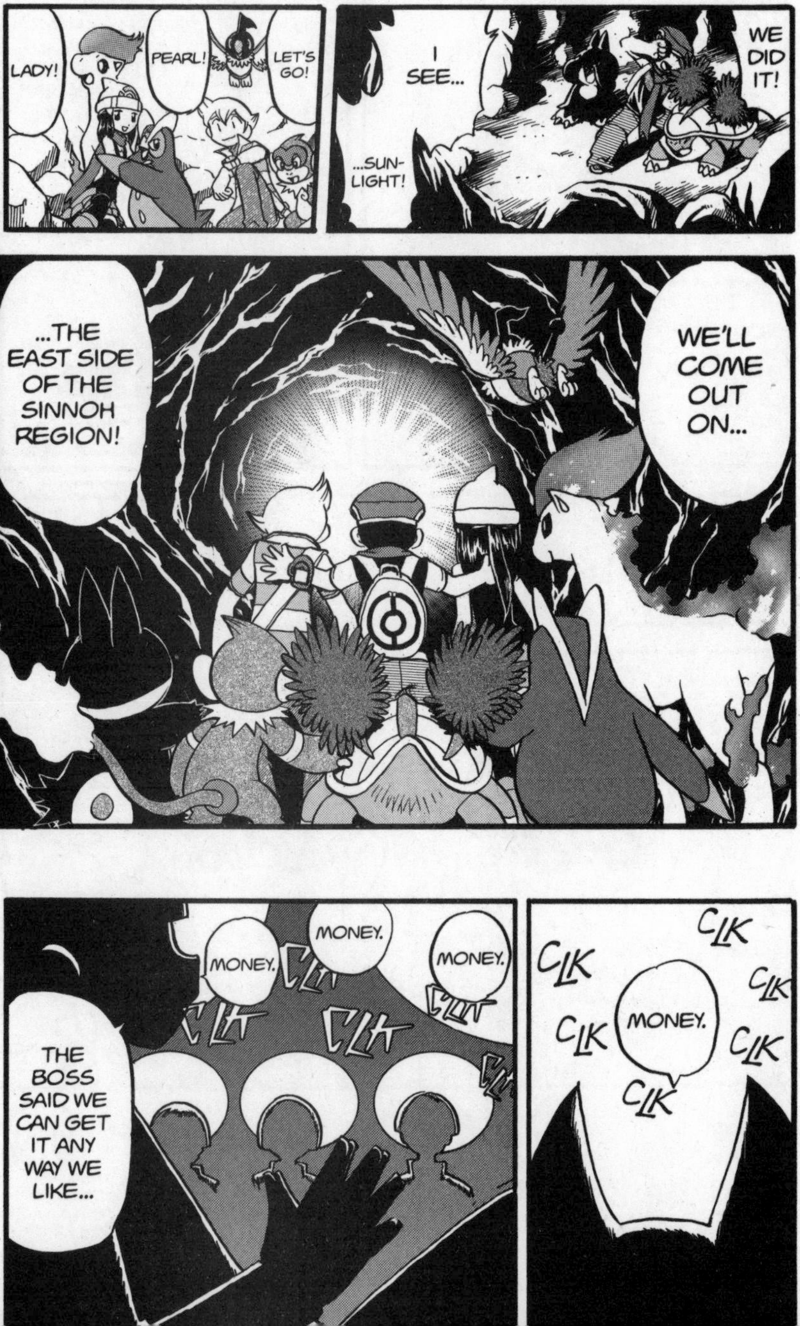
WE DID IT!
I SEE...
...SUN-LIGHT!
LET'S GO!
PEARL!
LADY!
WE'LL COME OUT ON...
...THE EAST SIDE OF THE SINNOH REGION!
CLK
CLK
CLK
CLK
MONEY.
CLK
CLK
MONEY.
MONEY.
CLK
MONEY.
CLK
THE BOSS SAID WE CAN GET IT ANY WAY WE LIKE...

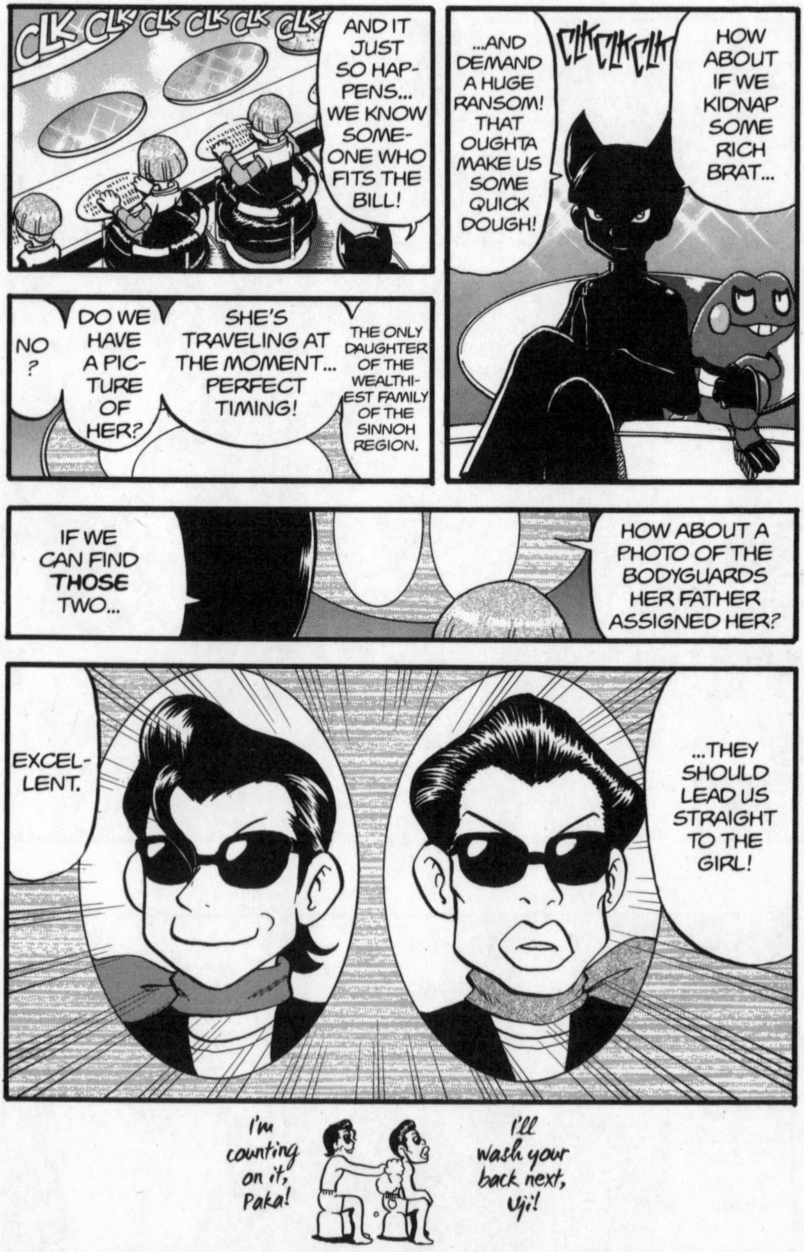
HOW ABOUT IF WE KIDNAP SOME RICH BRAT...
CLK CLK CLK
...AND DEMAND A HUGE RANSOM! THAT OUGHTA MAKE US SOME QUICK DOUGH!
CLK CLK CLK CLK CLK CLK
AND IT JUST SO HAPPENS... WE KNOW SOMEONE WHO FITS THE BILL!
THE ONLY DAUGHTER OF THE WEALTHIEST FAMILY OF THE SINNOH REGION.
SHE'S TRAVELING AT THE MOMENT... PERFECT TIMING!
DO WE HAVE A PICTURE OF HER?
NO ?
HOW ABOUT A PHOTO OF THE BODYGUARDS HER FATHER ASSIGNED HER?
IF WE CAN FIND **THOSE** TWO...
...THEY SHOULD LEAD US STRAIGHT TO THE GIRL!
EXCELLENT.
I'll wash your back next, Uji!
I'm counting on it, Paka!

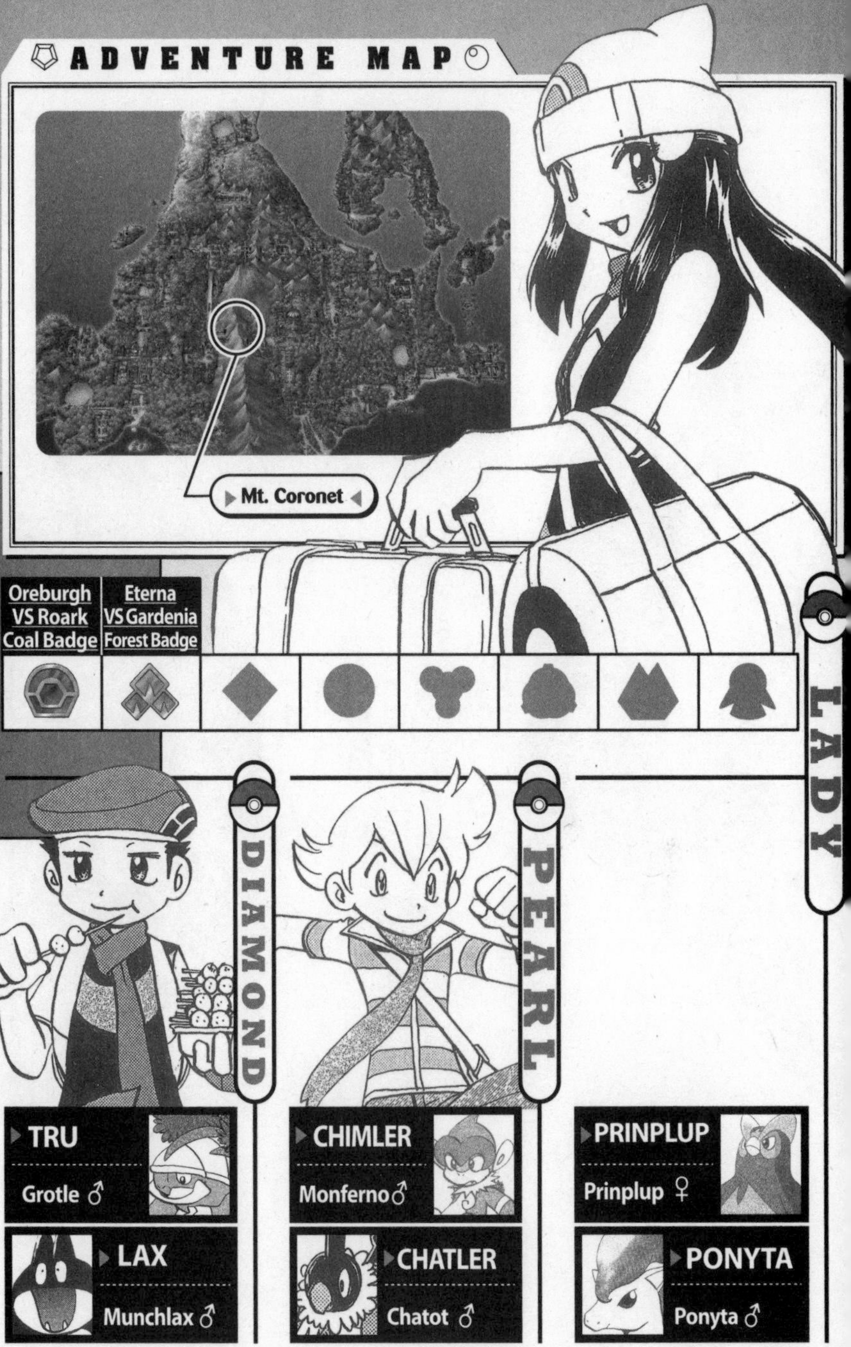
ADVENTURE MAP
Mt. Coronet
Oreburgh
VS Roark
Coal Badge
Eterna
VS Gardenia
Forest Badge
LADY
DIAMOND
PEARL
TRU
Grotle ♂
LAX
Munchlax ♂
CHIMLER
Monferno ♂
CHATLER
Chatot ♂
PRINPLUP
Prinplup ♀
PONYTA
Ponyta ♂

13

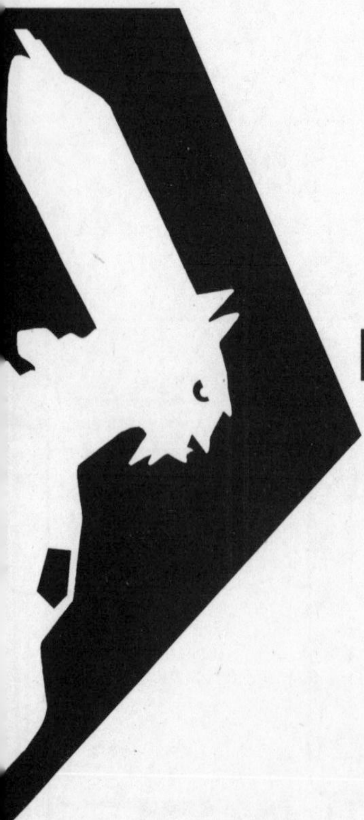

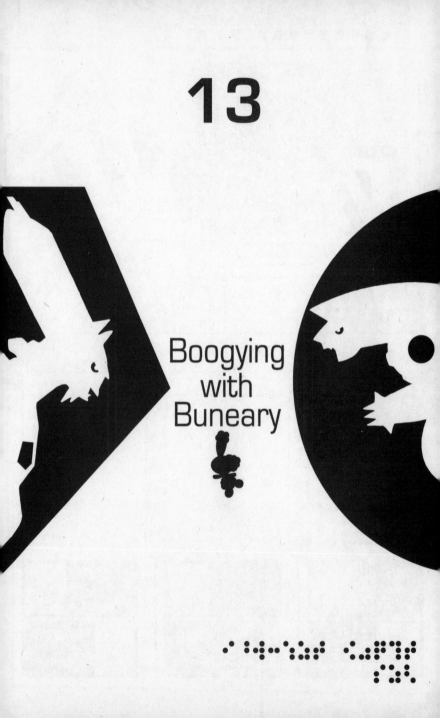

Boogying with Buneary

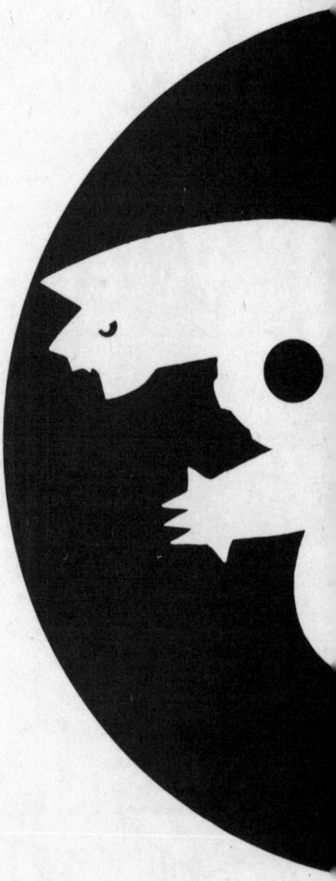

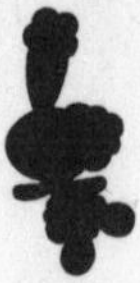

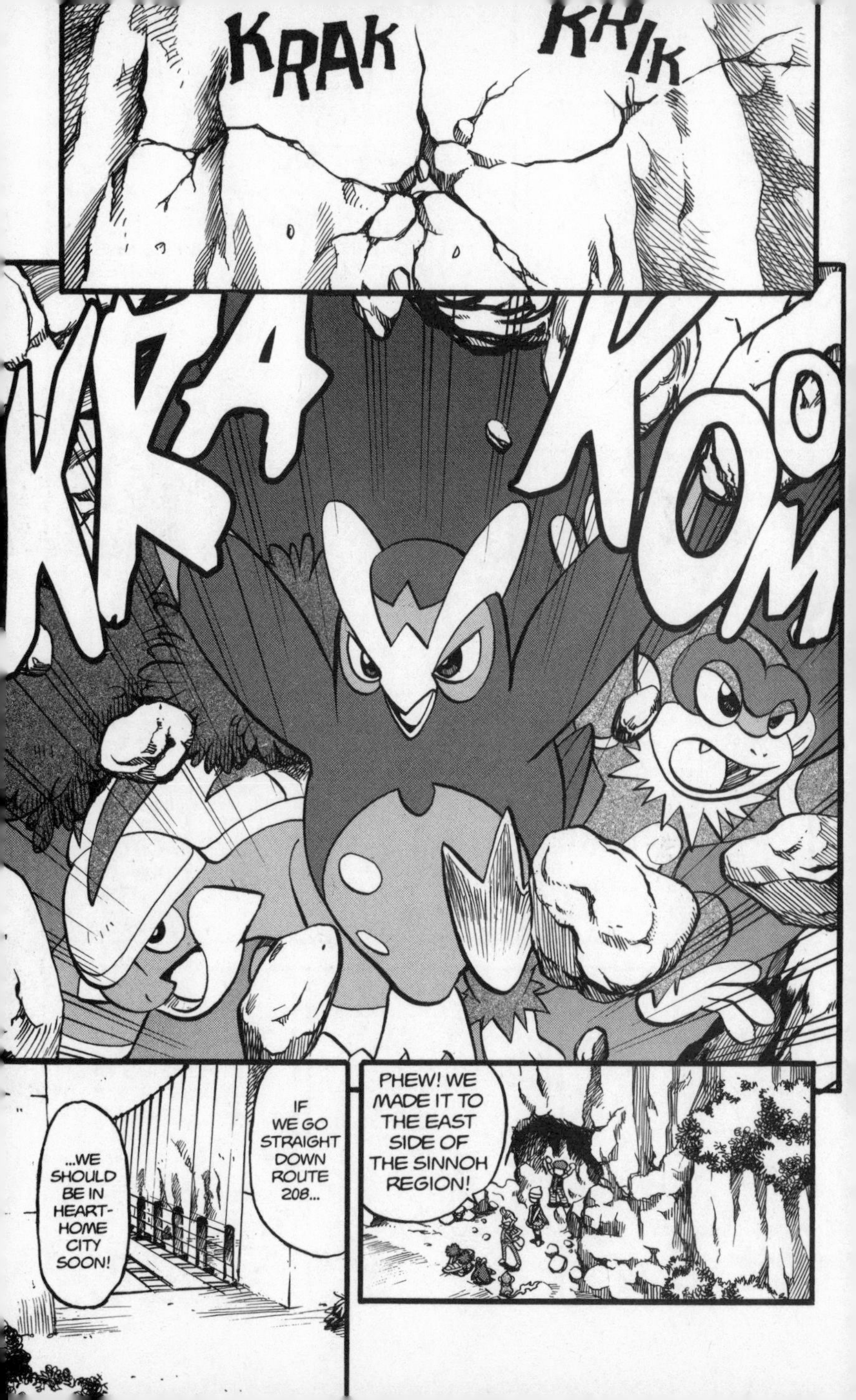
KRIK
KRAK
KRA-KOOM
PHEW! WE MADE IT TO THE EAST SIDE OF THE SINNOH REGION!
IF WE GO STRAIGHT DOWN ROUTE 208...
...WE SHOULD BE IN HEART-HOME CITY SOON!

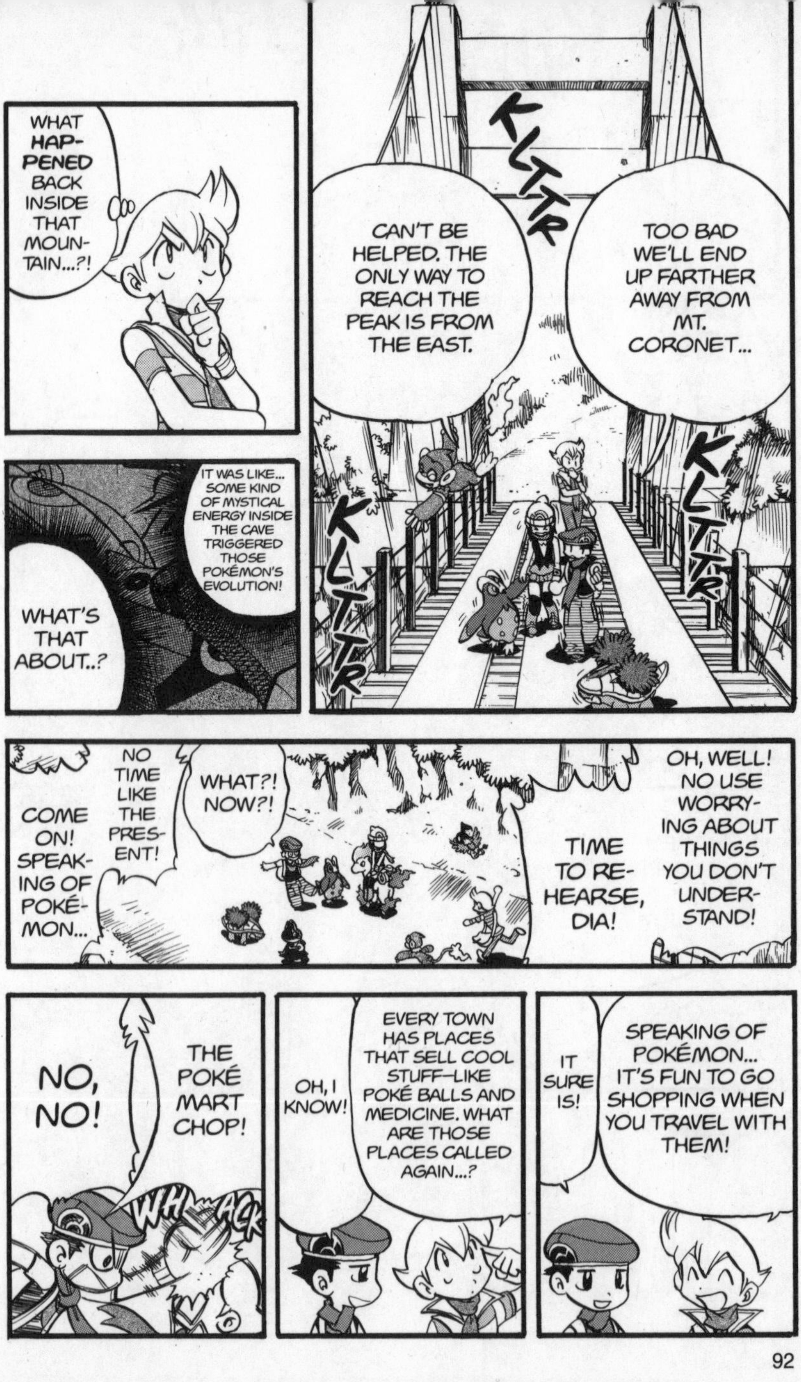
TOO BAD WE'LL END UP FARTHER AWAY FROM MT. CORONET...
CAN'T BE HELPED. THE ONLY WAY TO REACH THE PEAK IS FROM THE EAST.
KLTTR
KLTTR
KLTTR
WHAT HAPPENED BACK INSIDE THAT MOUNTAIN...?!
IT WAS LIKE... SOME KIND OF MYSTICAL ENERGY INSIDE THE CAVE TRIGGERED THOSE POKÉMON'S EVOLUTION!
WHAT'S THAT ABOUT..?
OH, WELL! NO USE WORRYING ABOUT THINGS YOU DON'T UNDERSTAND!
TIME TO REHEARSE, DIA!
WHAT?! NOW?!
NO TIME LIKE THE PRESENT!
COME ON! SPEAKING OF POKÉMON...
SPEAKING OF POKÉMON... IT'S FUN TO GO SHOPPING WHEN YOU TRAVEL WITH THEM!
IT SURE IS!
EVERY TOWN HAS PLACES THAT SELL COOL STUFF—LIKE POKÉ BALLS AND MEDICINE. WHAT ARE THOSE PLACES CALLED AGAIN...?
OH, I KNOW!
THE POKÉ MART CHOP!
NO, NO!
WHACK

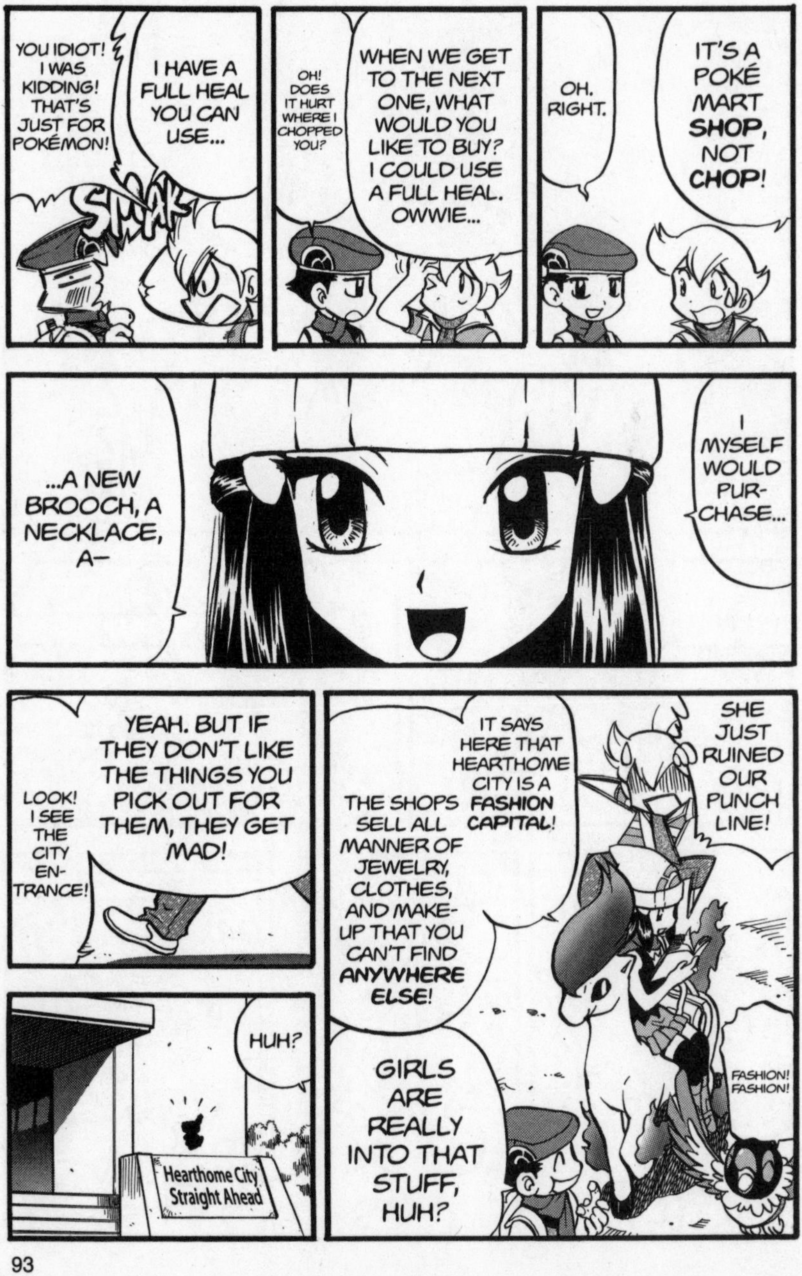
IT'S A POKÉ MART **SHOP**, NOT **CHOP**!
OH. RIGHT.
WHEN WE GET TO THE NEXT ONE, WHAT WOULD YOU LIKE TO BUY? I COULD USE A FULL HEAL. OWWIE...
OH! DOES IT HURT WHERE I CHOPPED YOU?
I HAVE A FULL HEAL YOU CAN USE...
YOU IDIOT! I WAS KIDDING! THAT'S JUST FOR POKÉMON!
I MYSELF WOULD PUR-CHASE...
...A NEW BROOCH, A NECKLACE, A—
SHE JUST RUINED OUR PUNCH LINE!
IT SAYS HERE THAT HEARTHOME CITY IS A **FASHION CAPITAL**!
THE SHOPS SELL ALL MANNER OF JEWELRY, CLOTHES, AND MAKE-UP THAT YOU CAN'T FIND **ANYWHERE ELSE**!
FASHION! FASHION!
GIRLS ARE REALLY INTO THAT STUFF, HUH?
YEAH. BUT IF THEY DON'T LIKE THE THINGS YOU PICK OUT FOR THEM, THEY GET MAD!
LOOK! I SEE THE CITY EN-TRANCE!
HUH?
Hearthome City Straight Ahead

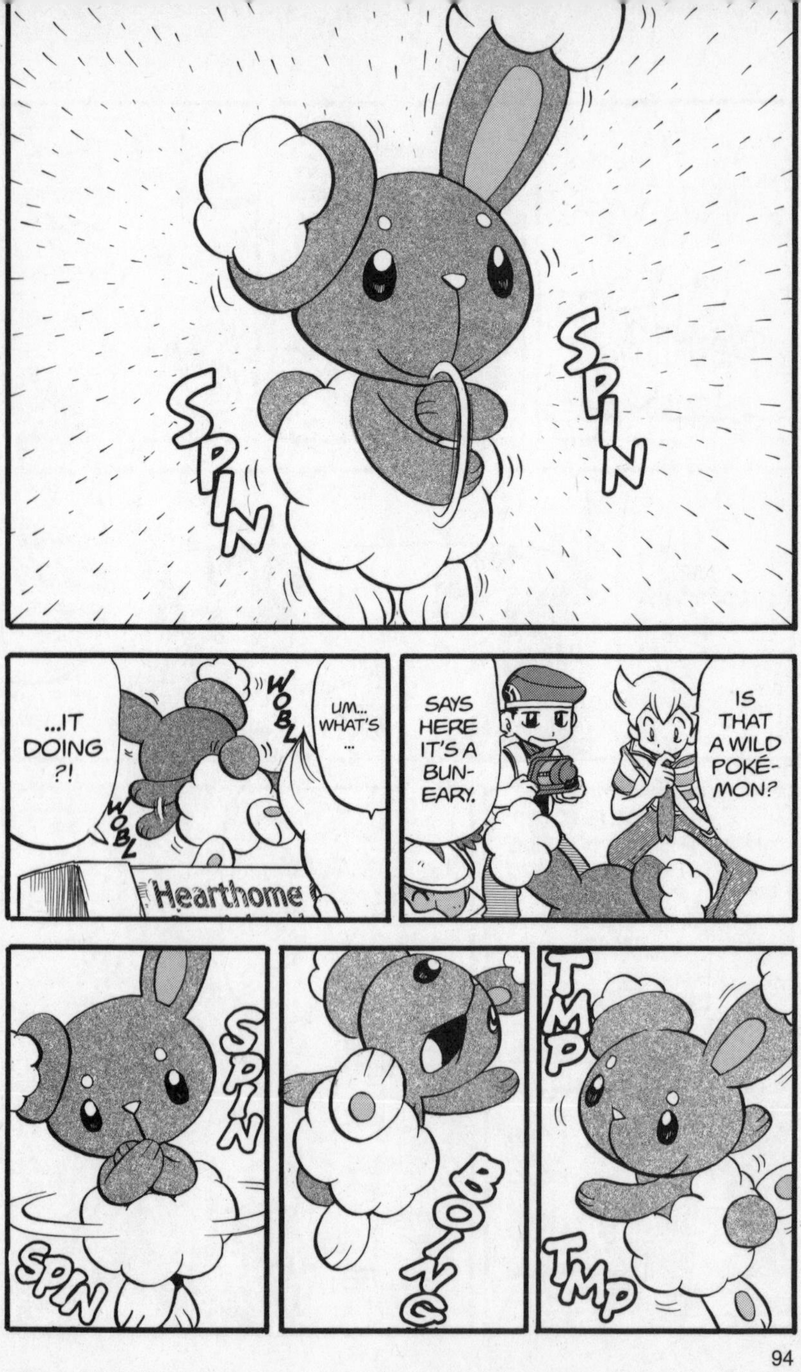
SPIN
SPIN
IS THAT A WILD POKÉMON?
SAYS HERE IT'S A BUNEARY.
UM... WHAT'S ...
WOBL
...IT DOING ?!
WOBL
Hearthome
TMP
TMP
BOING
SPIN
SPIN

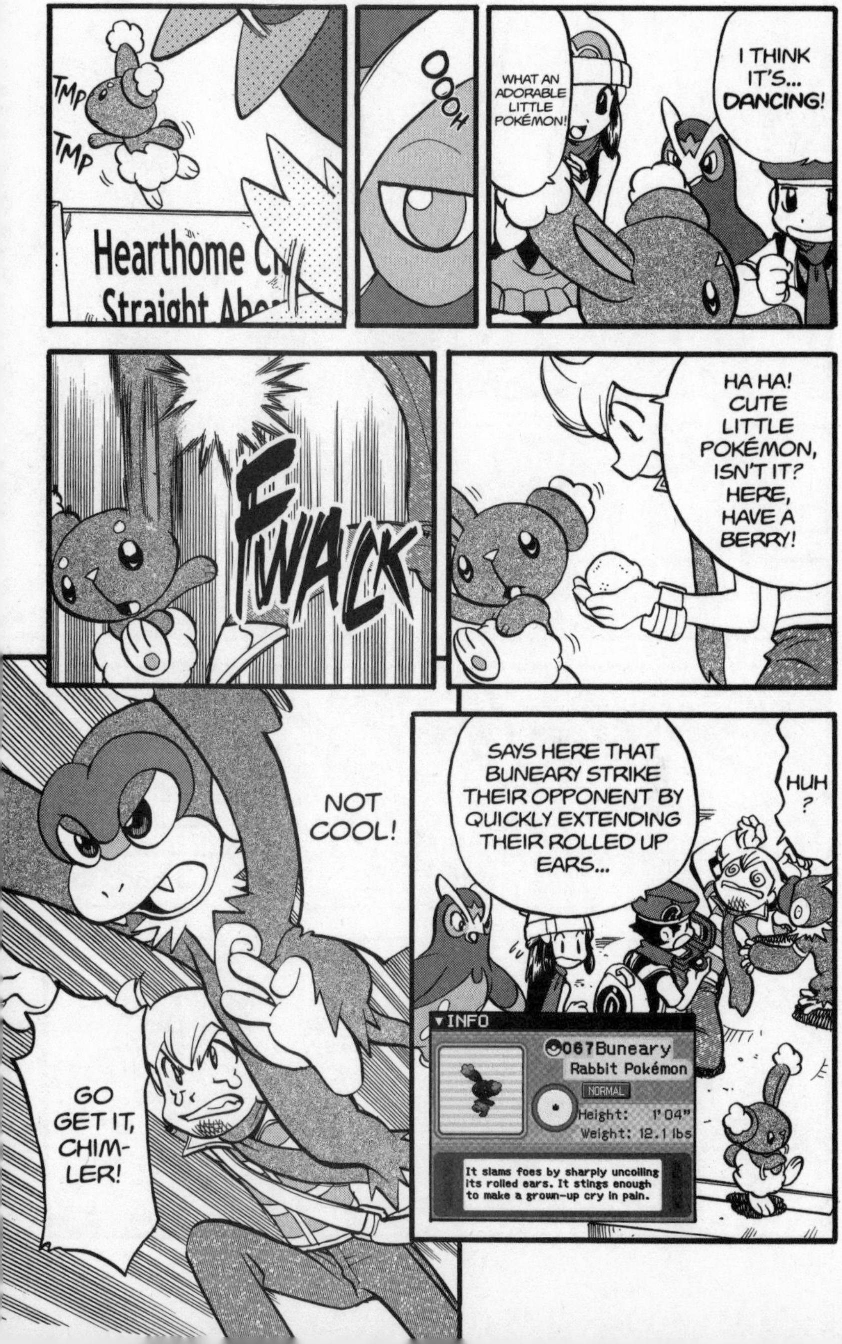

I THINK IT'S... DANCING!
WHAT AN ADORABLE LITTLE POKÉMON!
OOOH
TMP
TMP
Hearthome Ci
Straight Ahe
HA HA! CUTE LITTLE POKÉMON, ISN'T IT? HERE, HAVE A BERRY!
FWACK
HUH?
SAYS HERE THAT BUNEARY STRIKE THEIR OPPONENT BY QUICKLY EXTENDING THEIR ROLLED UP EARS...
▼INFO
067 Buneary
Rabbit Pokémon
NORMAL
Height: 1'04"
Weight: 12.1 lbs
It slams foes by sharply uncoiling its rolled ears. It stings enough to make a grown-up cry in pain.
NOT COOL!
GO GET IT, CHIMLER!

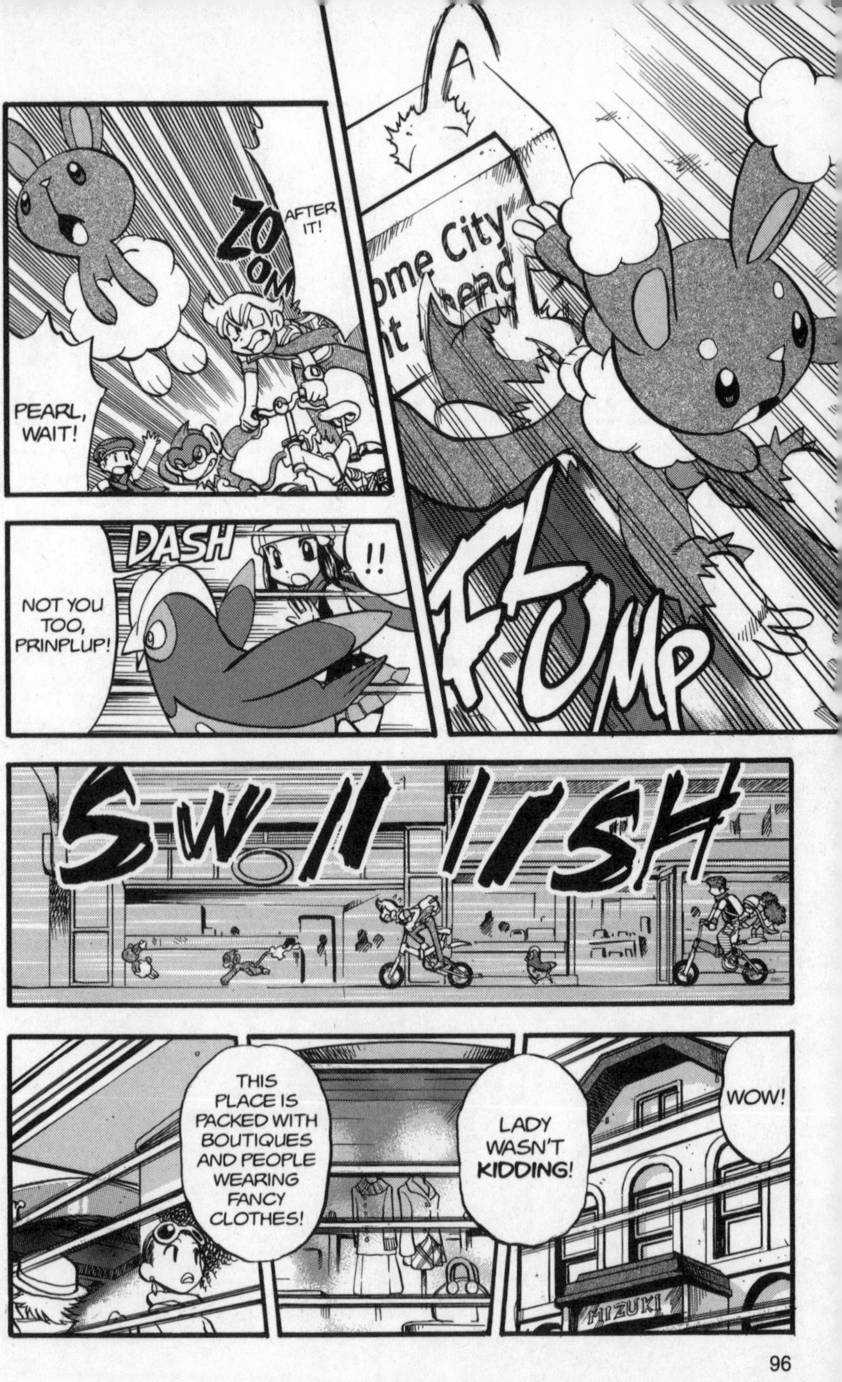
ome City
FUMP
ZOOM
AFTER IT!
PEARL, WAIT!
DASH
!!
NOT YOU TOO, PRINPLUP!
SWIISH
WOW!
MIZUKI
LADY WASN'T **KIDDING**!
THIS PLACE IS PACKED WITH BOUTIQUES AND PEOPLE WEARING FANCY CLOTHES!

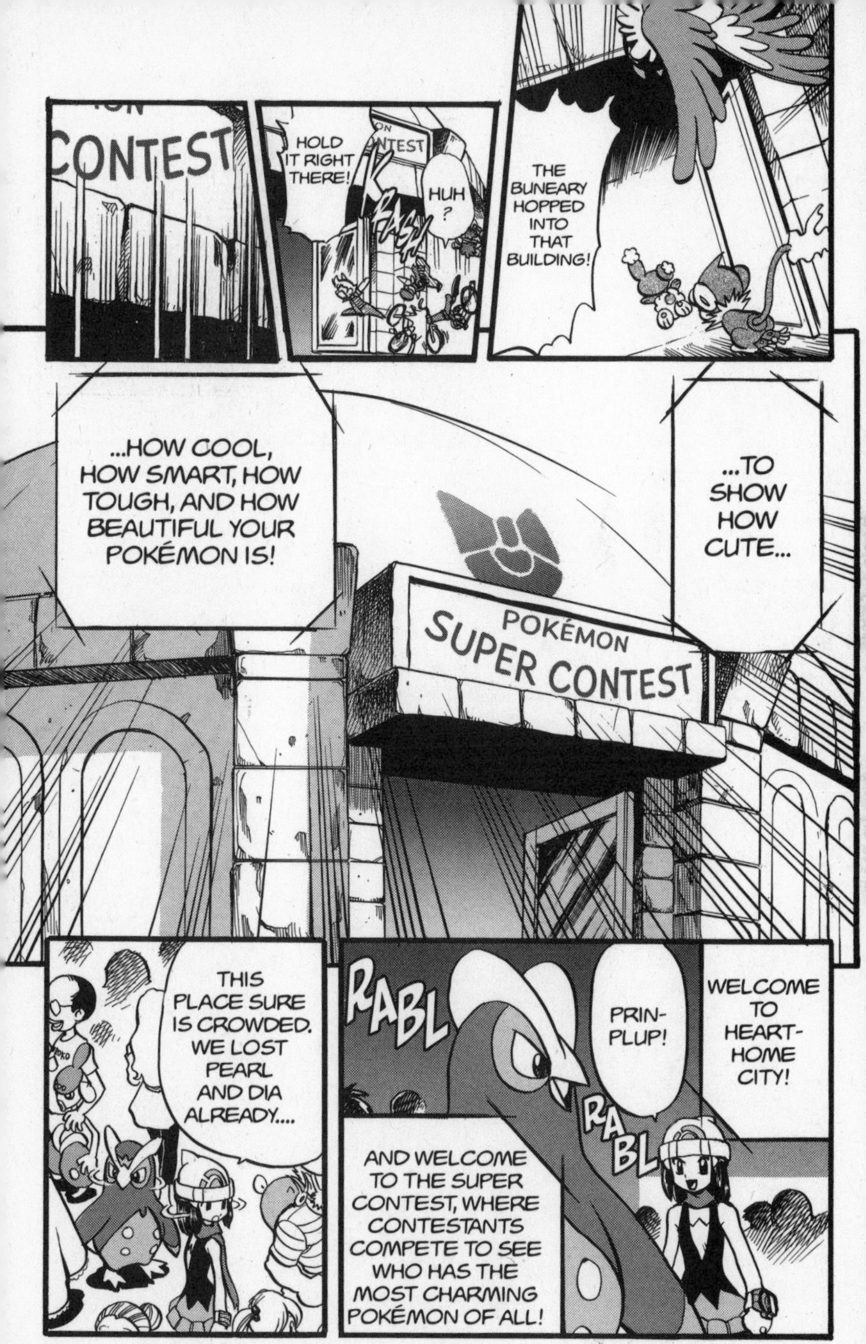
THE BUNEARY HOPPED INTO THAT BUILDING!
HOLD IT RIGHT THERE!
HUH ?
CONTEST
...TO SHOW HOW CUTE...
...HOW COOL, HOW SMART, HOW TOUGH, AND HOW BEAUTIFUL YOUR POKÉMON IS!
POKÉMON SUPER CONTEST
WELCOME TO HEART-HOME CITY!
PRIN-PLUP!
RABL
RABL
AND WELCOME TO THE SUPER CONTEST, WHERE CONTESTANTS COMPETE TO SEE WHO HAS THE MOST CHARMING POKÉMON OF ALL!
THIS PLACE SURE IS CROWDED. WE LOST PEARL AND DIA ALREADY....

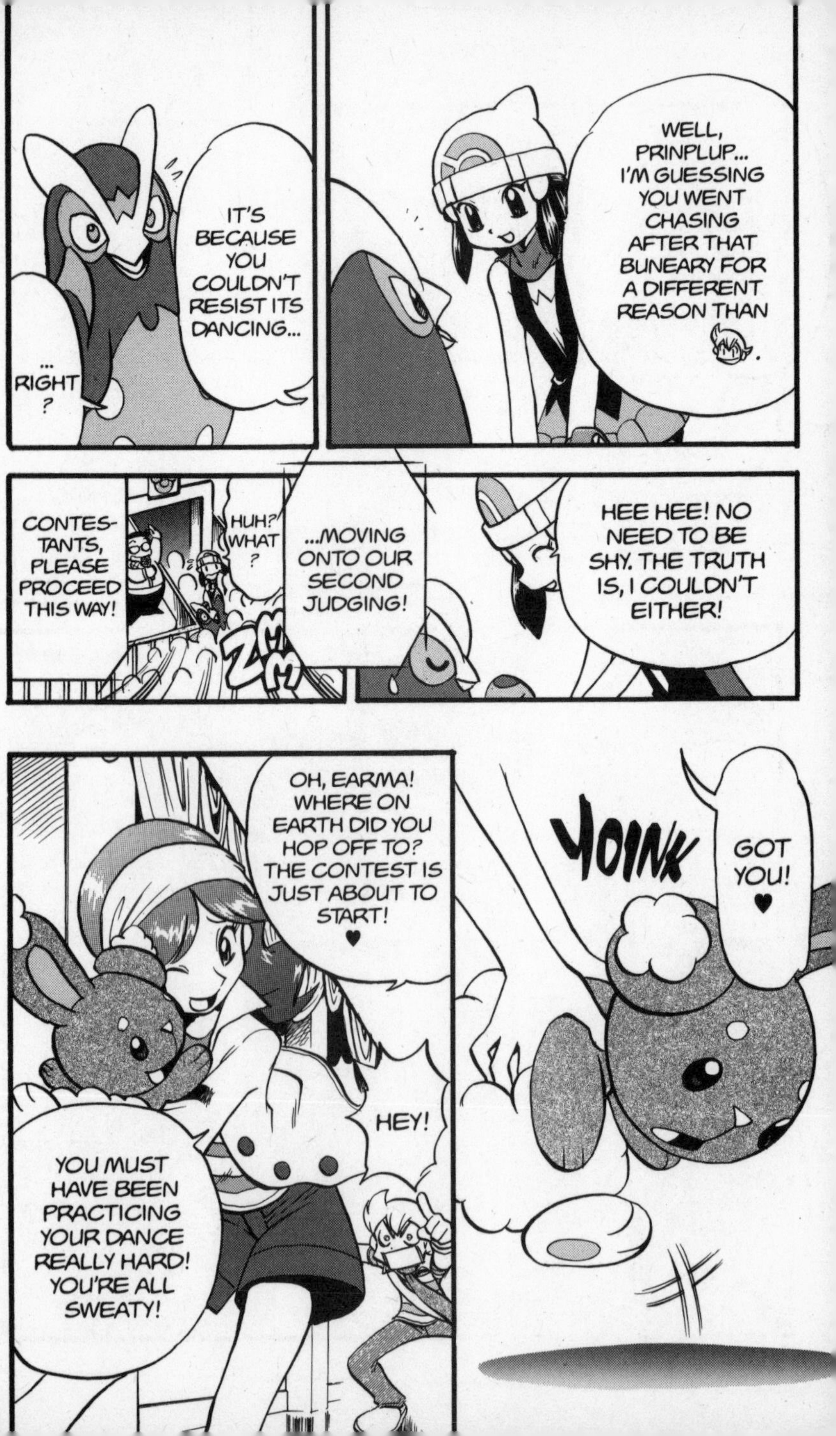
WELL, PRINPLUP... I'M GUESSING YOU WENT CHASING AFTER THAT BUNEARY FOR A DIFFERENT REASON THAN .
IT'S BECAUSE YOU COULDN'T RESIST ITS DANCING...
...RIGHT?
HEE HEE! NO NEED TO BE SHY. THE TRUTH IS, I COULDN'T EITHER!
...MOVING ONTO OUR SECOND JUDGING!
HUH? WHAT?
CONTES-TANTS, PLEASE PROCEED THIS WAY!
YOINK
GOT YOU! ♥
OH, EARMA! WHERE ON EARTH DID YOU HOP OFF TO? THE CONTEST IS JUST ABOUT TO START! ♥
HEY!
YOU MUST HAVE BEEN PRACTICING YOUR DANCE REALLY HARD! YOU'RE ALL SWEATY!

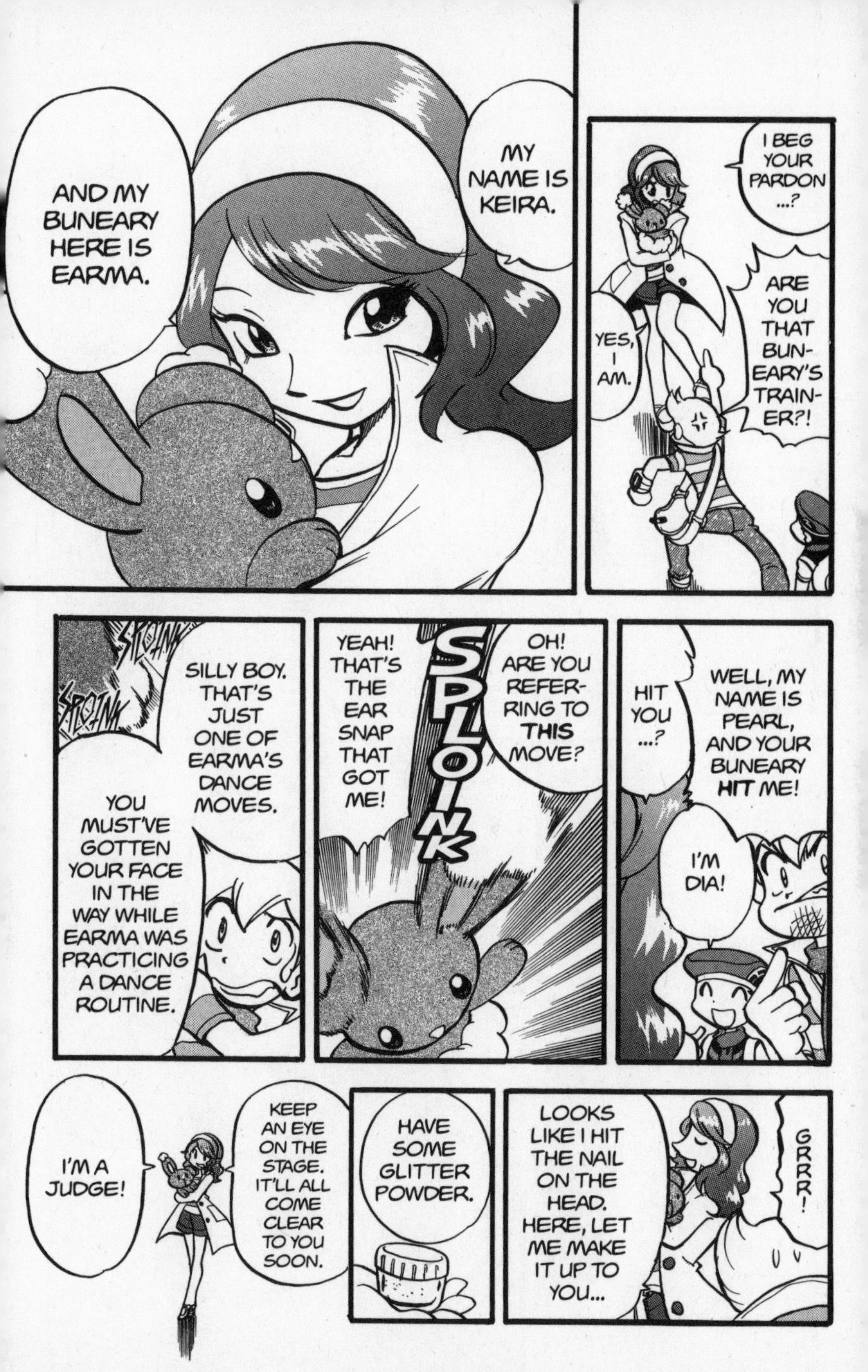
I BEG YOUR PARDON ...?
ARE YOU THAT BUNEARY'S TRAINER?!
YES, I AM.
MY NAME IS KEIRA.
AND MY BUNEARY HERE IS EARMA.
WELL, MY NAME IS PEARL, AND YOUR BUNEARY HIT ME!
HIT YOU ...?
I'M DIA!
OH! ARE YOU REFERRING TO THIS MOVE?
SPLOINK
YEAH! THAT'S THE EAR SNAP THAT GOT ME!
SILLY BOY. THAT'S JUST ONE OF EARMA'S DANCE MOVES.
YOU MUST'VE GOTTEN YOUR FACE IN THE WAY WHILE EARMA WAS PRACTICING A DANCE ROUTINE.
GRRR!
LOOKS LIKE I HIT THE NAIL ON THE HEAD. HERE, LET ME MAKE IT UP TO YOU...
HAVE SOME GLITTER POWDER.
KEEP AN EYE ON THE STAGE. IT'LL ALL COME CLEAR TO YOU SOON.
I'M A JUDGE!

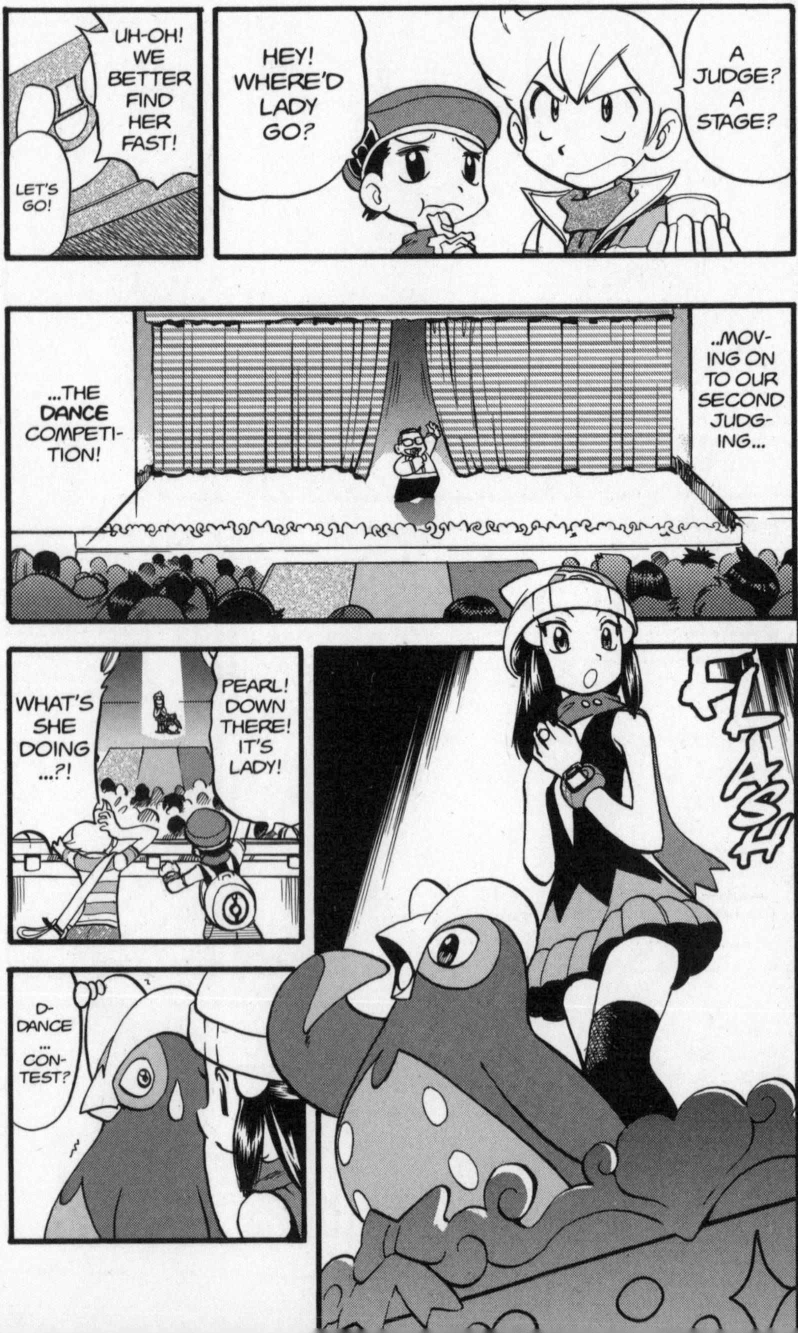
A JUDGE? A STAGE?
HEY! WHERE'D LADY GO?
UH-OH! WE BETTER FIND HER FAST!
LET'S GO!
..MOV-ING ON TO OUR SECOND JUDG-ING...
...THE DANCE COMPETI-TION!
FLASH
PEARL! DOWN THERE! IT'S LADY!
WHAT'S SHE DOING ...?!
D-DANCE ... CON-TEST?

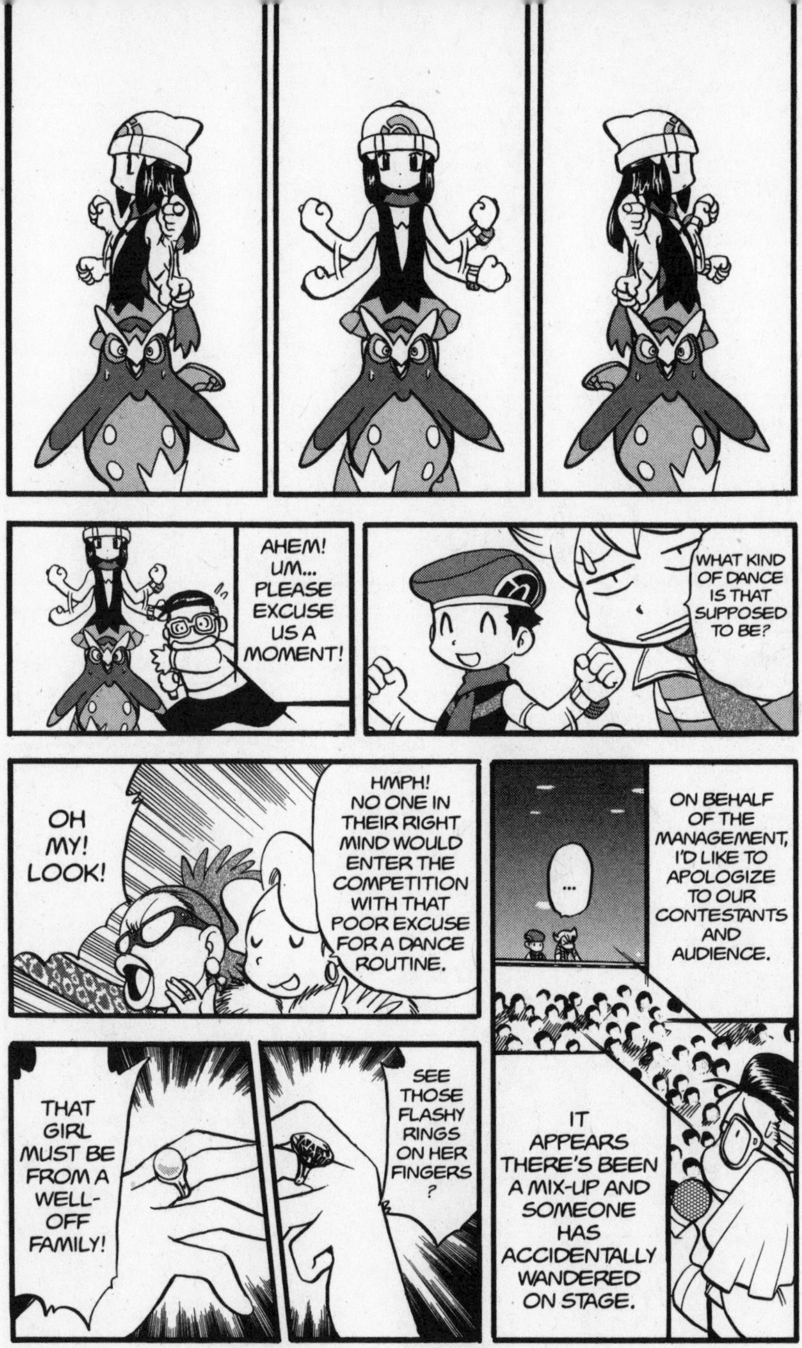
WHAT KIND OF DANCE IS THAT SUPPOSED TO BE?
AHEM! UM... PLEASE EXCUSE US A MOMENT!
...
ON BEHALF OF THE MANAGEMENT, I'D LIKE TO APOLOGIZE TO OUR CONTESTANTS AND AUDIENCE.
HMPH! NO ONE IN THEIR RIGHT MIND WOULD ENTER THE COMPETITION WITH THAT POOR EXCUSE FOR A DANCE ROUTINE.
OH MY! LOOK!
IT APPEARS THERE'S BEEN A MIX-UP AND SOMEONE HAS ACCIDENTALLY WANDERED ON STAGE.
SEE THOSE FLASHY RINGS ON HER FINGERS?
THAT GIRL MUST BE FROM A WELL-OFF FAMILY!

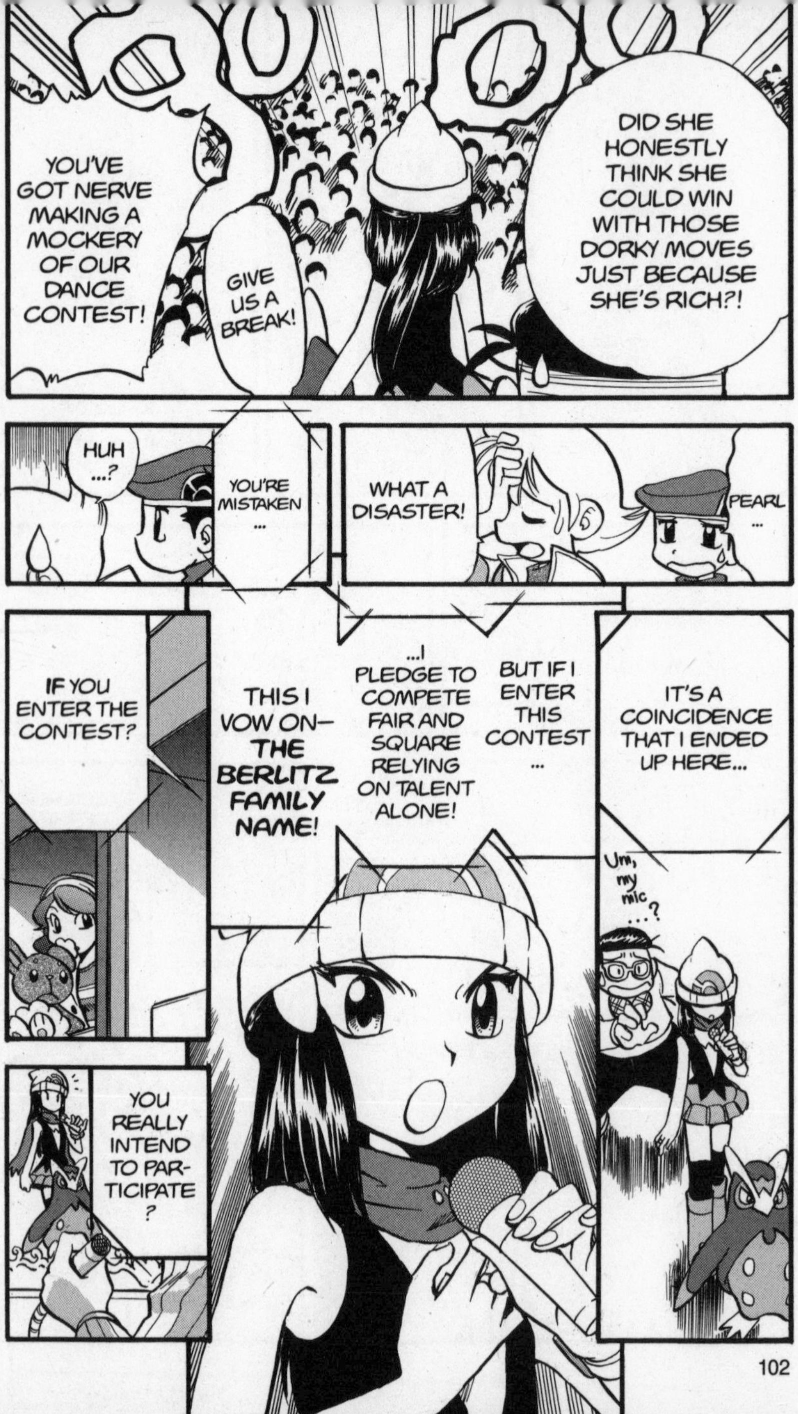

DID SHE HONESTLY THINK SHE COULD WIN WITH THOSE DORKY MOVES JUST BECAUSE SHE'S RICH?!
GIVE US A BREAK!
YOU'VE GOT NERVE MAKING A MOCKERY OF OUR DANCE CONTEST!
PEARL ...
WHAT A DISASTER!
YOU'RE MISTAKEN ...
HUH ...?
IT'S A COINCIDENCE THAT I ENDED UP HERE...
Um, my mic ...?
BUT IF I ENTER THIS CONTEST ...
...I PLEDGE TO COMPETE FAIR AND SQUARE RELYING ON TALENT ALONE!
THIS I VOW ON— THE BERLITZ FAMILY NAME!
IF YOU ENTER THE CONTEST?
YOU REALLY INTEND TO PARTICIPATE ?

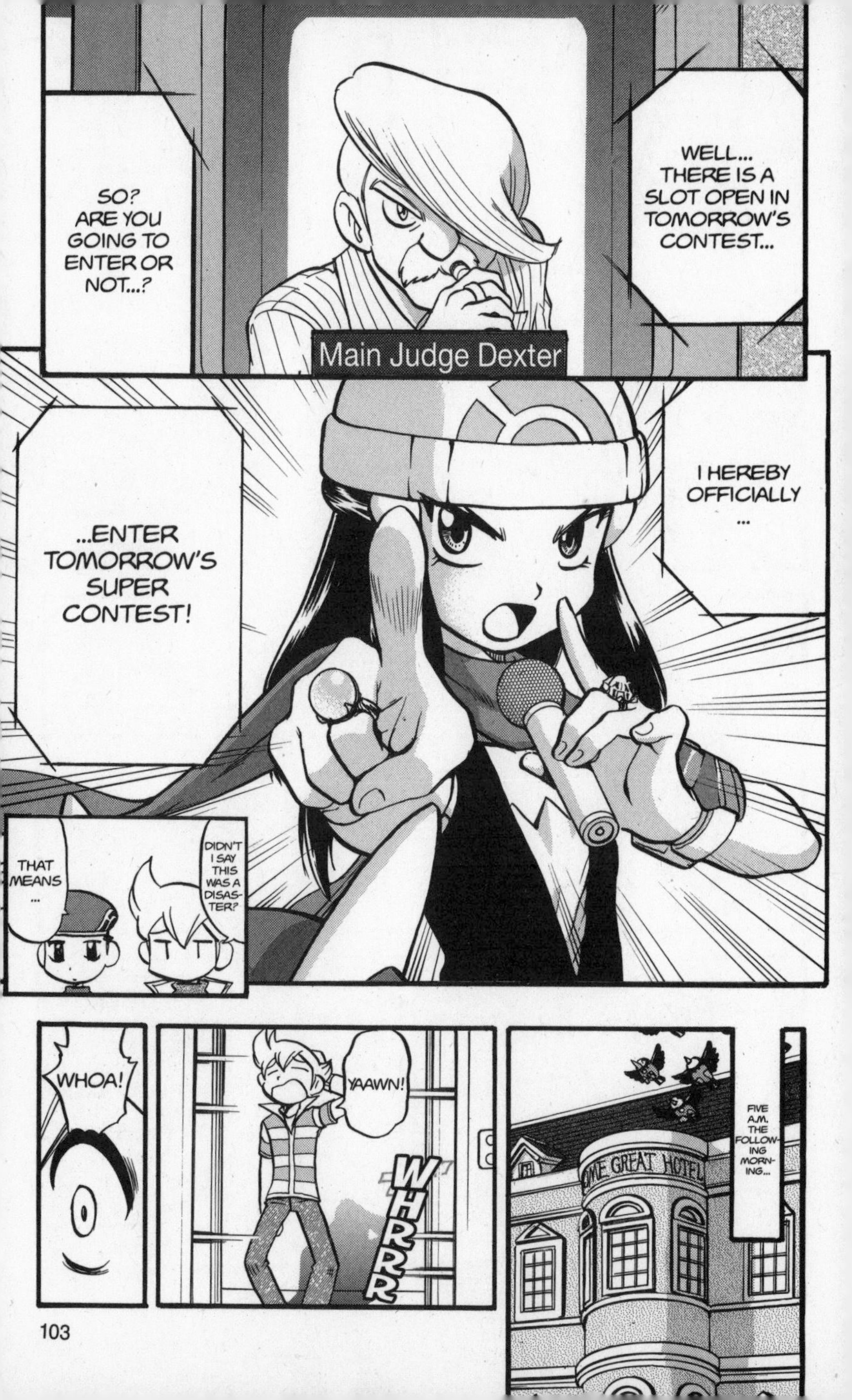
WELL... THERE IS A SLOT OPEN IN TOMORROW'S CONTEST...
SO? ARE YOU GOING TO ENTER OR NOT...?
Main Judge Dexter
I HEREBY OFFICIALLY ...
...ENTER TOMORROW'S SUPER CONTEST!
DIDN'T I SAY THIS WAS A DISAS-TER?
THAT MEANS ...
FIVE A.M. THE FOLLOW-ING MORN-ING...
YAAWN!
WHRRR
WHOA!

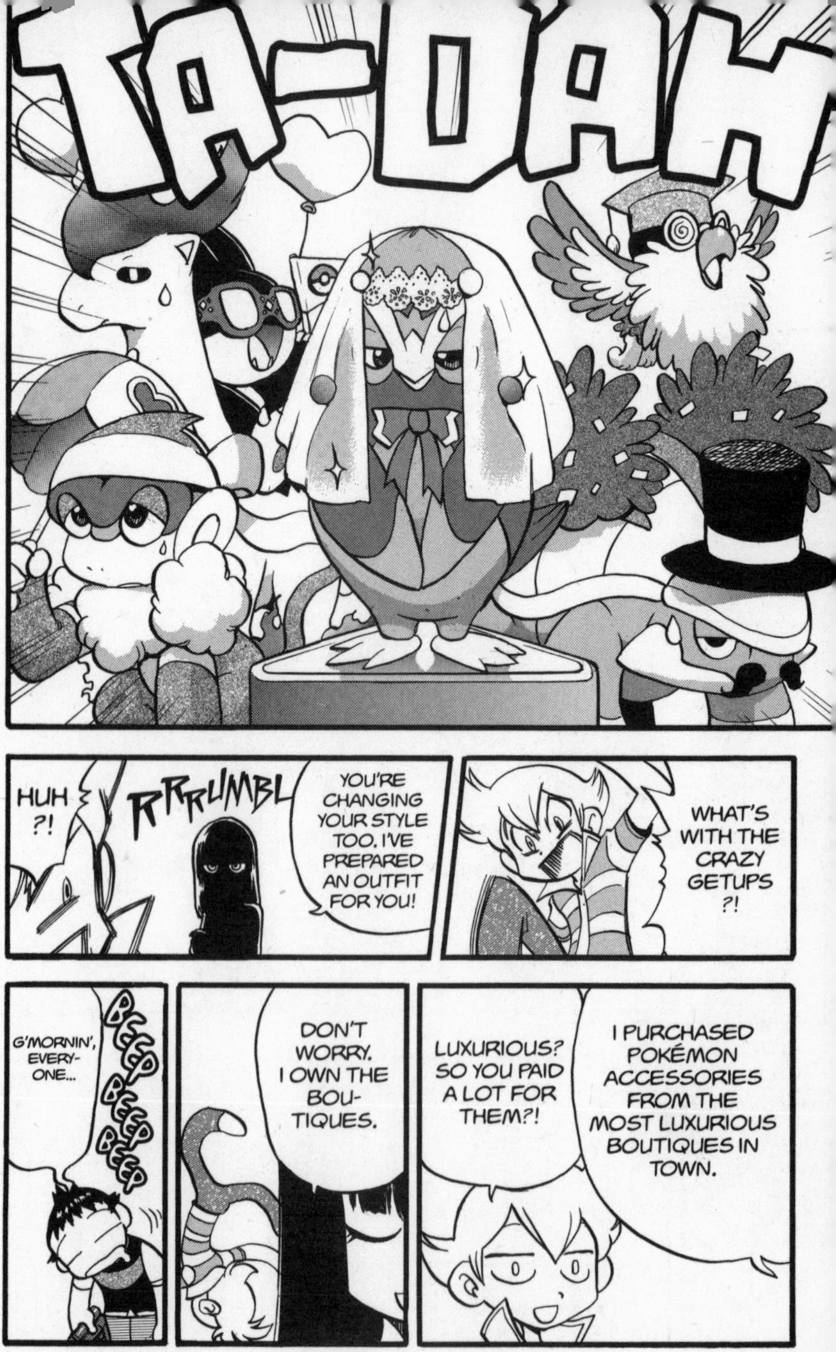
TA-DAH
WHAT'S WITH THE CRAZY GETUPS?!
YOU'RE CHANGING YOUR STYLE TOO. I'VE PREPARED AN OUTFIT FOR YOU!
RRRUMBL
HUH?!
I PURCHASED POKÉMON ACCESSORIES FROM THE MOST LUXURIOUS BOUTIQUES IN TOWN.
LUXURIOUS? SO YOU PAID A LOT FOR THEM?!
DON'T WORRY. I OWN THE BOU-TIQUES.
BEEP BEEP BEEP
G'MORNIN', EVERY-ONE...

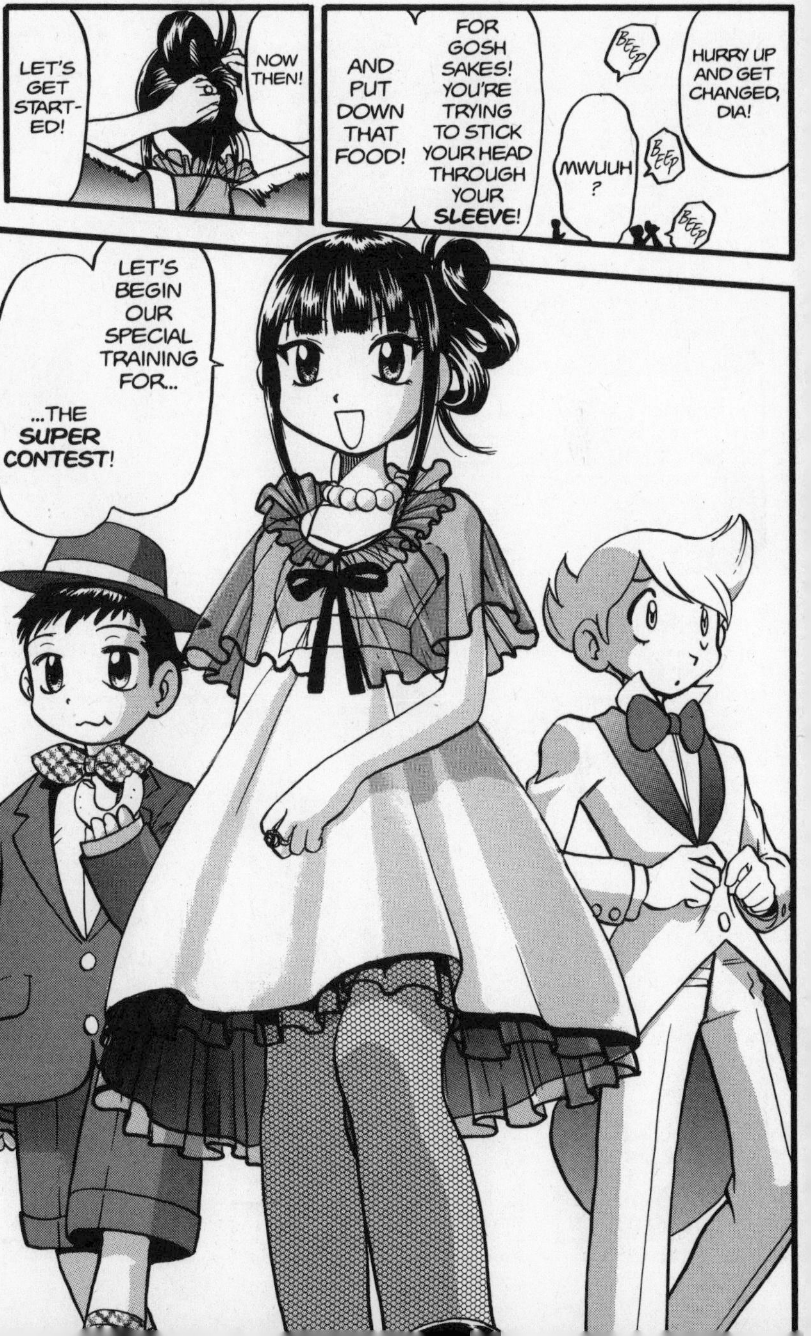
HURRY UP AND GET CHANGED, DIA!
BEEP
MWUUH?
BEEP
BEEP
FOR GOSH SAKES! YOU'RE TRYING TO STICK YOUR HEAD THROUGH YOUR **SLEEVE**!
AND PUT DOWN THAT FOOD!
NOW THEN!
LET'S GET START-ED!
LET'S BEGIN OUR SPECIAL TRAINING FOR...
...THE **SUPER CONTEST**!

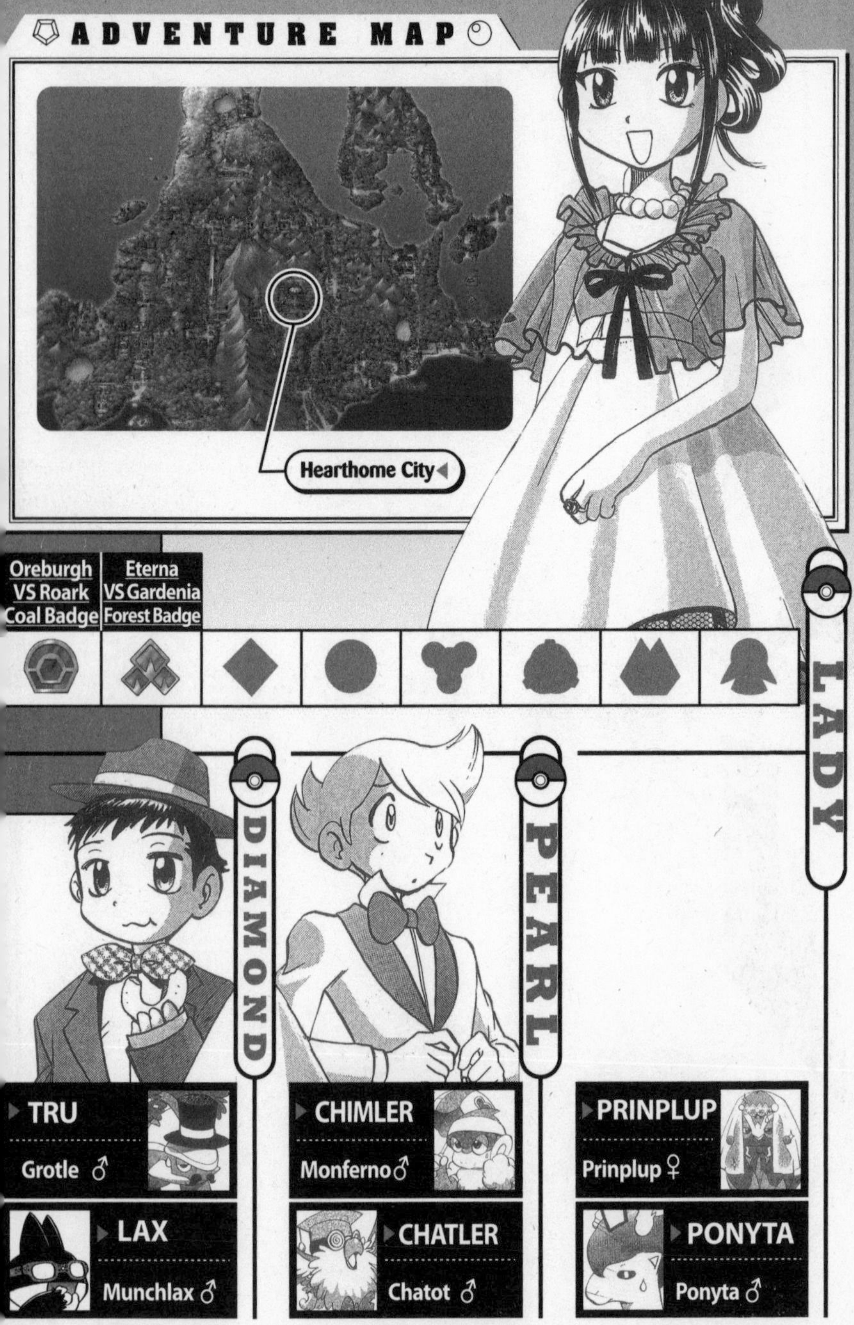
ADVENTURE MAP
Hearthome City
Oreburgh
VS Roark
Coal Badge
Eterna
VS Gardenia
Forest Badge
LADY
DIAMOND
PEARL
TRU
Grotle ♂
LAX
Munchlax ♂
CHIMLER
Monferno ♂
CHATLER
Chatot ♂
PRINPLUP
Prinplup ♀
PONYTA
Ponyta ♂

14

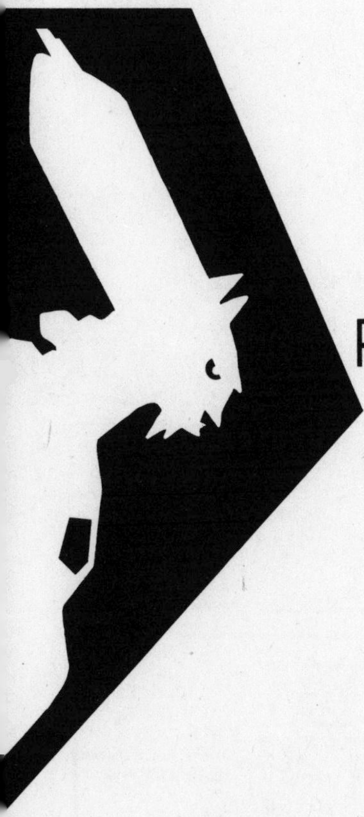

Perturbed by Pachirisu

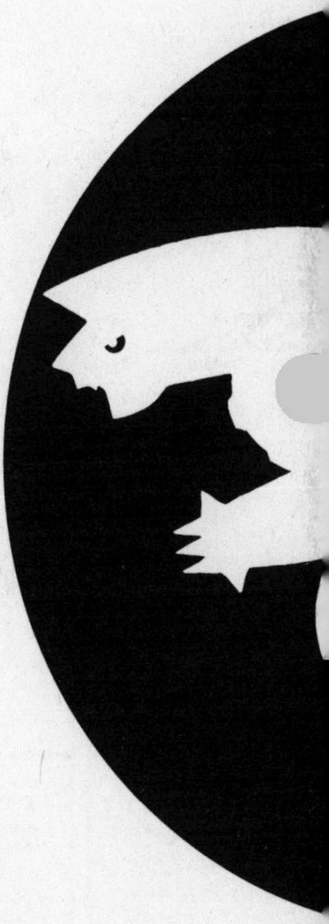

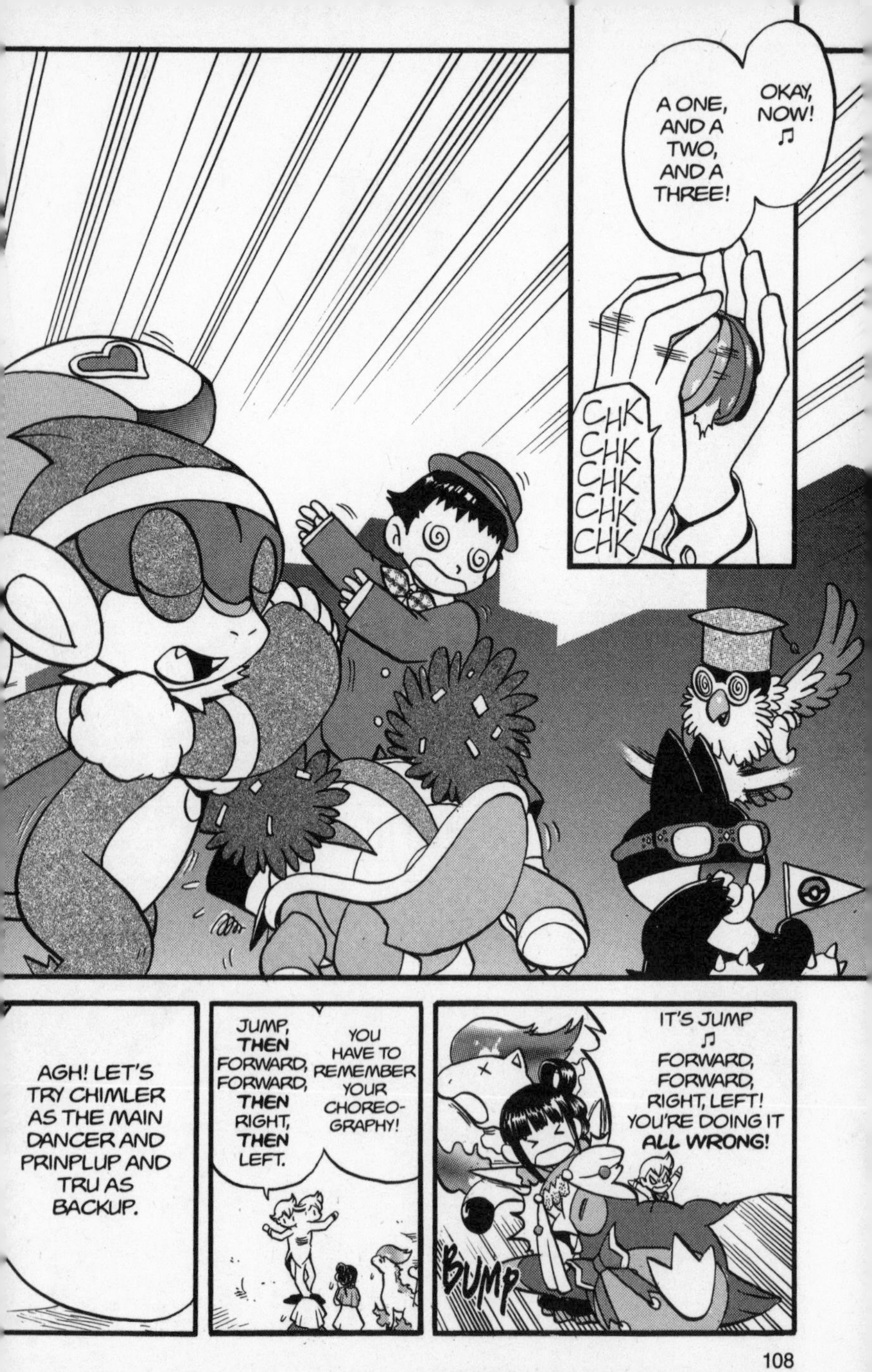
OKAY, NOW! ♫
A ONE, AND A TWO, AND A THREE!
CHK CHK CHK CHK CHK
IT'S JUMP ♫ FORWARD, FORWARD, RIGHT, LEFT! YOU'RE DOING IT **ALL WRONG**!
BUMP
YOU HAVE TO REMEMBER YOUR CHOREOGRAPHY!
JUMP, **THEN** FORWARD, FORWARD, **THEN** RIGHT, **THEN** LEFT.
AGH! LET'S TRY CHIMLER AS THE MAIN DANCER AND PRINPLUP AND TRU AS BACKUP.

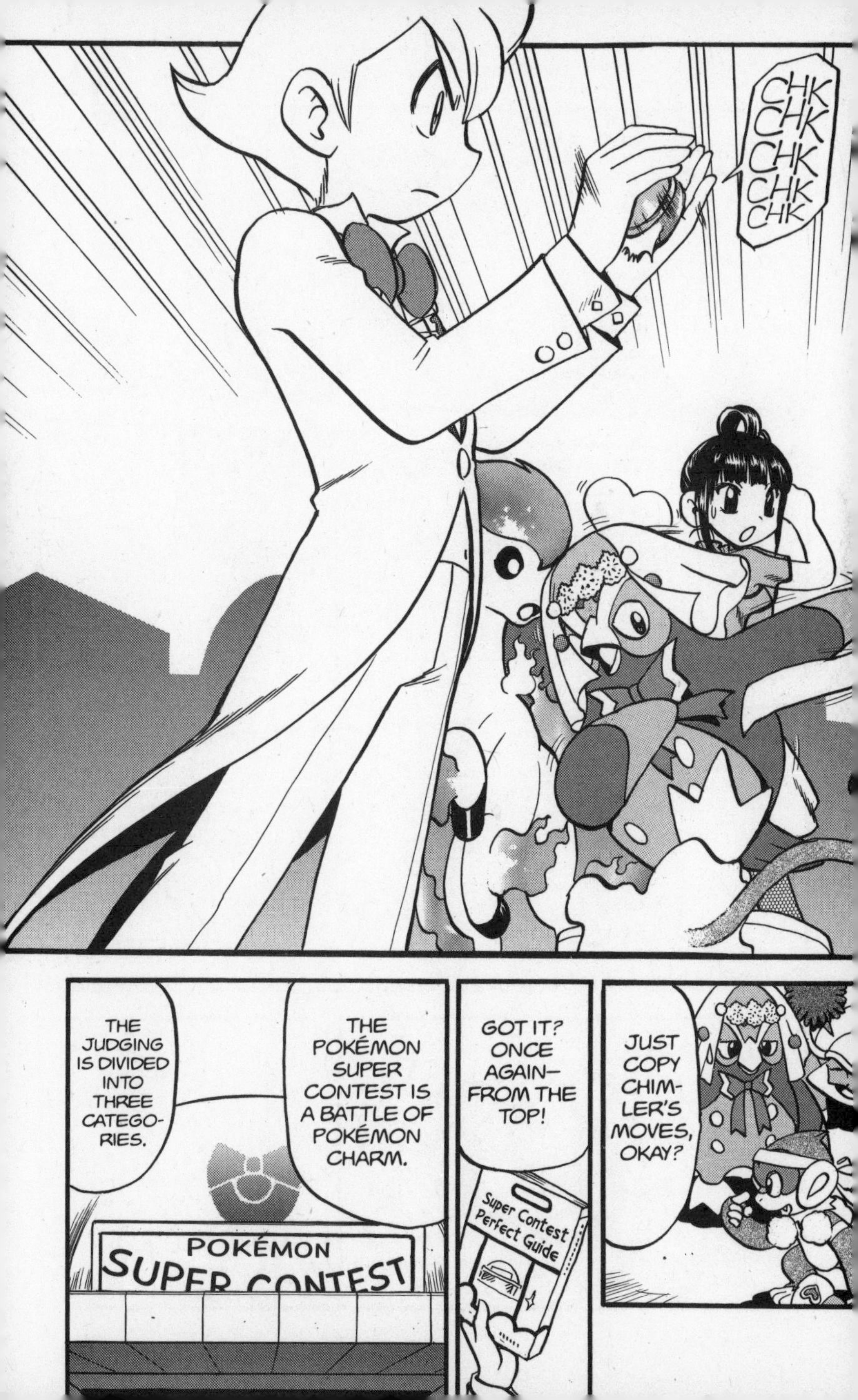
CHK CHK CHK CHK CHK
JUST COPY CHIMLER'S MOVES, OKAY?
GOT IT? ONCE AGAIN— FROM THE TOP!
Super Contest Perfect Guide
THE POKÉMON SUPER CONTEST IS A BATTLE OF POKÉMON CHARM.
THE JUDGING IS DIVIDED INTO THREE CATEGORIES.
POKÉMON SUPER CONTEST

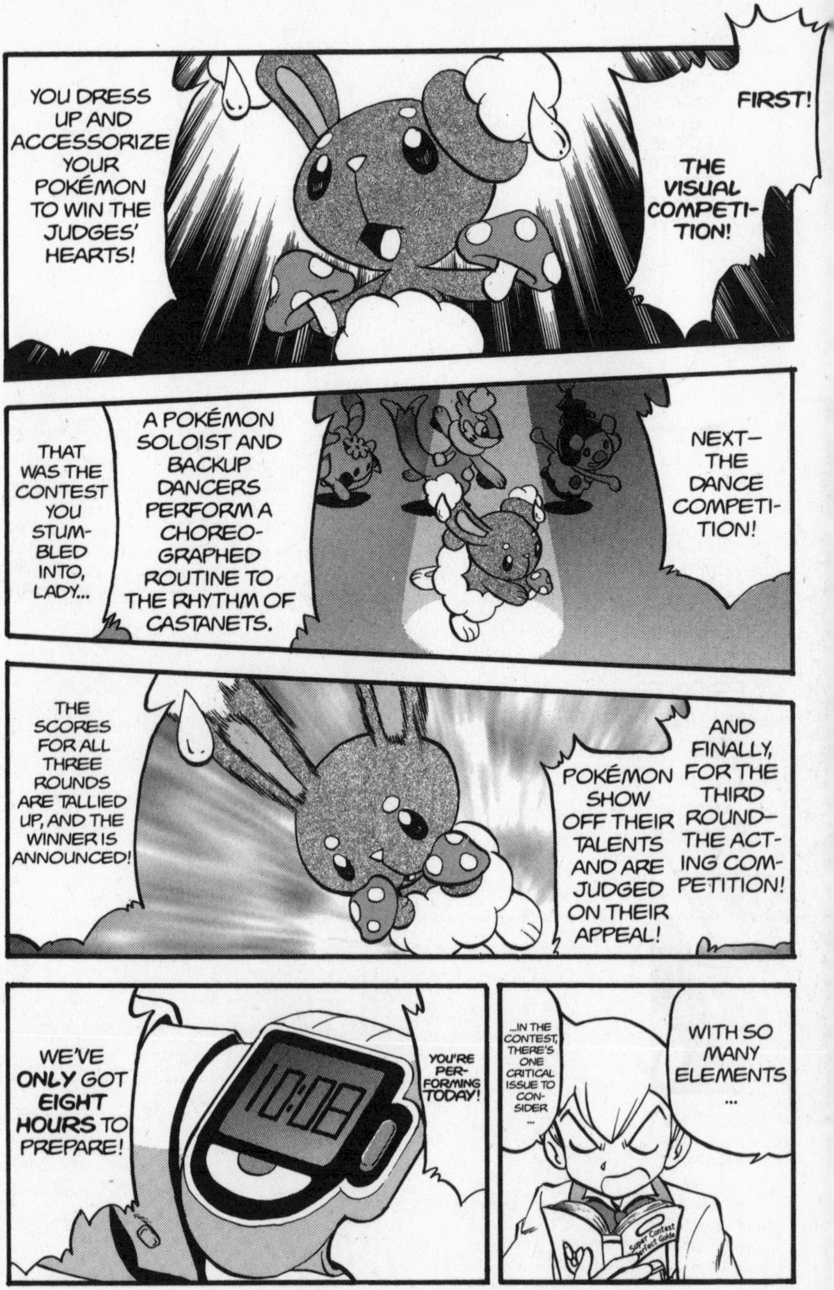

FIRST!
THE VISUAL COMPETITION!
YOU DRESS UP AND ACCESSORIZE YOUR POKÉMON TO WIN THE JUDGES' HEARTS!
NEXT—THE DANCE COMPETITION!
A POKÉMON SOLOIST AND BACKUP DANCERS PERFORM A CHOREOGRAPHED ROUTINE TO THE RHYTHM OF CASTANETS.
THAT WAS THE CONTEST YOU STUMBLED INTO, LADY...
AND FINALLY, FOR THE THIRD ROUND—THE ACTING COMPETITION!
POKÉMON SHOW OFF THEIR TALENTS AND ARE JUDGED ON THEIR APPEAL!
THE SCORES FOR ALL THREE ROUNDS ARE TALLIED UP, AND THE WINNER IS ANNOUNCED!
WITH SO MANY ELEMENTS...
...IN THE CONTEST, THERE'S ONE CRITICAL ISSUE TO CONSIDER...
Super Contest Perfect Guide
YOU'RE PERFORMING TODAY!
WE'VE ONLY GOT EIGHT HOURS TO PREPARE!
10:08

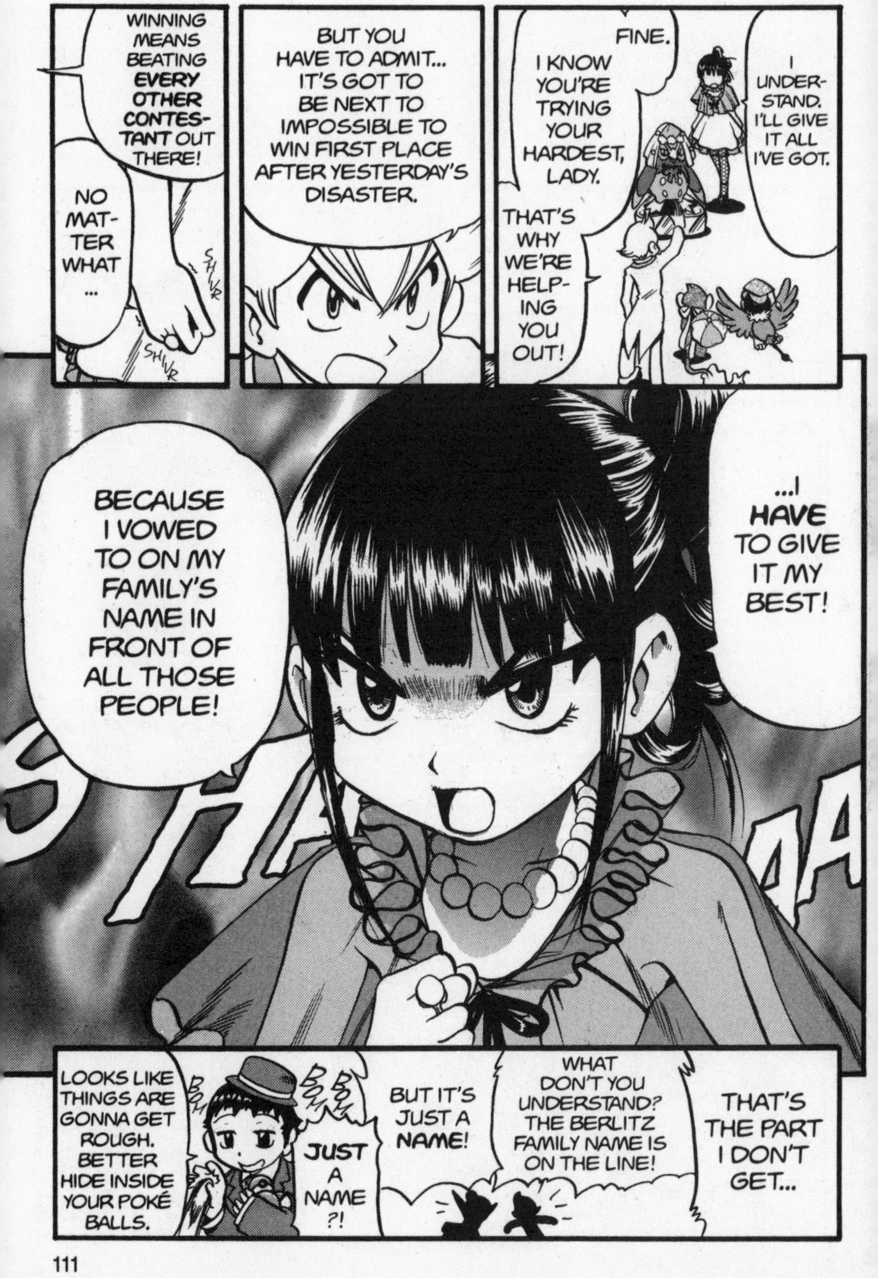
I UNDERSTAND. I'LL GIVE IT ALL I'VE GOT.
FINE. I KNOW YOU'RE TRYING YOUR HARDEST, LADY.
THAT'S WHY WE'RE HELPING YOU OUT!
BUT YOU HAVE TO ADMIT... IT'S GOT TO BE NEXT TO IMPOSSIBLE TO WIN FIRST PLACE AFTER YESTERDAY'S DISASTER.
WINNING MEANS BEATING **EVERY OTHER CONTESTANT** OUT THERE!
NO MATTER WHAT...
SHIVR
SHIVR
...I **HAVE** TO GIVE IT MY BEST!
BECAUSE I VOWED TO ON MY FAMILY'S NAME IN FRONT OF ALL THOSE PEOPLE!
THAT'S THE PART I DON'T GET...
WHAT DON'T YOU UNDERSTAND? THE BERLITZ FAMILY NAME IS ON THE LINE!
BUT IT'S JUST A **NAME**!
JUST A NAME?!
BOOM BOOM
LOOKS LIKE THINGS ARE GONNA GET ROUGH. BETTER HIDE INSIDE YOUR POKÉ BALLS.

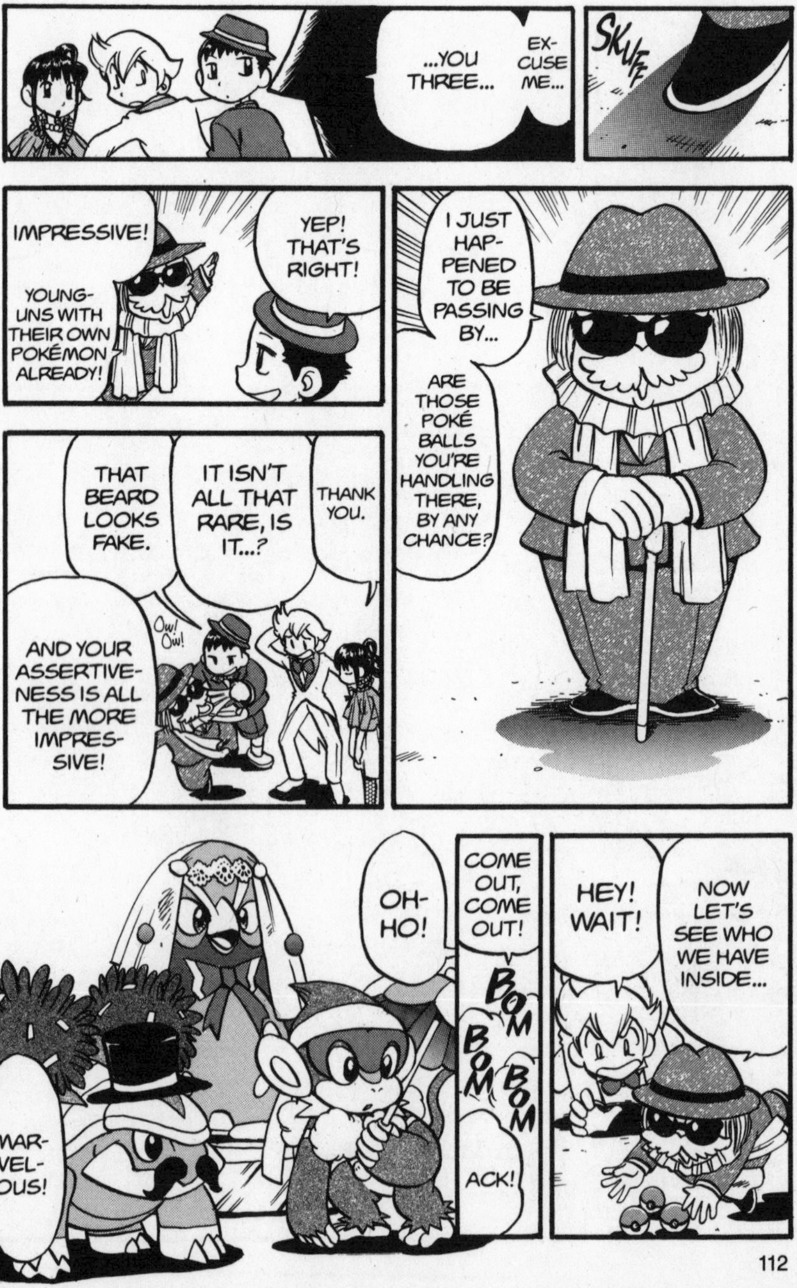
SKUFF
EXCUSE ME...
...YOU THREE...
I JUST HAPPENED TO BE PASSING BY...
ARE THOSE POKÉ BALLS YOU'RE HANDLING THERE, BY ANY CHANCE?
YEP! THAT'S RIGHT!
IMPRESSIVE!
YOUNGUNS WITH THEIR OWN POKÉMON ALREADY!
THANK YOU.
IT ISN'T ALL THAT RARE, IS IT...?
THAT BEARD LOOKS FAKE.
Ow! Ow!
AND YOUR ASSERTIVENESS IS ALL THE MORE IMPRESSIVE!
NOW LET'S SEE WHO WE HAVE INSIDE...
HEY! WAIT!
COME OUT, COME OUT!
BOM
BOM
BOM
ACK!
OH-HO!
MARVELOUS!

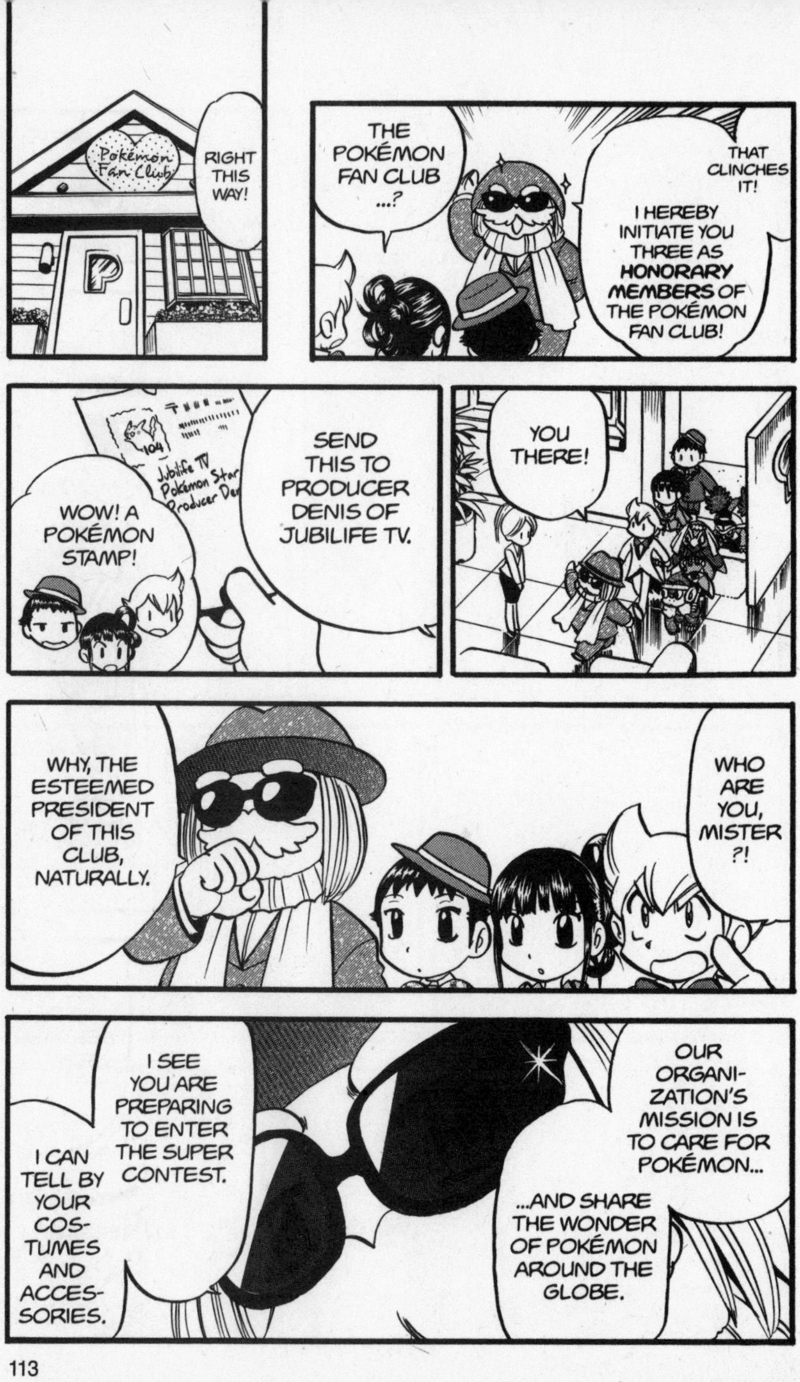
THAT CLINCHES IT!
I HEREBY INITIATE YOU THREE AS **HONORARY MEMBERS** OF THE POKÉMON FAN CLUB!
THE POKÉMON FAN CLUB ...?
Pokémon Fan Club
RIGHT THIS WAY!
YOU THERE!
SEND THIS TO PRODUCER DENIS OF JUBILIFE TV.
Jubilife TV Pokémon Star Producer Den
WOW! A POKÉMON STAMP!
WHO ARE YOU, MISTER ?!
WHY, THE ESTEEMED PRESIDENT OF THIS CLUB, NATURALLY.
OUR ORGANI-ZATION'S MISSION IS TO CARE FOR POKÉMON...
...AND SHARE THE WONDER OF POKÉMON AROUND THE GLOBE.
I SEE YOU ARE PREPARING TO ENTER THE SUPER CONTEST.
I CAN TELL BY YOUR COS-TUMES AND ACCES-SORIES.

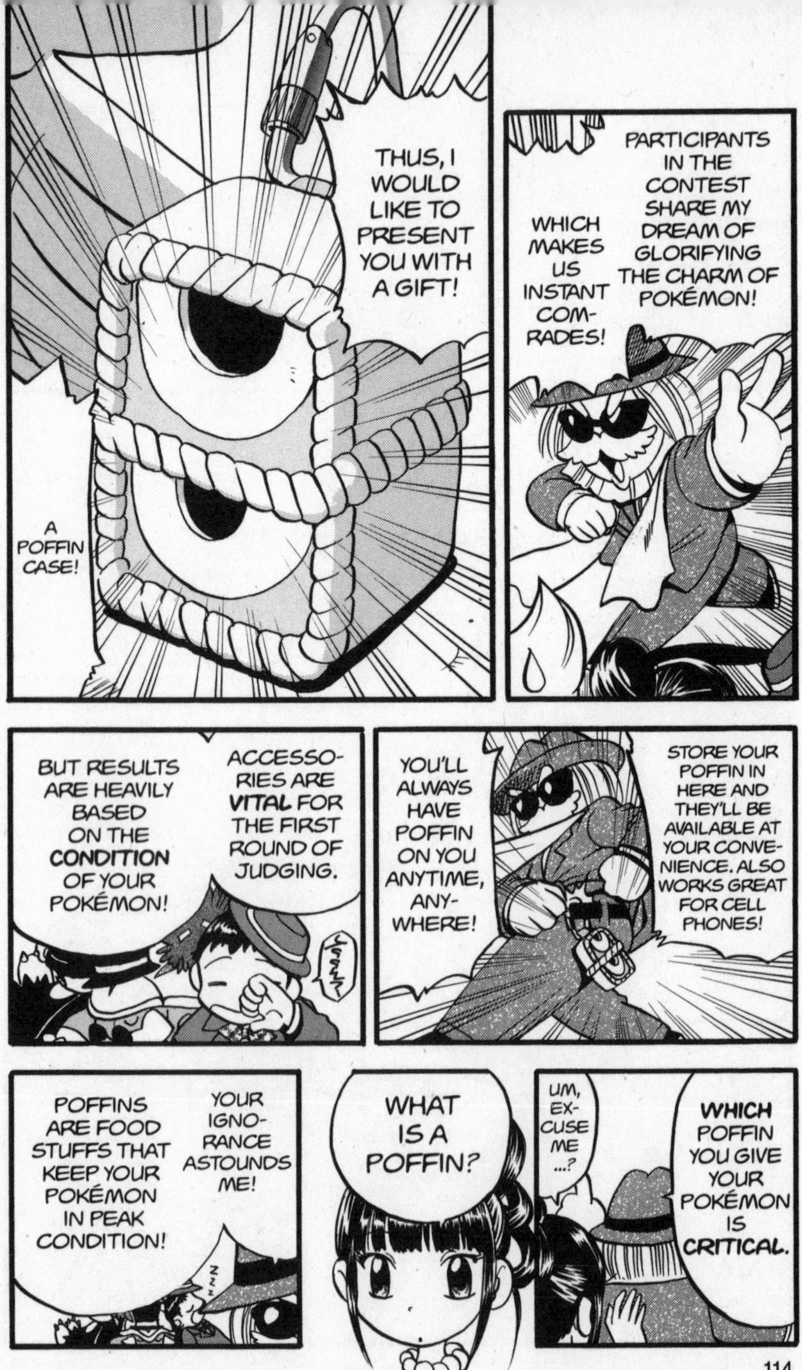
PARTICIPANTS IN THE CONTEST SHARE MY DREAM OF GLORIFYING THE CHARM OF POKéMON!
WHICH MAKES US INSTANT COM-RADES!
THUS, I WOULD LIKE TO PRESENT YOU WITH A GIFT!
A POFFIN CASE!
STORE YOUR POFFIN IN HERE AND THEY'LL BE AVAILABLE AT YOUR CONVE-NIENCE. ALSO WORKS GREAT FOR CELL PHONES!
YOU'LL ALWAYS HAVE POFFIN ON YOU ANYTIME, ANY-WHERE!
ACCESSO-RIES ARE **VITAL** FOR THE FIRST ROUND OF JUDGING.
BUT RESULTS ARE HEAVILY BASED ON THE **CONDITION** OF YOUR POKéMON!
WHICH POFFIN YOU GIVE YOUR POKéMON IS **CRITICAL.**
UM, EX-CUSE ME ...?
WHAT IS A POFFIN?
YOUR IGNO-RANCE ASTOUNDS ME!
POFFINS ARE FOOD STUFFS THAT KEEP YOUR POKéMON IN PEAK CONDITION!
ZZZ

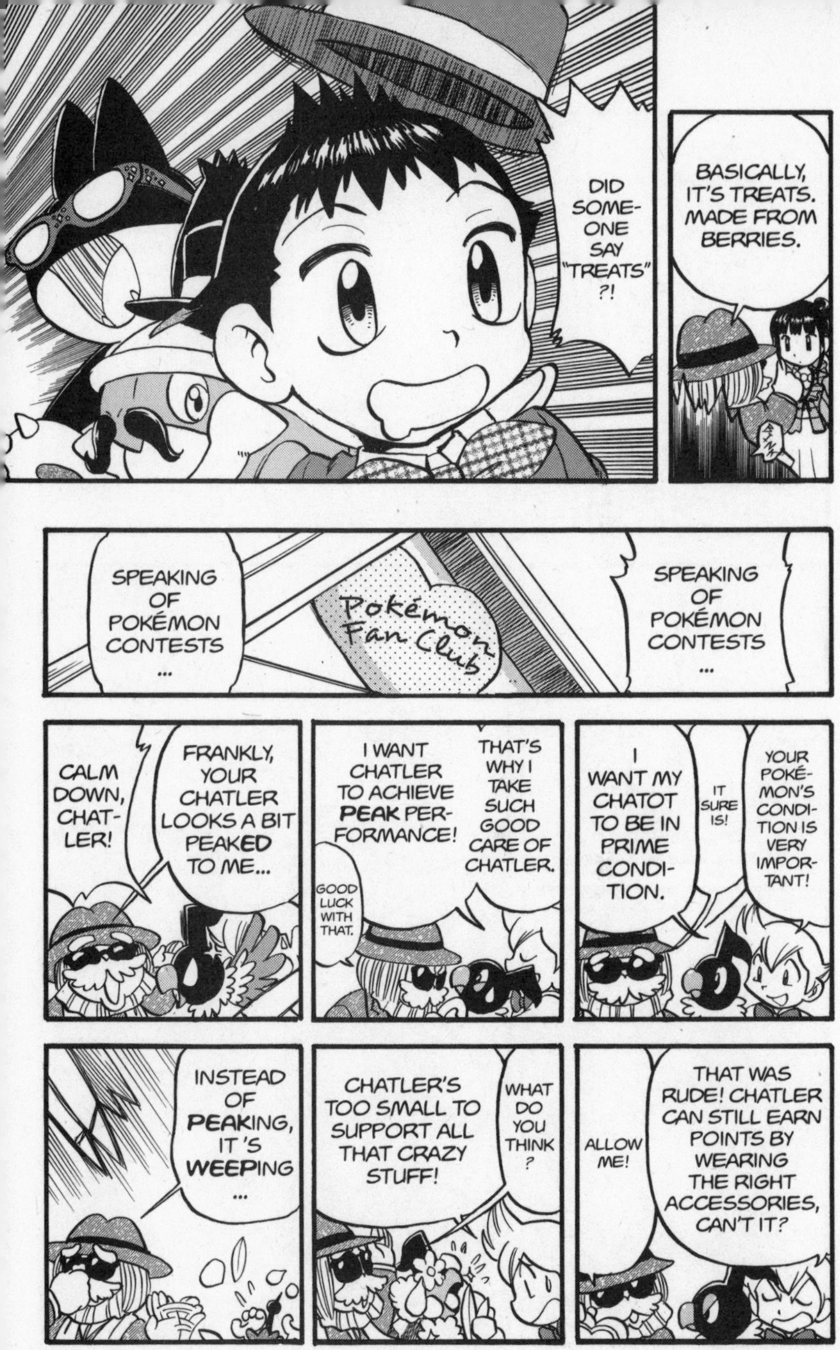
BASICALLY, IT'S TREATS. MADE FROM BERRIES.
DID SOMEONE SAY "TREATS"?!
SPEAKING OF POKÉMON CONTESTS ...
Pokémon Fan Club
SPEAKING OF POKÉMON CONTESTS ...
YOUR POKÉMON'S CONDITION IS VERY IMPORTANT!
IT SURE IS!
I WANT MY CHATOT TO BE IN PRIME CONDITION.
THAT'S WHY I TAKE SUCH GOOD CARE OF CHATLER.
I WANT CHATLER TO ACHIEVE PEAK PERFORMANCE!
GOOD LUCK WITH THAT.
FRANKLY, YOUR CHATLER LOOKS A BIT PEAKED TO ME...
CALM DOWN, CHATLER!
THAT WAS RUDE! CHATLER CAN STILL EARN POINTS BY WEARING THE RIGHT ACCESSORIES, CAN'T IT?
ALLOW ME!
WHAT DO YOU THINK?
CHATLER'S TOO SMALL TO SUPPORT ALL THAT CRAZY STUFF!
INSTEAD OF PEAKING, IT'S WEEPING ...

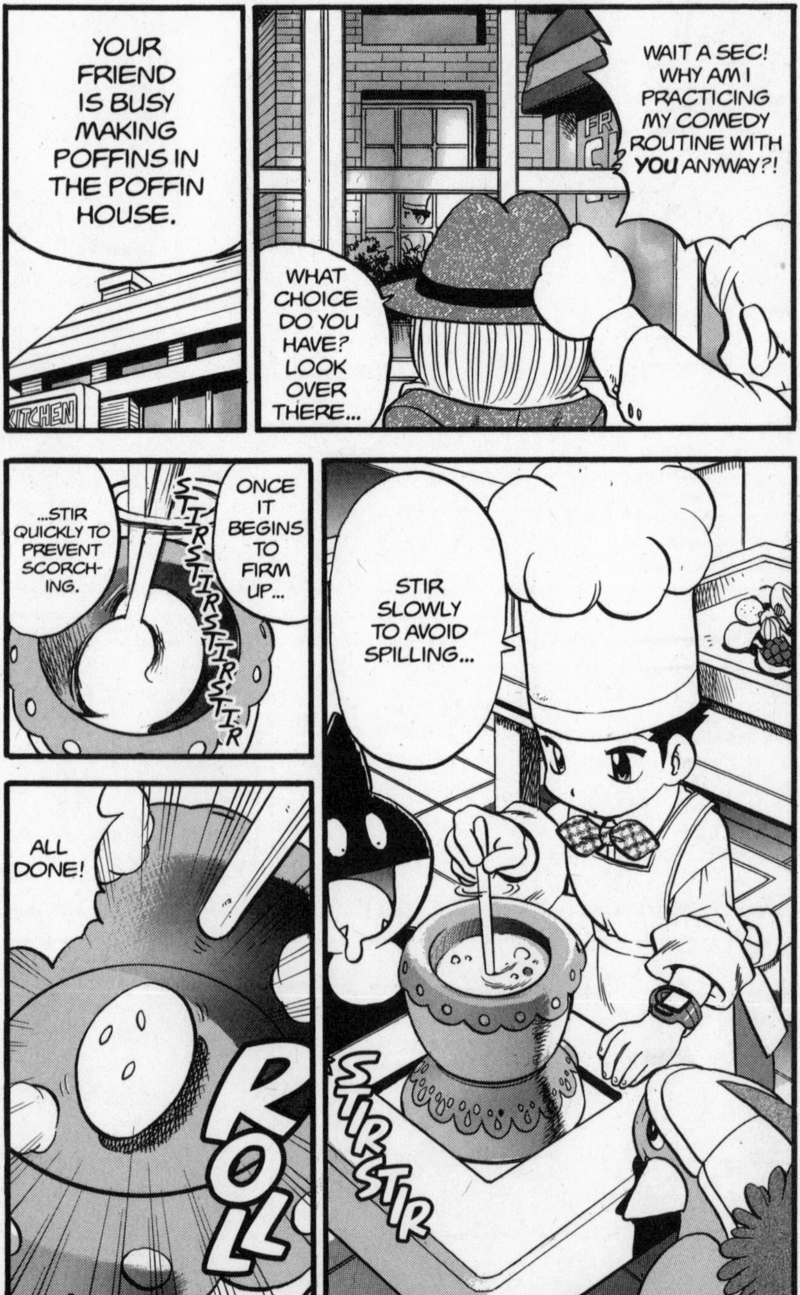
WAIT A SEC! WHY AM I PRACTICING MY COMEDY ROUTINE WITH **YOU** ANYWAY?!
WHAT CHOICE DO YOU HAVE? LOOK OVER THERE...
YOUR FRIEND IS BUSY MAKING POFFINS IN THE POFFIN HOUSE.
KITCHEN
STIR SLOWLY TO AVOID SPILLING...
STIRSTIR
ONCE IT BEGINS TO FIRM UP...
...STIR QUICKLY TO PREVENT SCORCH-ING.
STIRSTIRSTIRSTIRSTIRSTIR
ALL DONE!
ROLL

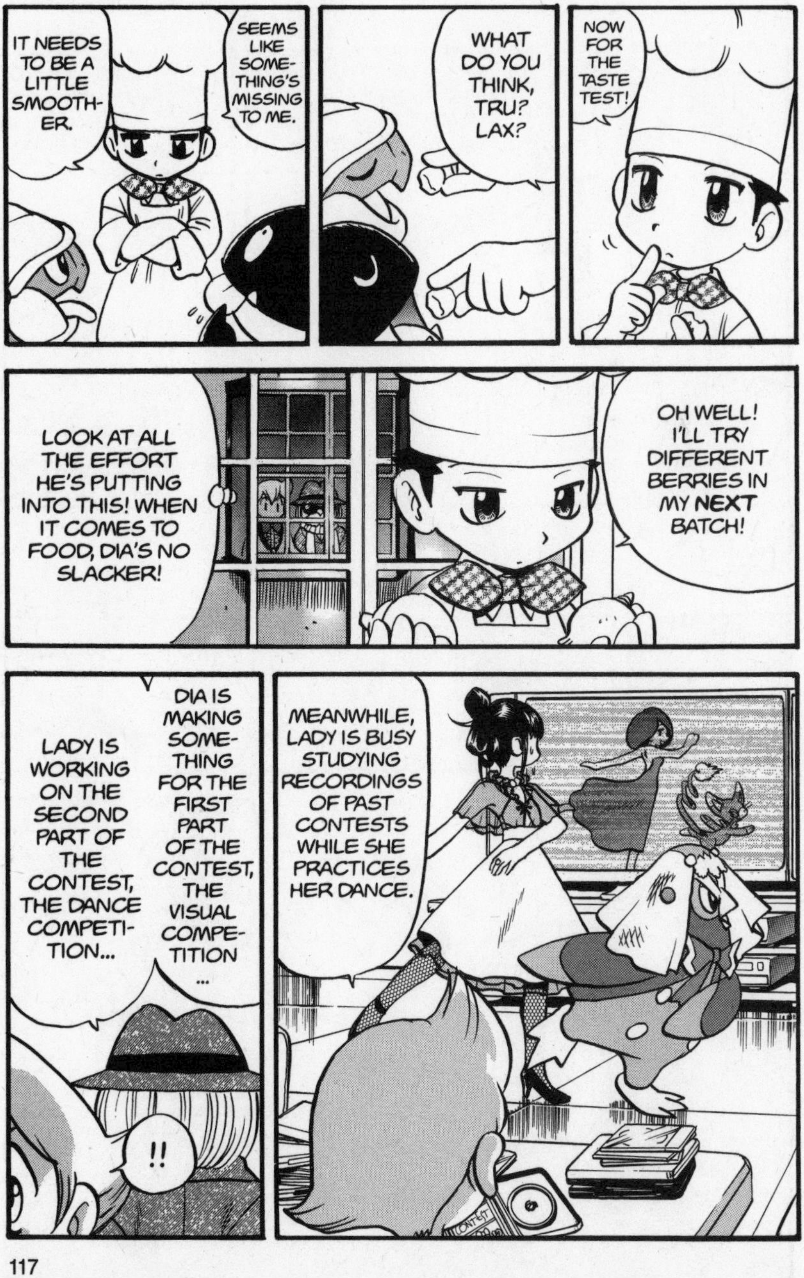
NOW FOR THE TASTE TEST!
WHAT DO YOU THINK, TRU? LAX?
SEEMS LIKE SOME-THING'S MISSING TO ME.
IT NEEDS TO BE A LITTLE SMOOTH-ER.
OH WELL! I'LL TRY DIFFERENT BERRIES IN MY **NEXT** BATCH!
LOOK AT ALL THE EFFORT HE'S PUTTING INTO THIS! WHEN IT COMES TO FOOD, DIA'S NO SLACKER!
MEANWHILE, LADY IS BUSY STUDYING RECORDINGS OF PAST CONTESTS WHILE SHE PRACTICES HER DANCE.
DIA IS MAKING SOME-THING FOR THE FIRST PART OF THE CONTEST, THE VISUAL COMPE-TITION ...
LADY IS WORKING ON THE SECOND PART OF THE CONTEST, THE DANCE COMPETI-TION...
!!

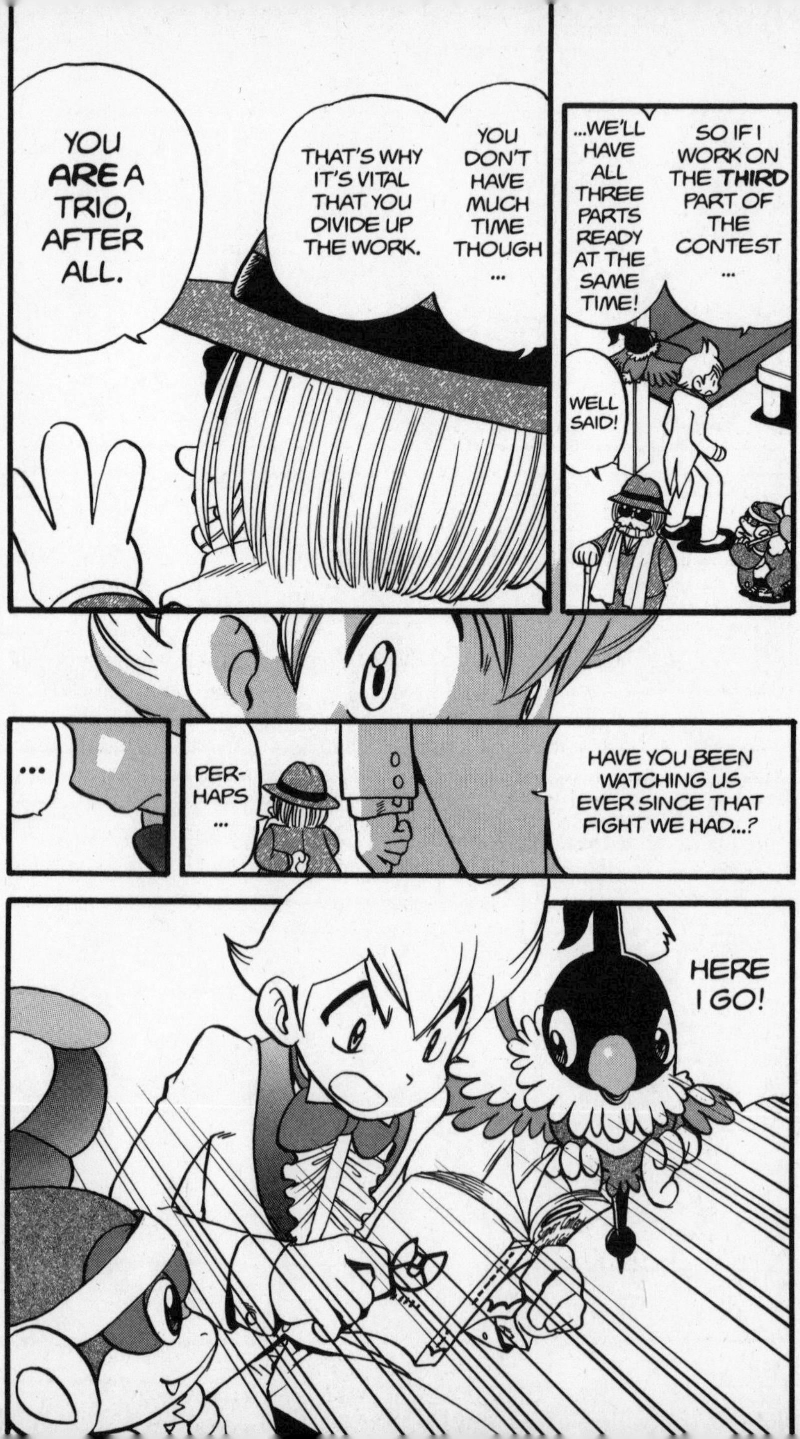

SO IF I WORK ON THE THIRD PART OF THE CONTEST...
...WE'LL HAVE ALL THREE PARTS READY AT THE SAME TIME!
WELL SAID!
YOU DON'T HAVE MUCH TIME THOUGH...
THAT'S WHY IT'S VITAL THAT YOU DIVIDE UP THE WORK.
YOU ARE A TRIO, AFTER ALL.
HAVE YOU BEEN WATCHING US EVER SINCE THAT FIGHT WE HAD...?
PER-HAPS...
...
HERE I GO!

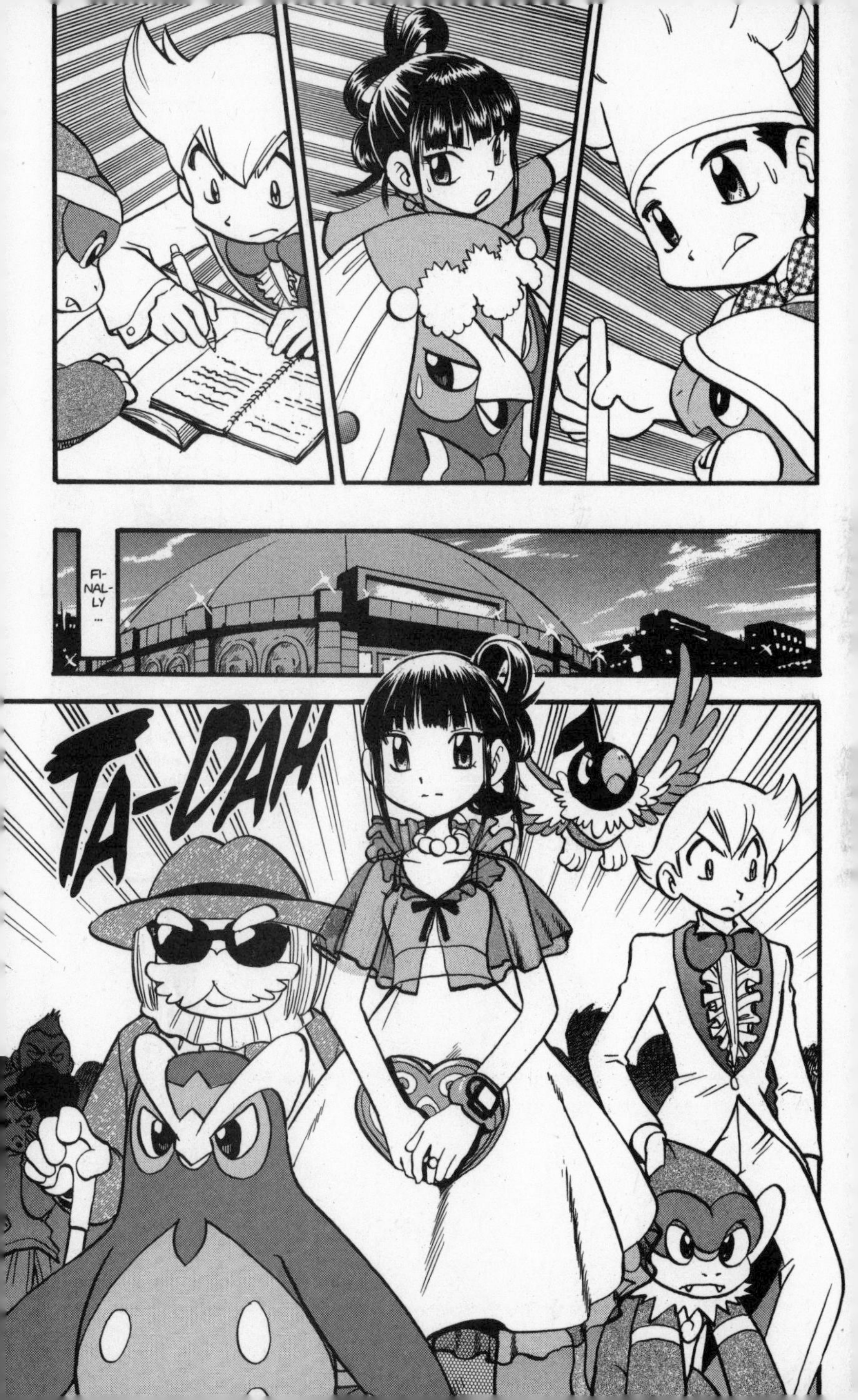
FI-
NAL-
LY
...
TA-DAH

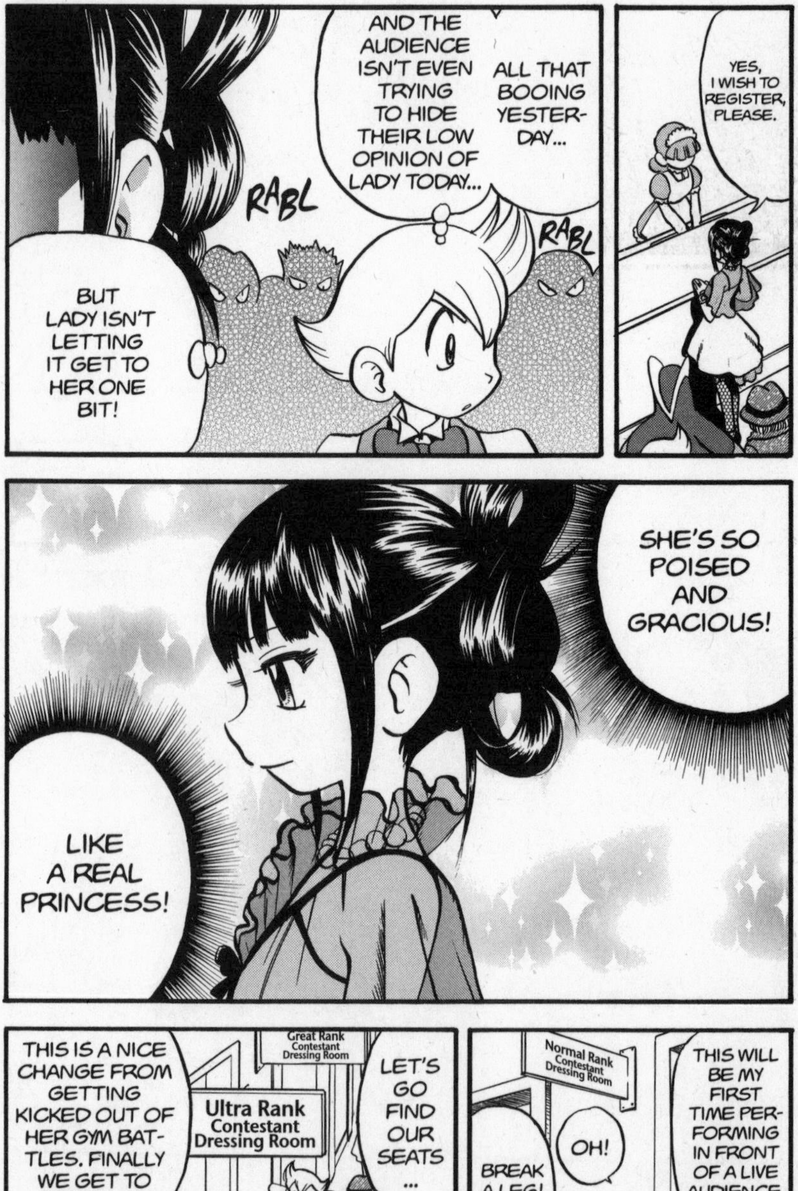

YES, I WISH TO REGISTER, PLEASE.
ALL THAT BOOING YESTERDAY...
AND THE AUDIENCE ISN'T EVEN TRYING TO HIDE THEIR LOW OPINION OF LADY TODAY...
RABL
RABL
BUT LADY ISN'T LETTING IT GET TO HER ONE BIT!
SHE'S SO POISED AND GRACIOUS!
LIKE A REAL PRINCESS!
THIS WILL BE MY FIRST TIME PERFORMING IN FRONT OF A LIVE AUDIENCE.
Normal Rank Contestant Dressing Room
OH!
BREAK A LEG!
Great Rank Contestant Dressing Room
LET'S GO FIND OUR SEATS...
Ultra Rank Contestant Dressing Room
THIS IS A NICE CHANGE FROM GETTING KICKED OUT OF HER GYM BATTLES. FINALLY WE GET TO CHEER HER ON!

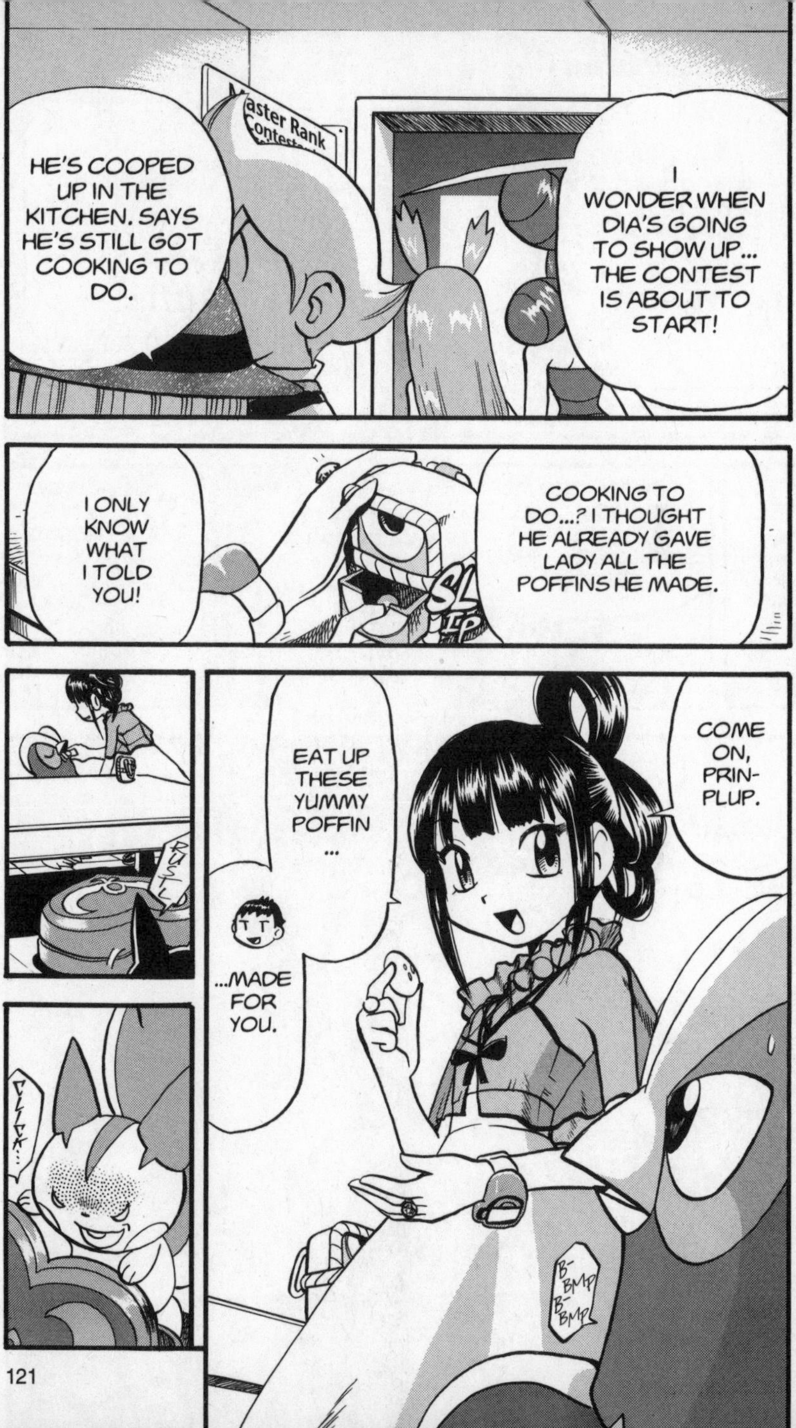
Master Rank
I WONDER WHEN DIA'S GOING TO SHOW UP... THE CONTEST IS ABOUT TO START!
HE'S COOPED UP IN THE KITCHEN. SAYS HE'S STILL GOT COOKING TO DO.
COOKING TO DO...? I THOUGHT HE ALREADY GAVE LADY ALL THE POFFINS HE MADE.
SLIP
I ONLY KNOW WHAT I TOLD YOU!
COME ON, PRIN-PLUP.
EAT UP THESE YUMMY POFFIN...
...MADE FOR YOU.
B-BMP B-BMP
RUSTL
CLICK...

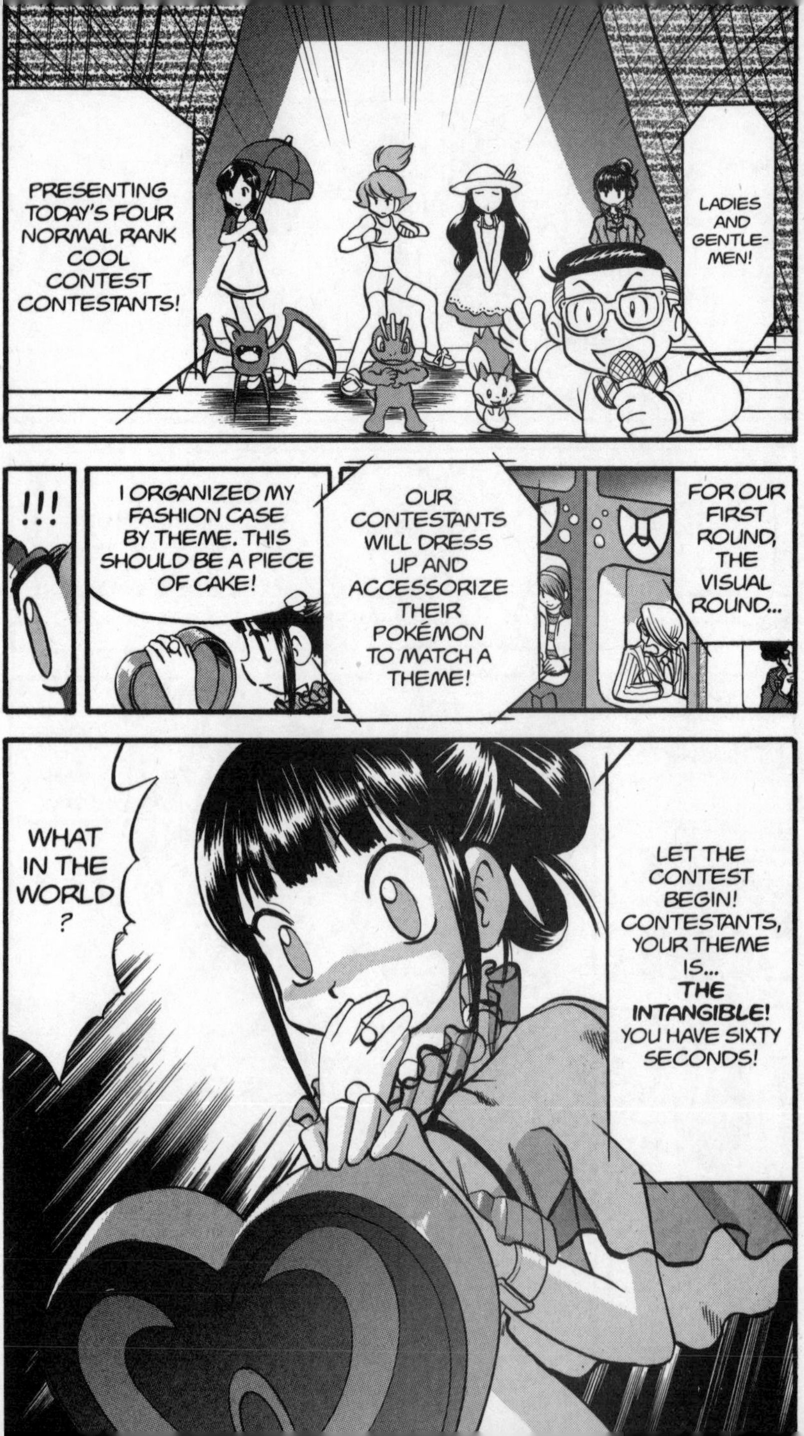
LADIES AND GENTLEMEN!
PRESENTING TODAY'S FOUR NORMAL RANK COOL CONTEST CONTESTANTS!
FOR OUR FIRST ROUND, THE VISUAL ROUND...
OUR CONTESTANTS WILL DRESS UP AND ACCESSORIZE THEIR POKÉMON TO MATCH A THEME!
I ORGANIZED MY FASHION CASE BY THEME. THIS SHOULD BE A PIECE OF CAKE!
!!!
LET THE CONTEST BEGIN! CONTESTANTS, YOUR THEME IS... **THE INTANGIBLE!** YOU HAVE SIXTY SECONDS!
WHAT IN THE WORLD?

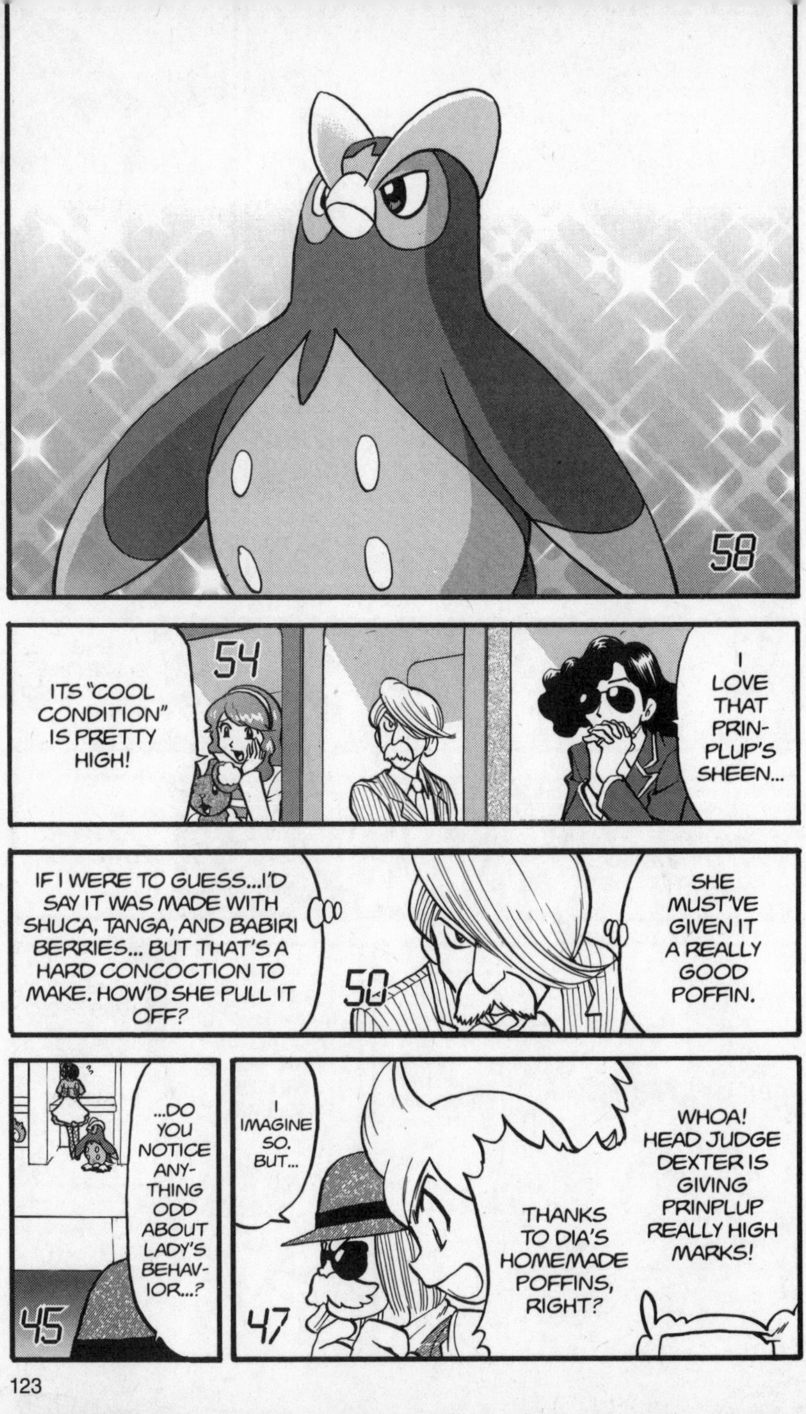
58
I LOVE THAT PRIN-PLUP'S SHEEN...
54
ITS "COOL CONDITION" IS PRETTY HIGH!
SHE MUST'VE GIVEN IT A REALLY GOOD POFFIN.
IF I WERE TO GUESS...I'D SAY IT WAS MADE WITH SHUCA, TANGA, AND BABIRI BERRIES... BUT THAT'S A HARD CONCOCTION TO MAKE. HOW'D SHE PULL IT OFF?
50
WHOA! HEAD JUDGE DEXTER IS GIVING PRINPLUP REALLY HIGH MARKS!
THANKS TO DIA'S HOMEMADE POFFINS, RIGHT?
I IMAGINE SO. BUT...
47
...DO YOU NOTICE ANY-THING ODD ABOUT LADY'S BEHAV-IOR...?
45

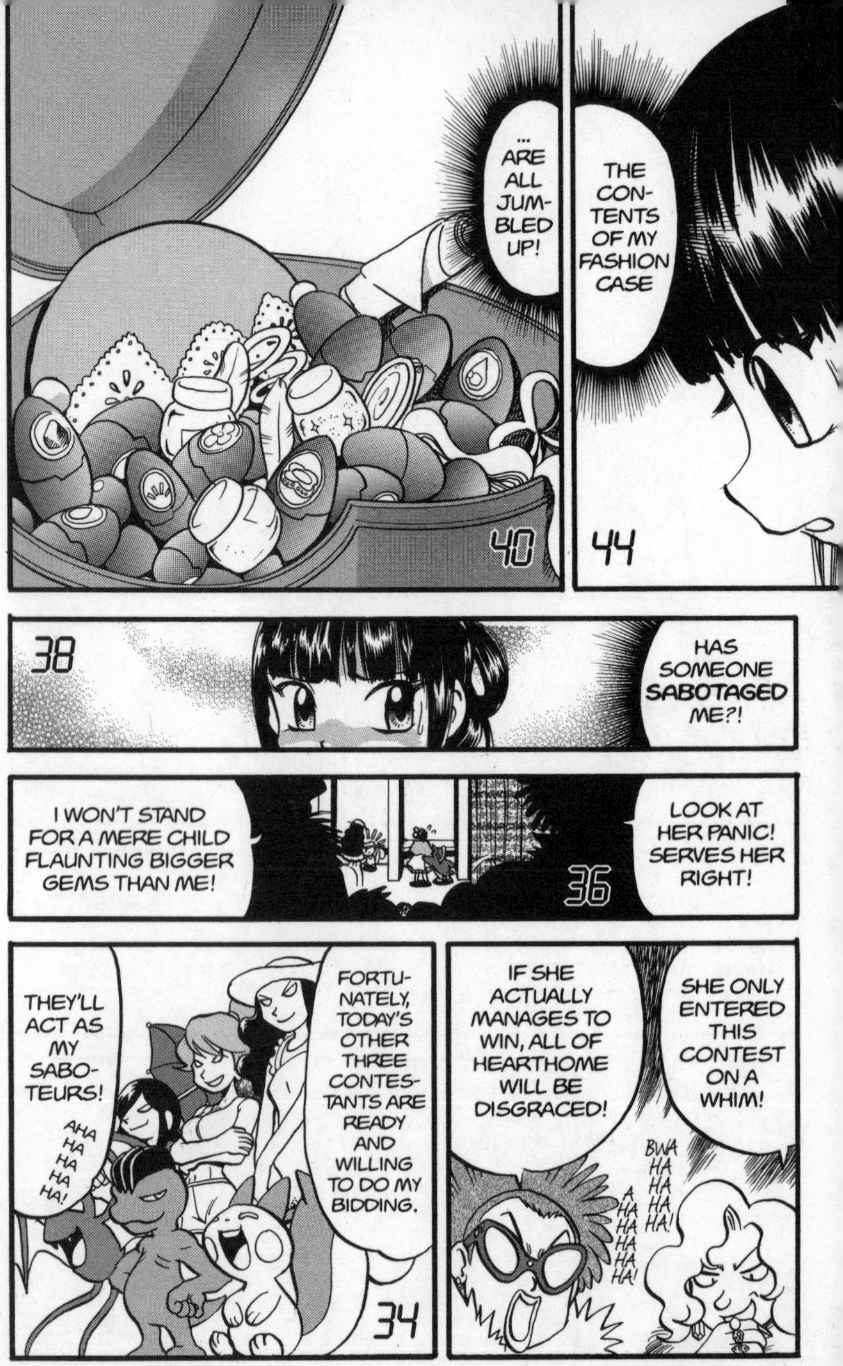
THE CONTENTS OF MY FASHION CASE
44
... ARE ALL JUMBLED UP!
40
HAS SOMEONE SABOTAGED ME?!
38
LOOK AT HER PANIC! SERVES HER RIGHT!
36
I WON'T STAND FOR A MERE CHILD FLAUNTING BIGGER GEMS THAN ME!
SHE ONLY ENTERED THIS CONTEST ON A WHIM!
IF SHE ACTUALLY MANAGES TO WIN, ALL OF HEARTHOME WILL BE DISGRACED!
BWA HA HA HA HA HA!
A HA HA HA HA HA HA!
FORTUNATELY, TODAY'S OTHER THREE CONTESTANTS ARE READY AND WILLING TO DO MY BIDDING.
THEY'LL ACT AS MY SABOTEURS!
AHA HA HA HA HA!
34

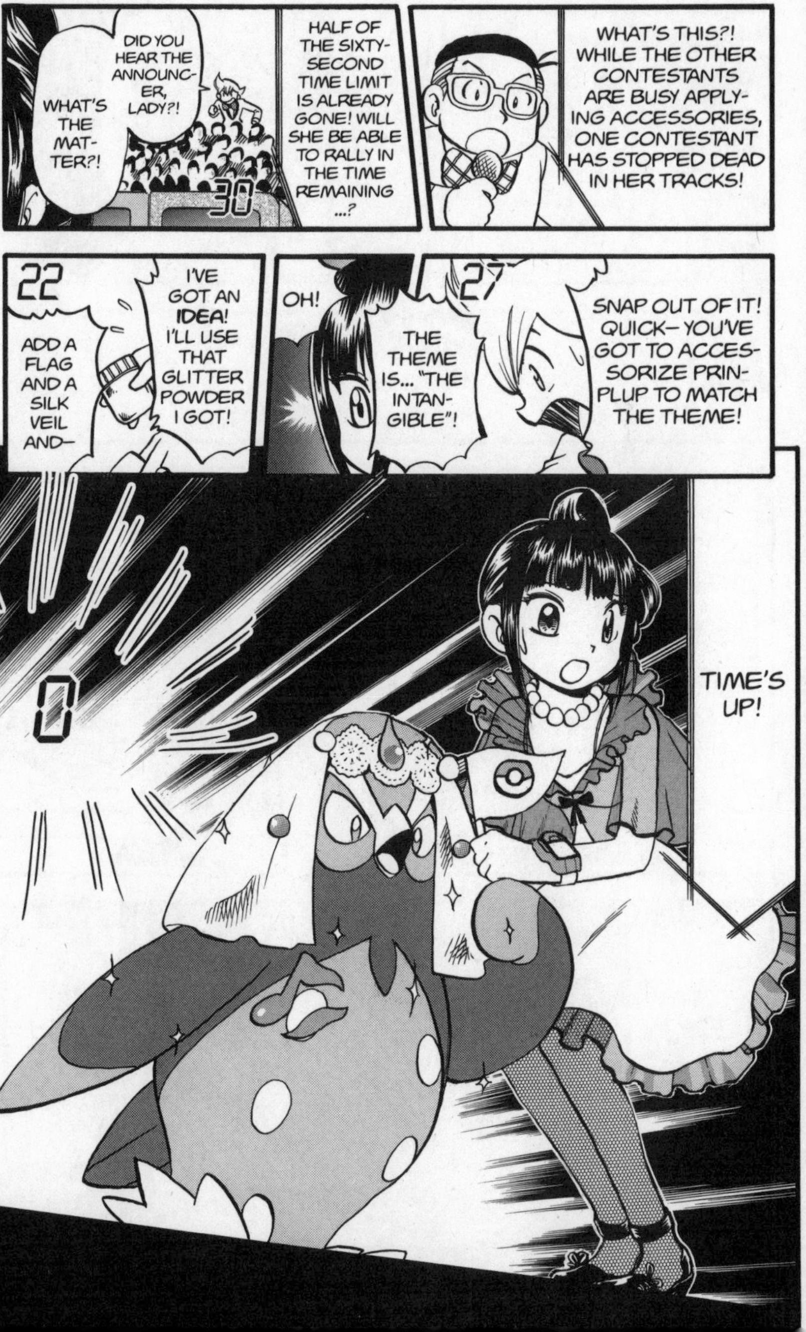
WHAT'S THIS?! WHILE THE OTHER CONTESTANTS ARE BUSY APPLYING ACCESSORIES, ONE CONTESTANT HAS STOPPED DEAD IN HER TRACKS!
HALF OF THE SIXTY-SECOND TIME LIMIT IS ALREADY GONE! WILL SHE BE ABLE TO RALLY IN THE TIME REMAINING ...?
DID YOU HEAR THE ANNOUNCER, LADY?!
WHAT'S THE MATTER?!
30
27
SNAP OUT OF IT! QUICK— YOU'VE GOT TO ACCESSORIZE PRINPLUP TO MATCH THE THEME!
THE THEME IS... "THE INTANGIBLE"!
OH!
22
I'VE GOT AN **IDEA**! I'LL USE THAT GLITTER POWDER I GOT!
ADD A FLAG AND A SILK VEIL AND—
TIME'S UP!
0

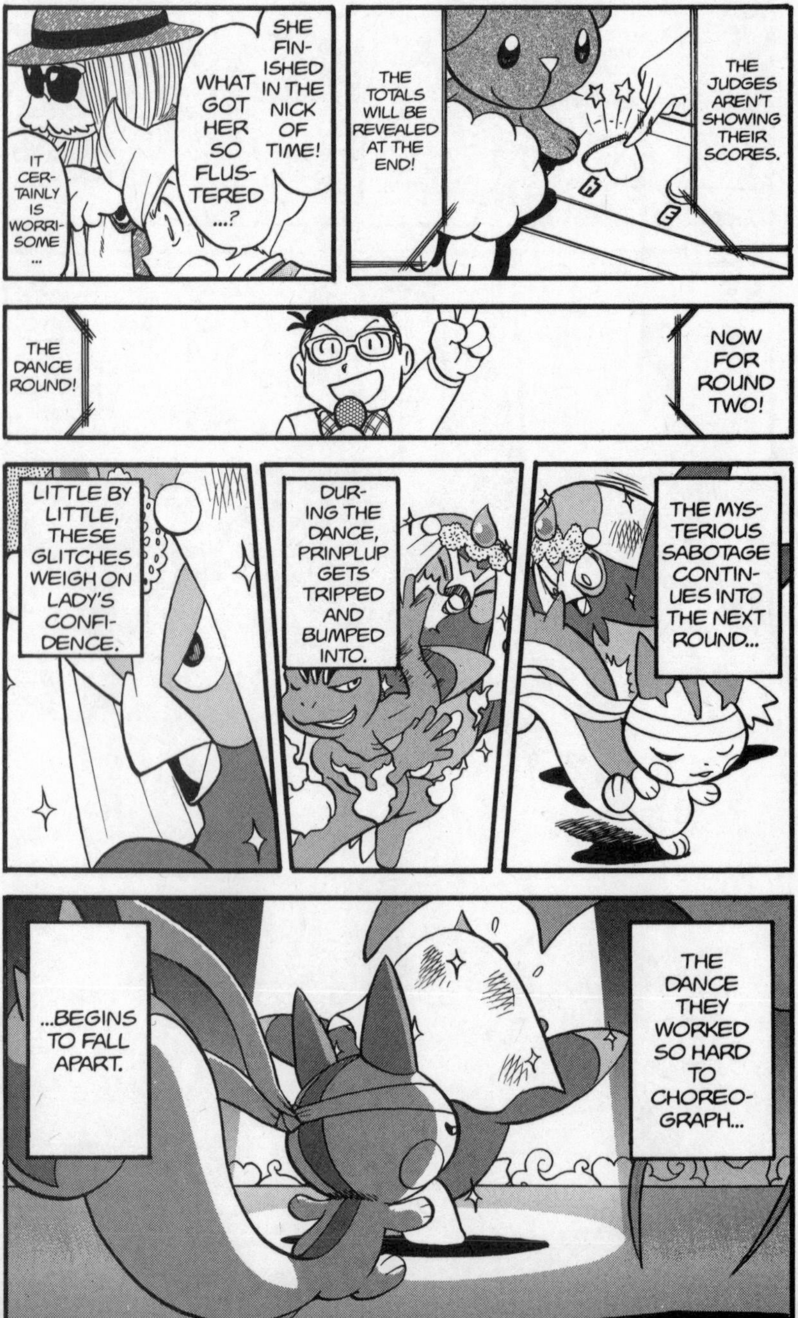
THE JUDGES AREN'T SHOWING THEIR SCORES.
THE TOTALS WILL BE REVEALED AT THE END!
SHE FINISHED IN THE NICK OF TIME!
WHAT GOT HER SO FLUSTERED...?
IT CERTAINLY IS WORRISOME...
NOW FOR ROUND TWO!
THE DANCE ROUND!
THE MYSTERIOUS SABOTAGE CONTINUES INTO THE NEXT ROUND...
DURING THE DANCE, PRINPLUP GETS TRIPPED AND BUMPED INTO.
LITTLE BY LITTLE, THESE GLITCHES WEIGH ON LADY'S CONFIDENCE.
THE DANCE THEY WORKED SO HARD TO CHOREOGRAPH...
...BEGINS TO FALL APART.

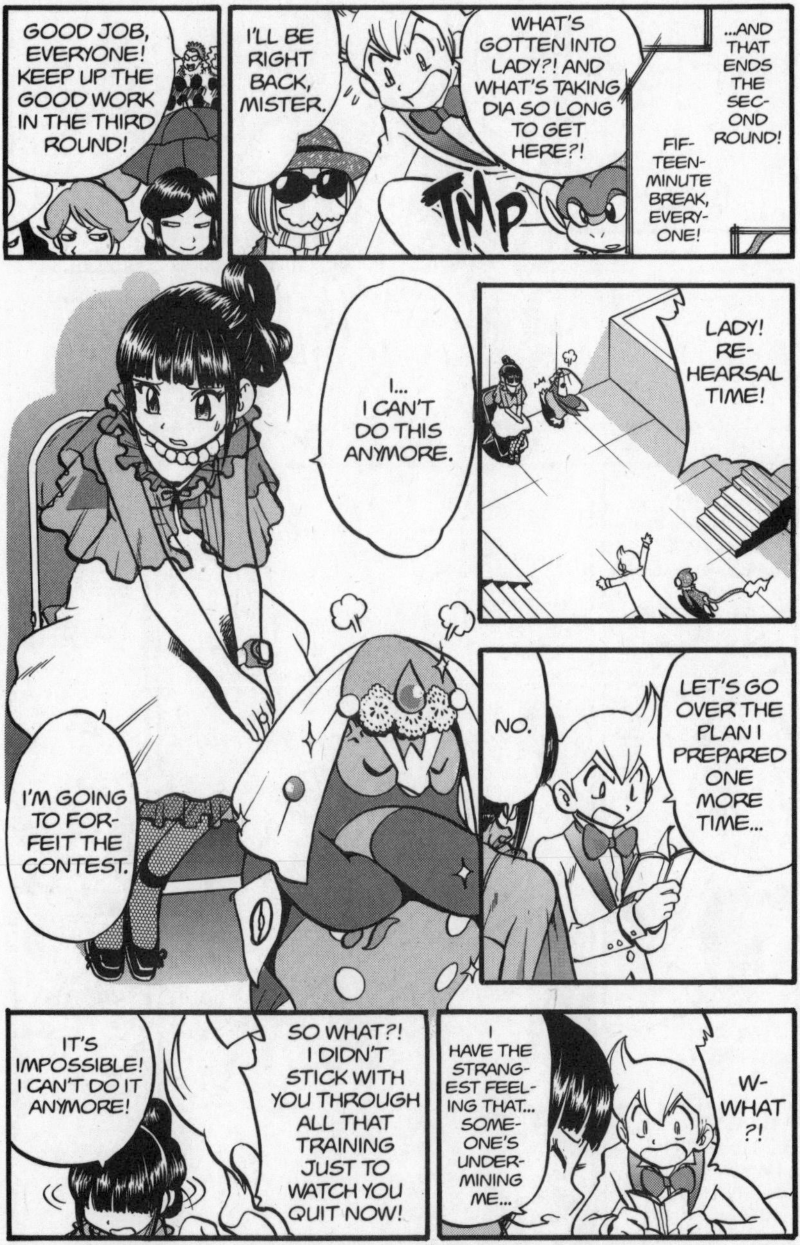
...AND THAT ENDS THE SECOND ROUND!
FIFTEEN-MINUTE BREAK, EVERYONE!
WHAT'S GOTTEN INTO LADY?! AND WHAT'S TAKING DIA SO LONG TO GET HERE?!
TMP
I'LL BE RIGHT BACK, MISTER.
GOOD JOB, EVERYONE! KEEP UP THE GOOD WORK IN THE THIRD ROUND!
LADY! REHEARSAL TIME!
LET'S GO OVER THE PLAN I PREPARED ONE MORE TIME...
NO.
I... I CAN'T DO THIS ANYMORE.
I'M GOING TO FORFEIT THE CONTEST.
W-WHAT?!
I HAVE THE STRANGEST FEELING THAT... SOMEONE'S UNDERMINING ME...
SO WHAT?! I DIDN'T STICK WITH YOU THROUGH ALL THAT TRAINING JUST TO WATCH YOU QUIT NOW!
IT'S IMPOSSIBLE! I CAN'T DO IT ANYMORE!

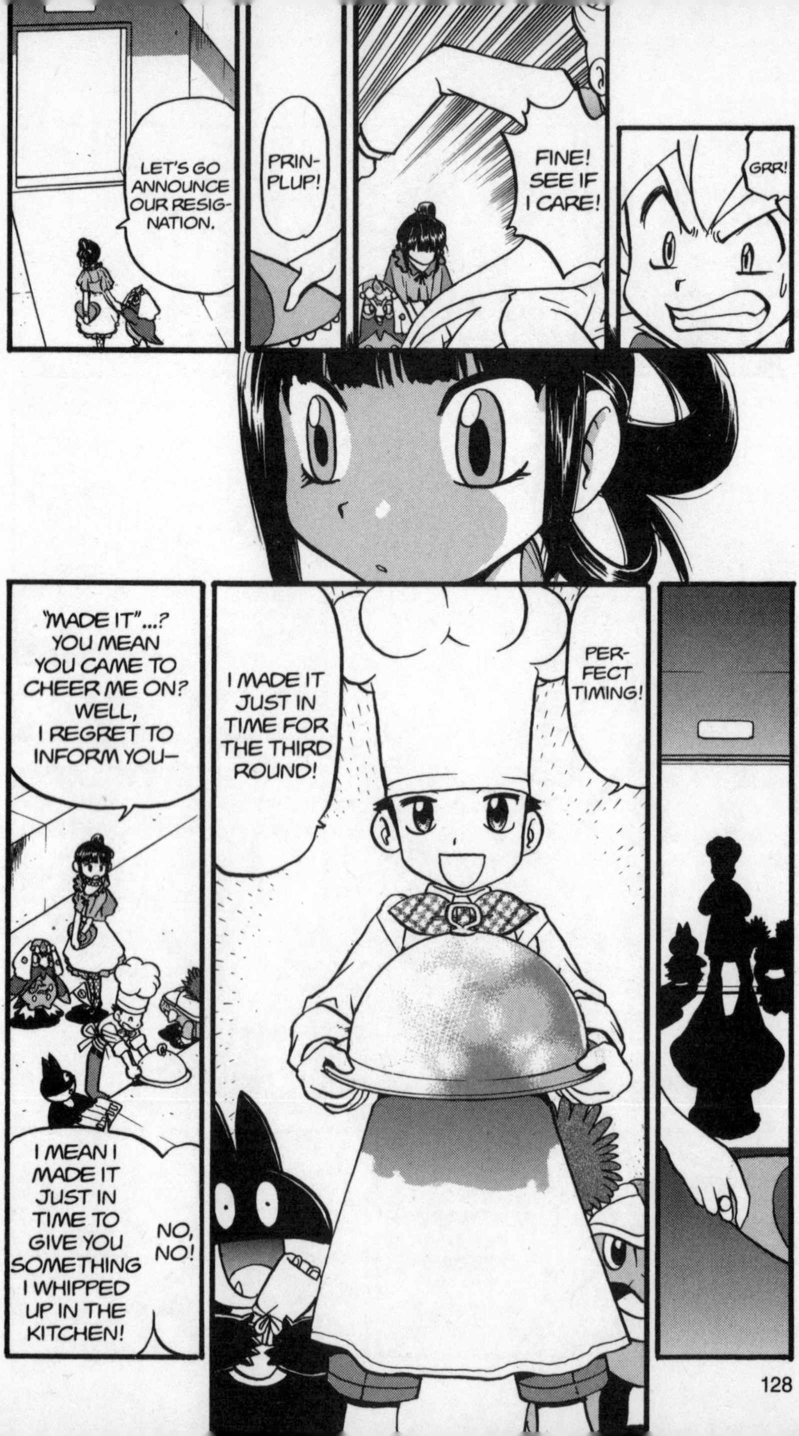
GRR!
FINE! SEE IF I CARE!
PRIN-PLUP!
LET'S GO ANNOUNCE OUR RESIG-NATION.
PER-FECT TIMING!
I MADE IT JUST IN TIME FOR THE THIRD ROUND!
"MADE IT"...? YOU MEAN YOU CAME TO CHEER ME ON? WELL, I REGRET TO INFORM YOU—
NO, NO!
I MEAN I MADE IT JUST IN TIME TO GIVE YOU SOMETHING I WHIPPED UP IN THE KITCHEN!

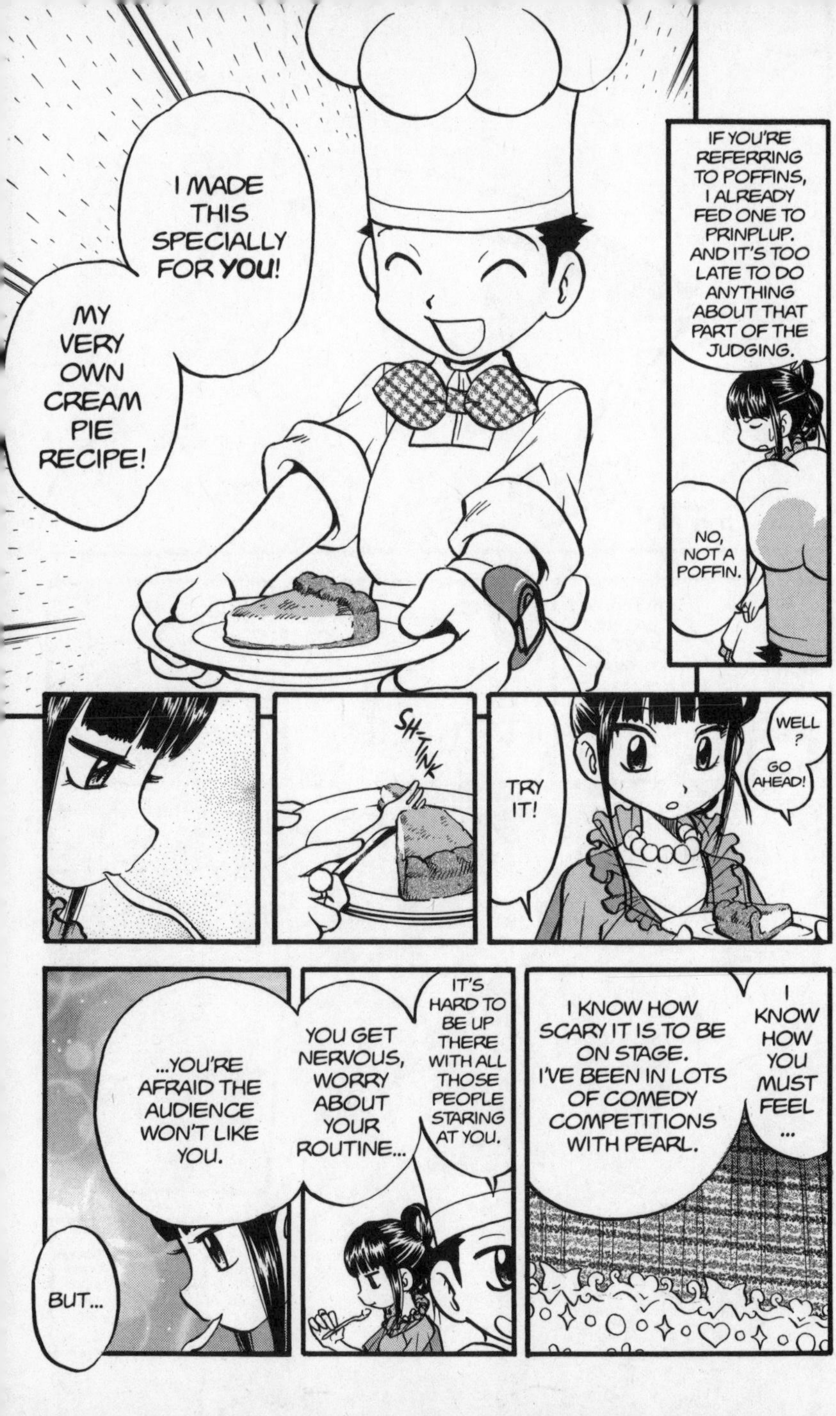
IF YOU'RE REFERRING TO POFFINS, I ALREADY FED ONE TO PRINPLUP. AND IT'S TOO LATE TO DO ANYTHING ABOUT THAT PART OF THE JUDGING.
NO, NOT A POFFIN.
I MADE THIS SPECIALLY FOR YOU!
MY VERY OWN CREAM PIE RECIPE!
WELL? GO AHEAD!
TRY IT!
SH-TINK
I KNOW HOW YOU MUST FEEL...
I KNOW HOW SCARY IT IS TO BE ON STAGE. I'VE BEEN IN LOTS OF COMEDY COMPETITIONS WITH PEARL.
IT'S HARD TO BE UP THERE WITH ALL THOSE PEOPLE STARING AT YOU.
YOU GET NERVOUS, WORRY ABOUT YOUR ROUTINE...
...YOU'RE AFRAID THE AUDIENCE WON'T LIKE YOU.
BUT...

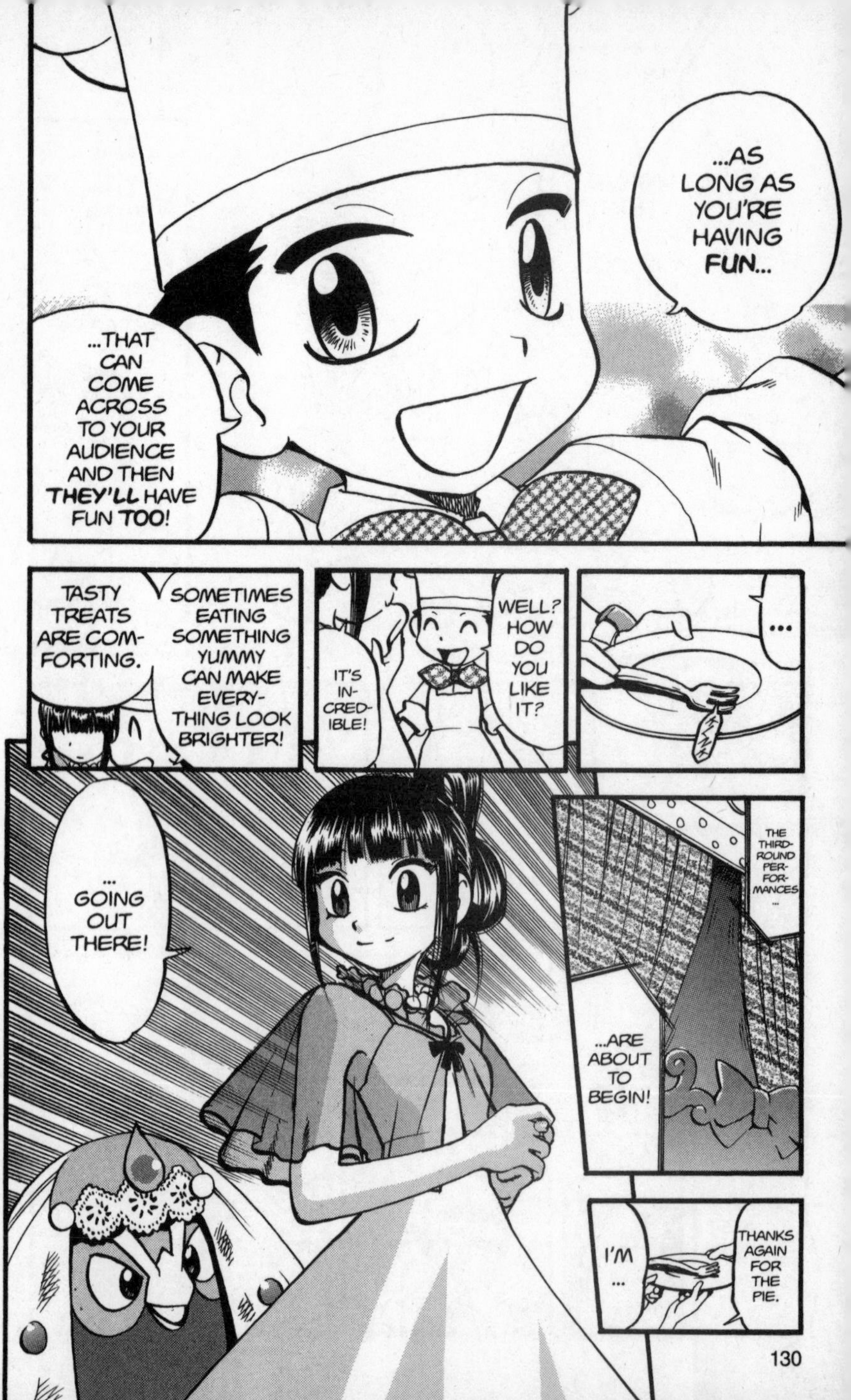
...AS LONG AS YOU'RE HAVING FUN...
...THAT CAN COME ACROSS TO YOUR AUDIENCE AND THEN THEY'LL HAVE FUN TOO!
...
WELL? HOW DO YOU LIKE IT?
IT'S INCREDIBLE!
SOMETIMES EATING SOMETHING YUMMY CAN MAKE EVERYTHING LOOK BRIGHTER!
TASTY TREATS ARE COMFORTING.
THE THIRD-ROUND PERFORMANCES...
...ARE ABOUT TO BEGIN!
THANKS AGAIN FOR THE PIE.
I'M ...
... GOING OUT THERE!

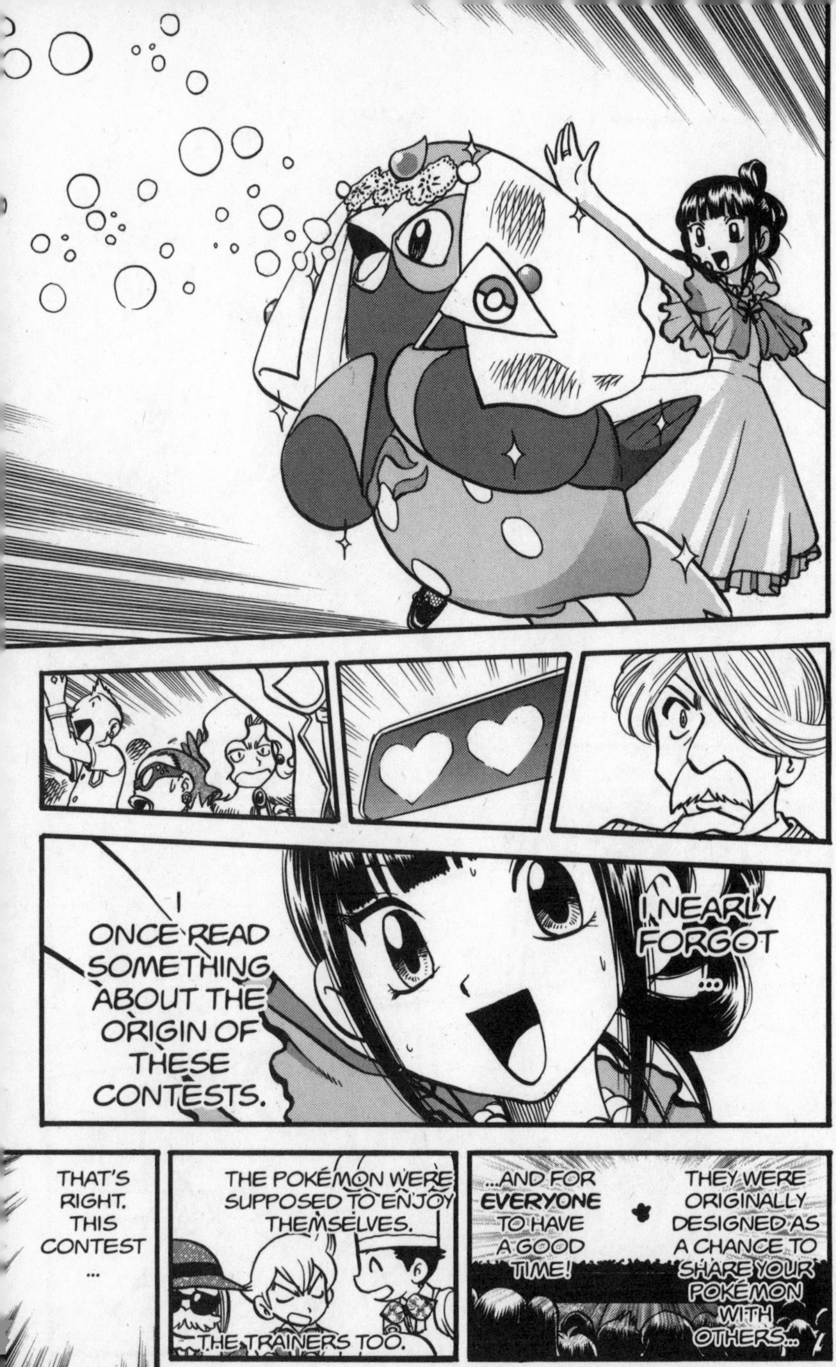
I NEARLY FORGOT ...
I ONCE READ SOMETHING ABOUT THE ORIGIN OF THESE CONTESTS.
THEY WERE ORIGINALLY DESIGNED AS A CHANCE TO SHARE YOUR POKÉMON WITH OTHERS...
...AND FOR **EVERYONE** TO HAVE A GOOD TIME!
THE POKÉMON WERE SUPPOSED TO ENJOY THEMSELVES.
THE TRAINERS TOO.
THAT'S RIGHT. THIS CONTEST ...

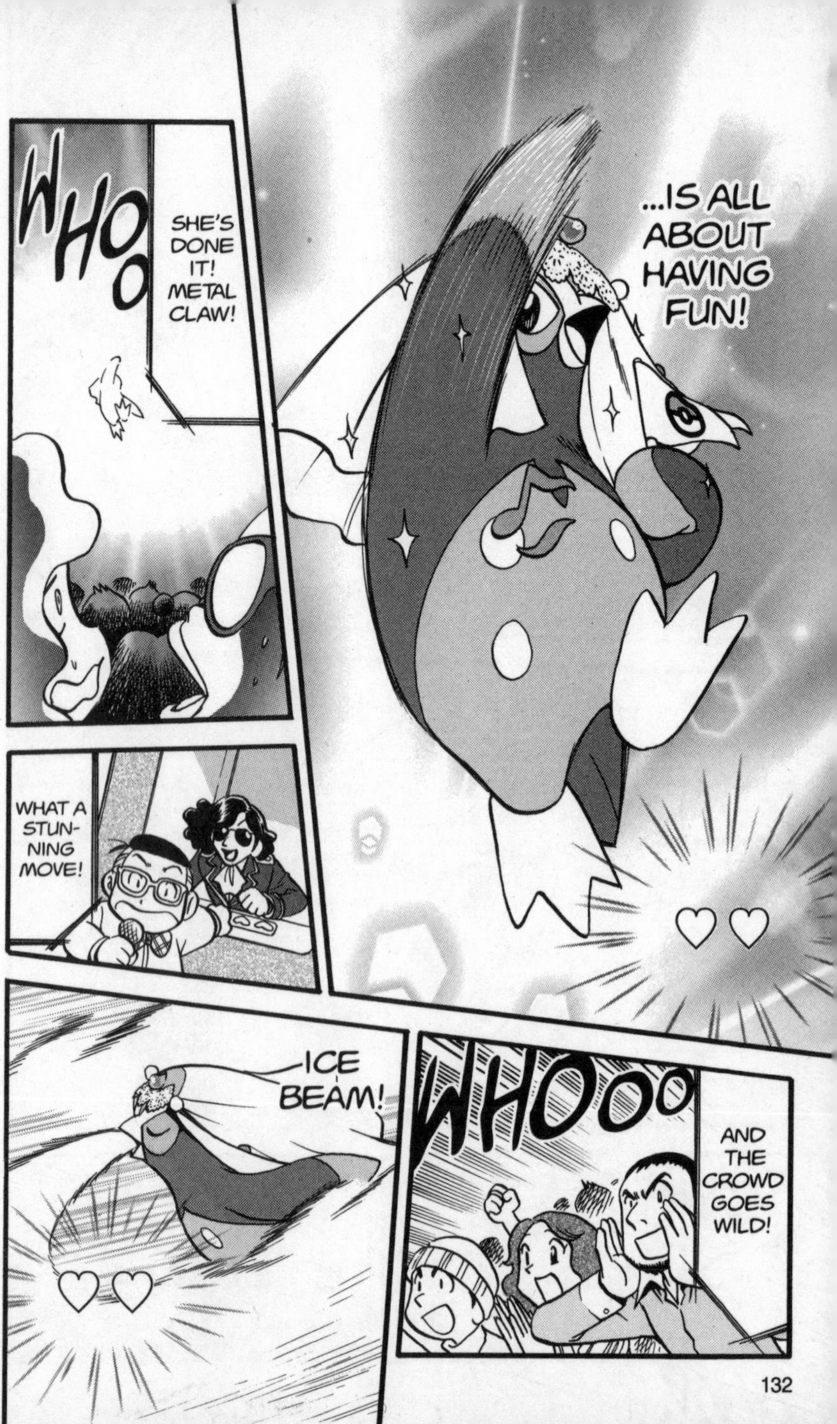
...IS ALL ABOUT HAVING FUN!
WHOO
SHE'S DONE IT! METAL CLAW!
WHAT A STUN-NING MOVE!
WHOOO
AND THE CROWD GOES WILD!
ICE BEAM!

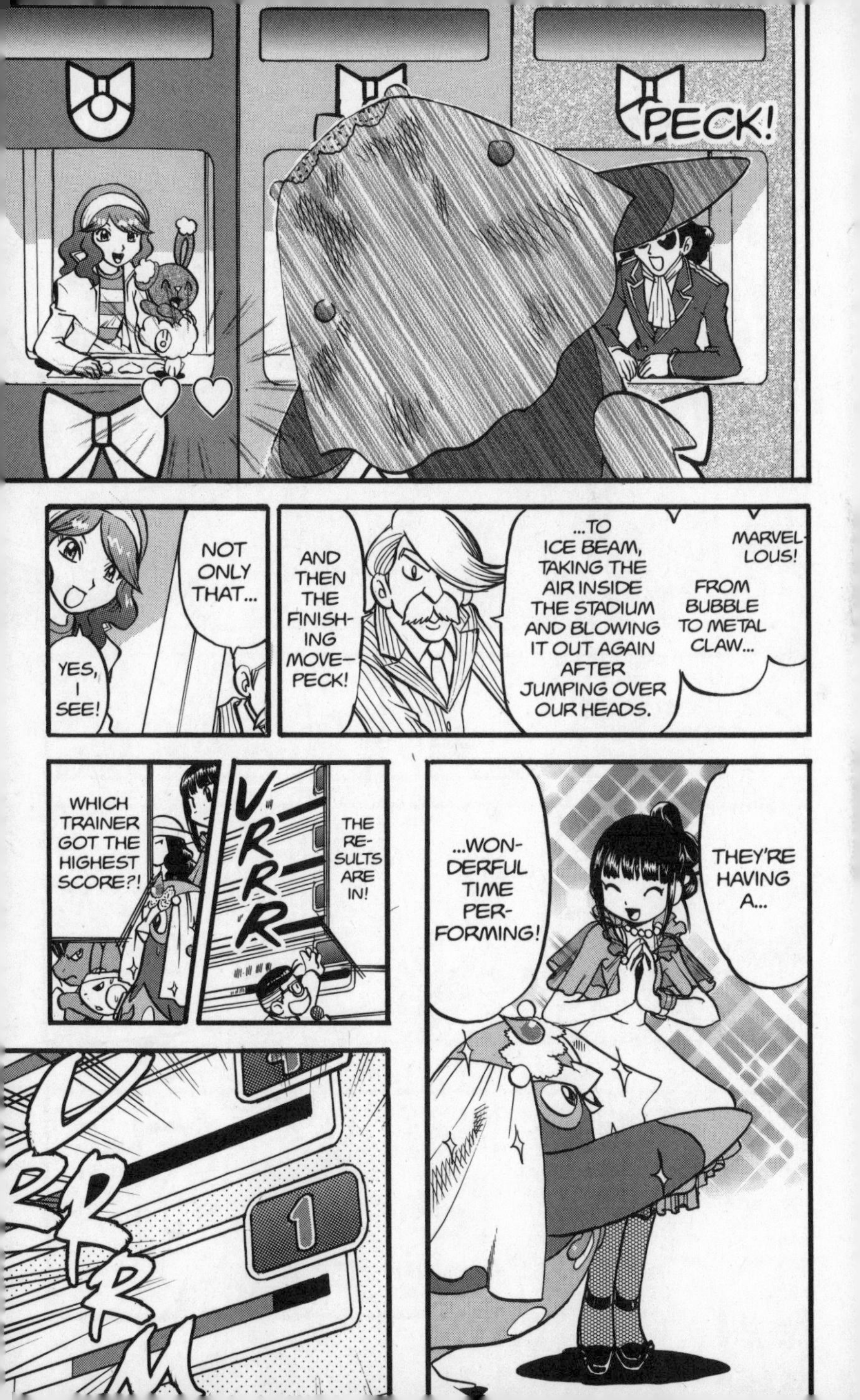
PECK!
MARVEL-LOUS!
FROM BUBBLE TO METAL CLAW...
...TO ICE BEAM, TAKING THE AIR INSIDE THE STADIUM AND BLOWING IT OUT AGAIN AFTER JUMPING OVER OUR HEADS.
AND THEN THE FINISHING MOVE—PECK!
NOT ONLY THAT...
YES, I SEE!
THEY'RE HAVING A...
...WONDERFUL TIME PERFORMING!
THE RESULTS ARE IN!
VRRR
WHICH TRAINER GOT THE HIGHEST SCORE?!
1

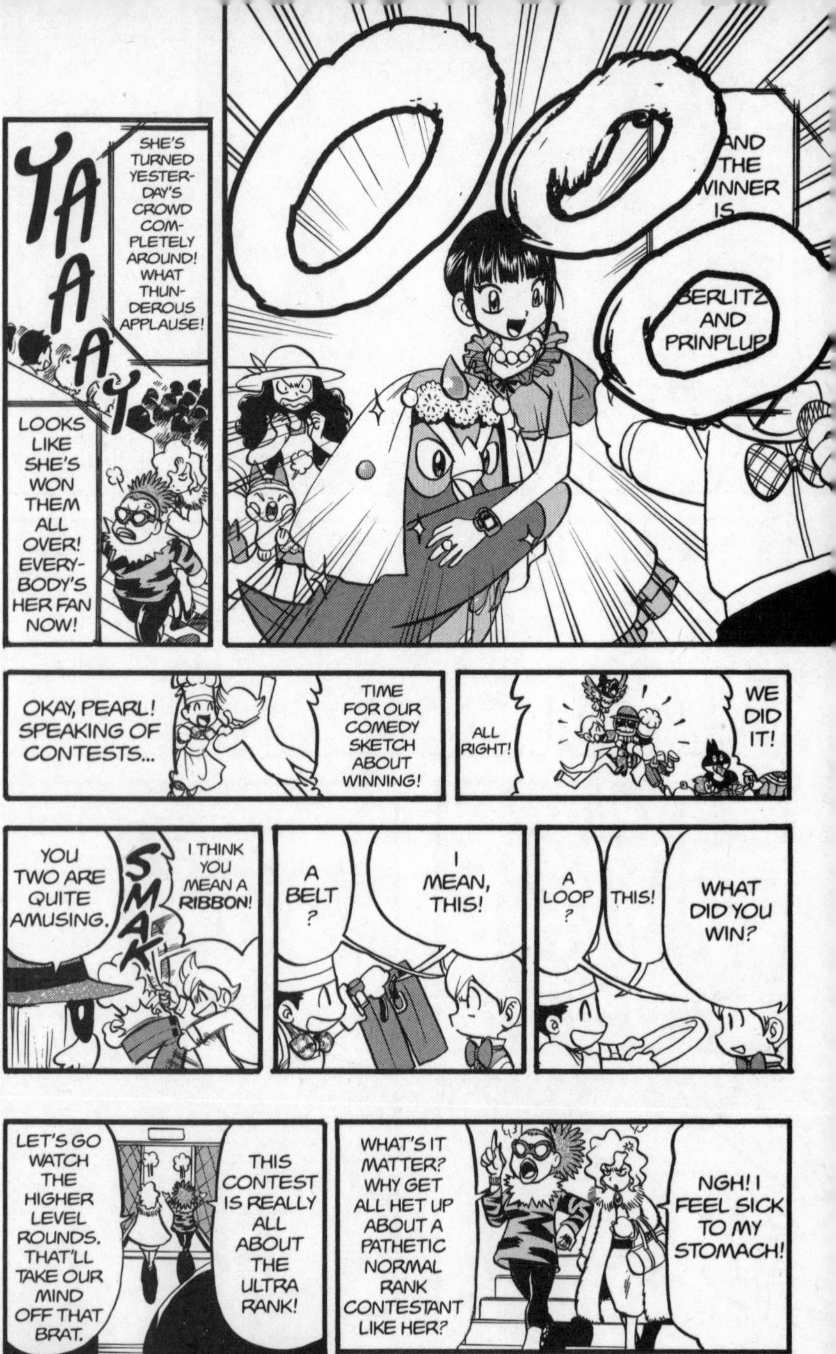
AND THE WINNER IS...
BERLITZ AND PRINPLUP!
YAAAY
SHE'S TURNED YESTERDAY'S CROWD COMPLETELY AROUND! WHAT THUNDEROUS APPLAUSE!
LOOKS LIKE SHE'S WON THEM ALL OVER! EVERYBODY'S HER FAN NOW!
WE DID IT!
ALL RIGHT!
TIME FOR OUR COMEDY SKETCH ABOUT WINNING!
OKAY, PEARL! SPEAKING OF CONTESTS...
WHAT DID YOU WIN?
THIS!
A LOOP?
I MEAN, THIS!
A BELT?
I THINK YOU MEAN A RIBBON!
SMAK
YOU TWO ARE QUITE AMUSING.
NGH! I FEEL SICK TO MY STOMACH!
WHAT'S IT MATTER? WHY GET ALL HET UP ABOUT A PATHETIC NORMAL RANK CONTESTANT LIKE HER?
THIS CONTEST IS REALLY ALL ABOUT THE ULTRA RANK!
LET'S GO WATCH THE HIGHER LEVEL ROUNDS. THAT'LL TAKE OUR MIND OFF THAT BRAT.

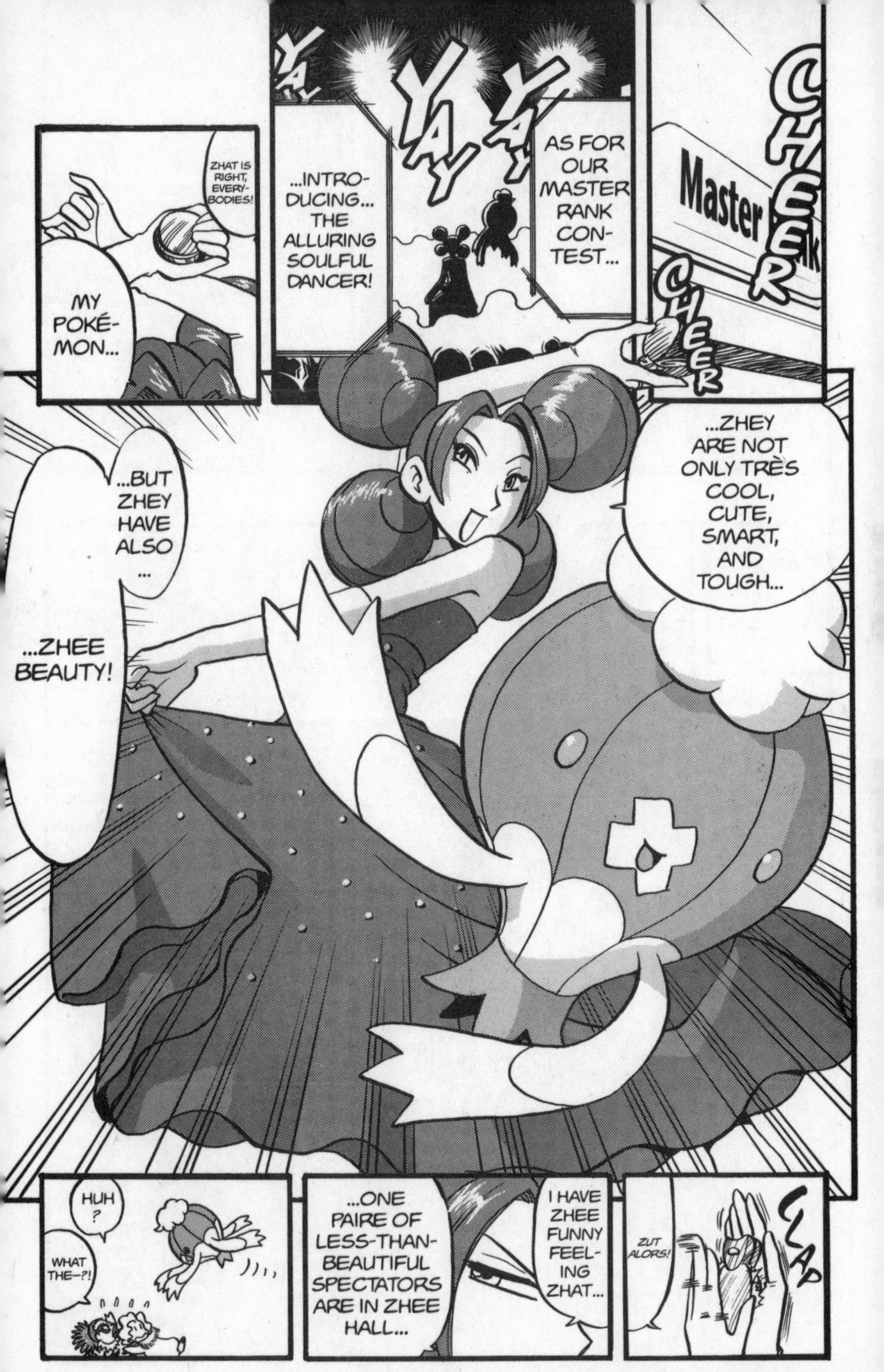
CHEER
CHEER
Master Rank
YAY
YAY
YAY
AS FOR OUR MASTER RANK CON-TEST...
...INTRO-DUCING... THE ALLURING SOULFUL DANCER!
ZHAT IS RIGHT, EVERY-BODIES!
MY POKÉ-MON...
...ZHEY ARE NOT ONLY TRÈS COOL, CUTE, SMART, AND TOUGH...
...BUT ZHEY HAVE ALSO ...
...ZHEE BEAUTY!
CLAP
ZUT ALORS!
I HAVE ZHEE FUNNY FEEL-ING ZHAT...
...ONE PAIRE OF LESS-THAN-BEAUTIFUL SPECTATORS ARE IN ZHEE HALL...
HUH ?
WHAT THE–?!

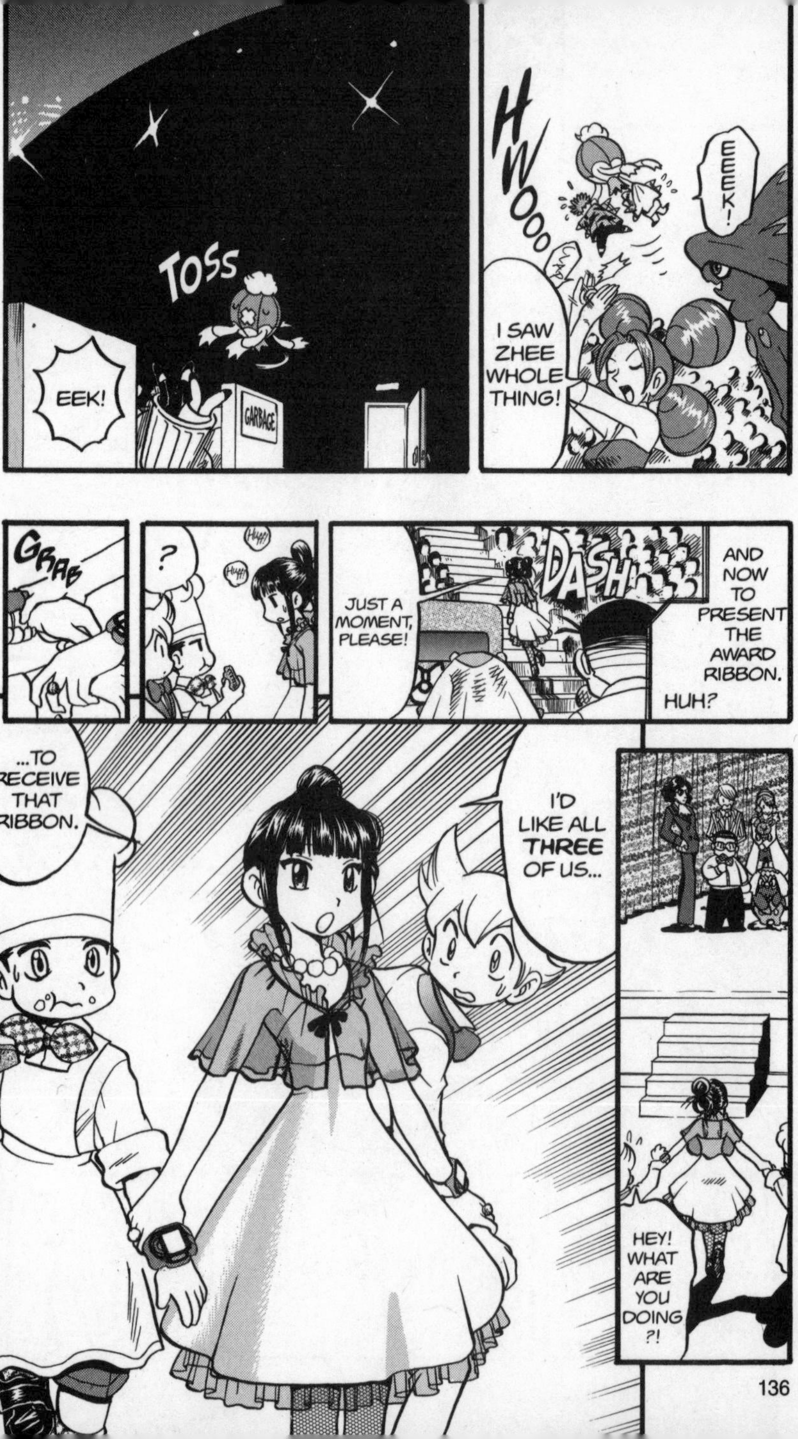
HWOOO
EEEK!
I SAW ZHEE WHOLE THING!
TOSS
EEK!
GARBAGE
AND NOW TO PRESENT THE AWARD RIBBON.
HUH?
DASH
JUST A MOMENT, PLEASE!
?
GRAB
HEY! WHAT ARE YOU DOING?!
I'D LIKE ALL THREE OF US...
...TO RECEIVE THAT RIBBON.

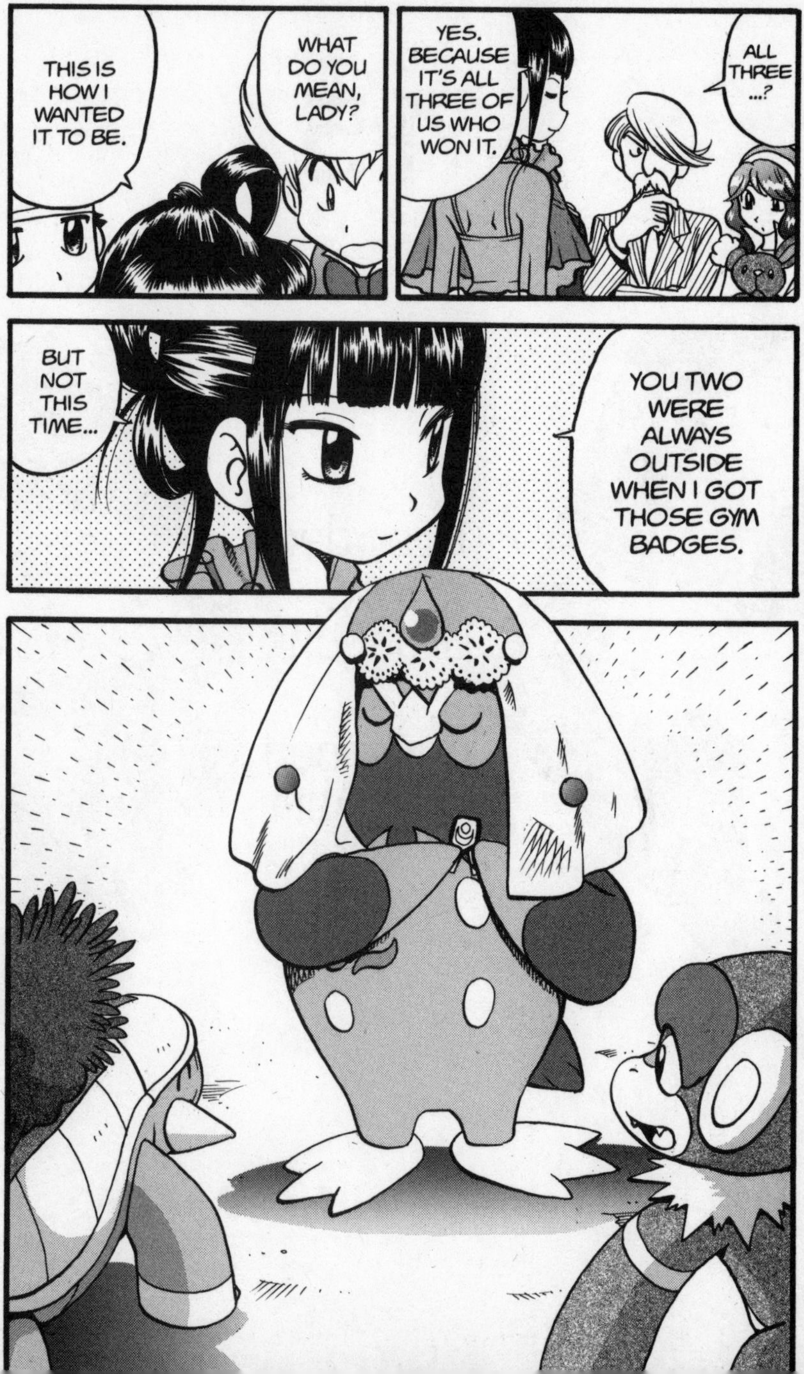
ALL THREE ...?
YES. BECAUSE IT'S ALL THREE OF US WHO WON IT.
WHAT DO YOU MEAN, LADY?
THIS IS HOW I WANTED IT TO BE.
YOU TWO WERE ALWAYS OUTSIDE WHEN I GOT THOSE GYM BADGES.
BUT NOT THIS TIME...

15

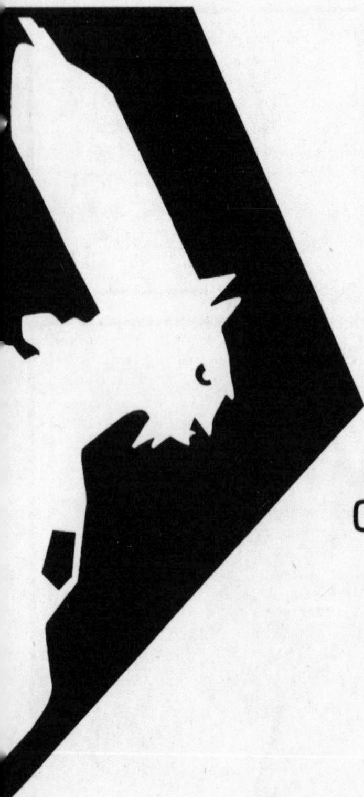

Crowded by Croagunk & Advanced on by Abra, Part I

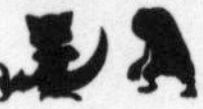

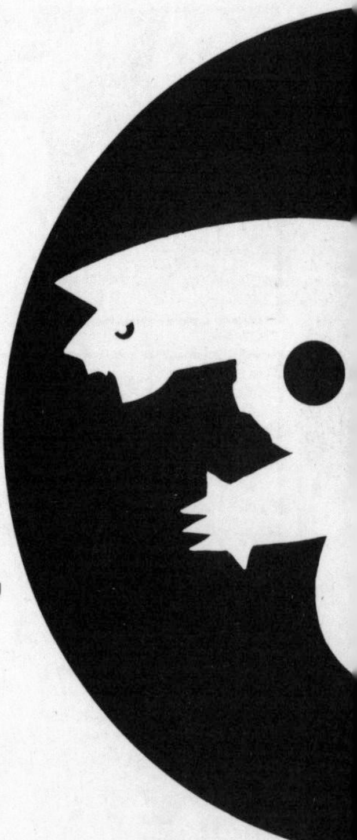

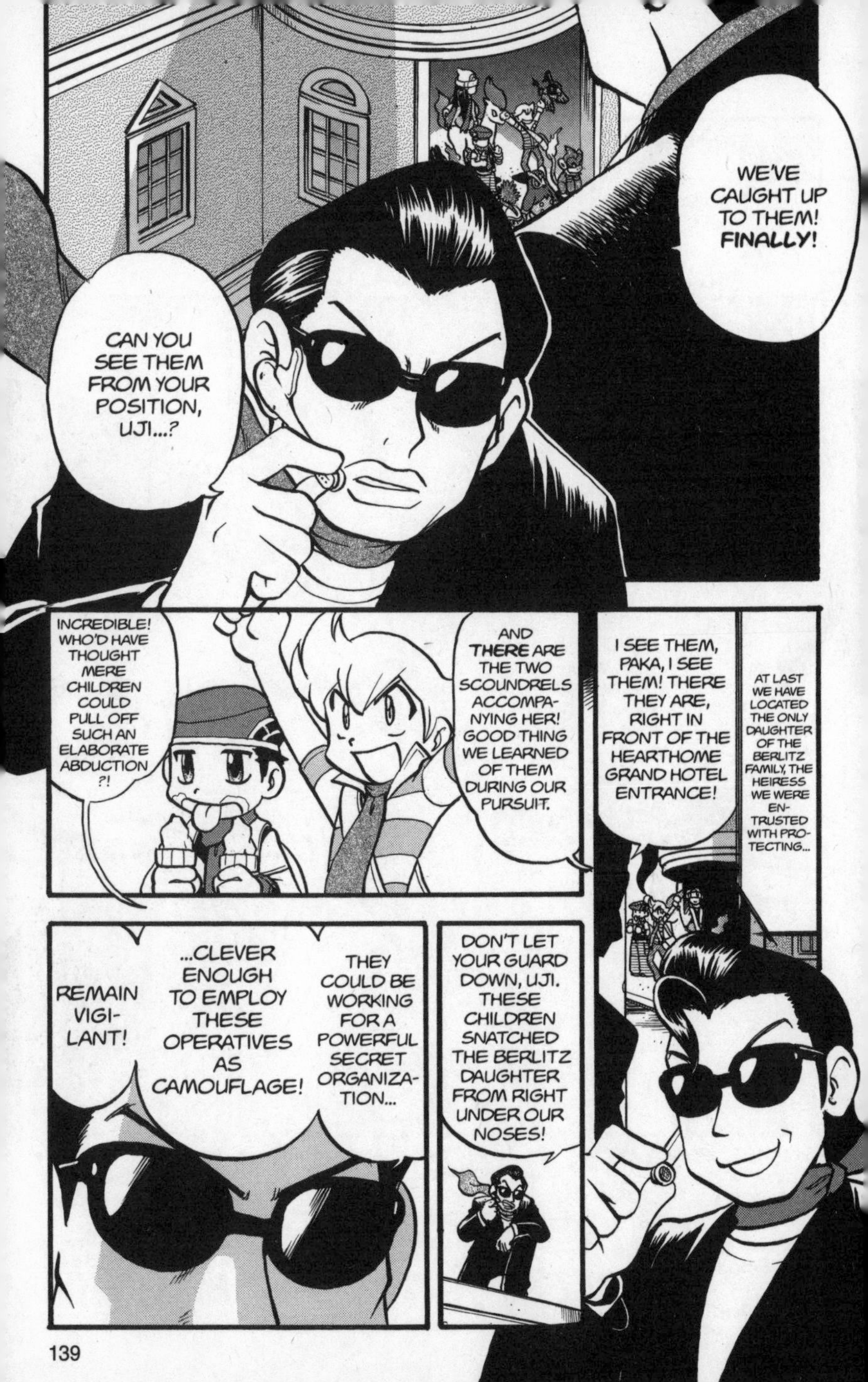
WE'VE CAUGHT UP TO THEM! FINALLY!
CAN YOU SEE THEM FROM YOUR POSITION, UJI...?
AT LAST WE HAVE LOCATED THE ONLY DAUGHTER OF THE BERLITZ FAMILY, THE HEIRESS WE WERE ENTRUSTED WITH PROTECTING...
I SEE THEM, PAKA, I SEE THEM! THERE THEY ARE, RIGHT IN FRONT OF THE HEARTHOME GRAND HOTEL ENTRANCE!
AND THERE ARE THE TWO SCOUNDRELS ACCOMPANYING HER! GOOD THING WE LEARNED OF THEM DURING OUR PURSUIT.
INCREDIBLE! WHO'D HAVE THOUGHT MERE CHILDREN COULD PULL OFF SUCH AN ELABORATE ABDUCTION?!
DON'T LET YOUR GUARD DOWN, UJI. THESE CHILDREN SNATCHED THE BERLITZ DAUGHTER FROM RIGHT UNDER OUR NOSES!
THEY COULD BE WORKING FOR A POWERFUL SECRET ORGANIZATION...
...CLEVER ENOUGH TO EMPLOY THESE OPERATIVES AS CAMOUFLAGE!
REMAIN VIGILANT!

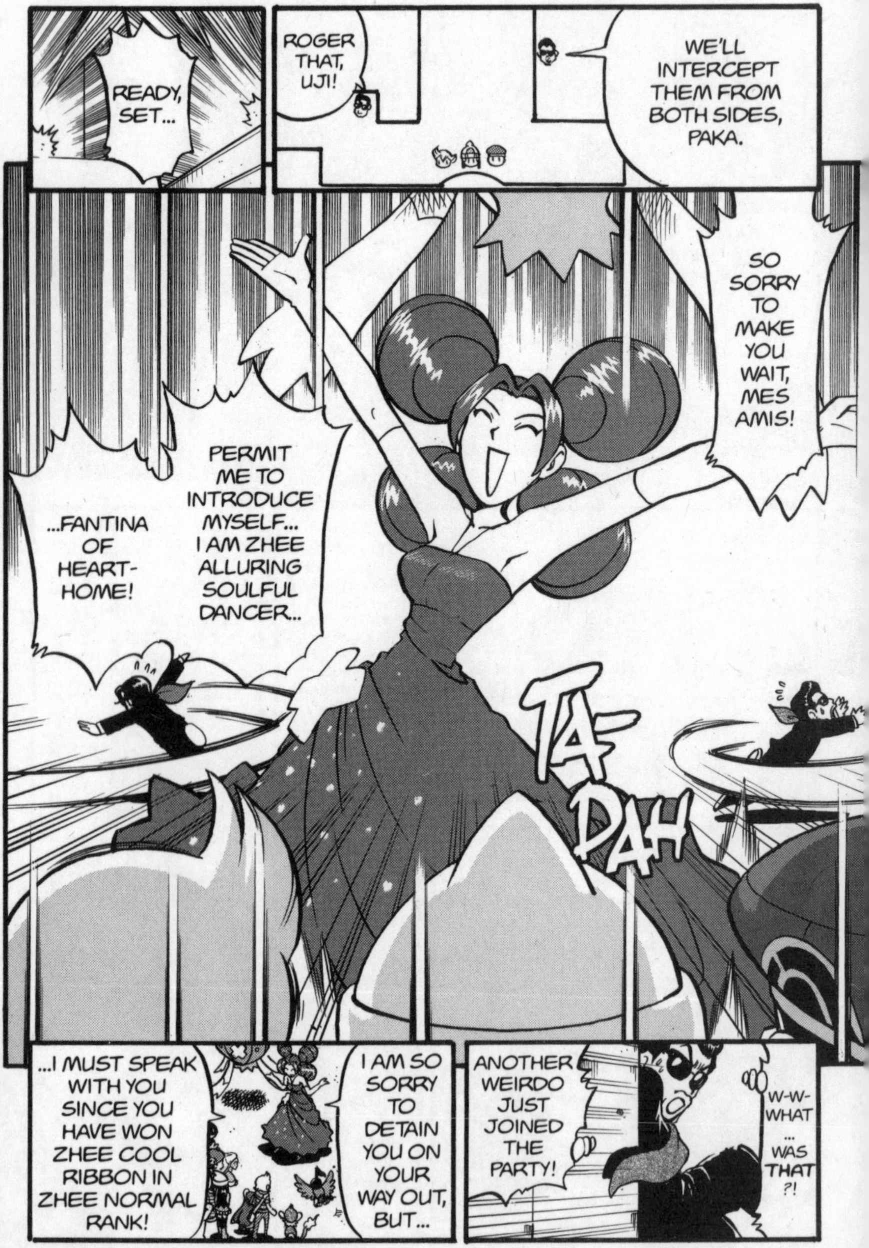
WE'LL INTERCEPT THEM FROM BOTH SIDES, PAKA.
ROGER THAT, UJI!
READY, SET...
SO SORRY TO MAKE YOU WAIT, MES AMIS!
PERMIT ME TO INTRODUCE MYSELF... I AM ZHEE ALLURING SOULFUL DANCER...
...FANTINA OF HEART-HOME!
TA-DAH
W-W-WHAT ... WAS THAT ?!
ANOTHER WEIRDO JUST JOINED THE PARTY!
I AM SO SORRY TO DETAIN YOU ON YOUR WAY OUT, BUT...
...I MUST SPEAK WITH YOU SINCE YOU HAVE WON ZHEE COOL RIBBON IN ZHEE NORMAL RANK!

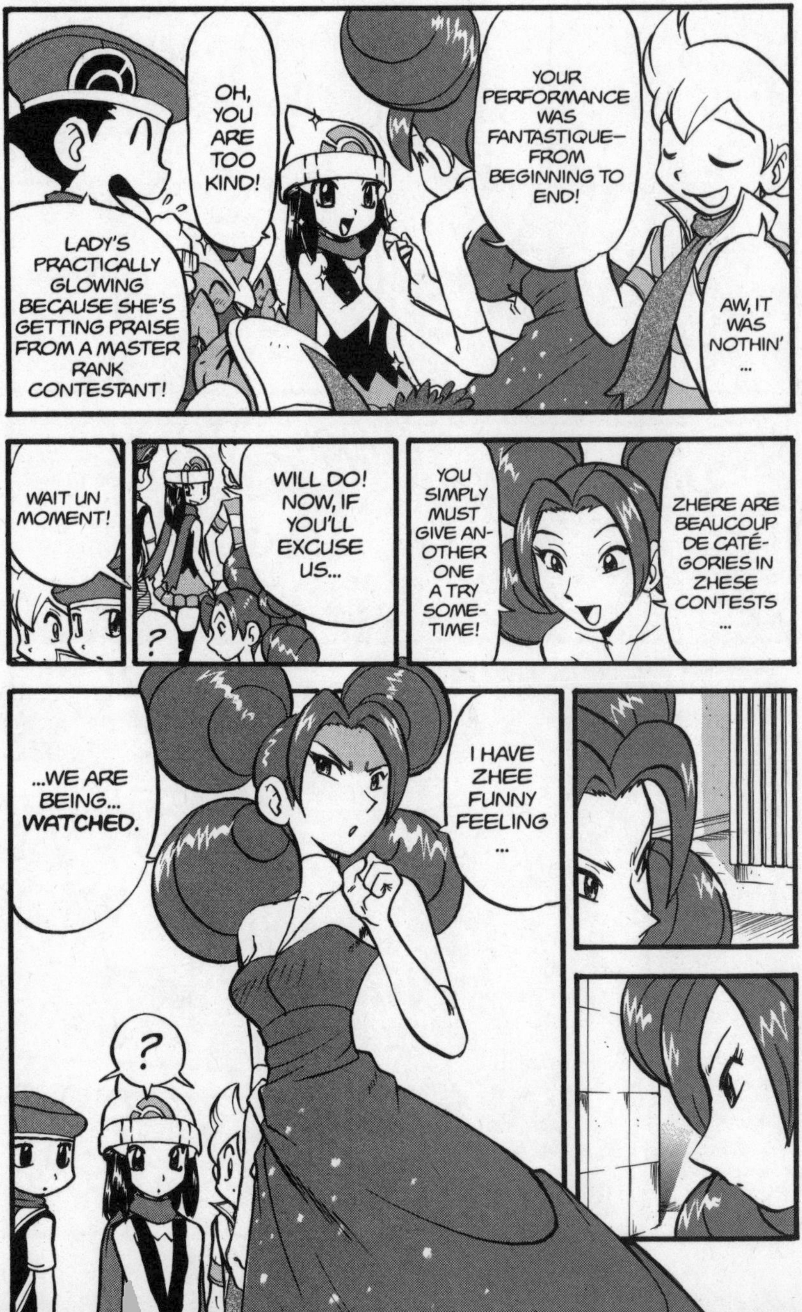
YOUR PERFORMANCE WAS FANTASTIQUE— FROM BEGINNING TO END!
AW, IT WAS NOTHIN' ...
OH, YOU ARE TOO KIND!
LADY'S PRACTICALLY GLOWING BECAUSE SHE'S GETTING PRAISE FROM A MASTER RANK CONTESTANT!
ZHERE ARE BEAUCOUP DE CATÉ-GORIES IN ZHESE CONTESTS ...
YOU SIMPLY MUST GIVE AN-OTHER ONE A TRY SOME-TIME!
WILL DO! NOW, IF YOU'LL EXCUSE US...
?
WAIT UN MOMENT!
I HAVE ZHEE FUNNY FEELING ...
...WE ARE BEING... **WATCHED.**
?

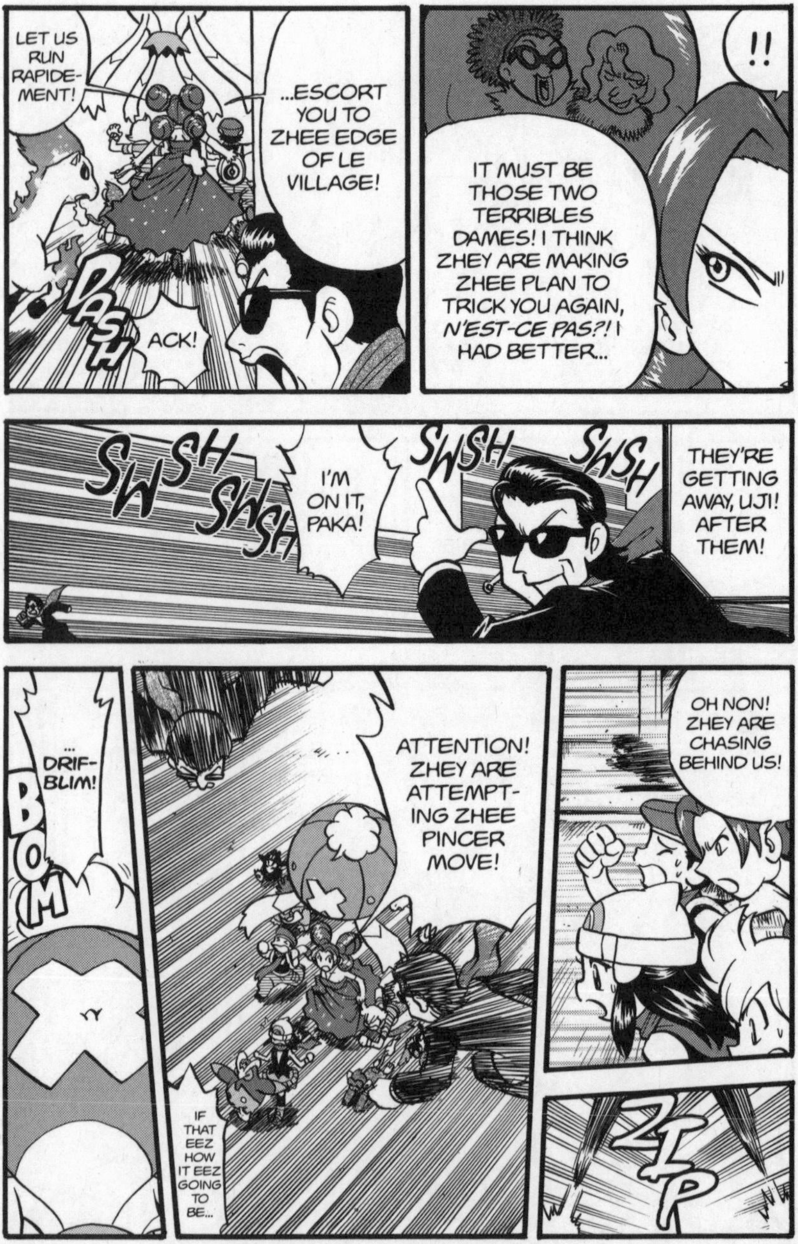
!!
IT MUST BE THOSE TWO TERRIBLES DAMES! I THINK ZHEY ARE MAKING ZHEE PLAN TO TRICK YOU AGAIN, *N'EST-CE PAS?!* I HAD BETTER...
...ESCORT YOU TO ZHEE EDGE OF LE VILLAGE!
LET US RUN RAPIDEMENT!
DASH
ACK!
THEY'RE GETTING AWAY, UJI! AFTER THEM!
SWSH
SWSH
I'M ON IT, PAKA!
SWSH
SWSH
OH NON! ZHEY ARE CHASING BEHIND US!
ZIP
ATTENTION! ZHEY ARE ATTEMPTING ZHEE PINCER MOVE!
IF THAT EEZ HOW IT EEZ GOING TO BE...
... DRIFBLIM!
BOOM

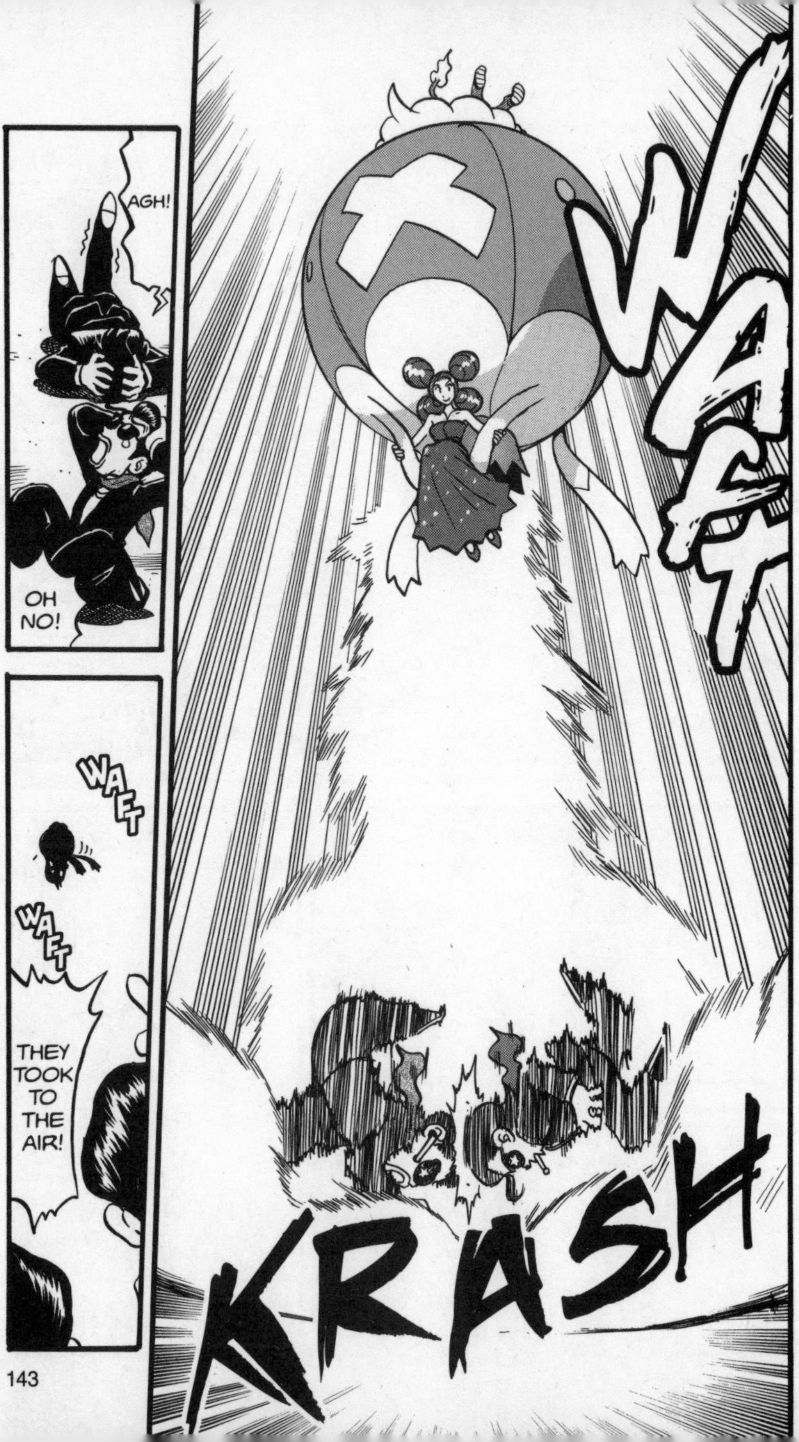
WAFT
KRASH
AGH!
OH NO!
WAFT
WAFT
THEY TOOK TO THE AIR!

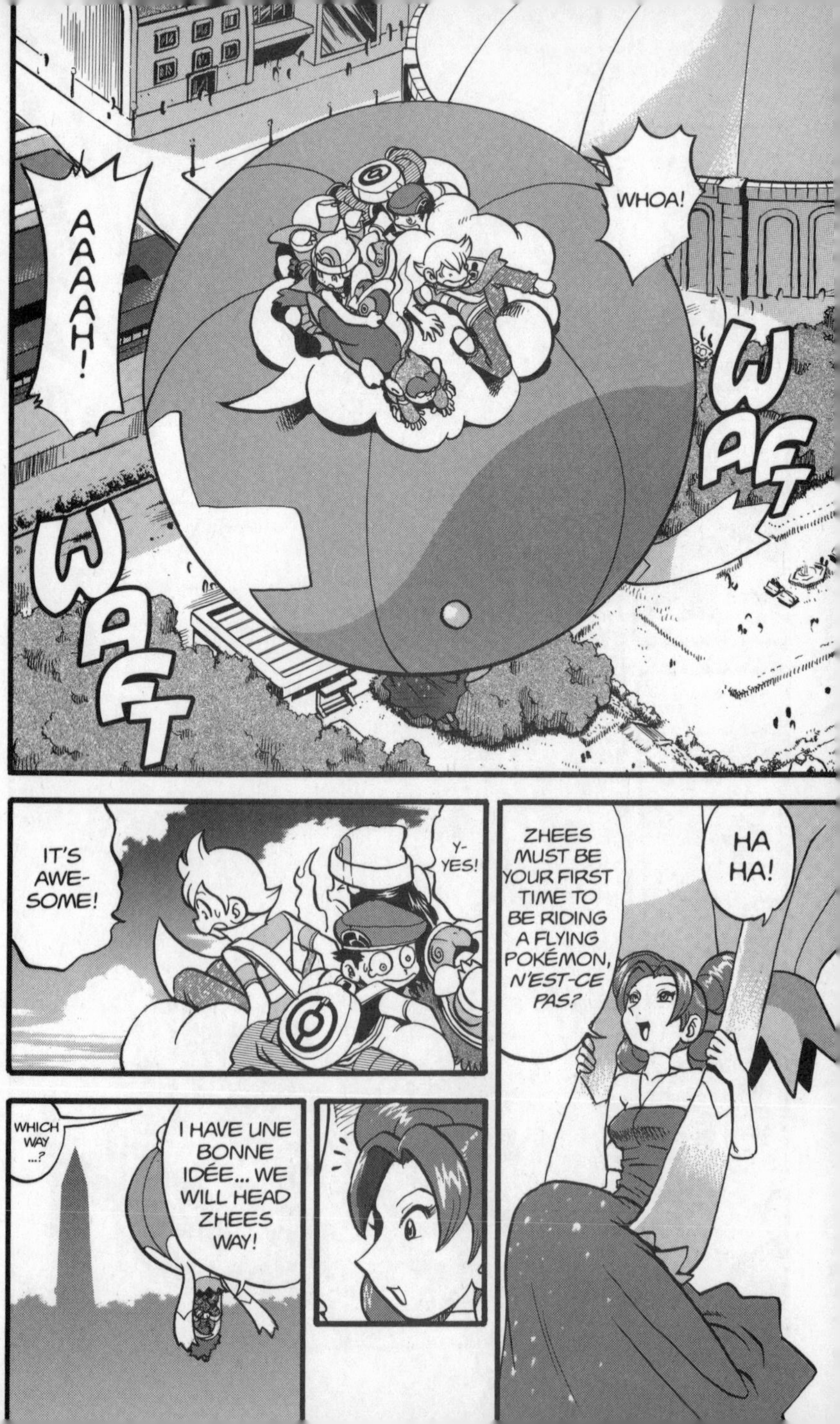
WHOA!
WAFT
AAAAAH!
WAFT
HA HA!
ZHEES MUST BE YOUR FIRST TIME TO BE RIDING A FLYING POKÉMON, N'EST-CE PAS?
Y-YES!
IT'S AWE-SOME!
WHICH WAY ...?
I HAVE UNE BONNE IDÉE... WE WILL HEAD ZHEES WAY!

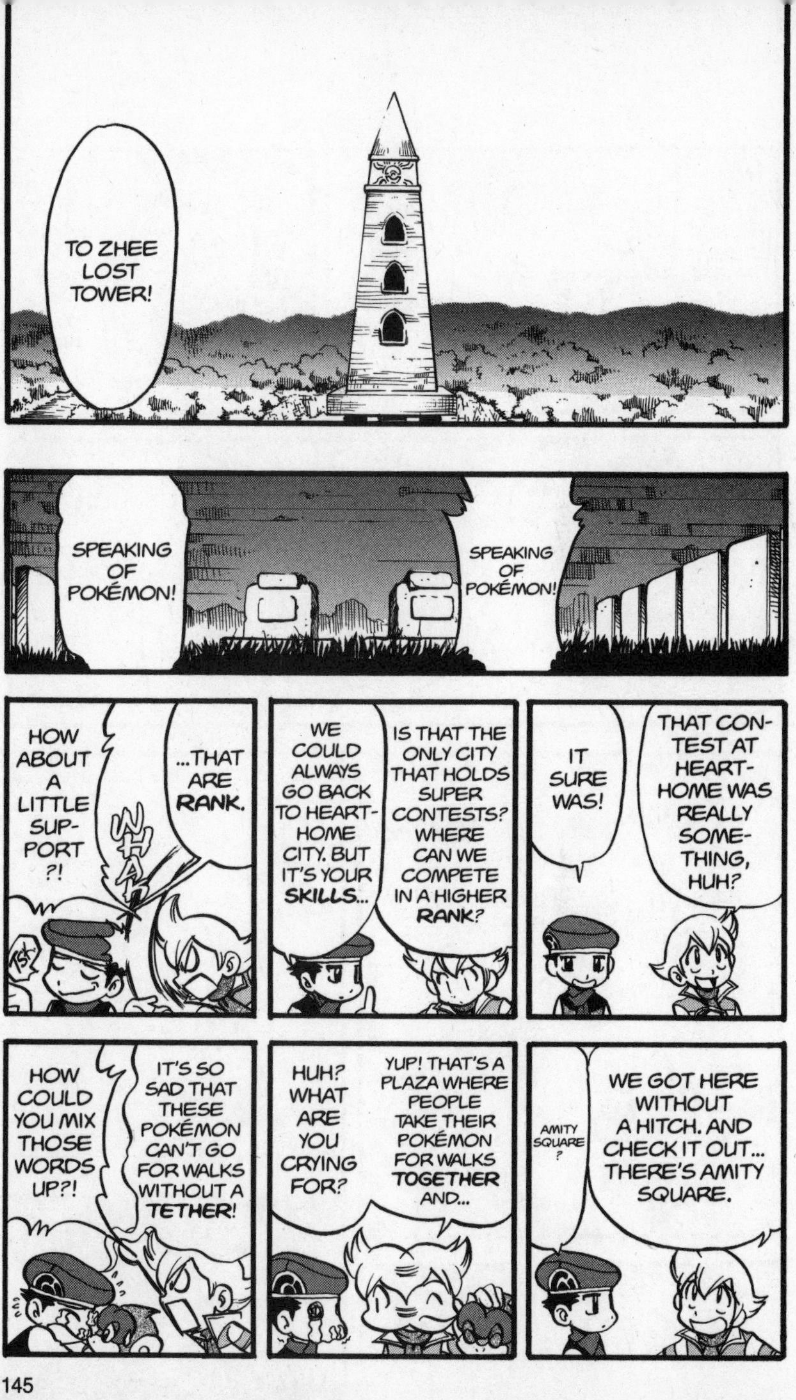
TO ZHEE LOST TOWER!
SPEAKING OF POKÉMON!
SPEAKING OF POKÉMON!
THAT CONTEST AT HEARTHOME WAS REALLY SOMETHING, HUH?
IT SURE WAS!
IS THAT THE ONLY CITY THAT HOLDS SUPER CONTESTS? WHERE CAN WE COMPETE IN A HIGHER RANK?
WE COULD ALWAYS GO BACK TO HEARTHOME CITY. BUT IT'S YOUR SKILLS...
...THAT ARE RANK.
WHAP
TSK
HOW ABOUT A LITTLE SUPPORT?!
WE GOT HERE WITHOUT A HITCH. AND CHECK IT OUT... THERE'S AMITY SQUARE.
AMITY SQUARE?
YUP! THAT'S A PLAZA WHERE PEOPLE TAKE THEIR POKÉMON FOR WALKS TOGETHER AND...
HUH? WHAT ARE YOU CRYING FOR?
IT'S SO SAD THAT THESE POKÉMON CAN'T GO FOR WALKS WITHOUT A TETHER!
HOW COULD YOU MIX THOSE WORDS UP?!

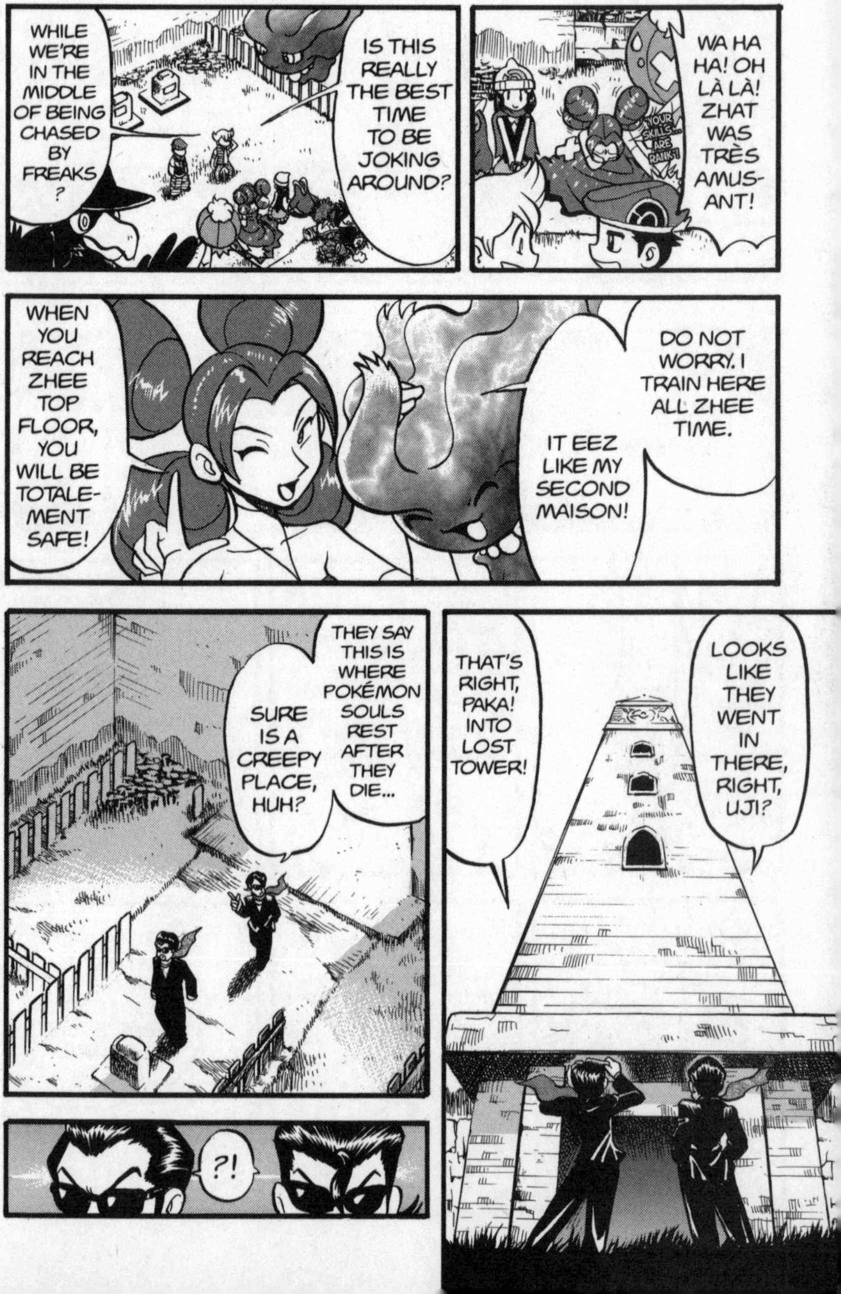
WA HA HA! OH LÀ LÀ! ZHAT WAS TRÈS AMUS-ANT!
YOUR SKILLS... ARE RANK"!
IS THIS REALLY THE BEST TIME TO BE JOKING AROUND?
WHILE WE'RE IN THE MIDDLE OF BEING CHASED BY FREAKS?
DO NOT WORRY. I TRAIN HERE ALL ZHEE TIME.
IT EEZ LIKE MY SECOND MAISON!
WHEN YOU REACH ZHEE TOP FLOOR, YOU WILL BE TOTALE-MENT SAFE!
LOOKS LIKE THEY WENT IN THERE, RIGHT, UJI?
THAT'S RIGHT, PAKA! INTO LOST TOWER!
THEY SAY THIS IS WHERE POKÉMON SOULS REST AFTER THEY DIE...
SURE IS A CREEPY PLACE, HUH?
?!

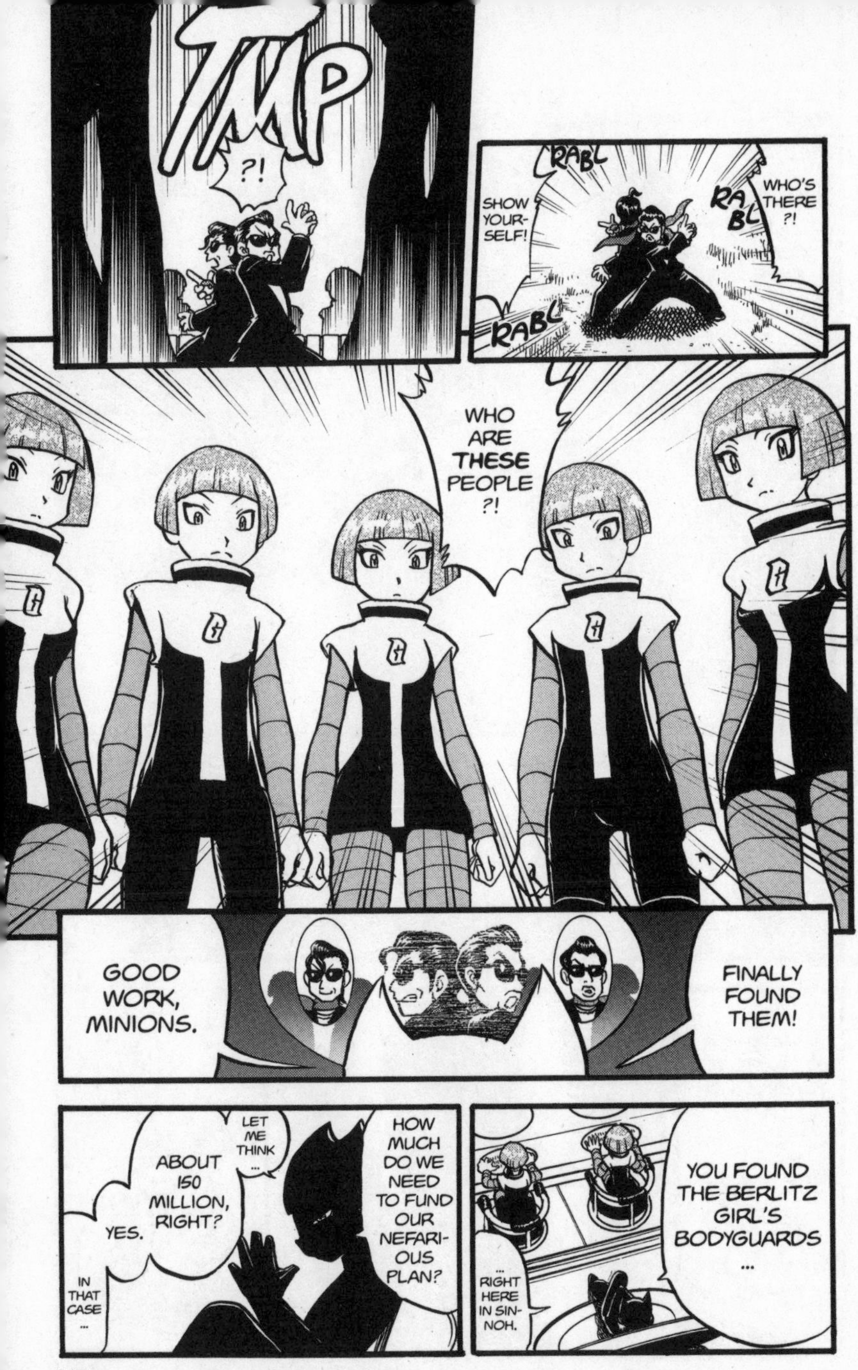
RABL
WHO'S THERE ?!
RABL
SHOW YOURSELF!
RABL
TMP
?!
WHO ARE THESE PEOPLE ?!
FINALLY FOUND THEM!
GOOD WORK, MINIONS.
YOU FOUND THE BERLITZ GIRL'S BODYGUARDS ...
... RIGHT HERE IN SINNOH.
HOW MUCH DO WE NEED TO FUND OUR NEFARIOUS PLAN?
LET ME THINK ...
ABOUT 150 MILLION, RIGHT?
YES.
IN THAT CASE ...

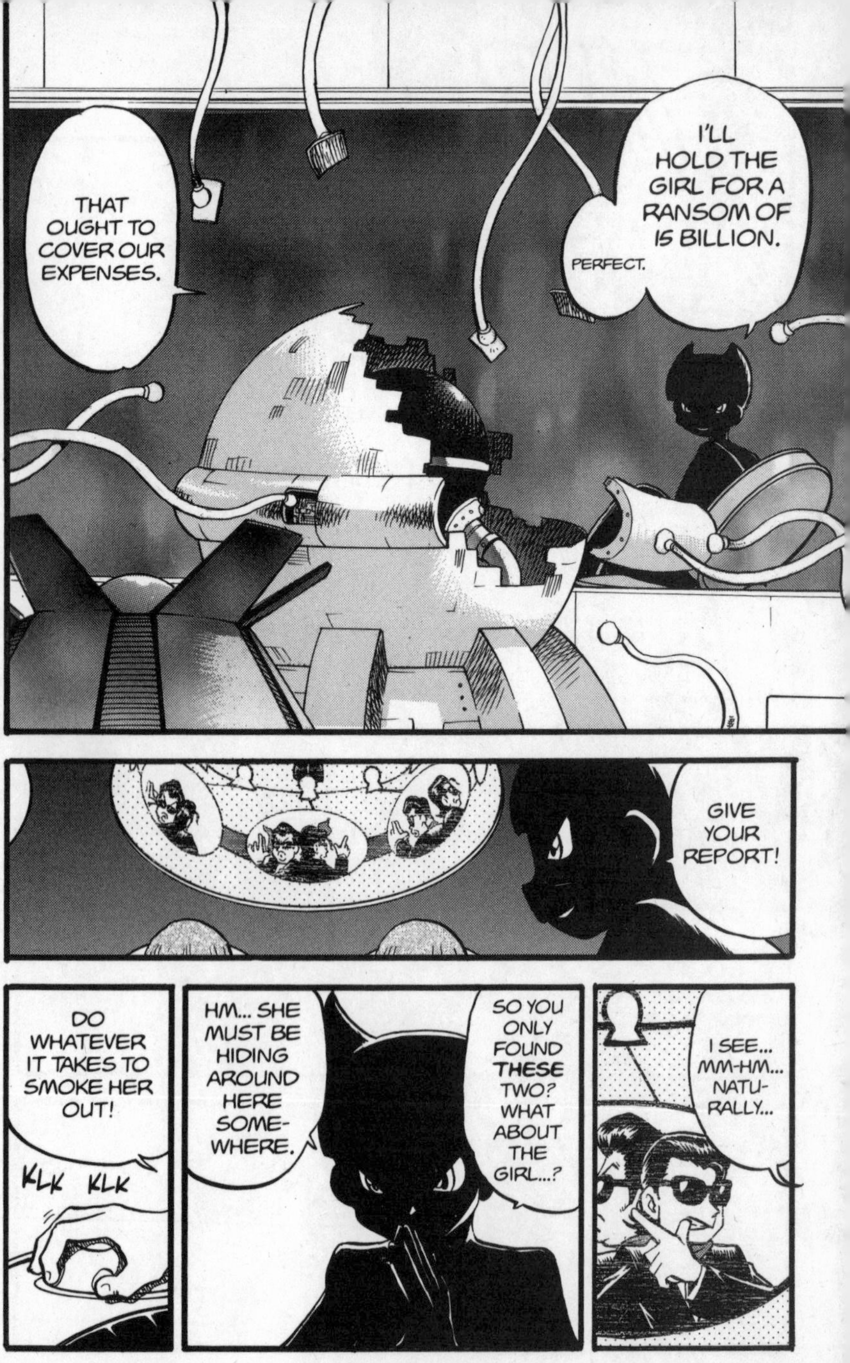
I'LL HOLD THE GIRL FOR A RANSOM OF 15 BILLION.
PERFECT.
THAT OUGHT TO COVER OUR EXPENSES.
GIVE YOUR REPORT!
I SEE... MM-HM... NATU-RALLY...
SO YOU ONLY FOUND **THESE** TWO? WHAT ABOUT THE GIRL...?
HM... SHE MUST BE HIDING AROUND HERE SOME-WHERE.
DO WHATEVER IT TAKES TO SMOKE HER OUT!
KLK KLK

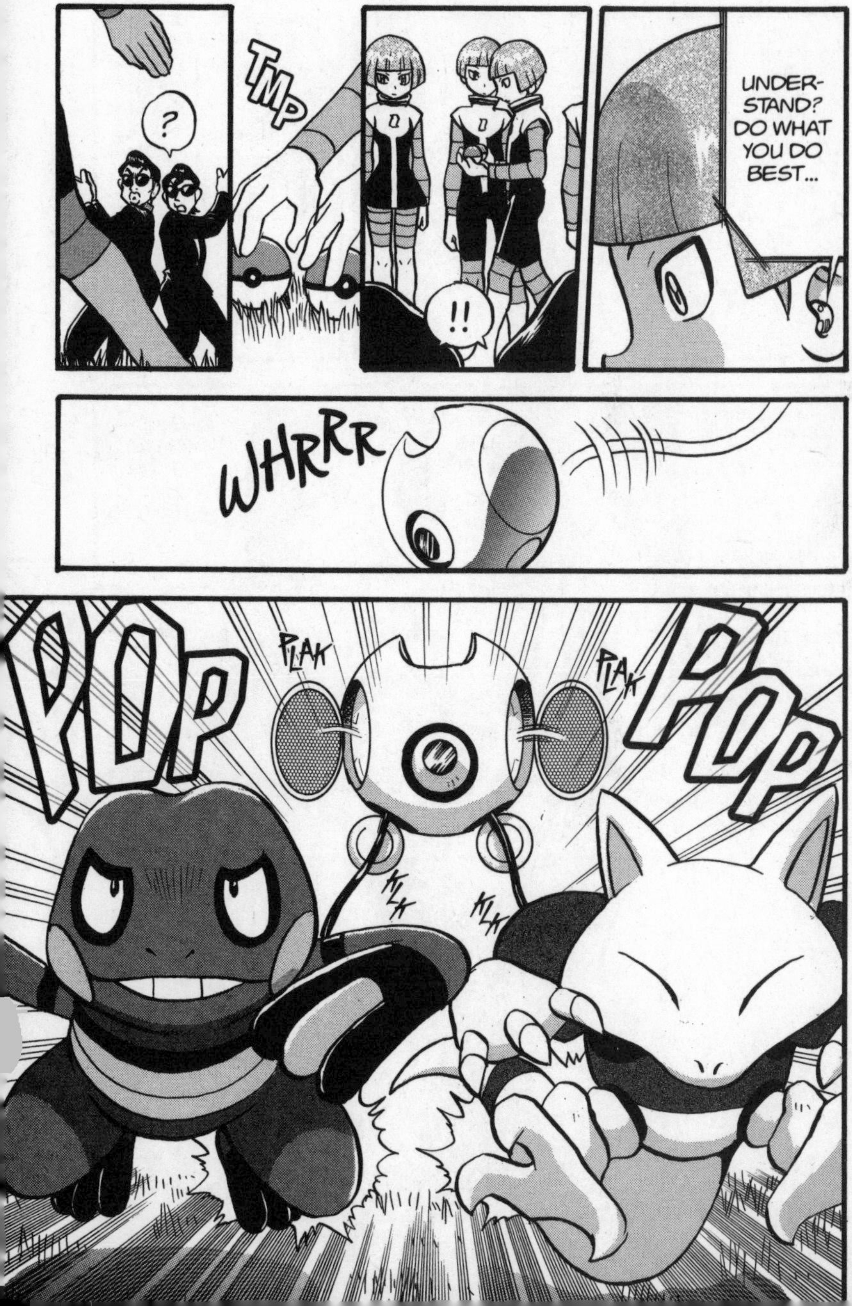
UNDER-STAND? DO WHAT YOU DO BEST...
!!
TMP
?
WHRRR
POP
PLAK
PLAK
POP
KLK
KLK

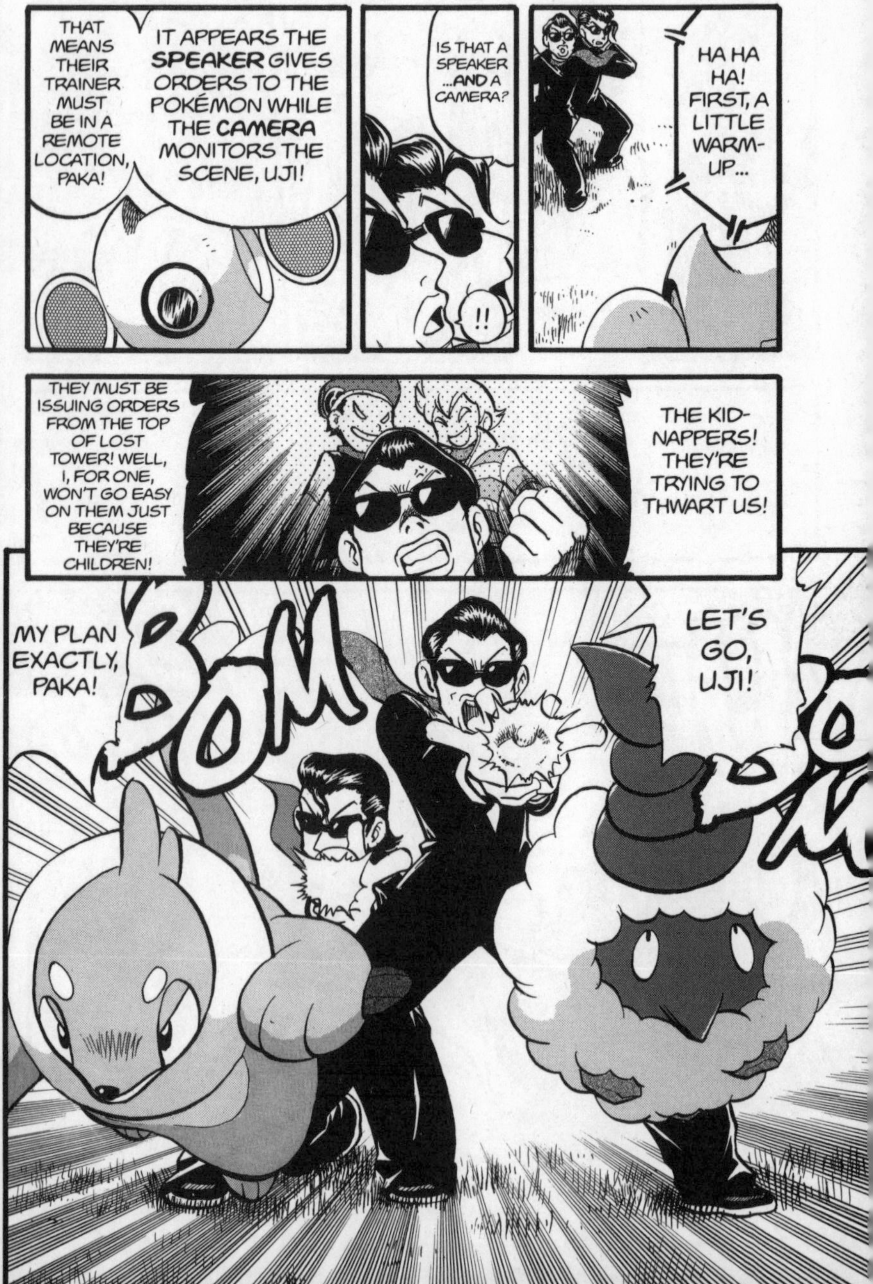
HA HA HA! FIRST, A LITTLE WARM-UP...
IS THAT A SPEAKER ...AND A CAMERA?
!!
IT APPEARS THE SPEAKER GIVES ORDERS TO THE POKÉMON WHILE THE CAMERA MONITORS THE SCENE, UJI!
THAT MEANS THEIR TRAINER MUST BE IN A REMOTE LOCATION, PAKA!
THE KID-NAPPERS! THEY'RE TRYING TO THWART US!
THEY MUST BE ISSUING ORDERS FROM THE TOP OF LOST TOWER! WELL, I, FOR ONE, WON'T GO EASY ON THEM JUST BECAUSE THEY'RE CHILDREN!
LET'S GO, UJI!
BOM
MY PLAN EXACTLY, PAKA!

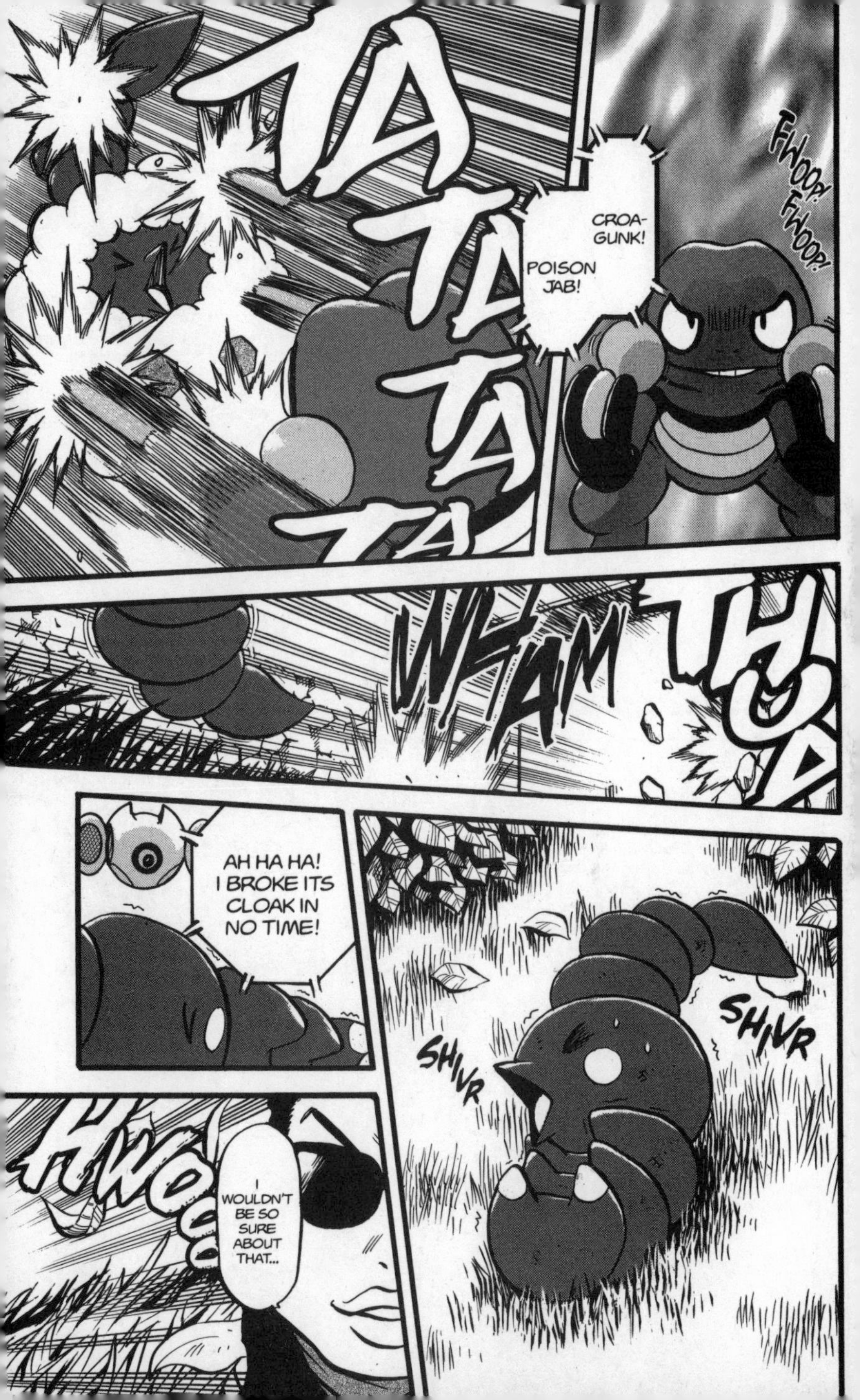
CROA-GUNK!
POISON JAB!
FWOOP! FWOOP!
TA TA TA TA TA
WHAM
SHIVR
SHIVR
AH HA HA! I BROKE ITS CLOAK IN NO TIME!
I WOULDN'T BE SO SURE ABOUT THAT...

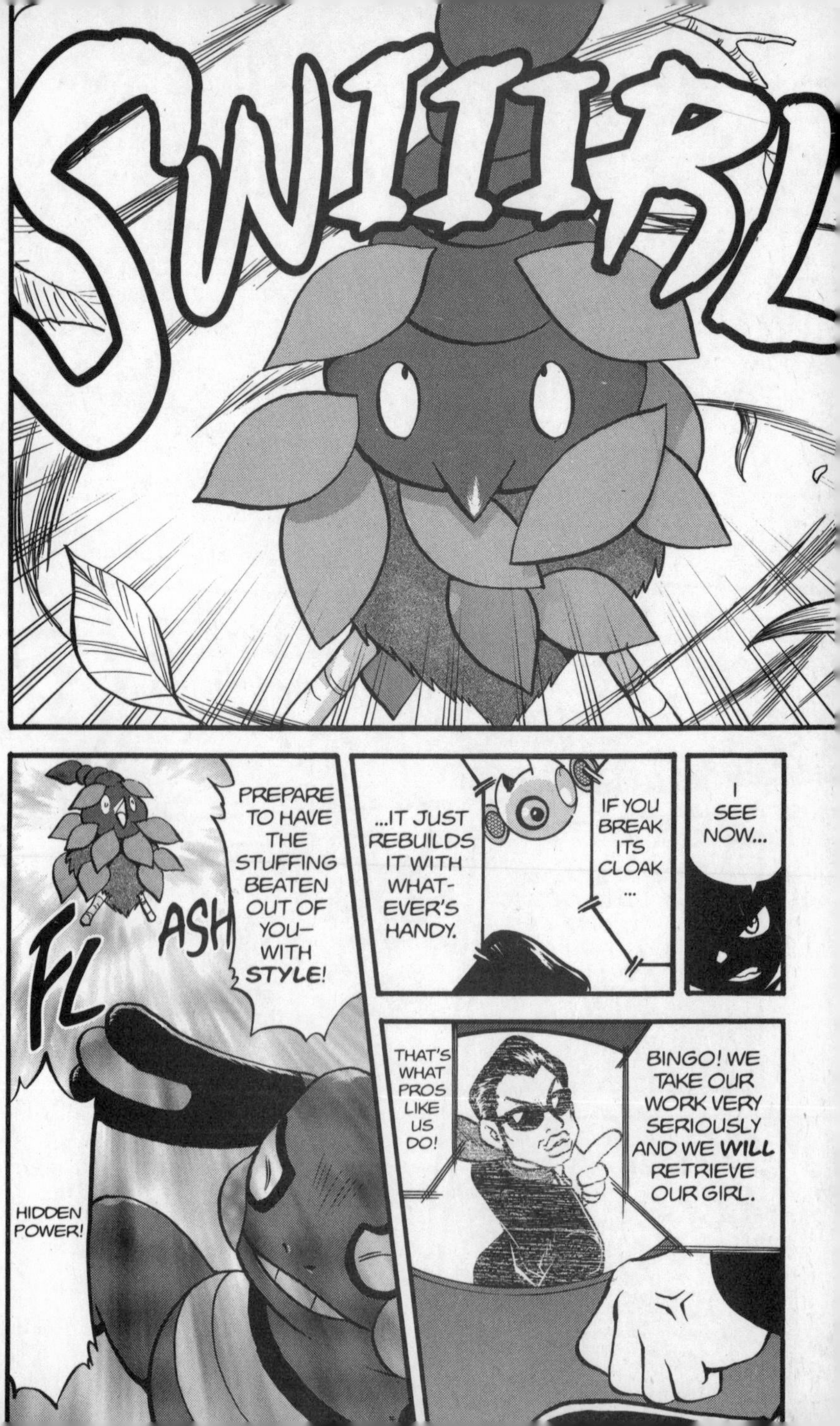
SWIIIRL
I SEE NOW...
IF YOU BREAK ITS CLOAK...
...IT JUST REBUILDS IT WITH WHATEVER'S HANDY.
BINGO! WE TAKE OUR WORK VERY SERIOUSLY AND WE **WILL** RETRIEVE OUR GIRL.
THAT'S WHAT PROS LIKE US DO!
PREPARE TO HAVE THE STUFFING BEATEN OUT OF YOU—WITH **STYLE!**
FLASH
HIDDEN POWER!

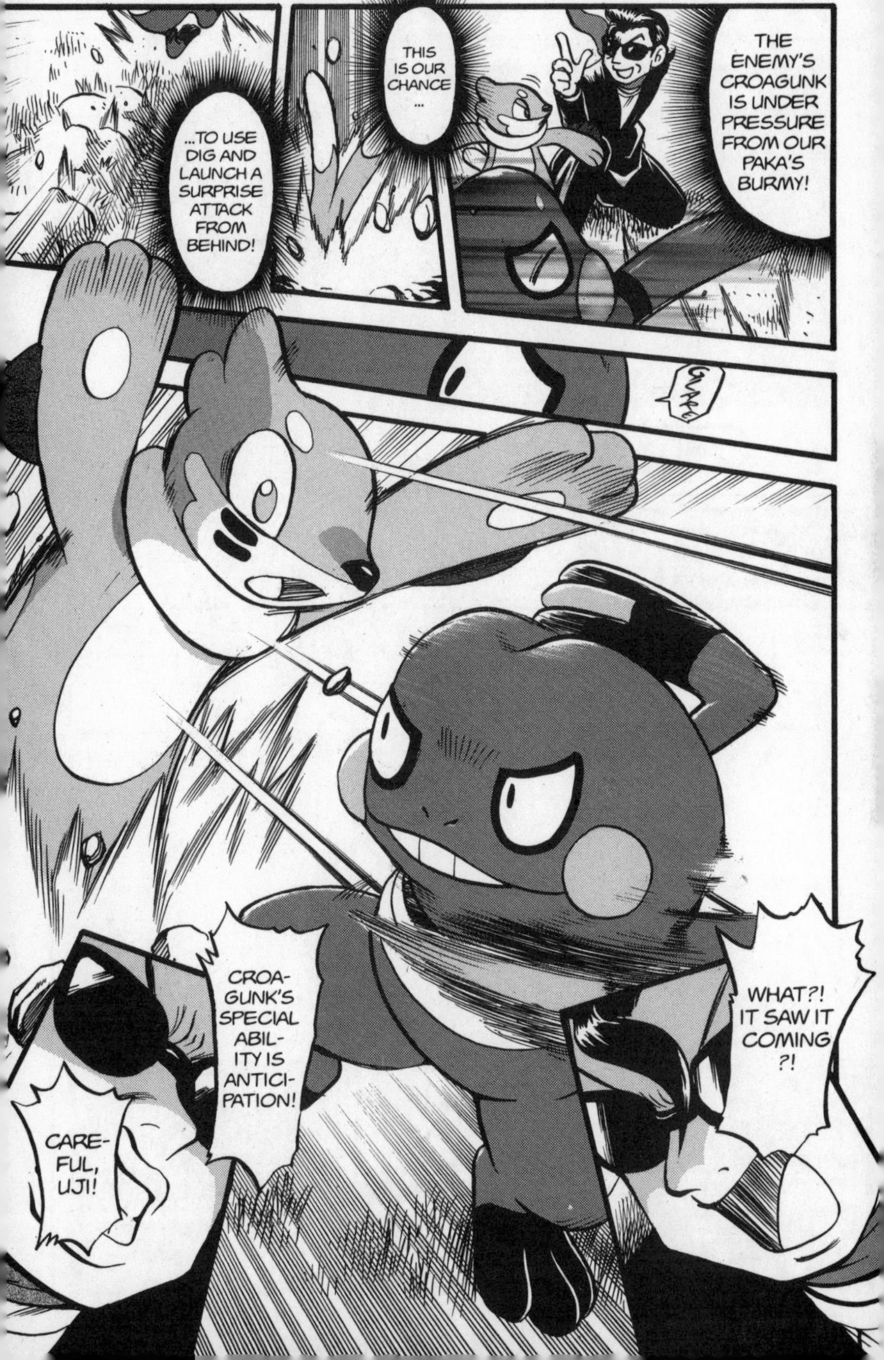
THE ENEMY'S CROAGUNK IS UNDER PRESSURE FROM OUR PAKA'S BURMY!
THIS IS OUR CHANCE ...
...TO USE DIG AND LAUNCH A SURPRISE ATTACK FROM BEHIND!
WHAT?! IT SAW IT COMING?!
CROA-GUNK'S SPECIAL ABIL-ITY IS ANTICI-PATION!
CARE-FUL, UJI!

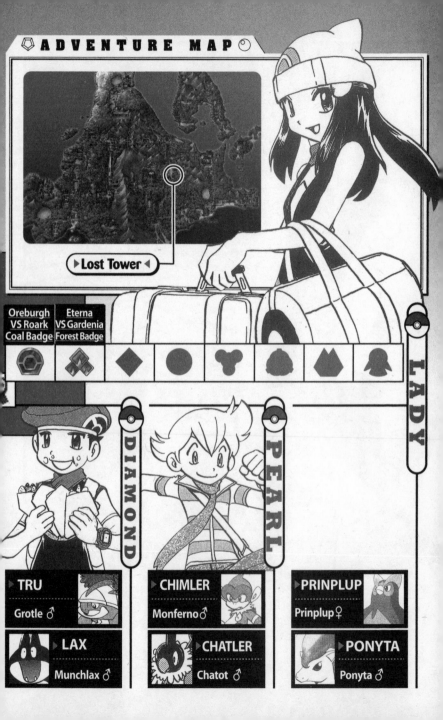

◇ ADVENTURE MAP ◎

▶ Lost Tower ◀

Oreburgh VS Roark Coal Badge	Eterna VS Gardenia Forest Badge						

LADY

DIAMOND

PEARL

▶ **TRU**
Grotle ♂

▶ **LAX**
Munchlax ♂

▶ **CHIMLER**
Monferno ♂

▶ **CHATLER**
Chatot ♂

▶ **PRINPLUP**
Prinplup ♀

▶ **PONYTA**
Ponyta ♂

16

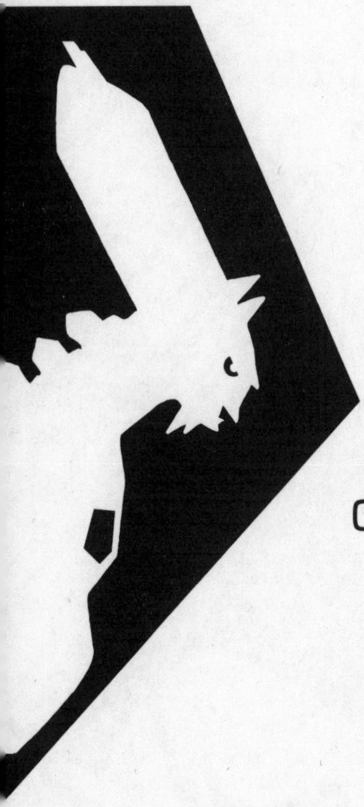

Crowded by Croagunk & Advanced on by Abra, Part II

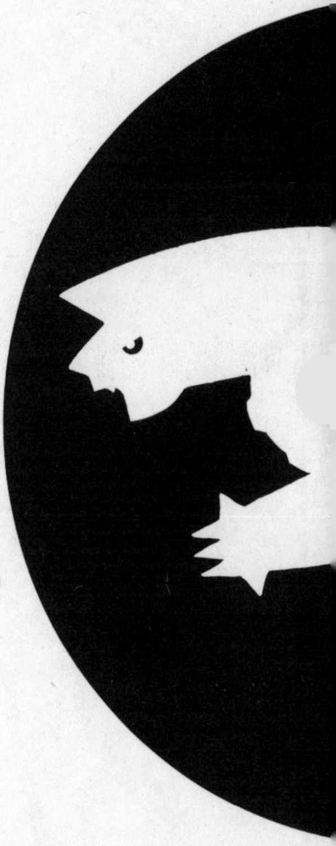

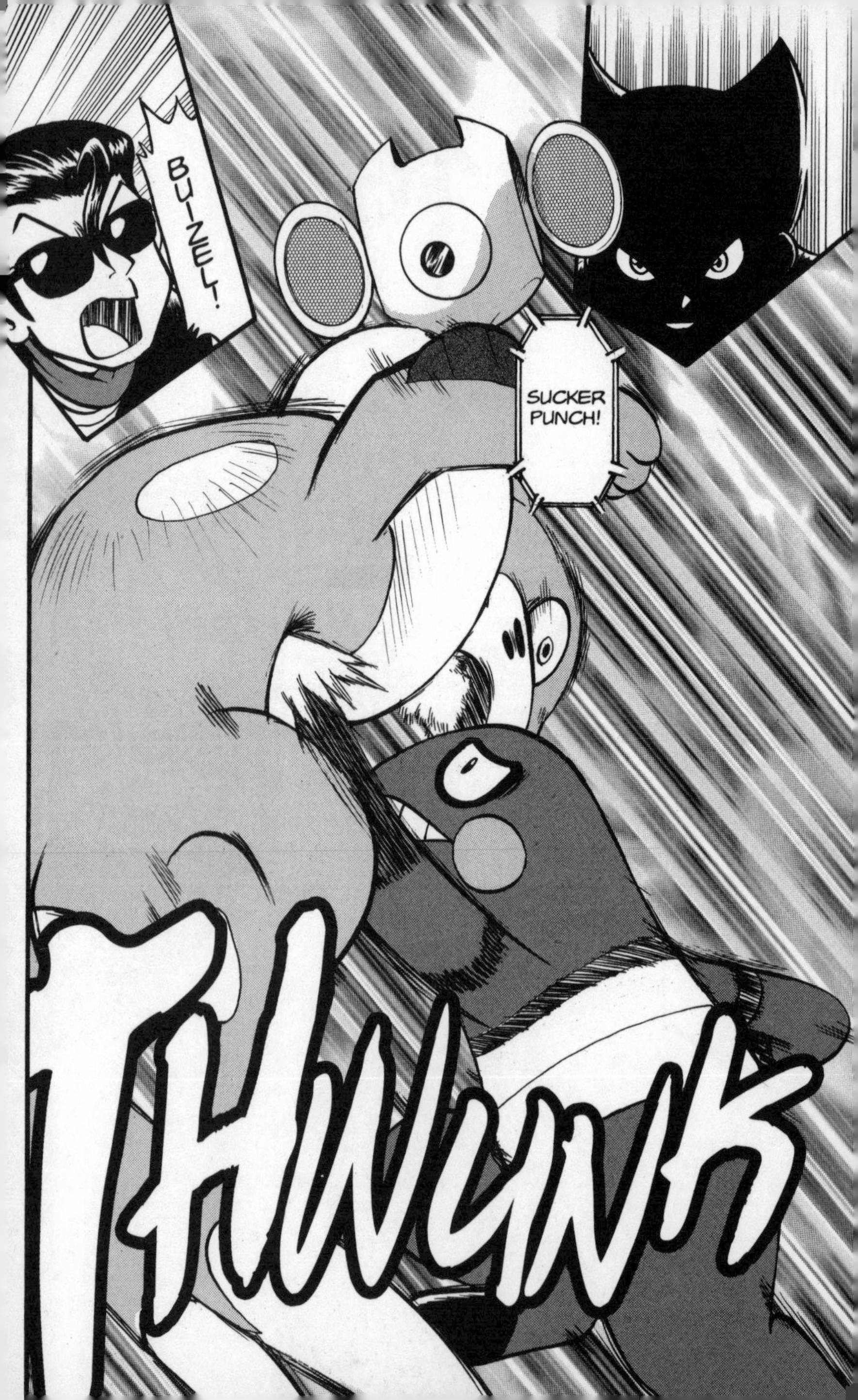
BUIZEL!
SUCKER PUNCH!
THWUNK

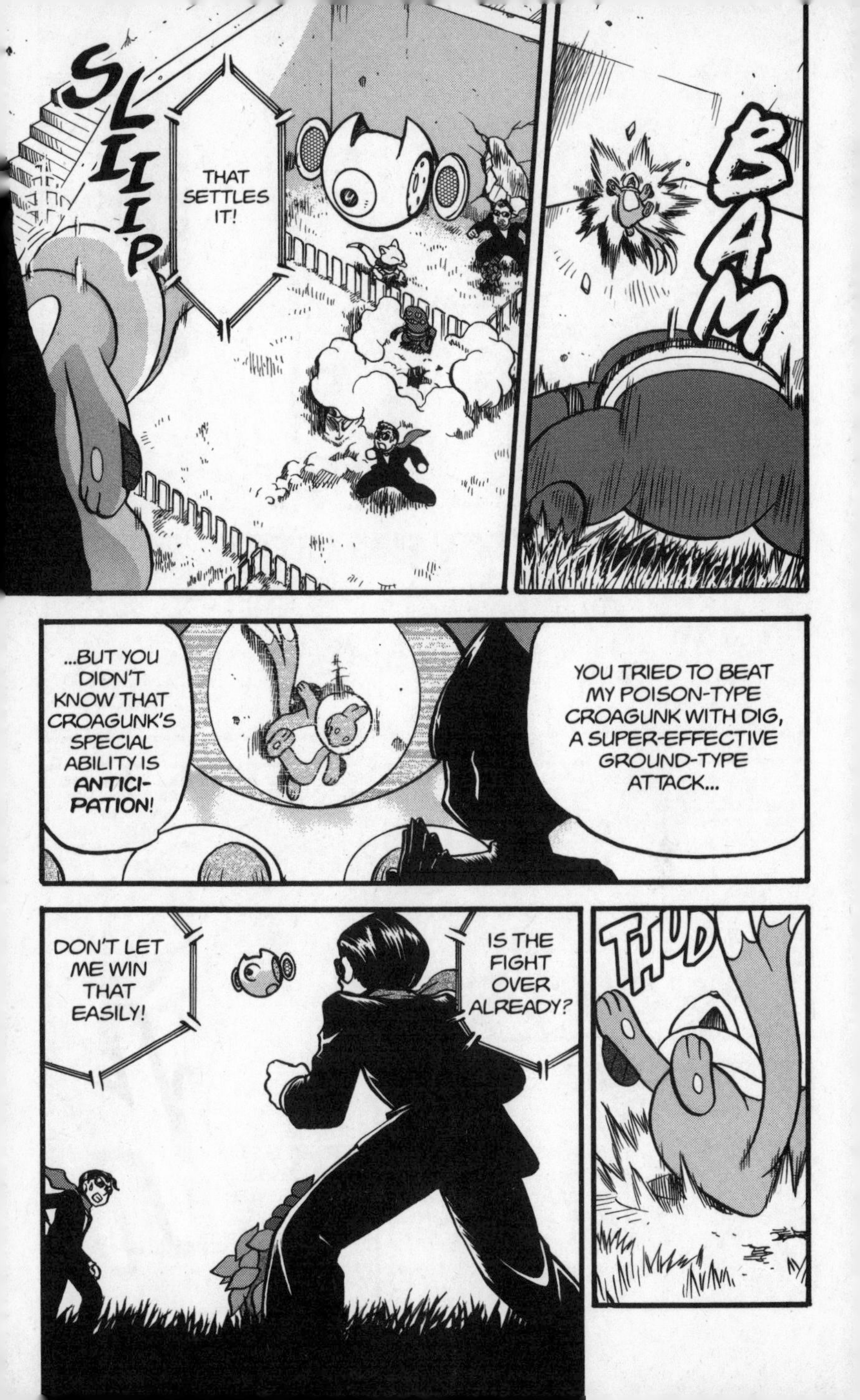
BAM
THAT SETTLES IT!
SLIIIP
YOU TRIED TO BEAT MY POISON-TYPE CROAGUNK WITH DIG, A SUPER-EFFECTIVE GROUND-TYPE ATTACK...
...BUT YOU DIDN'T KNOW THAT CROAGUNK'S SPECIAL ABILITY IS **ANTICIPATION!**
THUD
IS THE FIGHT OVER ALREADY?
DON'T LET ME WIN THAT EASILY!

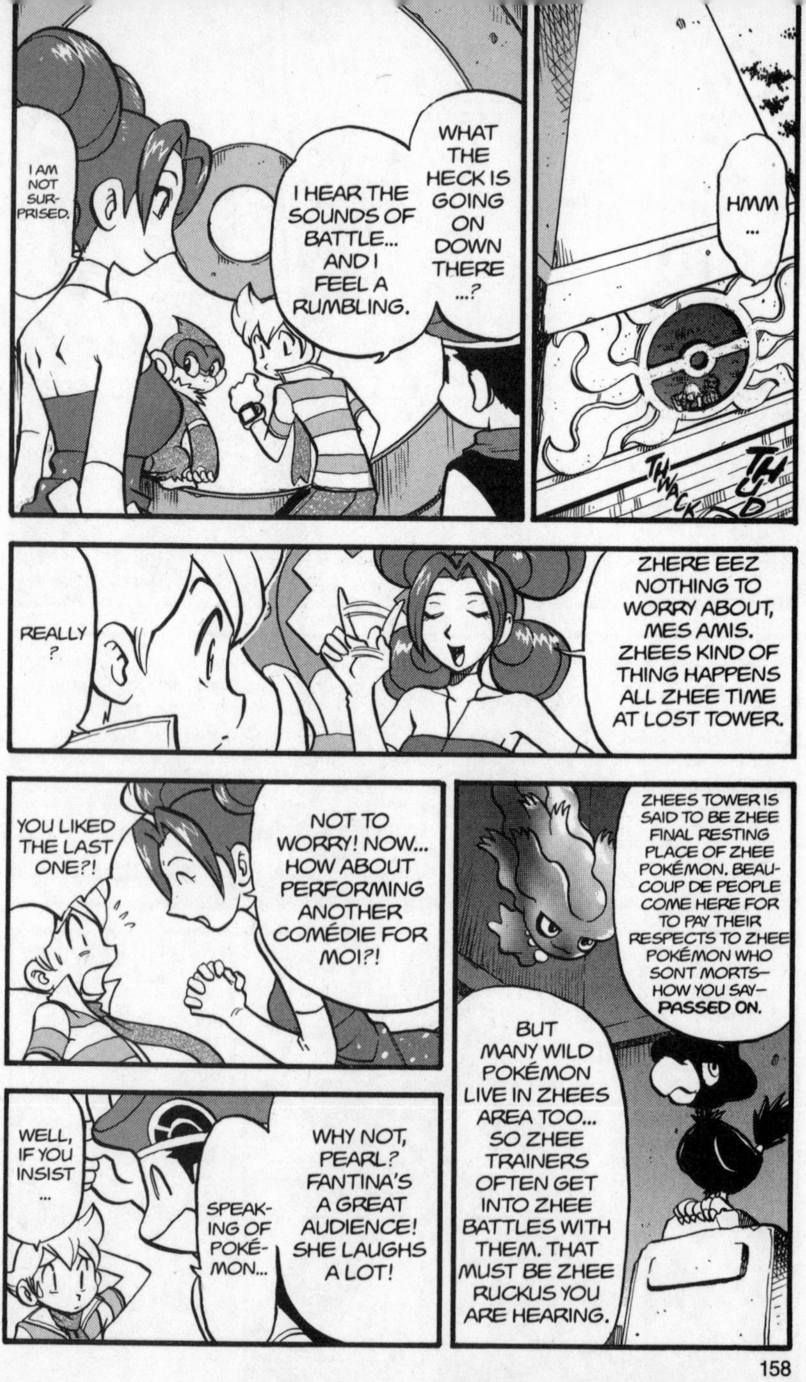
HMM...
THWACK
THUD
WHAT THE HECK IS GOING ON DOWN THERE ...?
I HEAR THE SOUNDS OF BATTLE... AND I FEEL A RUMBLING.
I AM NOT SURPRISED.
ZHERE EEZ NOTHING TO WORRY ABOUT, MES AMIS. ZHEES KIND OF THING HAPPENS ALL ZHEE TIME AT LOST TOWER.
REALLY?
ZHEES TOWER IS SAID TO BE ZHEE FINAL RESTING PLACE OF ZHEE POKÉMON. BEAUCOUP DE PEOPLE COME HERE FOR TO PAY THEIR RESPECTS TO ZHEE POKÉMON WHO SONT MORTS—HOW YOU SAY—PASSED ON.
BUT MANY WILD POKÉMON LIVE IN ZHEES AREA TOO... SO ZHEE TRAINERS OFTEN GET INTO ZHEE BATTLES WITH THEM. THAT MUST BE ZHEE RUCKUS YOU ARE HEARING.
NOT TO WORRY! NOW... HOW ABOUT PERFORMING ANOTHER COMÉDIE FOR MOI?!
YOU LIKED THE LAST ONE?!
WHY NOT, PEARL? FANTINA'S A GREAT AUDIENCE! SHE LAUGHS A LOT!
SPEAKING OF POKÉMON...
WELL, IF YOU INSIST...

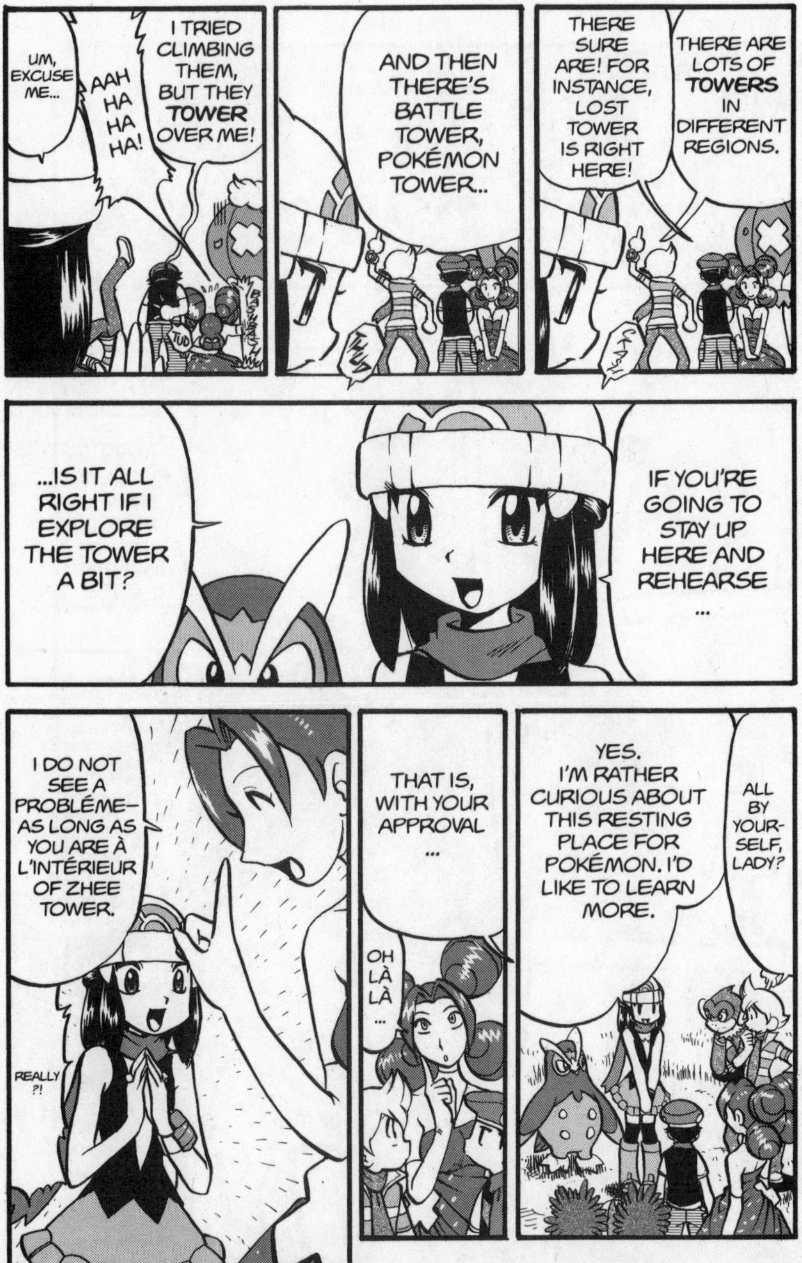
THERE ARE LOTS OF TOWERS IN DIFFERENT REGIONS.
THERE SURE ARE! FOR INSTANCE, LOST TOWER IS RIGHT HERE!
CLASH
AND THEN THERE'S BATTLE TOWER, POKÉMON TOWER...
THUD
I TRIED CLIMBING THEM, BUT THEY TOWER OVER ME!
AAH HA HA HA!
UM, EXCUSE ME...
TUD
IF YOU'RE GOING TO STAY UP HERE AND REHEARSE ...
...IS IT ALL RIGHT IF I EXPLORE THE TOWER A BIT?
ALL BY YOURSELF, LADY?
YES. I'M RATHER CURIOUS ABOUT THIS RESTING PLACE FOR POKÉMON. I'D LIKE TO LEARN MORE.
THAT IS, WITH YOUR APPROVAL ...
OH LÀ LÀ ...
I DO NOT SEE A PROBLÉME—AS LONG AS YOU ARE À L'INTÉRIEUR OF ZHEE TOWER.
REALLY ?!

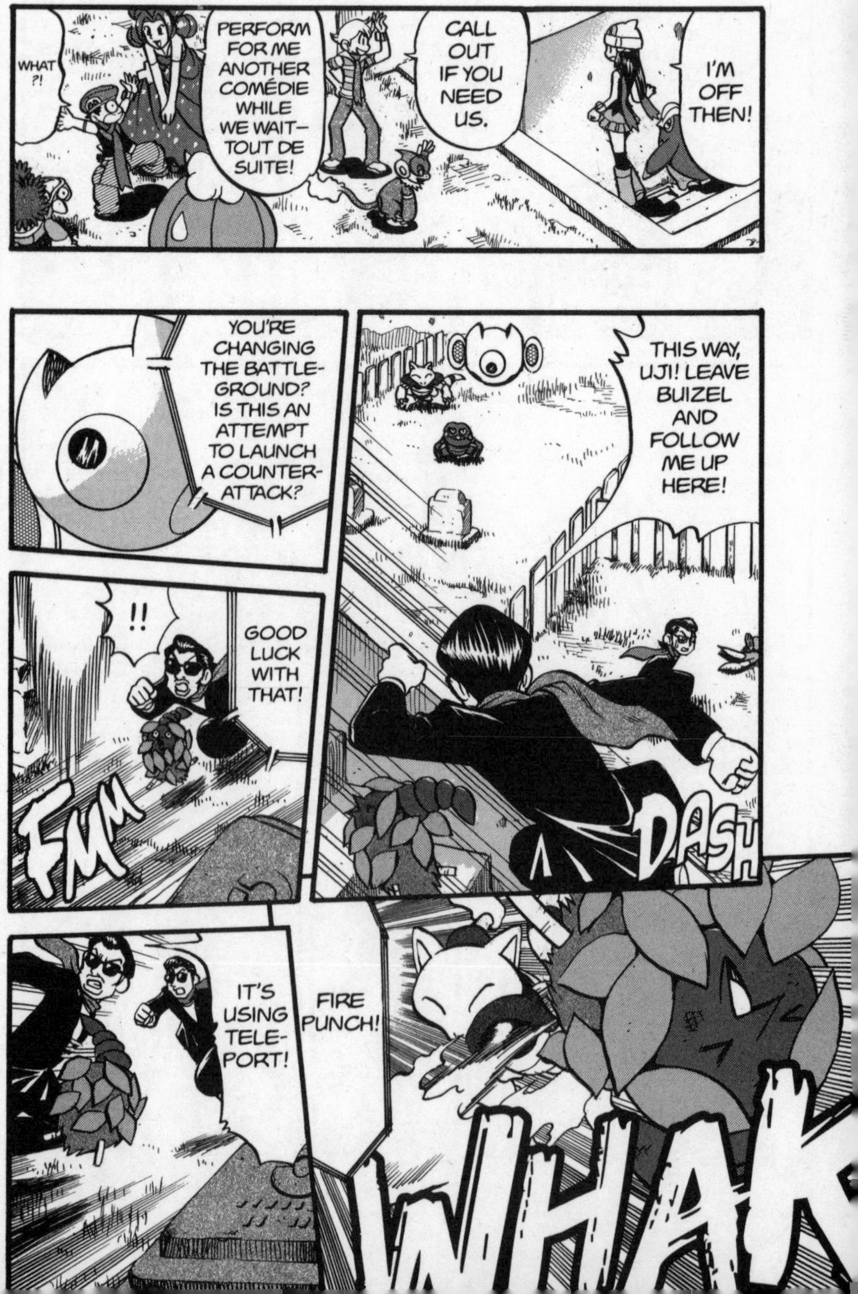
I'M OFF THEN!
CALL OUT IF YOU NEED US.
PERFORM FOR ME ANOTHER COMÉDIE WHILE WE WAIT—TOUT DE SUITE!
WHAT?!
THIS WAY, UJI! LEAVE BUIZEL AND FOLLOW ME UP HERE!
DASH
YOU'RE CHANGING THE BATTLE-GROUND? IS THIS AN ATTEMPT TO LAUNCH A COUNTER-ATTACK?
!!
GOOD LUCK WITH THAT!
FMM
FIRE PUNCH!
WHAK
IT'S USING TELE-PORT!

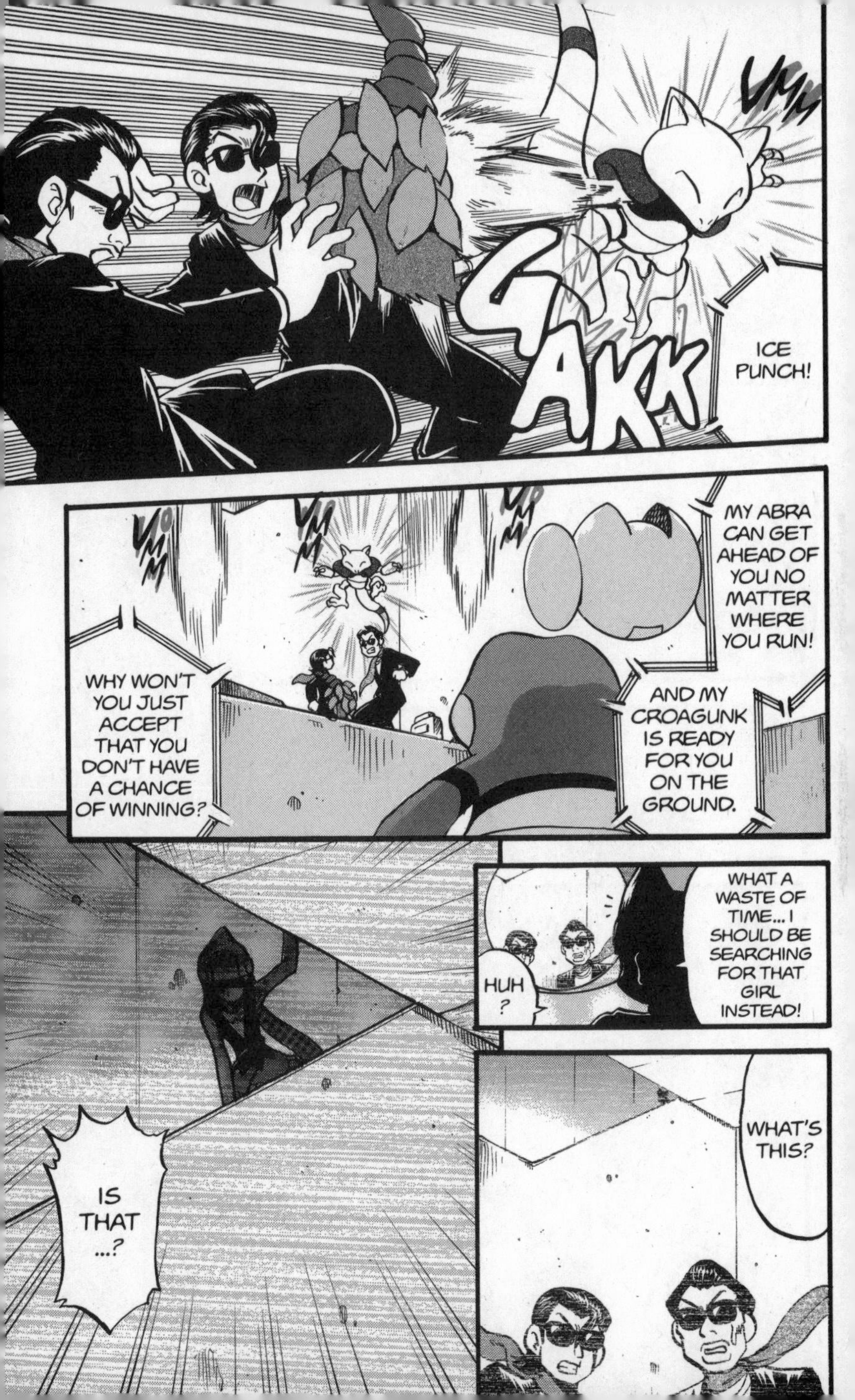
VMM
GAKK
ICE PUNCH!
MY ABRA CAN GET AHEAD OF YOU NO MATTER WHERE YOU RUN!
AND MY CROAGUNK IS READY FOR YOU ON THE GROUND.
WHY WON'T YOU JUST ACCEPT THAT YOU DON'T HAVE A CHANCE OF WINNING?
WHAT A WASTE OF TIME... I SHOULD BE SEARCHING FOR THAT GIRL INSTEAD!
HUH?
WHAT'S THIS?
IS THAT ...?

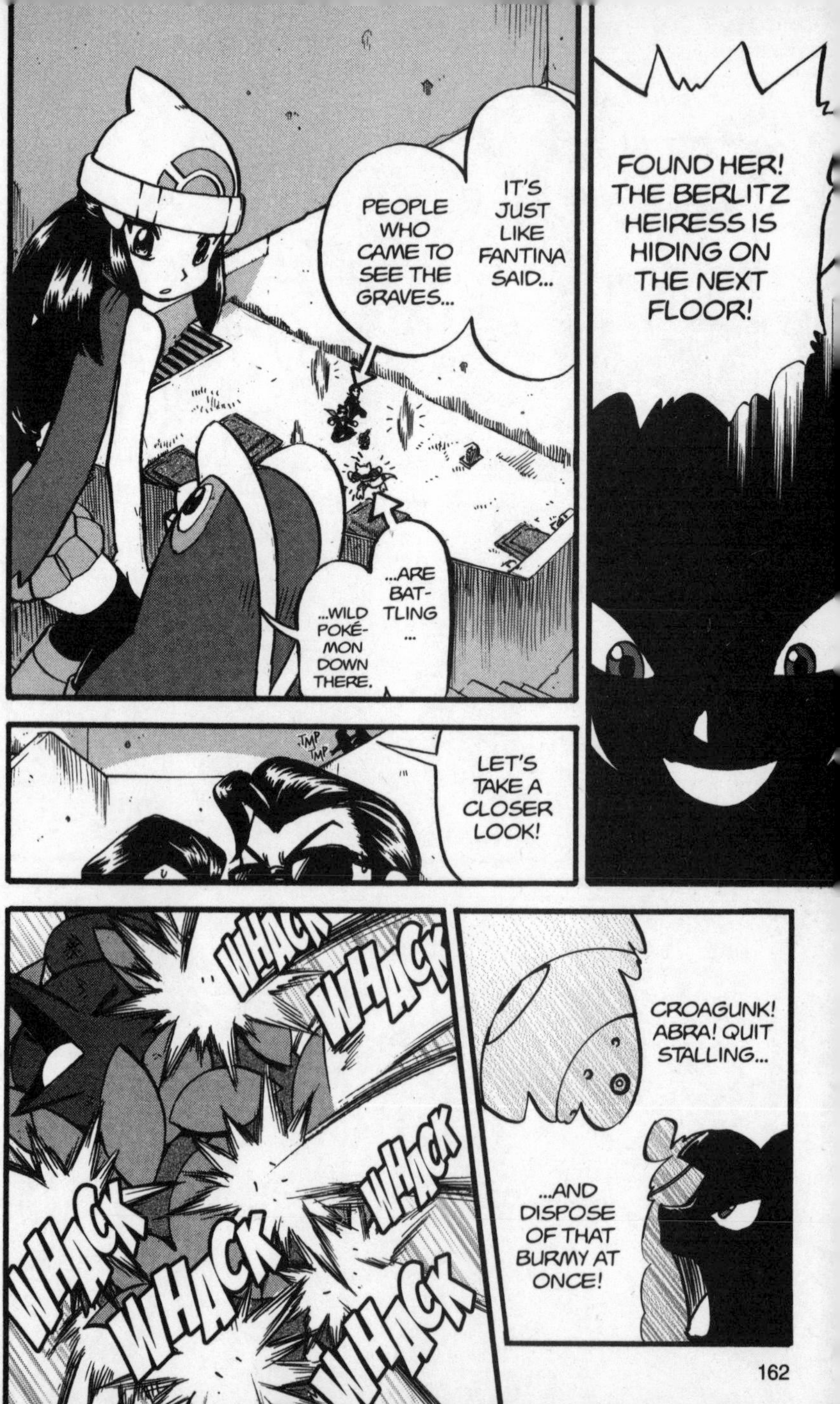
FOUND HER! THE BERLITZ HEIRESS IS HIDING ON THE NEXT FLOOR!
IT'S JUST LIKE FANTINA SAID...
PEOPLE WHO CAME TO SEE THE GRAVES...
...ARE BATTLING...
...WILD POKÉMON DOWN THERE.
TMP TMP
LET'S TAKE A CLOSER LOOK!
CROAGUNK! ABRA! QUIT STALLING...
...AND DISPOSE OF THAT BURMY AT ONCE!
WHACK
WHACK
WHACK
WHACK
WHACK
WHACK

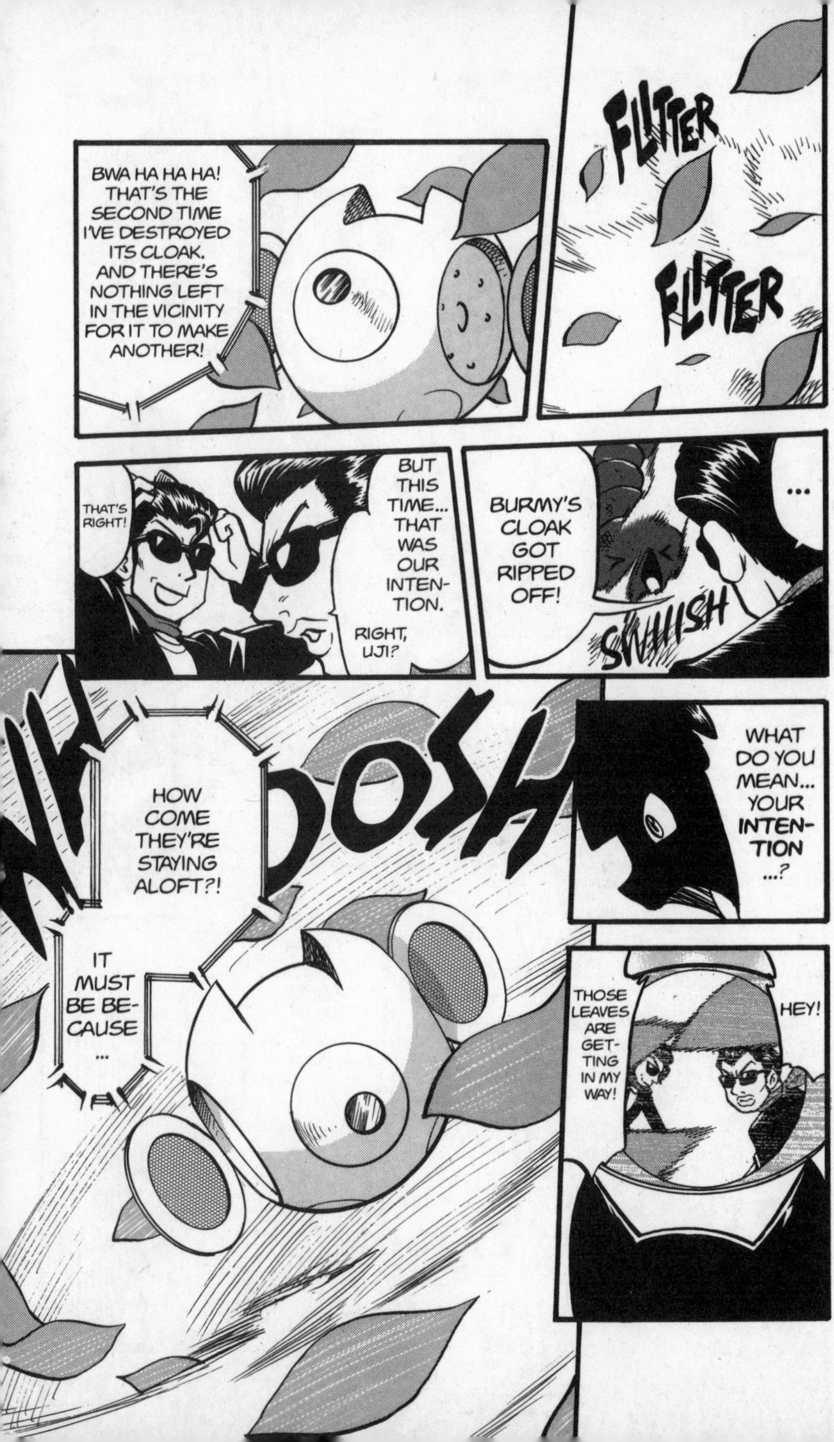
FLITTER
FLITTER
BWA HA HA HA! THAT'S THE SECOND TIME I'VE DESTROYED ITS CLOAK. AND THERE'S NOTHING LEFT IN THE VICINITY FOR IT TO MAKE ANOTHER!
...
BURMY'S CLOAK GOT RIPPED OFF!
SWIISH
BUT THIS TIME... THAT WAS OUR INTENTION.
RIGHT, UJI?
THAT'S RIGHT!
WHAT DO YOU MEAN... YOUR INTENTION ...?
HEY!
THOSE LEAVES ARE GETTING IN MY WAY!
HOW COME THEY'RE STAYING ALOFT?!
IT MUST BE BECAUSE ...

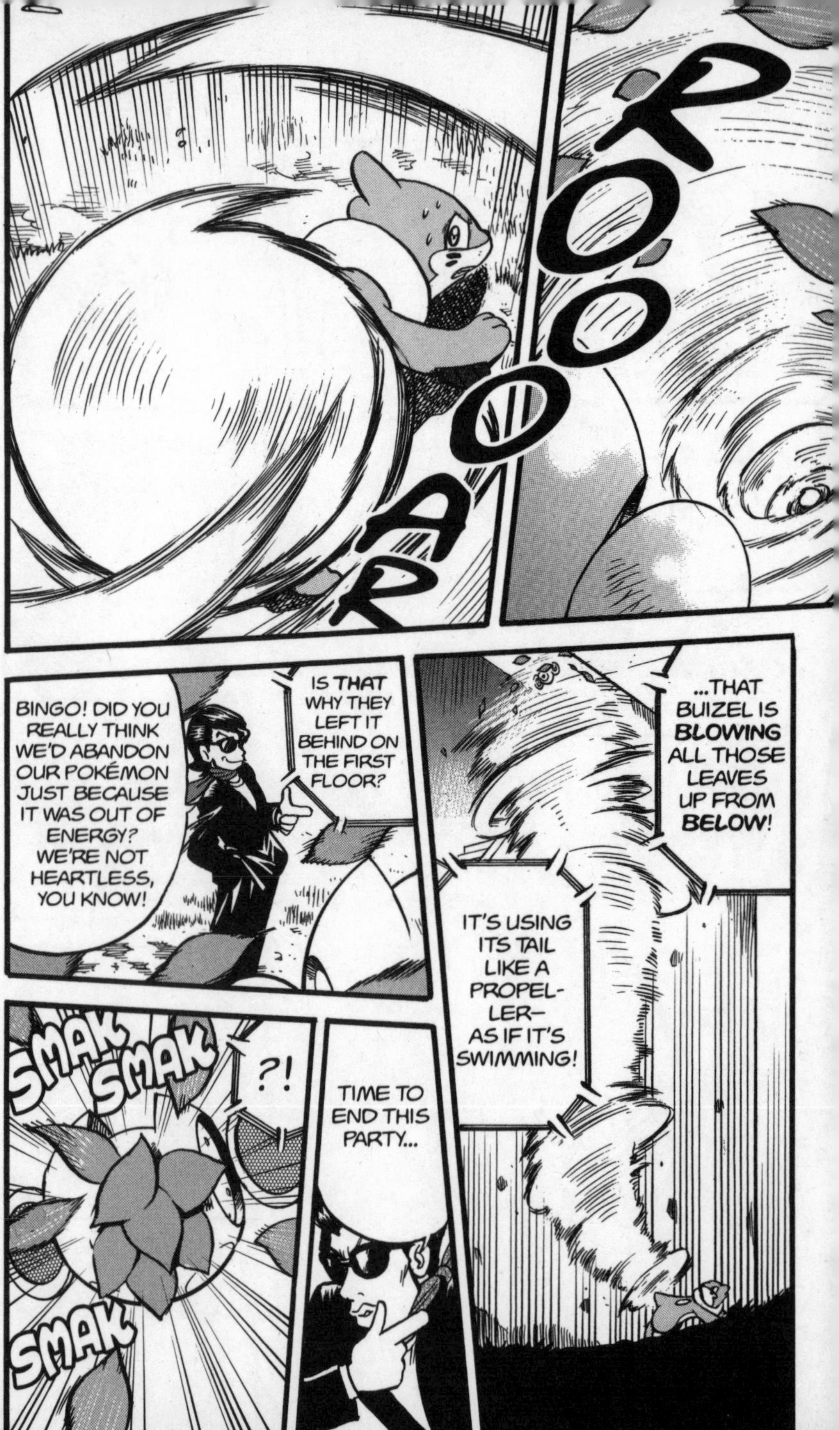
ROOOOAR
...THAT BUIZEL IS BLOWING ALL THOSE LEAVES UP FROM BELOW!
IT'S USING ITS TAIL LIKE A PROPELLER— AS IF IT'S SWIMMING!
IS THAT WHY THEY LEFT IT BEHIND ON THE FIRST FLOOR?
BINGO! DID YOU REALLY THINK WE'D ABANDON OUR POKÉMON JUST BECAUSE IT WAS OUT OF ENERGY? WE'RE NOT HEARTLESS, YOU KNOW!
TIME TO END THIS PARTY...
SMAK SMAK
?!
SMAK

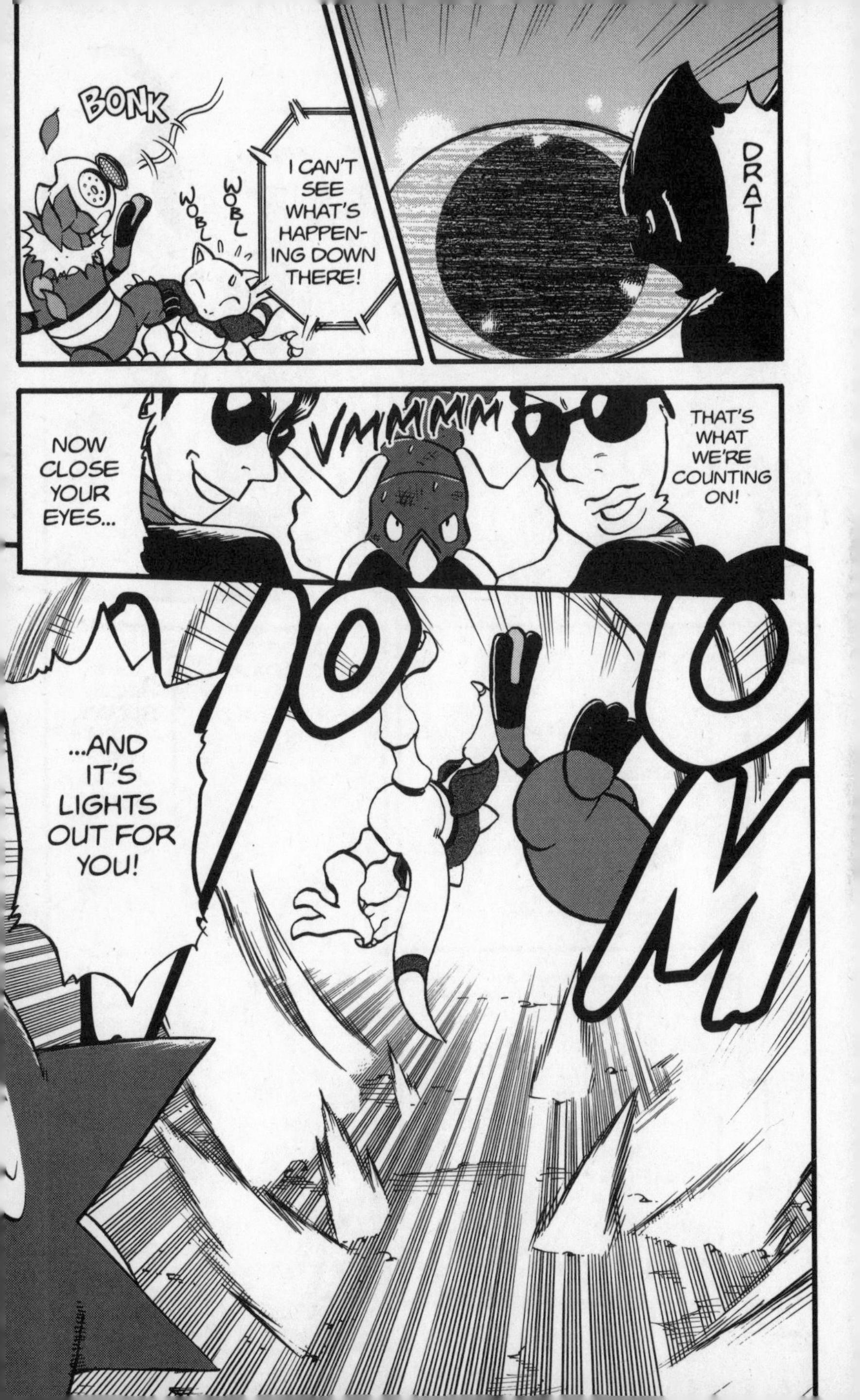
DRAT!
I CAN'T SEE WHAT'S HAPPENING DOWN THERE!
WOBL WOBL
BONK
THAT'S WHAT WE'RE COUNTING ON!
VMMMMM
NOW CLOSE YOUR EYES...
...AND IT'S LIGHTS OUT FOR YOU!

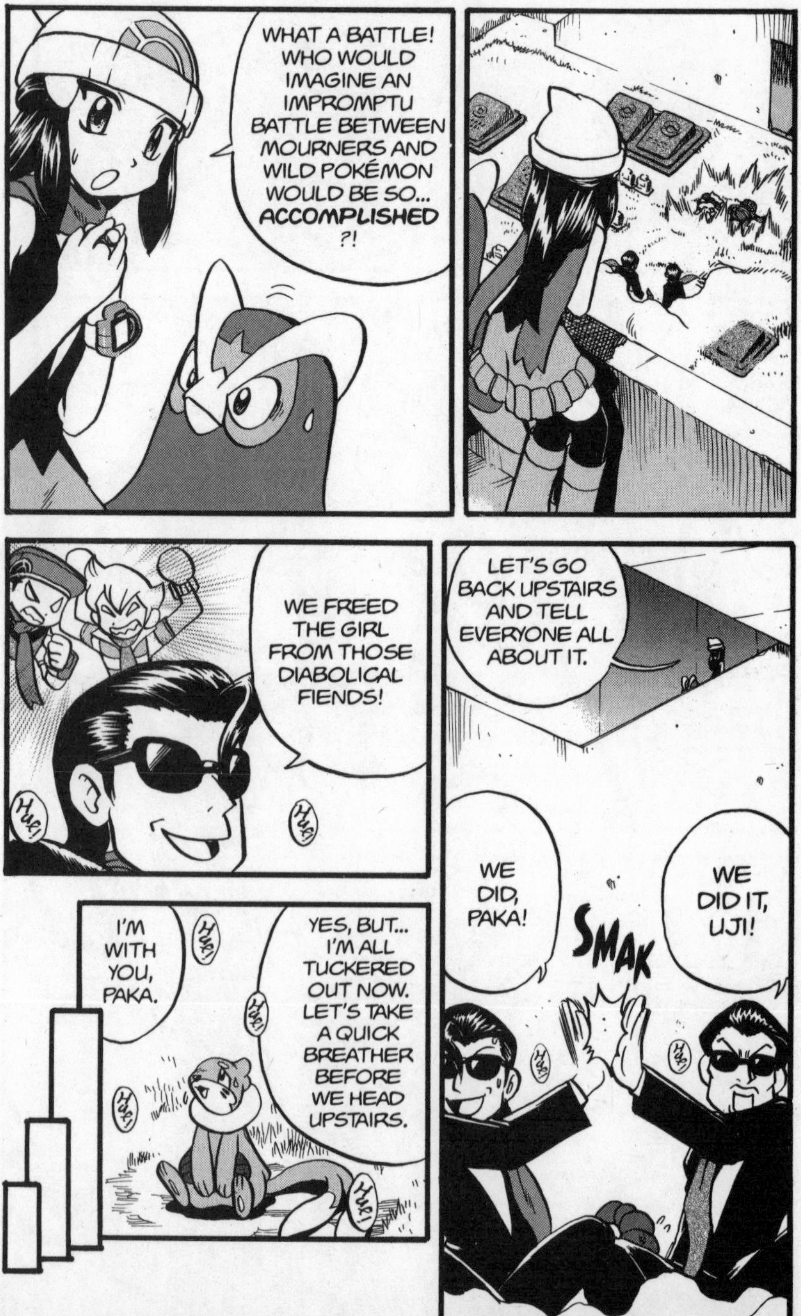
WHAT A BATTLE! WHO WOULD IMAGINE AN IMPROMPTU BATTLE BETWEEN MOURNERS AND WILD POKÉMON WOULD BE SO... **ACCOMPLISHED** ?!
LET'S GO BACK UPSTAIRS AND TELL EVERYONE ALL ABOUT IT.
WE DID IT, UJI!
WE DID, PAKA!
SMAK
Hue!
Hue!
WE FREED THE GIRL FROM THOSE DIABOLICAL FIENDS!
Hue!
Hue!
YES, BUT... I'M ALL TUCKERED OUT NOW. LET'S TAKE A QUICK BREATHER BEFORE WE HEAD UPSTAIRS.
I'M WITH YOU, PAKA.
Hue!
Hue!
Hue!
Hue!

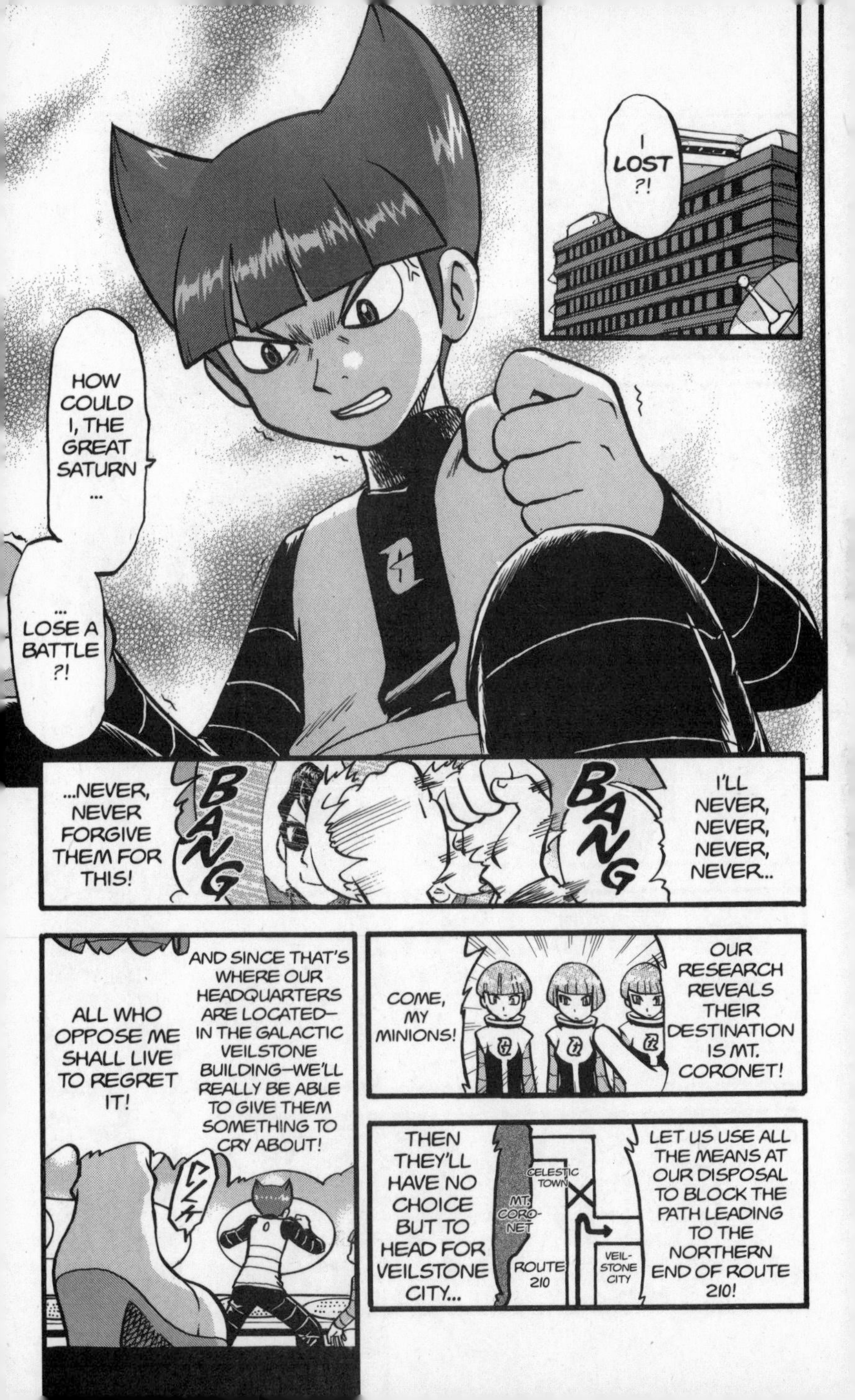
I LOST?!
HOW COULD I, THE GREAT SATURN...
...LOSE A BATTLE?!
I'LL NEVER, NEVER, NEVER, NEVER...
BANG
BANG
...NEVER, NEVER FORGIVE THEM FOR THIS!
OUR RESEARCH REVEALS THEIR DESTINATION IS MT. CORONET!
COME, MY MINIONS!
LET US USE ALL THE MEANS AT OUR DISPOSAL TO BLOCK THE PATH LEADING TO THE NORTHERN END OF ROUTE 210!
CELESTIC TOWN
MT. CORO-NET
ROUTE 210
VEIL-STONE CITY
THEN THEY'LL HAVE NO CHOICE BUT TO HEAD FOR VEILSTONE CITY...
AND SINCE THAT'S WHERE OUR HEADQUARTERS ARE LOCATED—IN THE GALACTIC VEILSTONE BUILDING—WE'LL REALLY BE ABLE TO GIVE THEM SOMETHING TO CRY ABOUT!
ALL WHO OPPOSE ME SHALL LIVE TO REGRET IT!

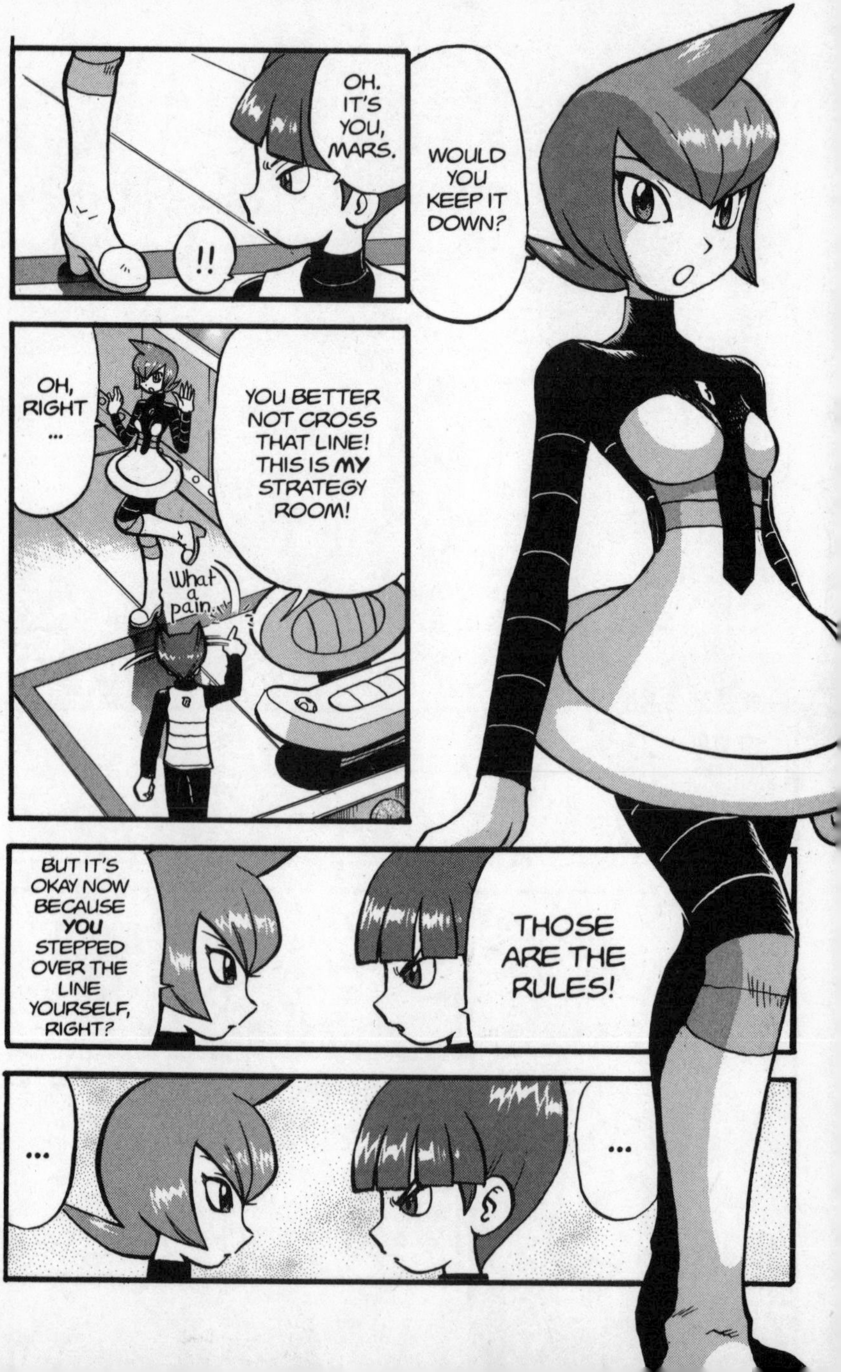

WOULD YOU KEEP IT DOWN?
OH. IT'S YOU, MARS.
!!
YOU BETTER NOT CROSS THAT LINE! THIS IS **MY** STRATEGY ROOM!
What a pain.
OH, RIGHT ...
THOSE ARE THE RULES!
BUT IT'S OKAY NOW BECAUSE **YOU** STEPPED OVER THE LINE YOURSELF, RIGHT?
...
...

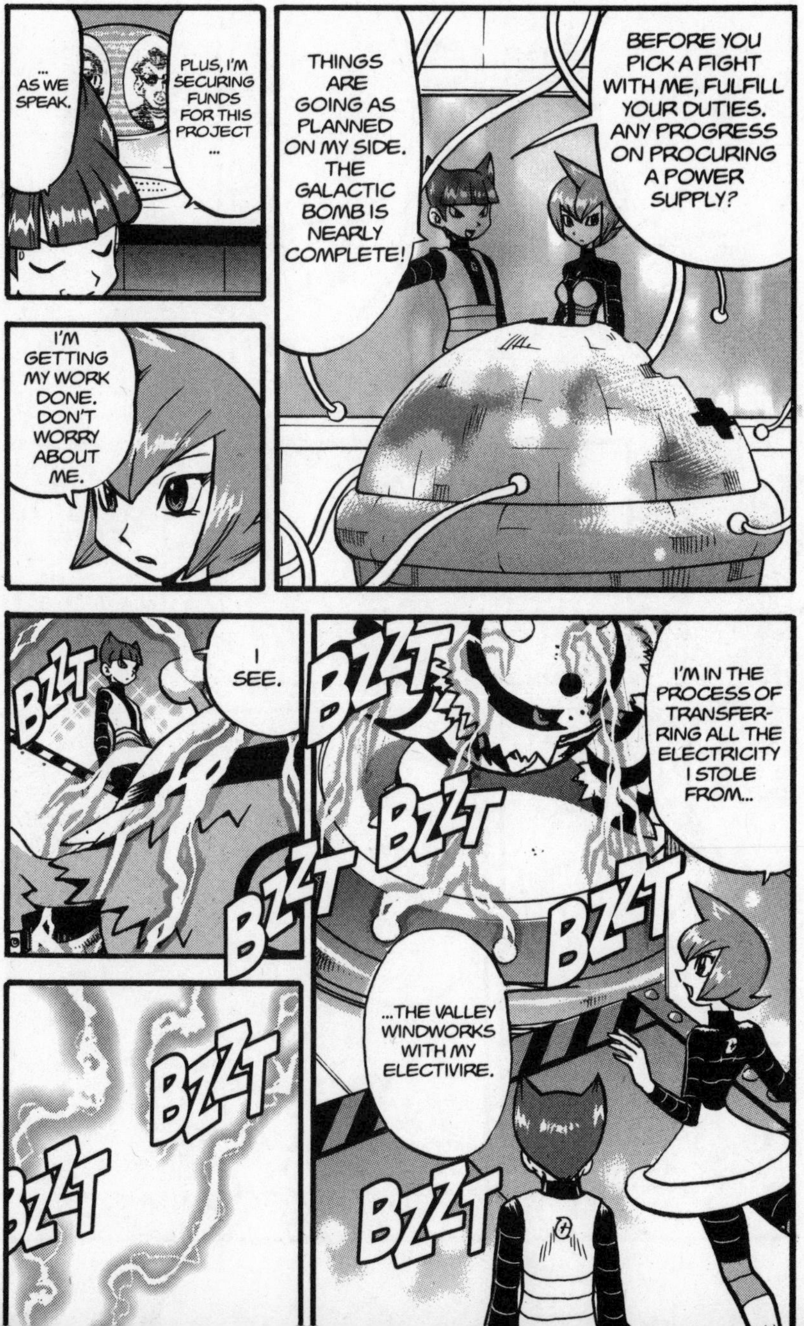
BEFORE YOU PICK A FIGHT WITH ME, FULFILL YOUR DUTIES. ANY PROGRESS ON PROCURING A POWER SUPPLY?
THINGS ARE GOING AS PLANNED ON MY SIDE. THE GALACTIC BOMB IS NEARLY COMPLETE!
PLUS, I'M SECURING FUNDS FOR THIS PROJECT ...
... AS WE SPEAK.
I'M GETTING MY WORK DONE. DON'T WORRY ABOUT ME.
I'M IN THE PROCESS OF TRANSFER-RING ALL THE ELECTRICITY I STOLE FROM...
BZZT
BZZT
BZZT
...THE VALLEY WINDWORKS WITH MY ELECTIVIRE.
BZZT
I SEE.
BZZT
BZZT
BZZT
BZZT

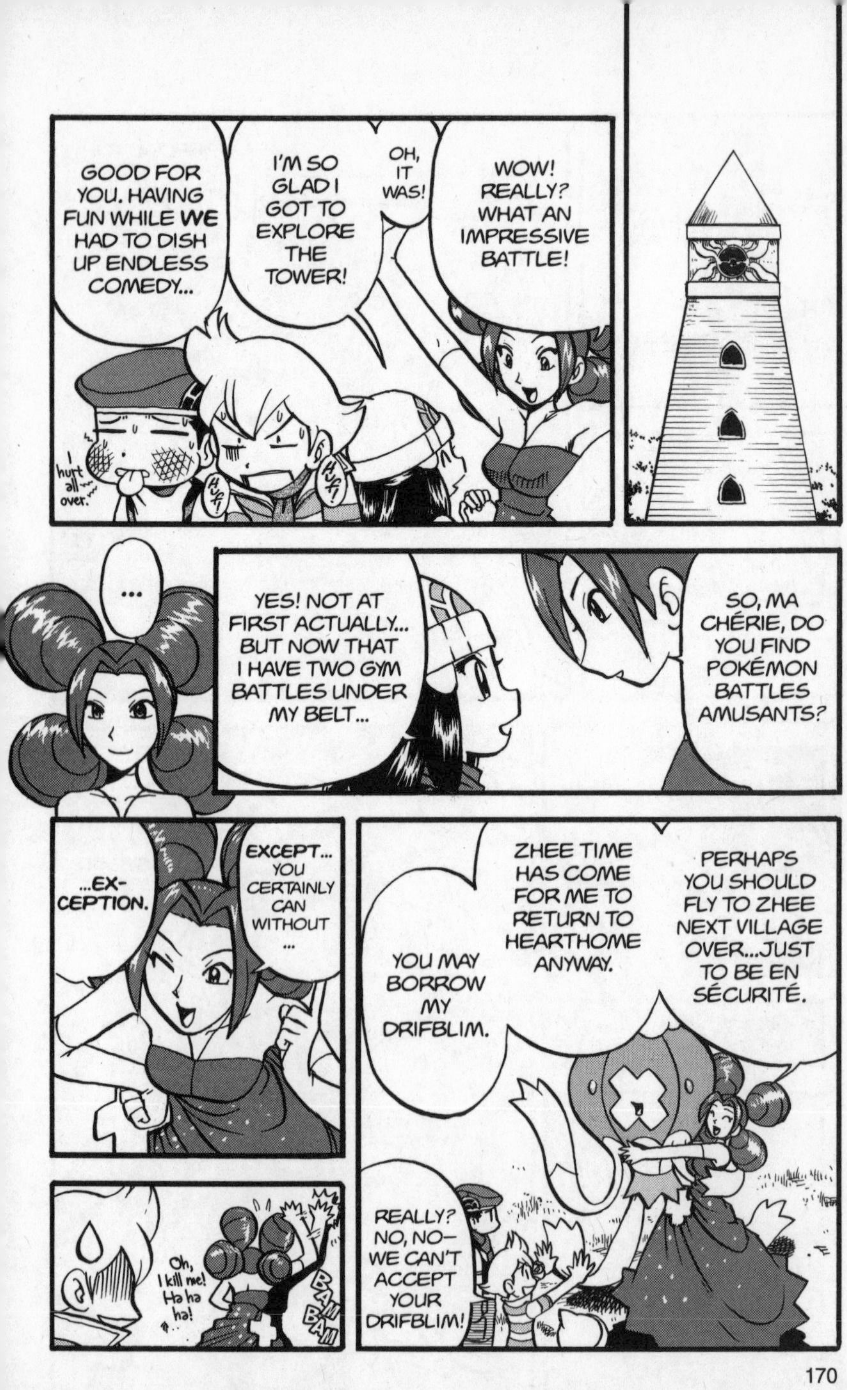
WOW! REALLY? WHAT AN IMPRESSIVE BATTLE!
OH, IT WAS!
I'M SO GLAD I GOT TO EXPLORE THE TOWER!
GOOD FOR YOU. HAVING FUN WHILE WE HAD TO DISH UP ENDLESS COMEDY...
HUF! HUF!
I hurt all over.
SO, MA CHÉRIE, DO YOU FIND POKÉMON BATTLES AMUSANTS?
YES! NOT AT FIRST ACTUALLY... BUT NOW THAT I HAVE TWO GYM BATTLES UNDER MY BELT...
...
PERHAPS YOU SHOULD FLY TO ZHEE NEXT VILLAGE OVER...JUST TO BE EN SÉCURITÉ.
ZHEE TIME HAS COME FOR ME TO RETURN TO HEARTHOME ANYWAY.
YOU MAY BORROW MY DRIFBLIM.
REALLY? NO, NO— WE CAN'T ACCEPT YOUR DRIFBLIM!
EXCEPT... YOU CERTAINLY CAN WITHOUT ...
...EX-CEPTION.
Oh, I kill me! Ha ha ha!
BAM BAM

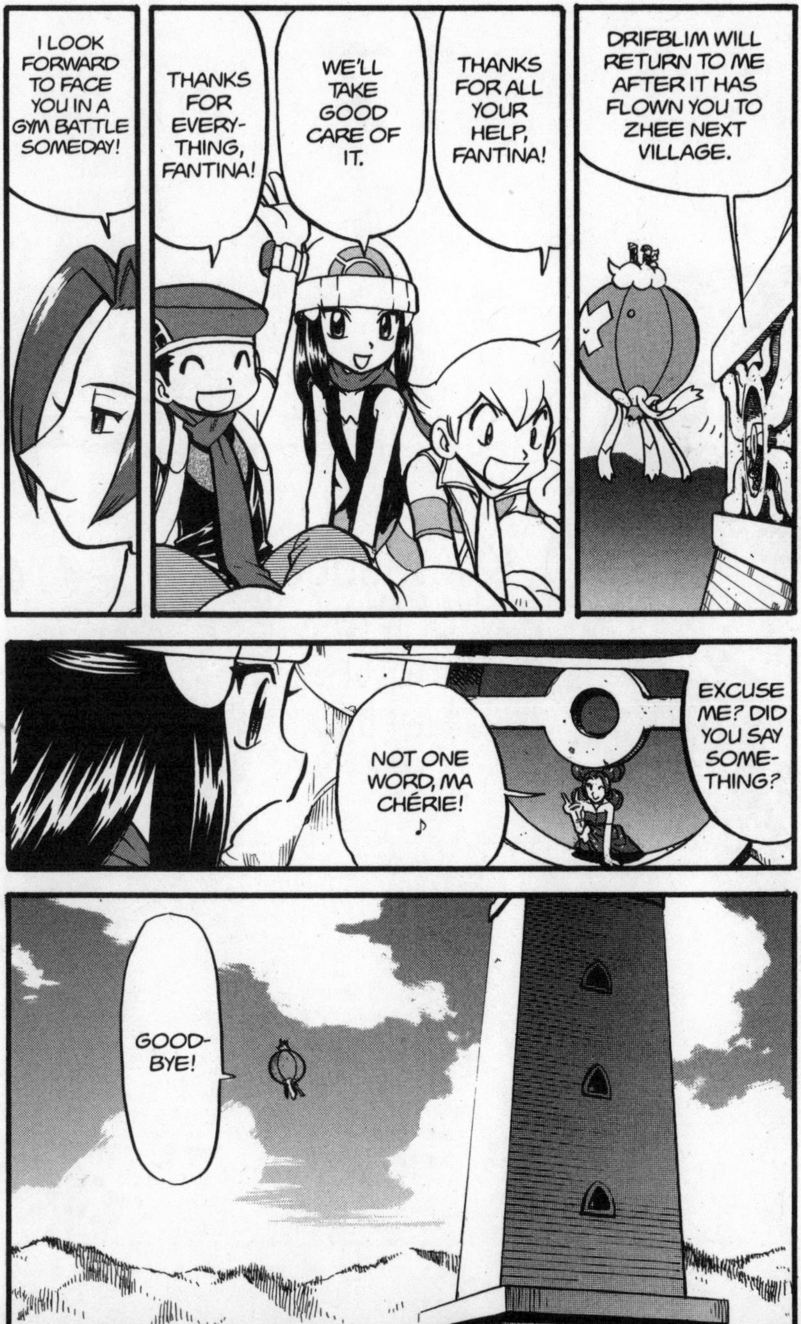
DRIFBLIM WILL RETURN TO ME AFTER IT HAS FLOWN YOU TO ZHEE NEXT VILLAGE.
THANKS FOR ALL YOUR HELP, FANTINA!
WE'LL TAKE GOOD CARE OF IT.
THANKS FOR EVERY-THING, FANTINA!
I LOOK FORWARD TO FACE YOU IN A GYM BATTLE SOMEDAY!
EXCUSE ME? DID YOU SAY SOME-THING?
NOT ONE WORD, MA CHÉRIE! ♪
GOOD-BYE!

17

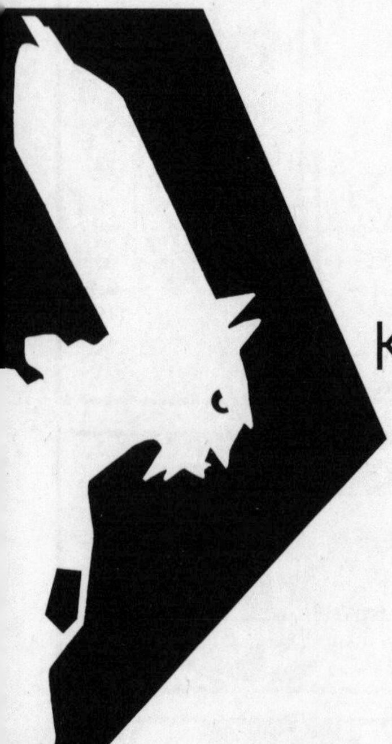

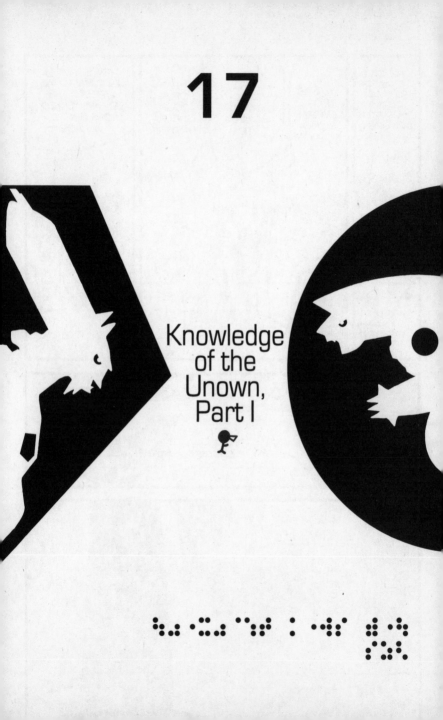

Knowledge of the Unown, Part I

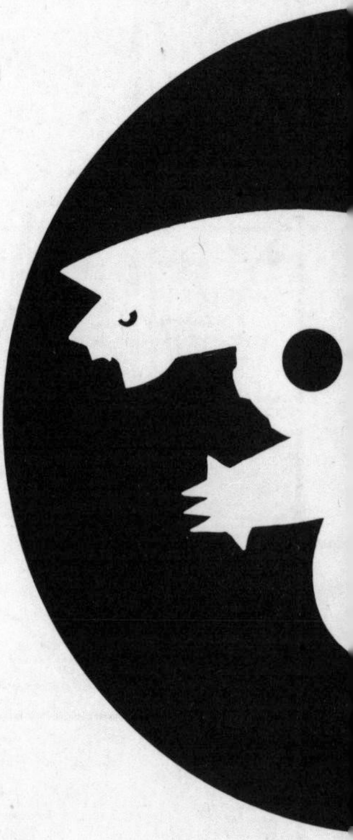

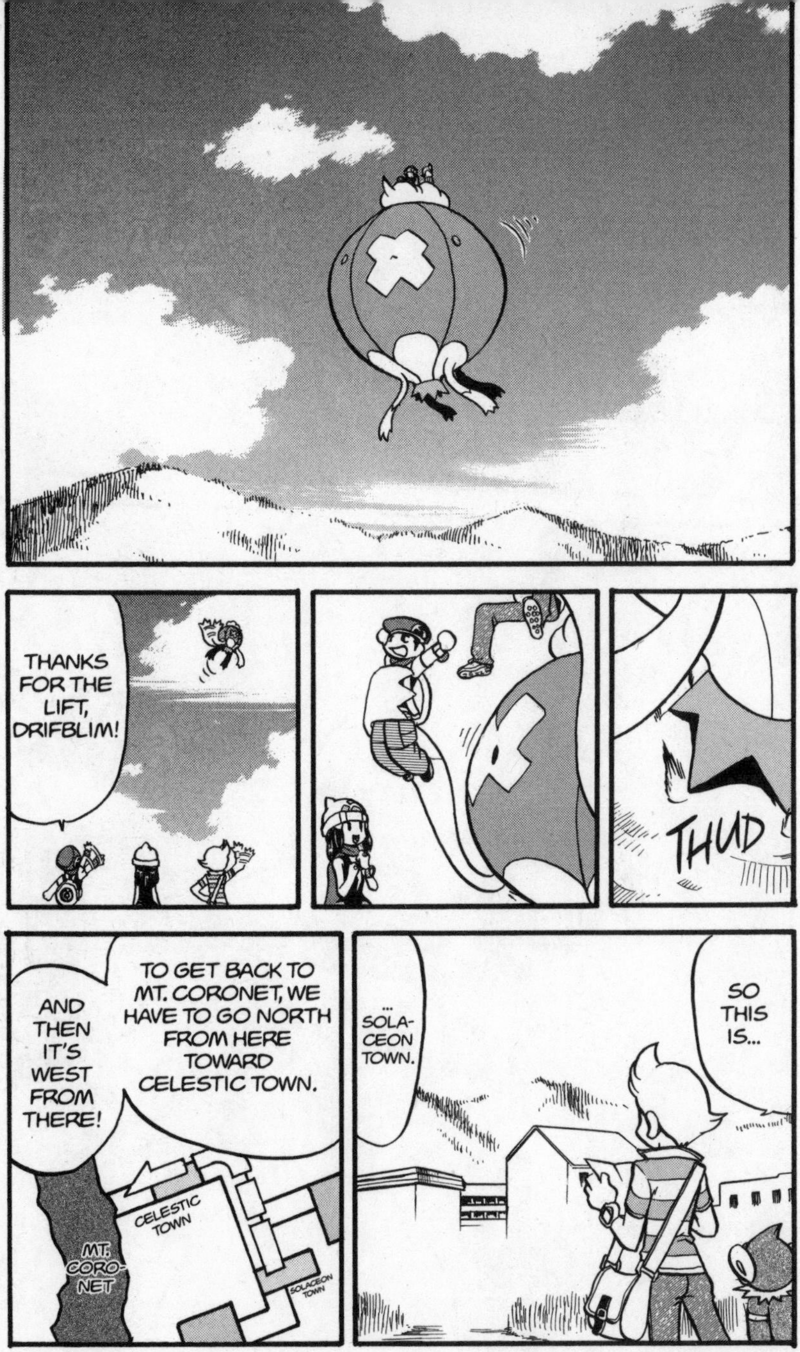
THUD
THANKS FOR THE LIFT, DRIFBLIM!
SO THIS IS...
... SOLACEON TOWN.
TO GET BACK TO MT. CORONET, WE HAVE TO GO NORTH FROM HERE TOWARD CELESTIC TOWN.
AND THEN IT'S WEST FROM THERE!
CELESTIC TOWN
MT. CORO-NET
SOLACEON TOWN

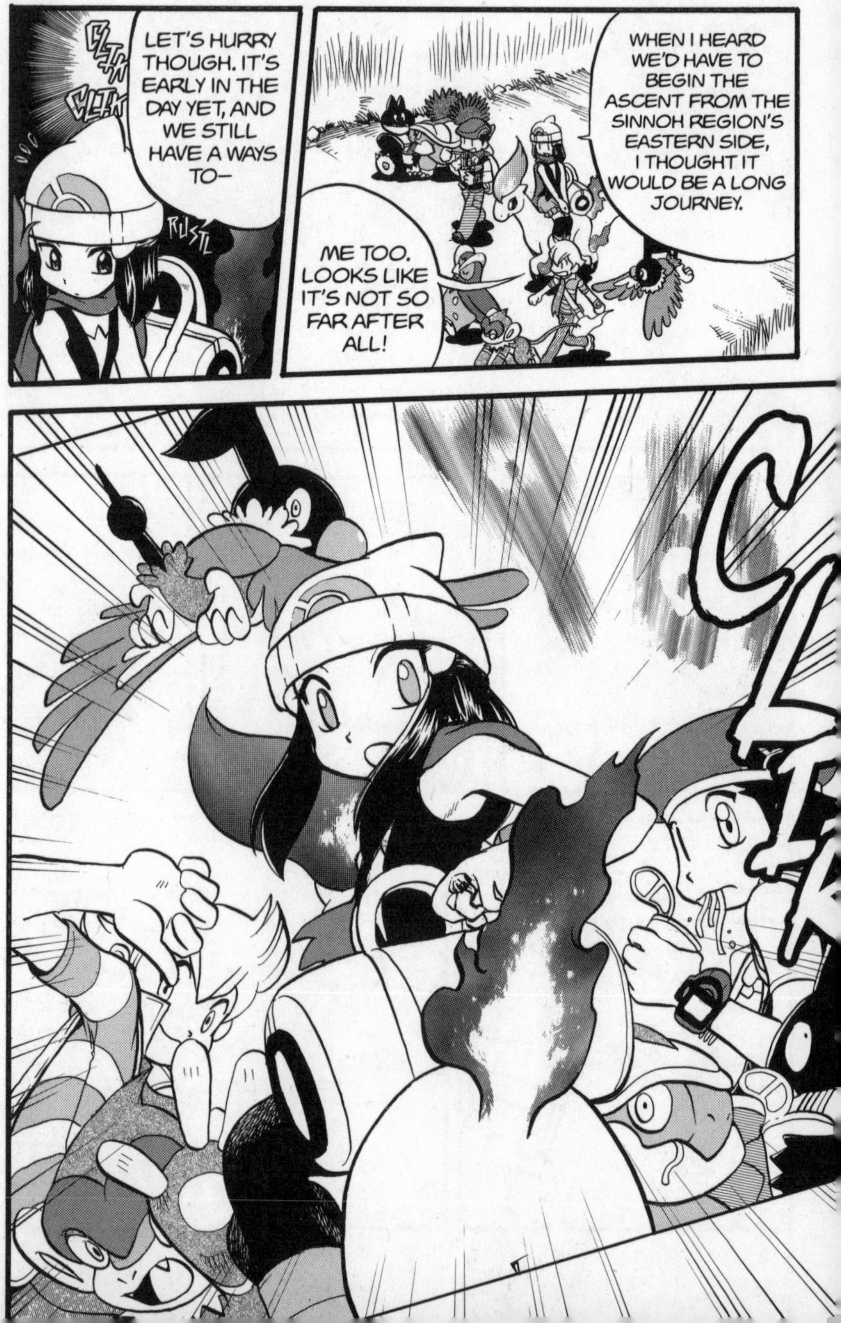
WHEN I HEARD WE'D HAVE TO BEGIN THE ASCENT FROM THE SINNOH REGION'S EASTERN SIDE, I THOUGHT IT WOULD BE A LONG JOURNEY.
ME TOO. LOOKS LIKE IT'S NOT SO FAR AFTER ALL!
CLIK
CLIK
LET'S HURRY THOUGH. IT'S EARLY IN THE DAY YET, AND WE STILL HAVE A WAYS TO—
RUSTL

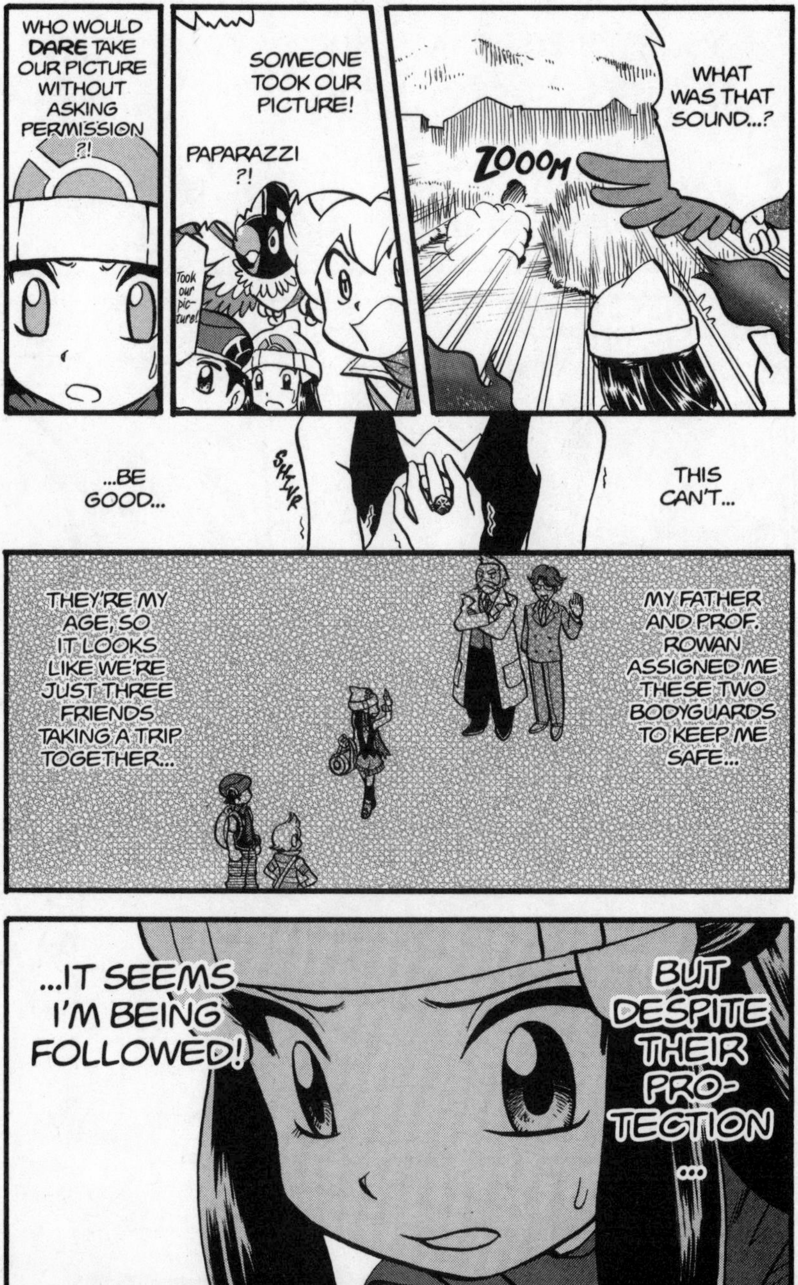
WHAT WAS THAT SOUND...?
ZOOOM
SOMEONE TOOK OUR PICTURE!
PAPARAZZI ?!
Took our picture!
WHO WOULD DARE TAKE OUR PICTURE WITHOUT ASKING PERMISSION ?!
THIS CAN'T...
SHWR
...BE GOOD...
MY FATHER AND PROF. ROWAN ASSIGNED ME THESE TWO BODYGUARDS TO KEEP ME SAFE...
THEY'RE MY AGE, SO IT LOOKS LIKE WE'RE JUST THREE FRIENDS TAKING A TRIP TOGETHER...
BUT DESPITE THEIR PRO-TECTION...
...IT SEEMS I'M BEING FOLLOWED!

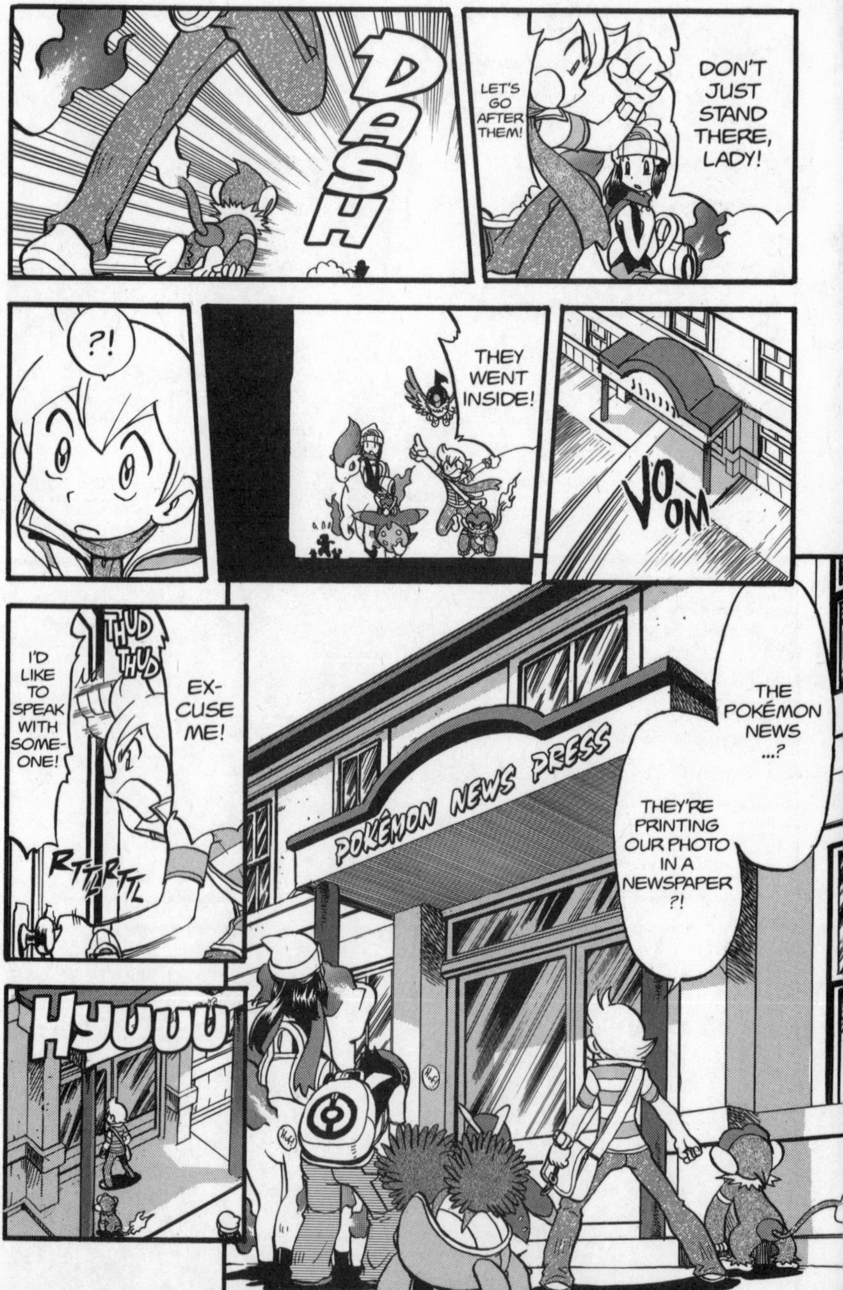
DON'T JUST STAND THERE, LADY!
LET'S GO AFTER THEM!
DASH
VOOM
THEY WENT INSIDE!
?!
THE POKÉMON NEWS ...?
THEY'RE PRINTING OUR PHOTO IN A NEWSPAPER ?!
POKÉMON NEWS PRESS
EX-CUSE ME!
I'D LIKE TO SPEAK WITH SOME-ONE!
THUD THUD
RTTLRTTL
HYUUU

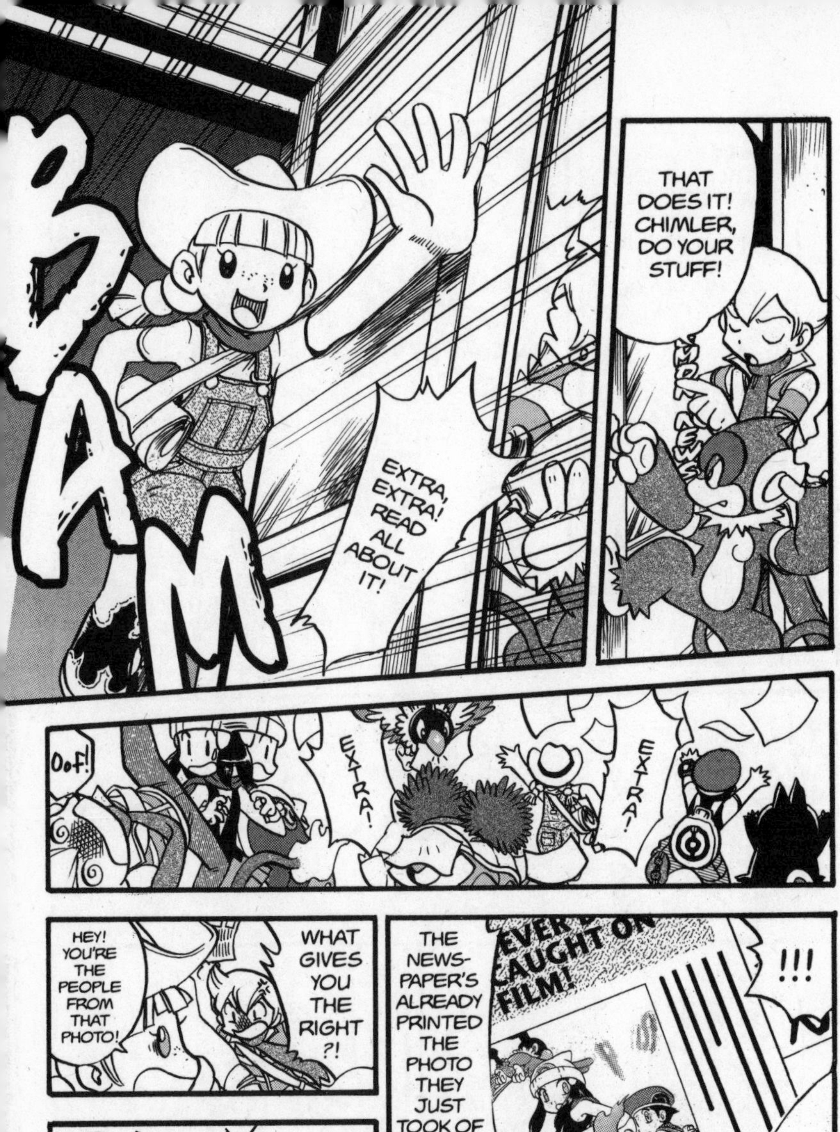

THAT DOES IT! CHIMLER, DO YOUR STUFF!
EXTRA, EXTRA! READ ALL ABOUT IT!
EXTRA!
EXTRA!
Oof!
!!!
CAUGHT ON FILM!
THE NEWSPAPER'S ALREADY PRINTED THE PHOTO THEY JUST TOOK OF US!
WHAT GIVES YOU THE RIGHT?!
HEY! YOU'RE THE PEOPLE FROM THAT PHOTO!
OH NO! THEY'RE GONNA SUE US BUT GOOD!
WHAT SEEMS TO BE THE TROUBLE HERE?!

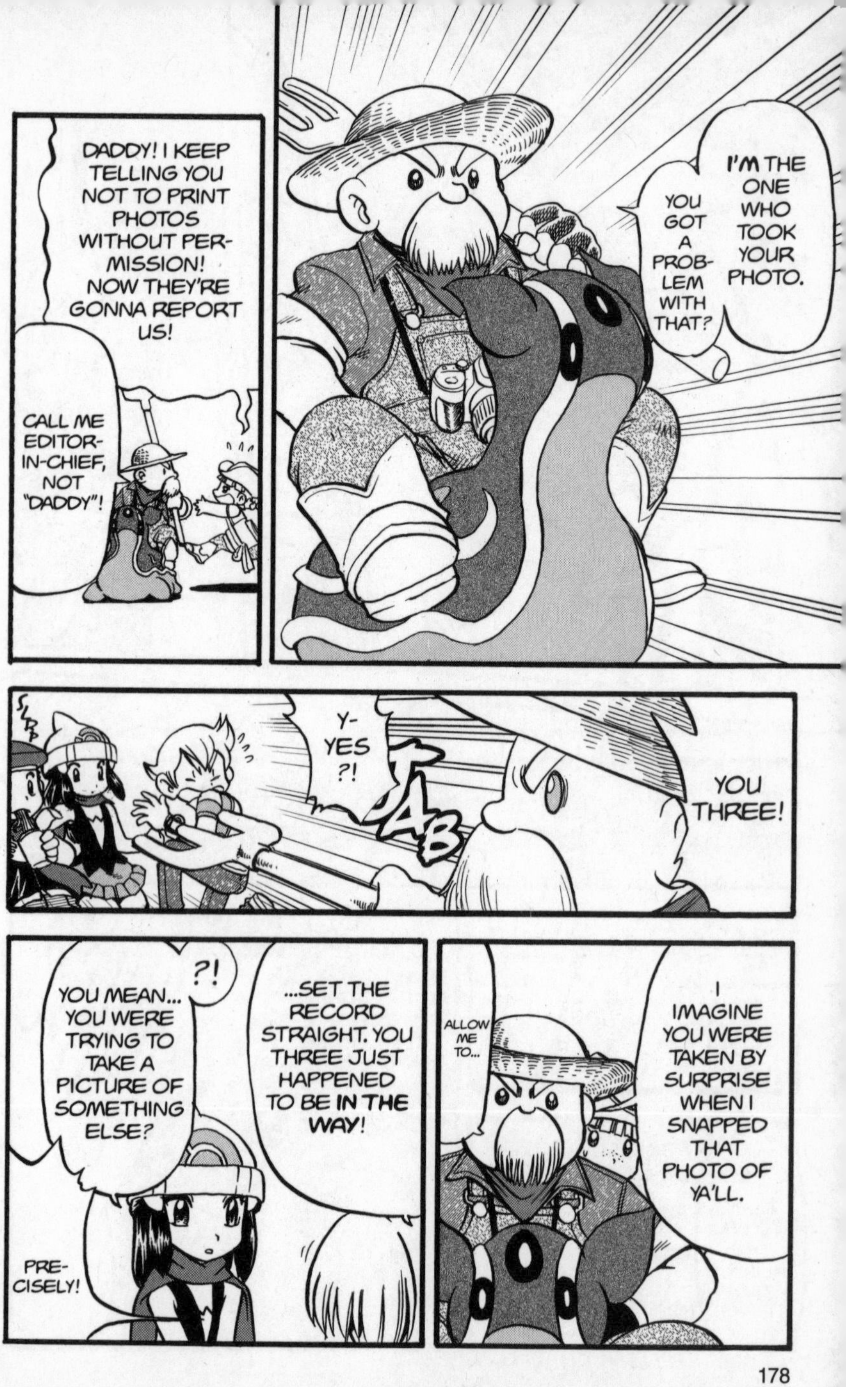

I'M THE ONE WHO TOOK YOUR PHOTO.
YOU GOT A PROBLEM WITH THAT?
DADDY! I KEEP TELLING YOU NOT TO PRINT PHOTOS WITHOUT PERMISSION! NOW THEY'RE GONNA REPORT US!
CALL ME EDITOR-IN-CHIEF, NOT "DADDY"!
YOU THREE!
JAB
Y-YES?!
I IMAGINE YOU WERE TAKEN BY SURPRISE WHEN I SNAPPED THAT PHOTO OF YA'LL.
ALLOW ME TO...
...SET THE RECORD STRAIGHT. YOU THREE JUST HAPPENED TO BE IN THE WAY!
?!
YOU MEAN... YOU WERE TRYING TO TAKE A PICTURE OF SOMETHING ELSE?
PRECISELY!

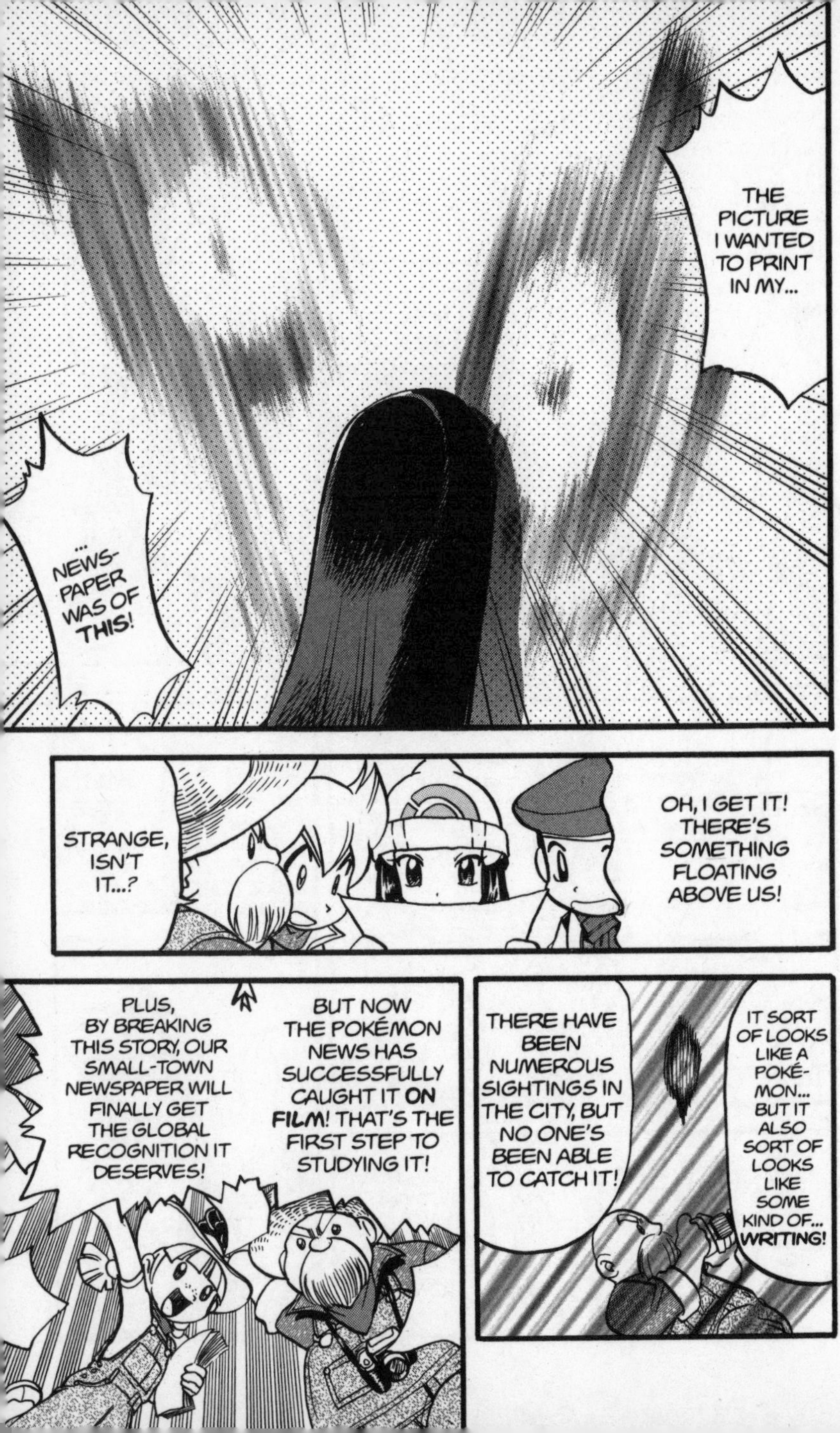
THE PICTURE I WANTED TO PRINT IN MY...
...NEWS-PAPER WAS OF **THIS**!
OH, I GET IT! THERE'S SOMETHING FLOATING ABOVE US!
STRANGE, ISN'T IT...?
IT SORT OF LOOKS LIKE A POKÉ-MON... BUT IT ALSO SORT OF LOOKS LIKE SOME KIND OF... **WRITING**!
THERE HAVE BEEN NUMEROUS SIGHTINGS IN THE CITY, BUT NO ONE'S BEEN ABLE TO CATCH IT!
BUT NOW THE POKÉMON NEWS HAS SUCCESSFULLY CAUGHT IT **ON FILM**! THAT'S THE FIRST STEP TO STUDYING IT!
PLUS, BY BREAKING THIS STORY, OUR SMALL-TOWN NEWSPAPER WILL FINALLY GET THE GLOBAL RECOGNITION IT DESERVES!

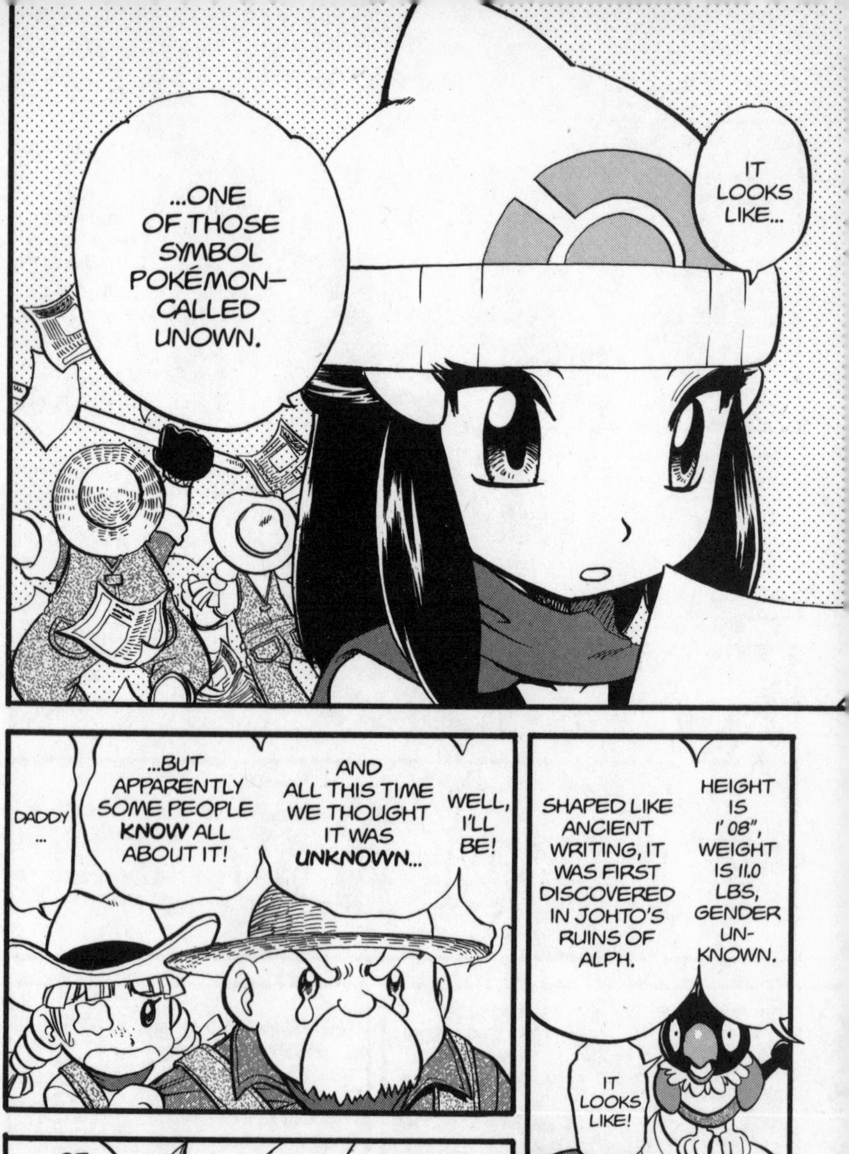
IT LOOKS LIKE...
...ONE OF THOSE SYMBOL POKÉMON—CALLED UNOWN.
HEIGHT IS 1' 08", WEIGHT IS 11.0 LBS, GENDER UN-KNOWN.
SHAPED LIKE ANCIENT WRITING, IT WAS FIRST DISCOVERED IN JOHTO'S RUINS OF ALPH.
IT LOOKS LIKE!
WELL, I'LL BE!
AND ALL THIS TIME WE THOUGHT IT WAS **UNKNOWN**...
...BUT APPARENTLY SOME PEOPLE **KNOW** ALL ABOUT IT!
DADDY...
OF COURSE I KNOW ALL ABOUT IT—THANKS TO PROFESSOR ROWAN!
OF COURSE SHE KNOWS ALL ABOUT IT—SHE'S A TOUR GUIDE!

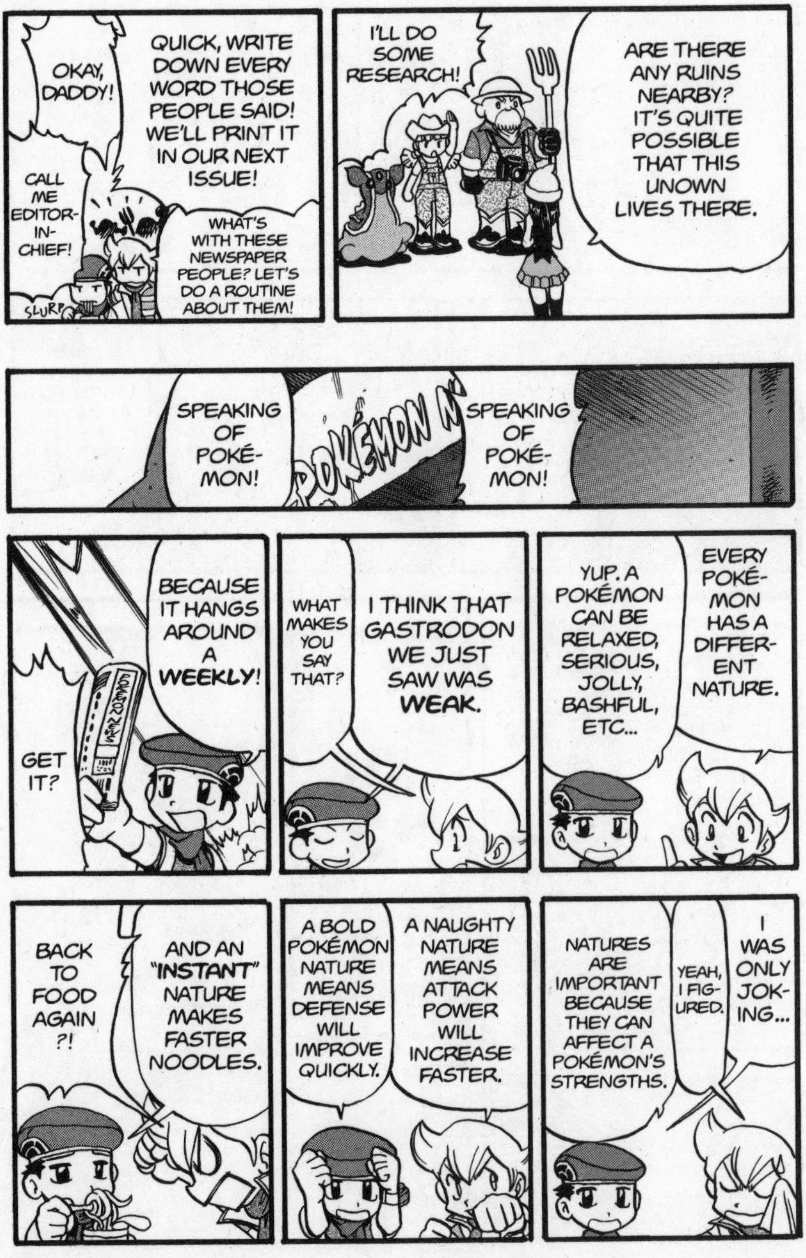

ARE THERE ANY RUINS NEARBY? IT'S QUITE POSSIBLE THAT THIS UNOWN LIVES THERE.
I'LL DO SOME RESEARCH!
QUICK, WRITE DOWN EVERY WORD THOSE PEOPLE SAID! WE'LL PRINT IT IN OUR NEXT ISSUE!
OKAY, DADDY!
WHAT'S WITH THESE NEWSPAPER PEOPLE? LET'S DO A ROUTINE ABOUT THEM!
CALL ME EDITOR-IN-CHIEF!
SLURP
SPEAKING OF POKÉMON!
POKÉMON N
SPEAKING OF POKÉMON!
EVERY POKÉMON HAS A DIFFERENT NATURE.
YUP. A POKÉMON CAN BE RELAXED, SERIOUS, JOLLY, BASHFUL, ETC...
I THINK THAT GASTRODON WE JUST SAW WAS WEAK.
WHAT MAKES YOU SAY THAT?
BECAUSE IT HANGS AROUND A WEEKLY!
POKÉMON NEWS
GET IT?
I WAS ONLY JOKING...
YEAH, I FIGURED.
NATURES ARE IMPORTANT BECAUSE THEY CAN AFFECT A POKÉMON'S STRENGTHS.
A NAUGHTY NATURE MEANS ATTACK POWER WILL INCREASE FASTER.
A BOLD POKÉMON NATURE MEANS DEFENSE WILL IMPROVE QUICKLY.
AND AN "INSTANT" NATURE MAKES FASTER NOODLES.
BACK TO FOOD AGAIN?!

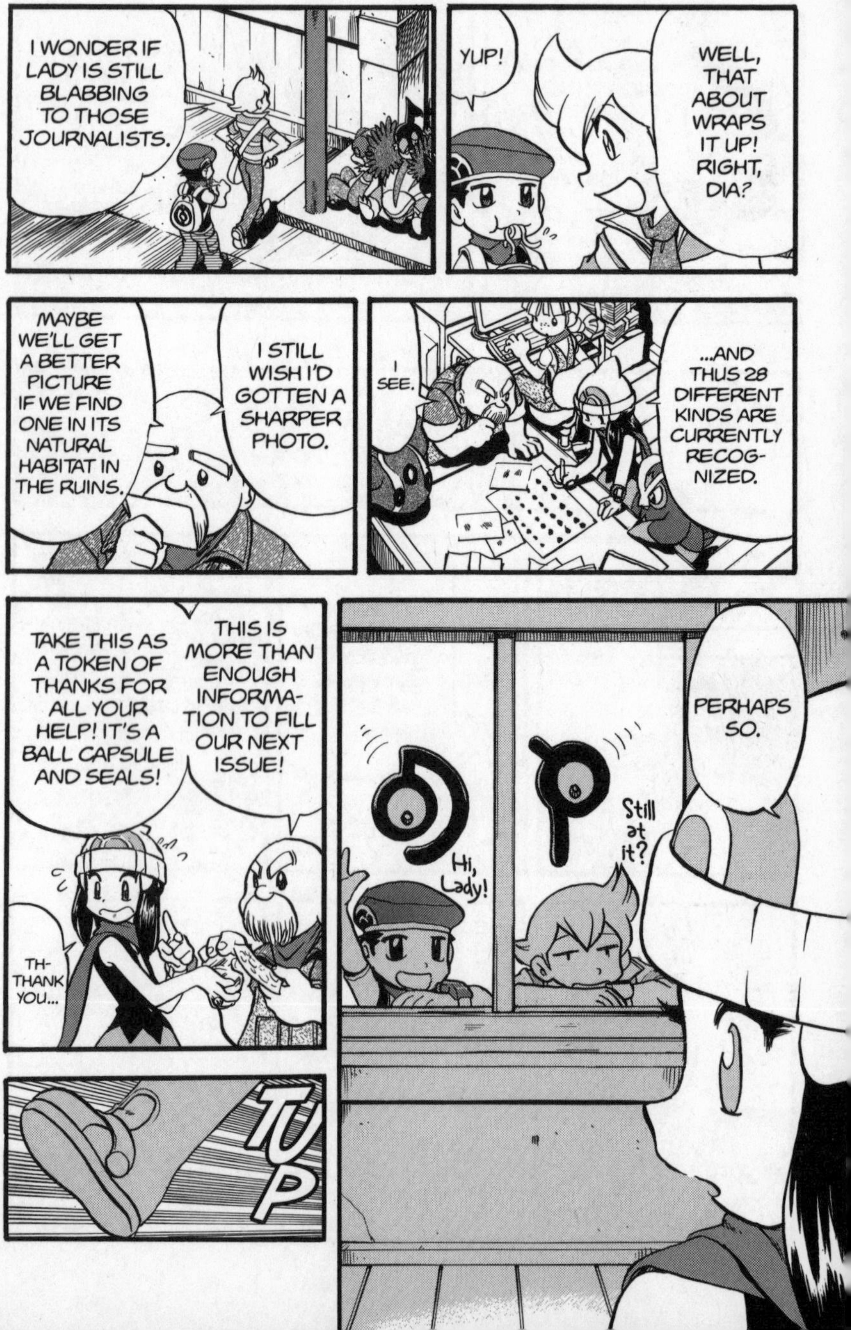
WELL, THAT ABOUT WRAPS IT UP! RIGHT, DIA?
YUP!
I WONDER IF LADY IS STILL BLABBING TO THOSE JOURNALISTS.
...AND THUS 28 DIFFERENT KINDS ARE CURRENTLY RECOG-NIZED.
I SEE.
I STILL WISH I'D GOTTEN A SHARPER PHOTO.
MAYBE WE'LL GET A BETTER PICTURE IF WE FIND ONE IN ITS NATURAL HABITAT IN THE RUINS.
PERHAPS SO.
Still at it?
Hi, Lady!
THIS IS MORE THAN ENOUGH INFORMA-TION TO FILL OUR NEXT ISSUE!
TAKE THIS AS A TOKEN OF THANKS FOR ALL YOUR HELP! IT'S A BALL CAPSULE AND SEALS!
TH-THANK YOU...
TUP

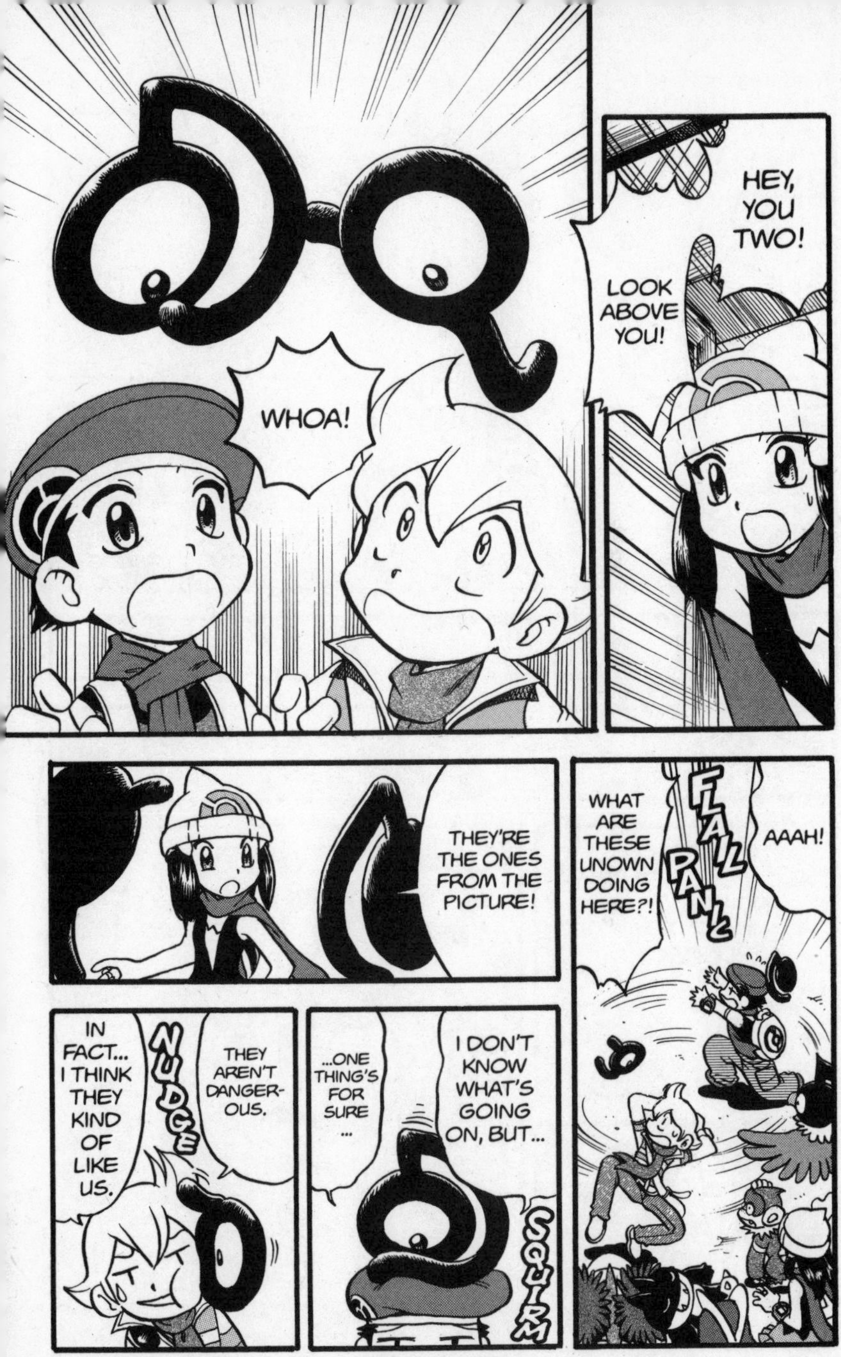
HEY, YOU TWO!
LOOK ABOVE YOU!
WHOA!
AAAH!
FLAIL
PANIC
WHAT ARE THESE UNOWN DOING HERE?!
THEY'RE THE ONES FROM THE PICTURE!
I DON'T KNOW WHAT'S GOING ON, BUT...
...ONE THING'S FOR SURE...
SQUIRM
THEY AREN'T DANGER-OUS.
NUDGE
IN FACT... I THINK THEY KIND OF LIKE US.

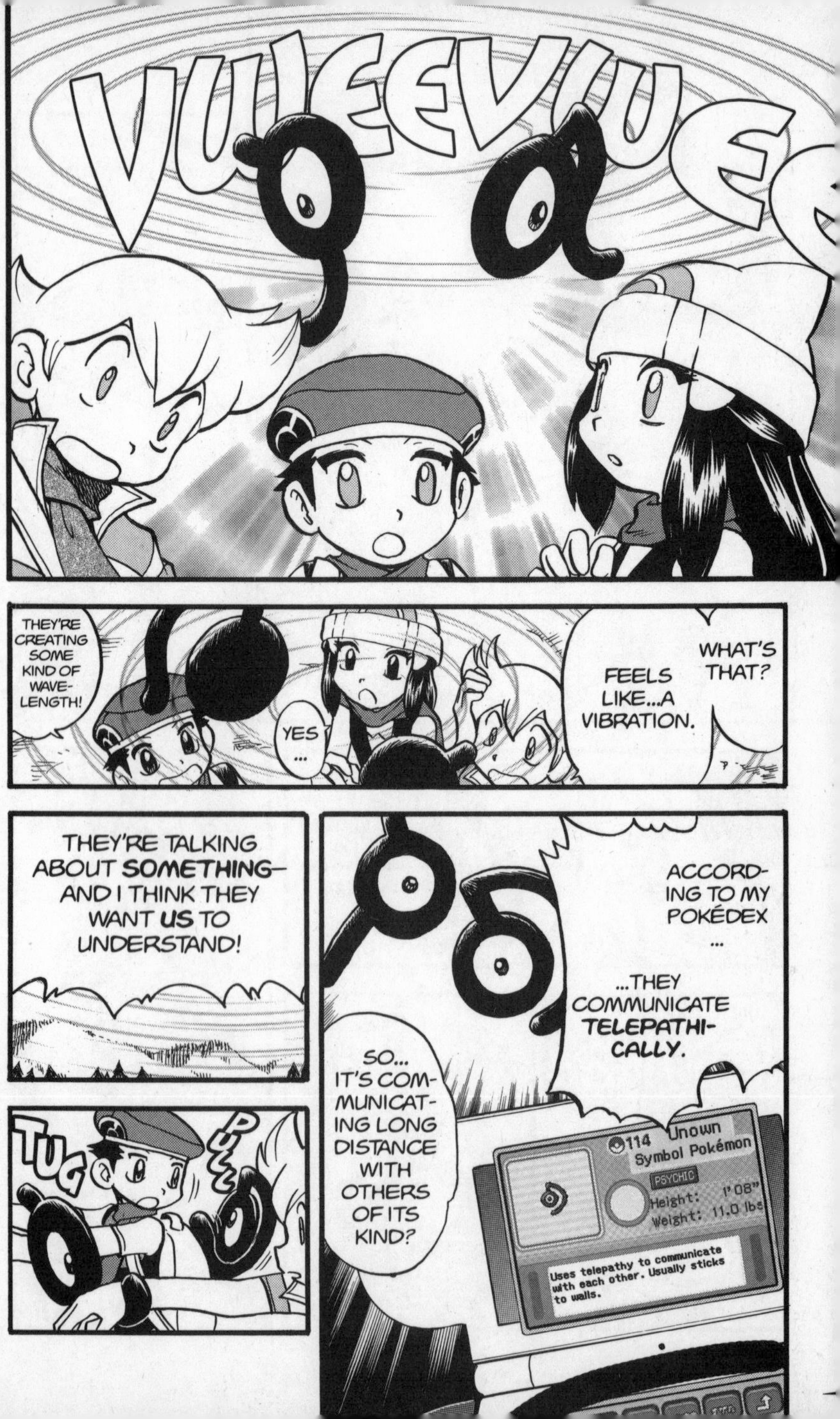
VUIEEVIUEE
WHAT'S THAT?
FEELS LIKE...A VIBRATION.
YES...
THEY'RE CREATING SOME KIND OF WAVE-LENGTH!
ACCORD-ING TO MY POKÉDEX...
...THEY COMMUNICATE **TELEPATHI-CALLY.**
114 Unown
Symbol Pokémon
PSYCHIC
Height: 1'08"
Weight: 11.0 lbs
Uses telepathy to communicate with each other. Usually sticks to walls.
SO... IT'S COM-MUNICAT-ING LONG DISTANCE WITH OTHERS OF ITS KIND?
THEY'RE TALKING ABOUT **SOMETHING**—AND I THINK THEY WANT **US** TO UNDERSTAND!
PULL
TUG

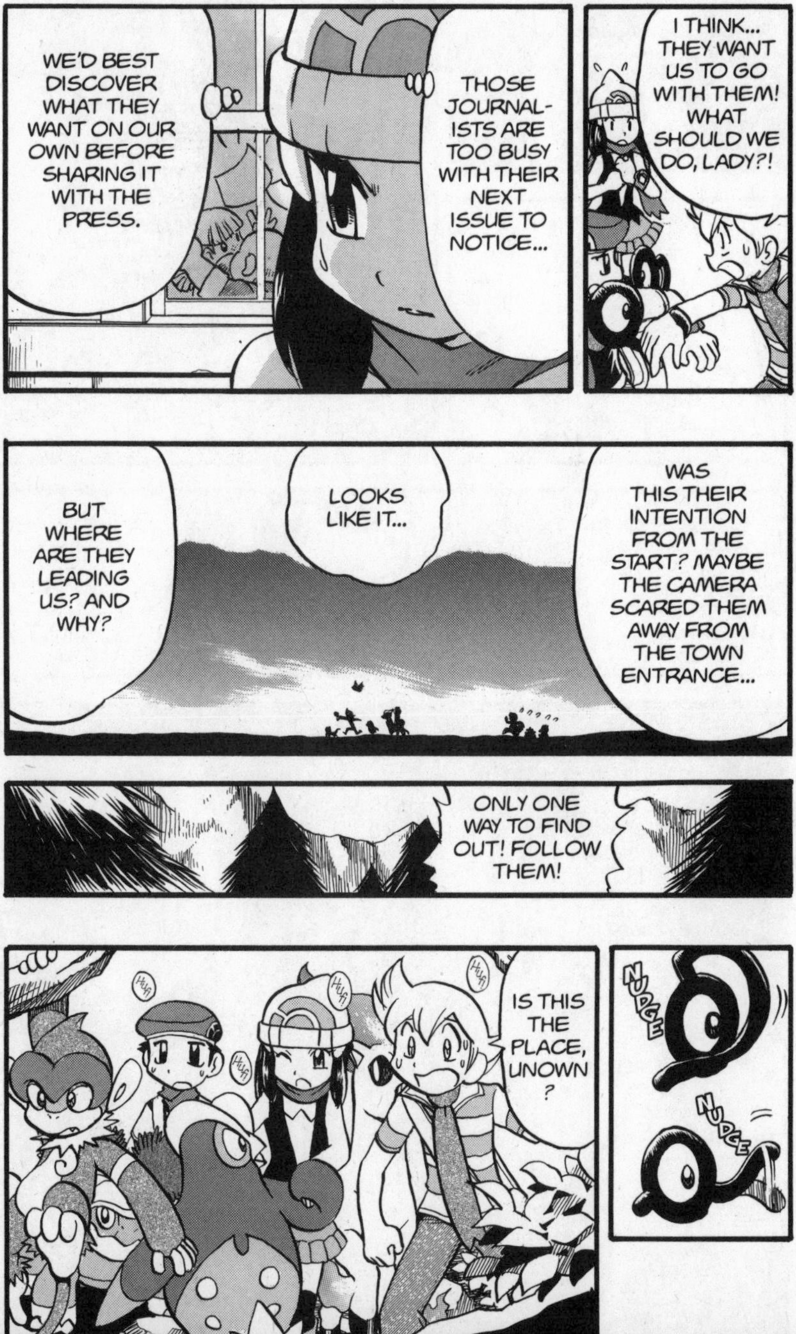
I THINK... THEY WANT US TO GO WITH THEM! WHAT SHOULD WE DO, LADY?!
THOSE JOURNAL-ISTS ARE TOO BUSY WITH THEIR NEXT ISSUE TO NOTICE...
WE'D BEST DISCOVER WHAT THEY WANT ON OUR OWN BEFORE SHARING IT WITH THE PRESS.
WAS THIS THEIR INTENTION FROM THE START? MAYBE THE CAMERA SCARED THEM AWAY FROM THE TOWN ENTRANCE...
LOOKS LIKE IT...
BUT WHERE ARE THEY LEADING US? AND WHY?
ONLY ONE WAY TO FIND OUT! FOLLOW THEM!
NUDGE
NUDGE
Huff
IS THIS THE PLACE, UNOWN?
Huff
Huff
Huff

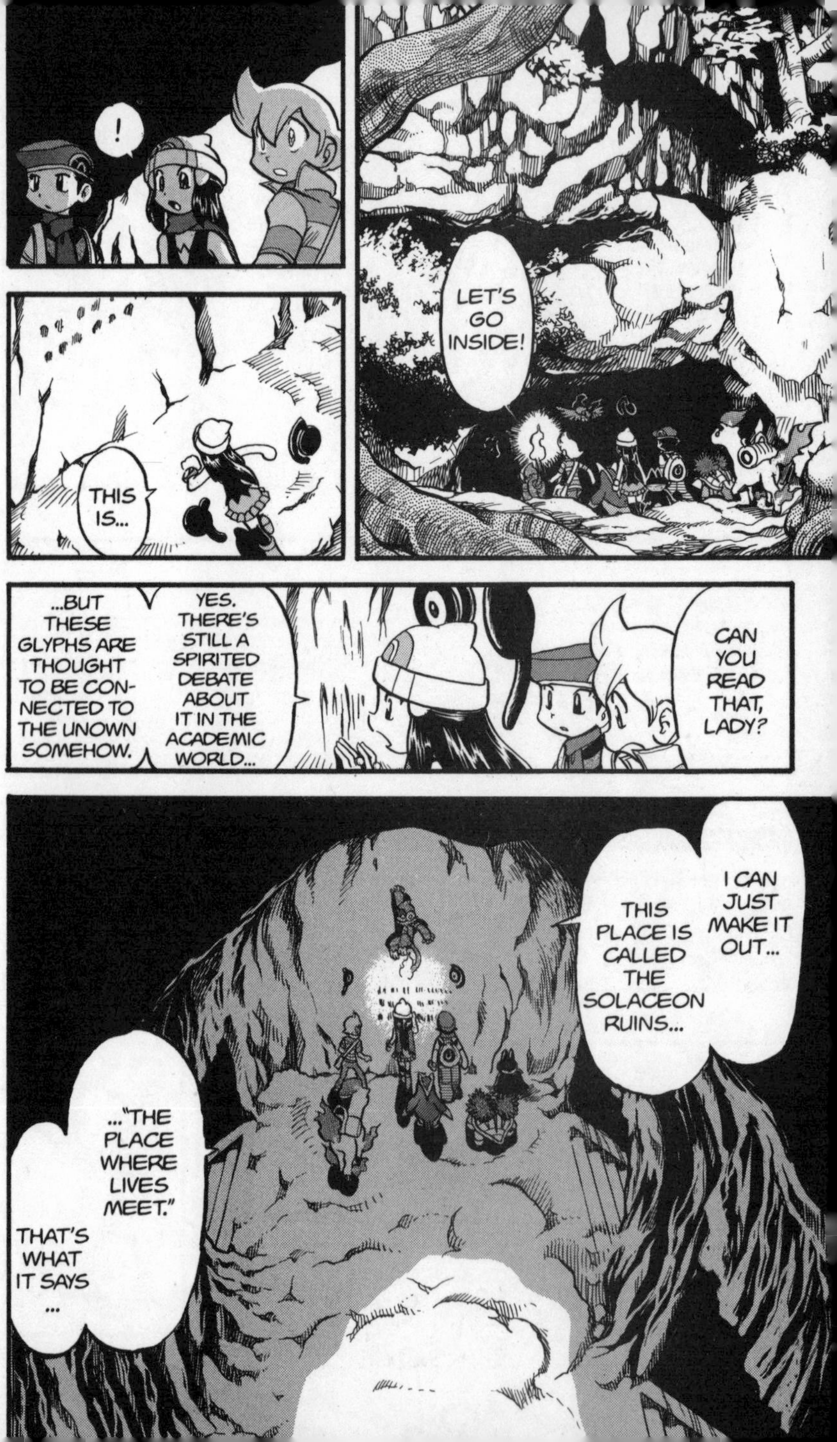
LET'S GO INSIDE!
!
THIS IS...
CAN YOU READ THAT, LADY?
YES. THERE'S STILL A SPIRITED DEBATE ABOUT IT IN THE ACADEMIC WORLD...
...BUT THESE GLYPHS ARE THOUGHT TO BE CON-NECTED TO THE UNOWN SOMEHOW.
I CAN JUST MAKE IT OUT...
THIS PLACE IS CALLED THE SOLACEON RUINS...
..."THE PLACE WHERE LIVES MEET."
THAT'S WHAT IT SAYS...

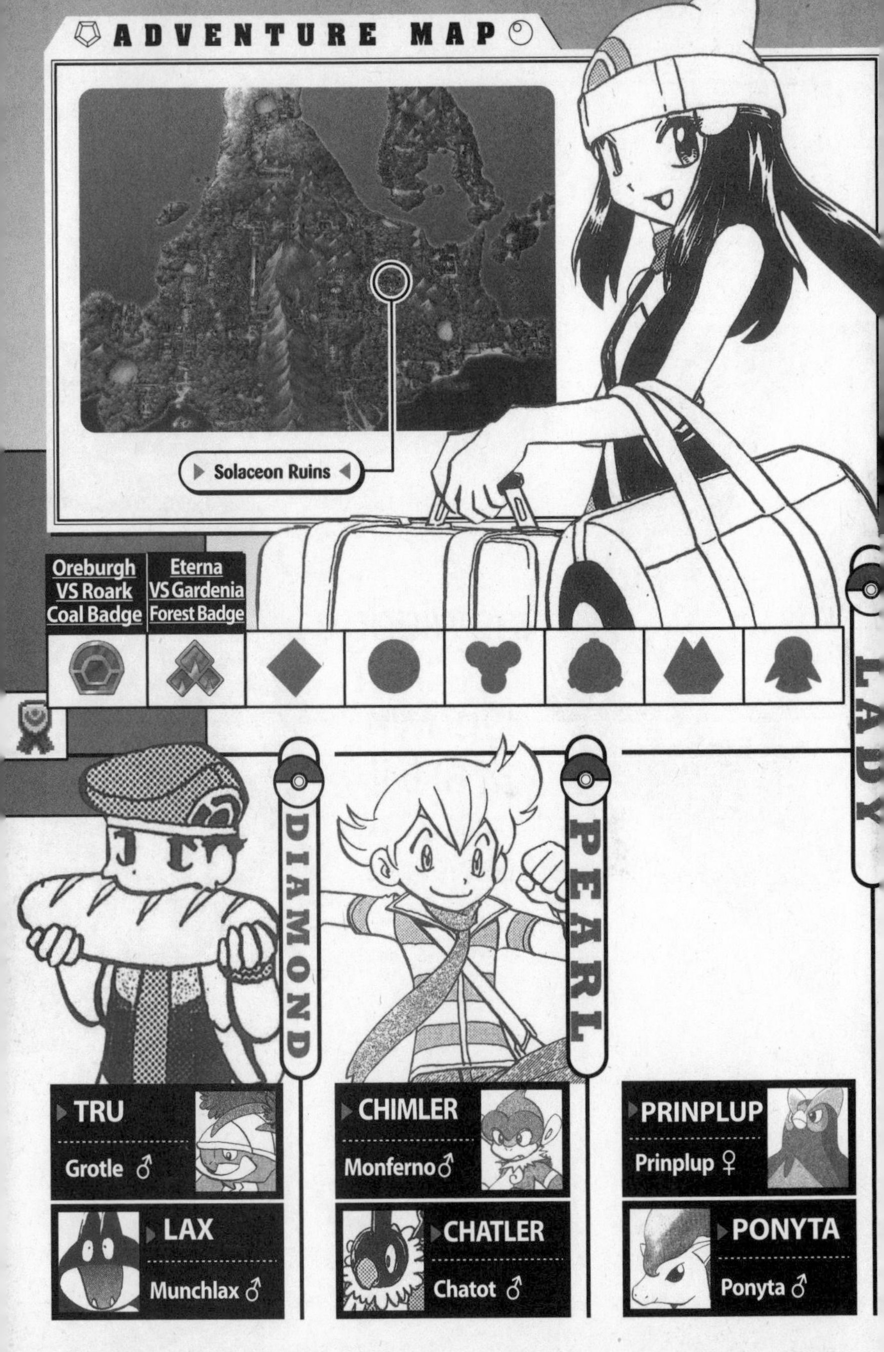
ADVENTURE MAP
Solaceon Ruins
Oreburgh VS Roark Coal Badge
Eterna VS Gardenia Forest Badge
LADY
DIAMOND
PEARL
TRU
Grotle ♂
LAX
Munchlax ♂
CHIMLER
Monferno ♂
CHATLER
Chatot ♂
PRINPLUP
Prinplup ♀
PONYTA
Ponyta ♂

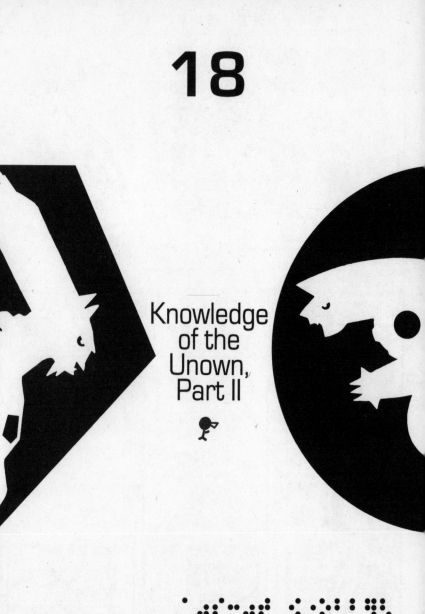

18

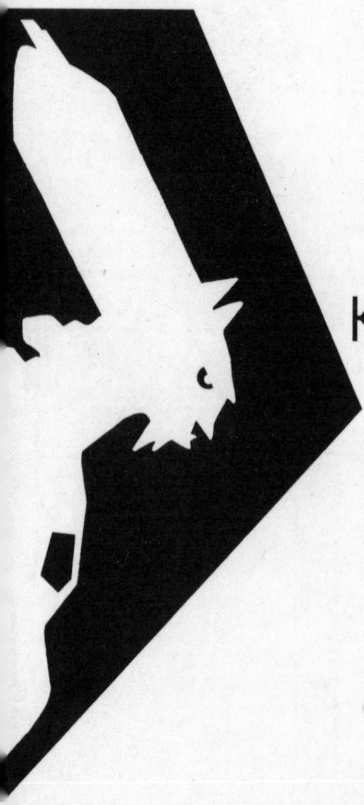

Knowledge of the Unown, Part II

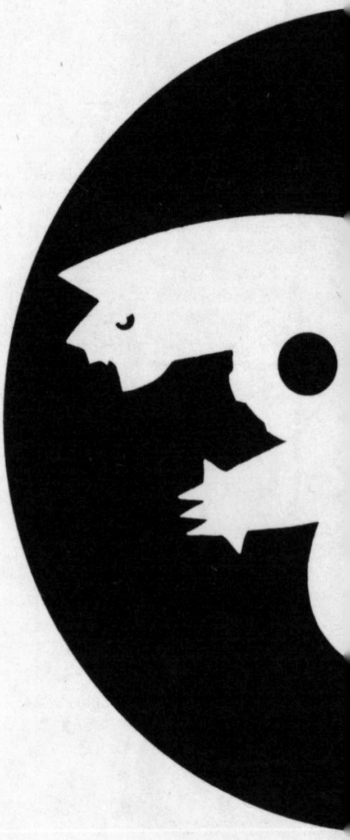

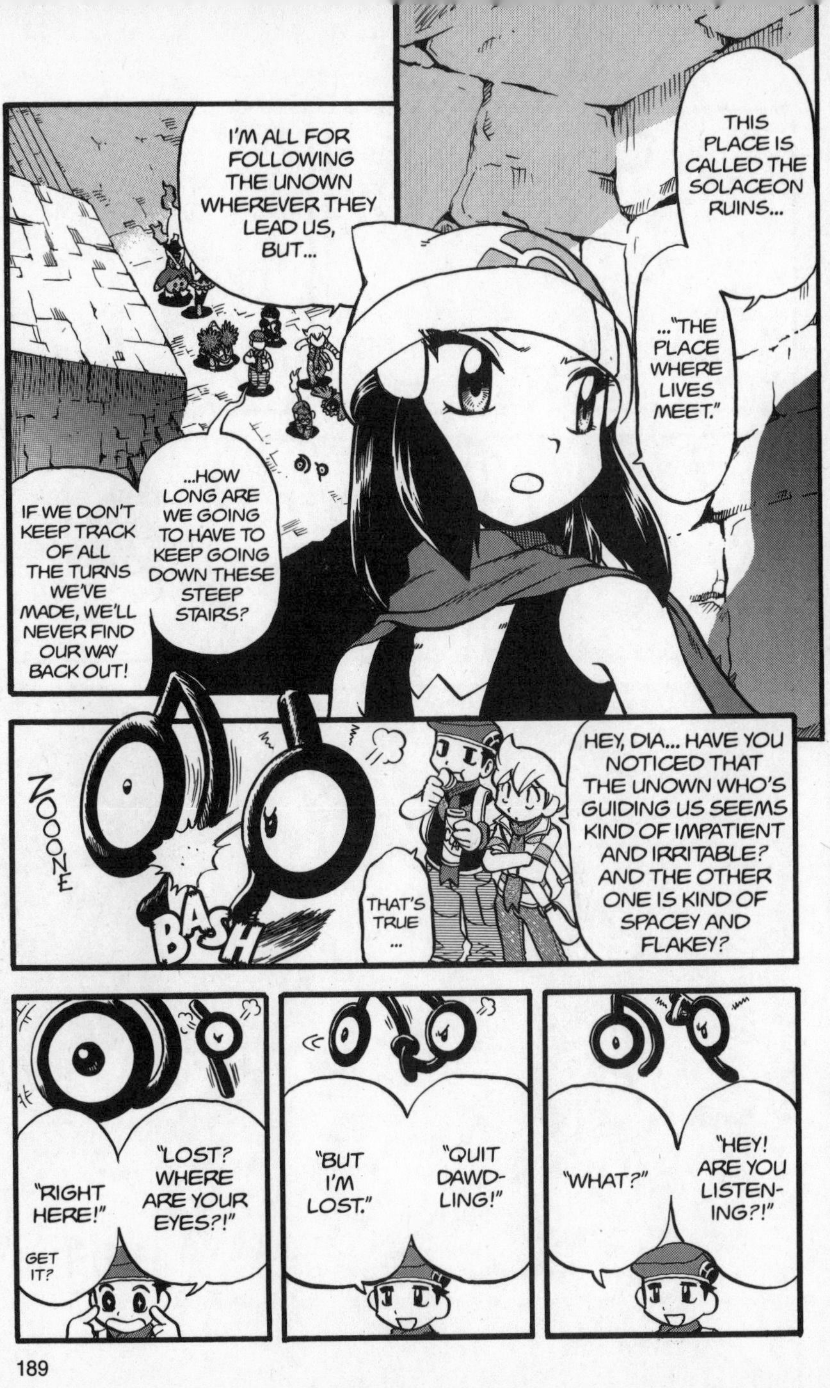
THIS PLACE IS CALLED THE SOLACEON RUINS...
..."THE PLACE WHERE LIVES MEET."
I'M ALL FOR FOLLOWING THE UNOWN WHEREVER THEY LEAD US, BUT...
...HOW LONG ARE WE GOING TO HAVE TO KEEP GOING DOWN THESE STEEP STAIRS?
IF WE DON'T KEEP TRACK OF ALL THE TURNS WE'VE MADE, WE'LL NEVER FIND OUR WAY BACK OUT!
HEY, DIA... HAVE YOU NOTICED THAT THE UNOWN WHO'S GUIDING US SEEMS KIND OF IMPATIENT AND IRRITABLE? AND THE OTHER ONE IS KIND OF SPACEY AND FLAKEY?
THAT'S TRUE ...
BASH
ZOOOONE
"HEY! ARE YOU LISTEN-ING?!"
"WHAT?"
"QUIT DAWD-LING!"
"BUT I'M LOST."
"LOST? WHERE ARE YOUR EYES?!"
"RIGHT HERE!"
GET IT?

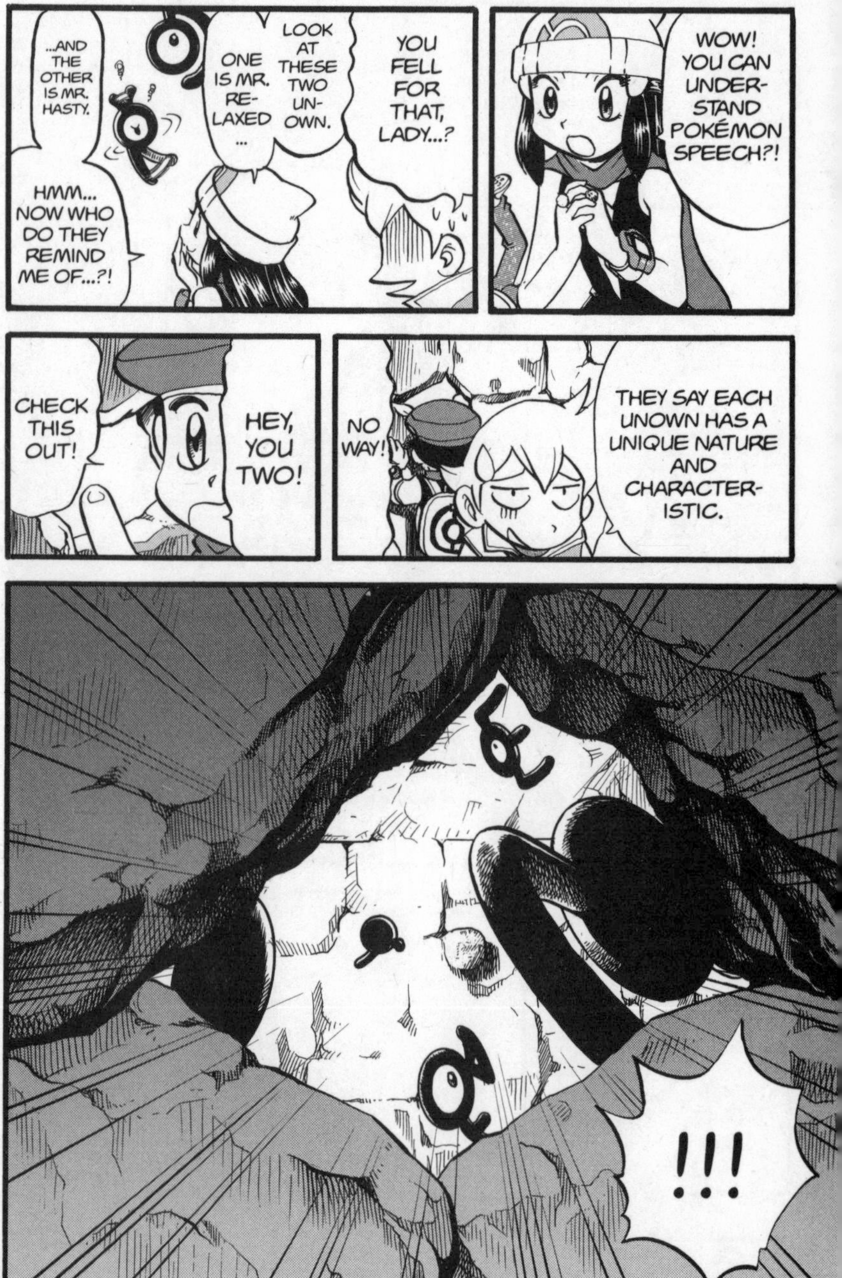
WOW! YOU CAN UNDERSTAND POKÉMON SPEECH?!
YOU FELL FOR THAT, LADY...?
LOOK AT THESE TWO UNOWN.
ONE IS MR. RELAXED...
...AND THE OTHER IS MR. HASTY.
HMM... NOW WHO DO THEY REMIND ME OF...?!
THEY SAY EACH UNOWN HAS A UNIQUE NATURE AND CHARACTERISTIC.
NO WAY!
HEY, YOU TWO!
CHECK THIS OUT!
!!!

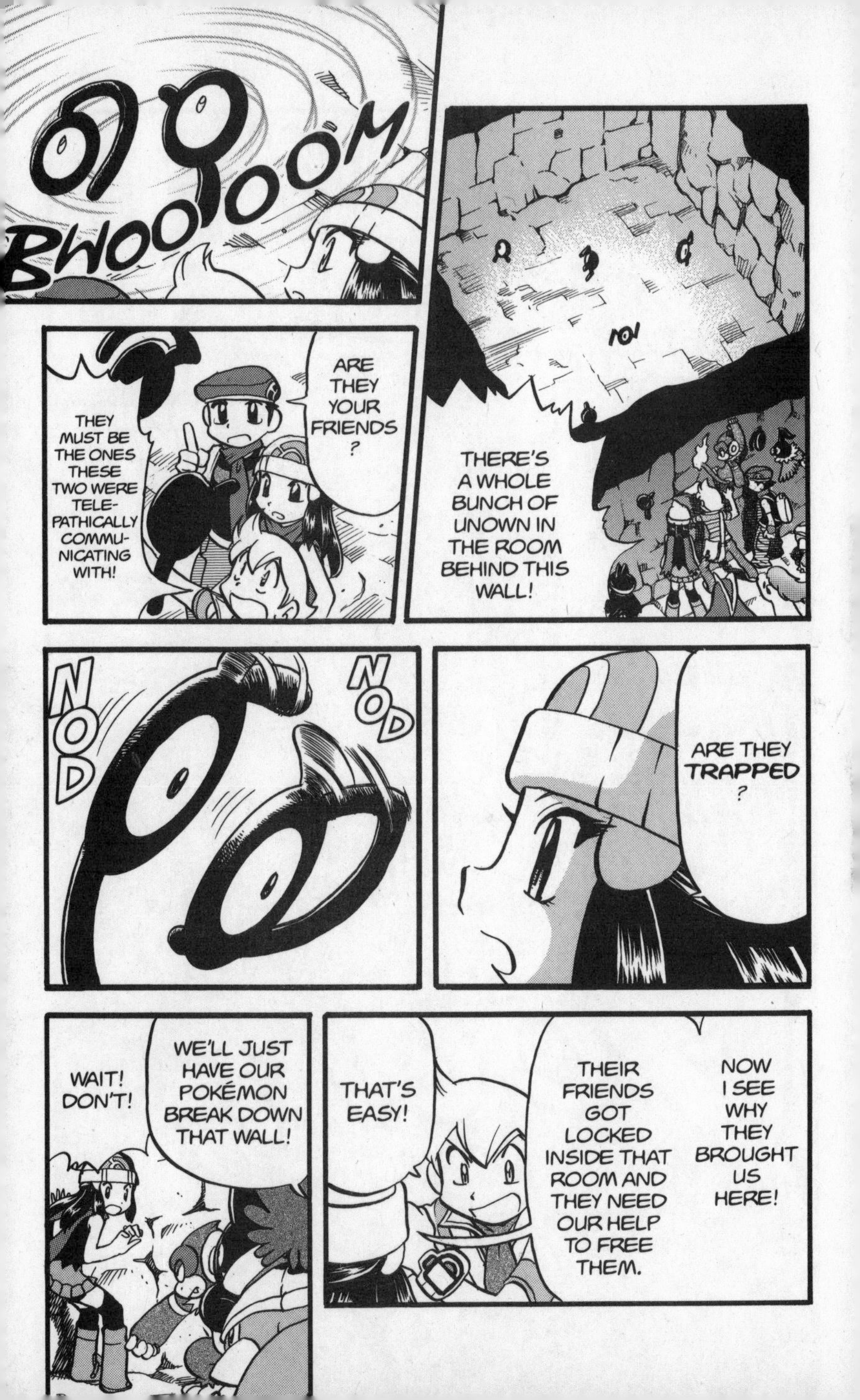
BWOOOOOOM
THERE'S A WHOLE BUNCH OF UNOWN IN THE ROOM BEHIND THIS WALL!
ARE THEY YOUR FRIENDS?
THEY MUST BE THE ONES THESE TWO WERE TELE-PATHICALLY COMMU-NICATING WITH!
ARE THEY **TRAPPED**?
NOD
NOD
NOW I SEE WHY THEY BROUGHT US HERE!
THEIR FRIENDS GOT LOCKED INSIDE THAT ROOM AND THEY NEED OUR HELP TO FREE THEM.
THAT'S EASY!
WE'LL JUST HAVE OUR POKÉMON BREAK DOWN THAT WALL!
WAIT! DON'T!

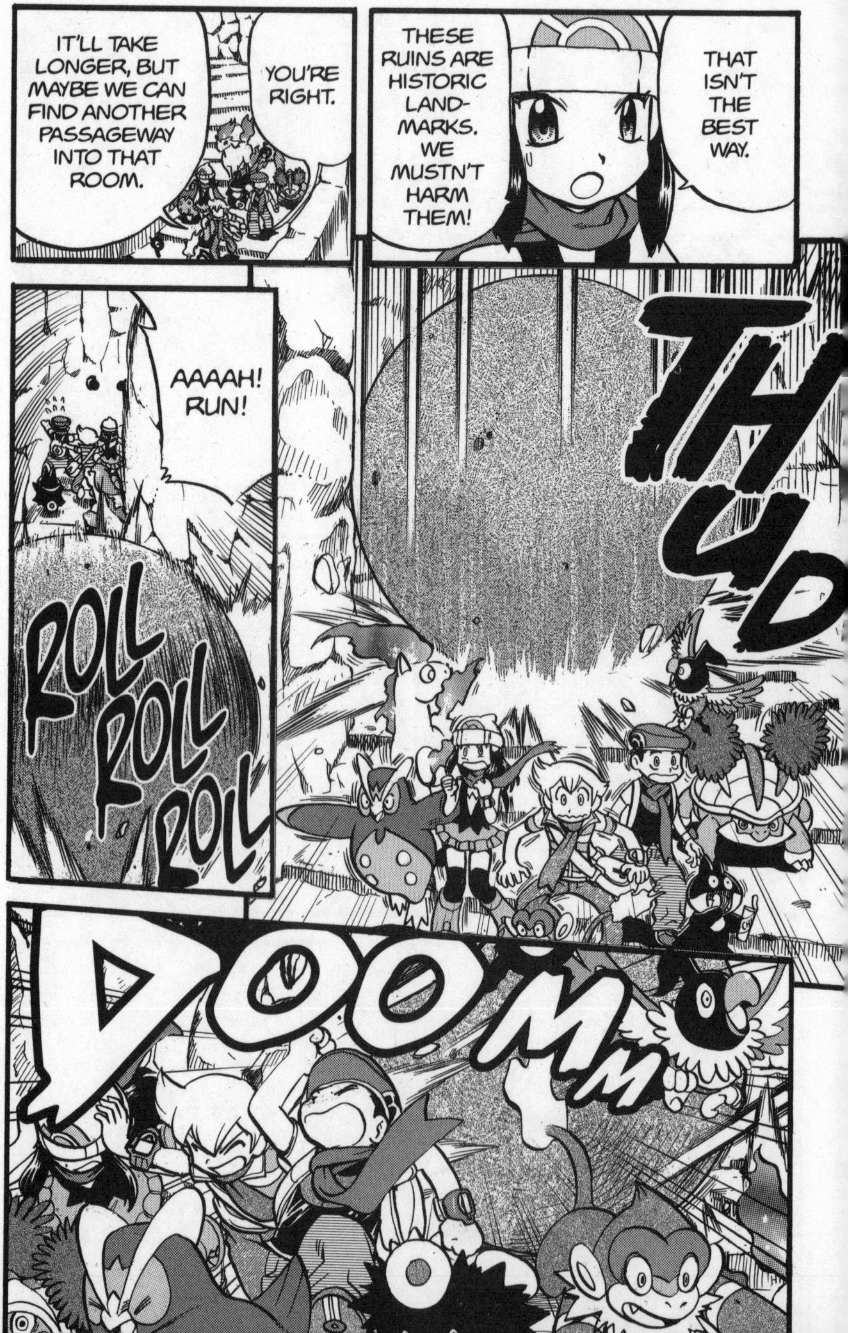
THAT ISN'T THE BEST WAY.
THESE RUINS ARE HISTORIC LAND-MARKS. WE MUSTN'T HARM THEM!
YOU'RE RIGHT.
IT'LL TAKE LONGER, BUT MAYBE WE CAN FIND ANOTHER PASSAGEWAY INTO THAT ROOM.
THUD
AAAAH! RUN!
ROLL ROLL ROLL
DOOMM

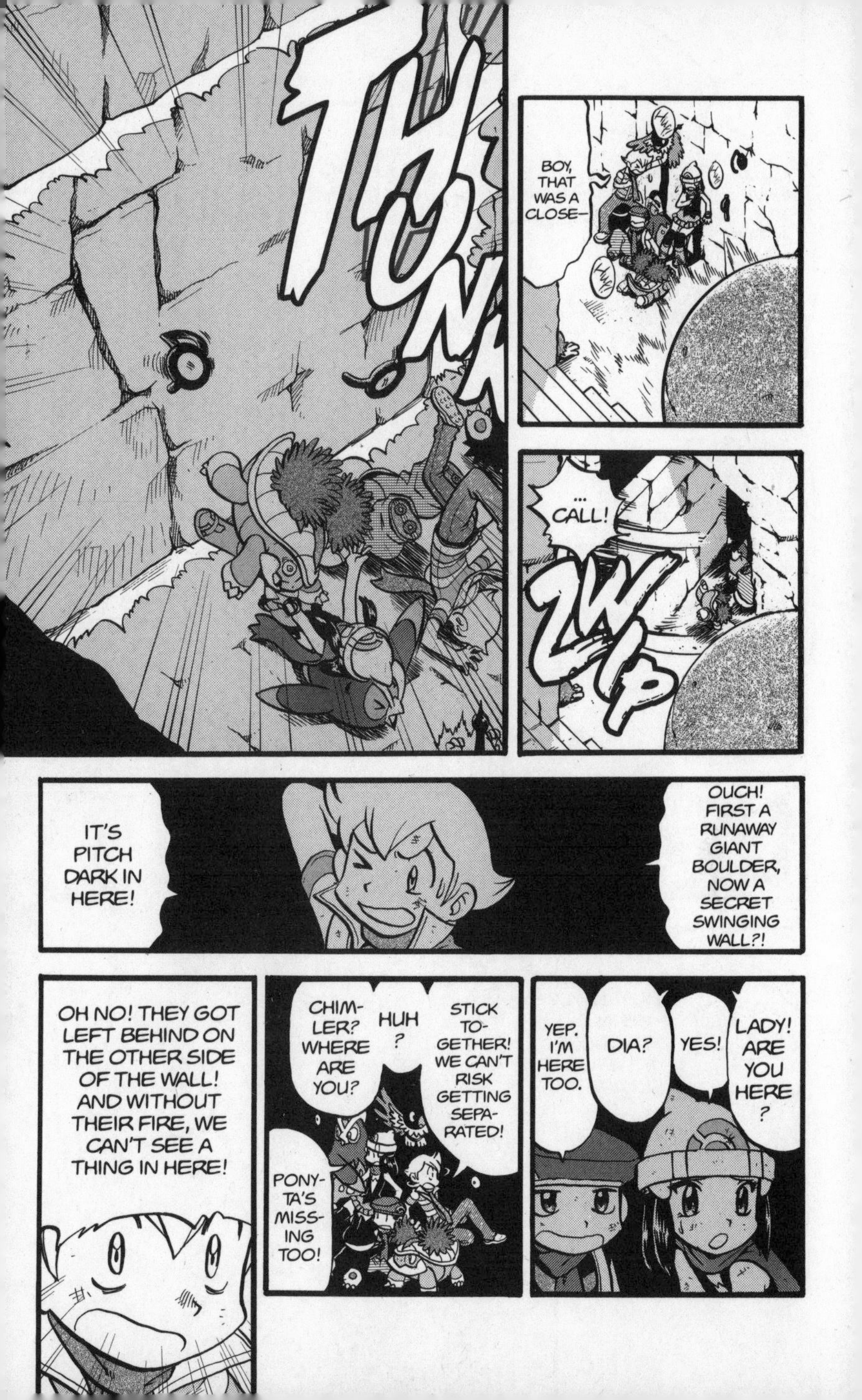
BOY, THAT WAS A CLOSE—
... CALL!
ZWIP
OUCH! FIRST A RUNAWAY GIANT BOULDER, NOW A SECRET SWINGING WALL?!
IT'S PITCH DARK IN HERE!
LADY! ARE YOU HERE?
YES!
DIA?
YEP. I'M HERE TOO.
STICK TO-GETHER! WE CAN'T RISK GETTING SEPA-RATED!
HUH?
CHIM-LER? WHERE ARE YOU?
PONY-TA'S MISS-ING TOO!
OH NO! THEY GOT LEFT BEHIND ON THE OTHER SIDE OF THE WALL! AND WITHOUT THEIR FIRE, WE CAN'T SEE A THING IN HERE!

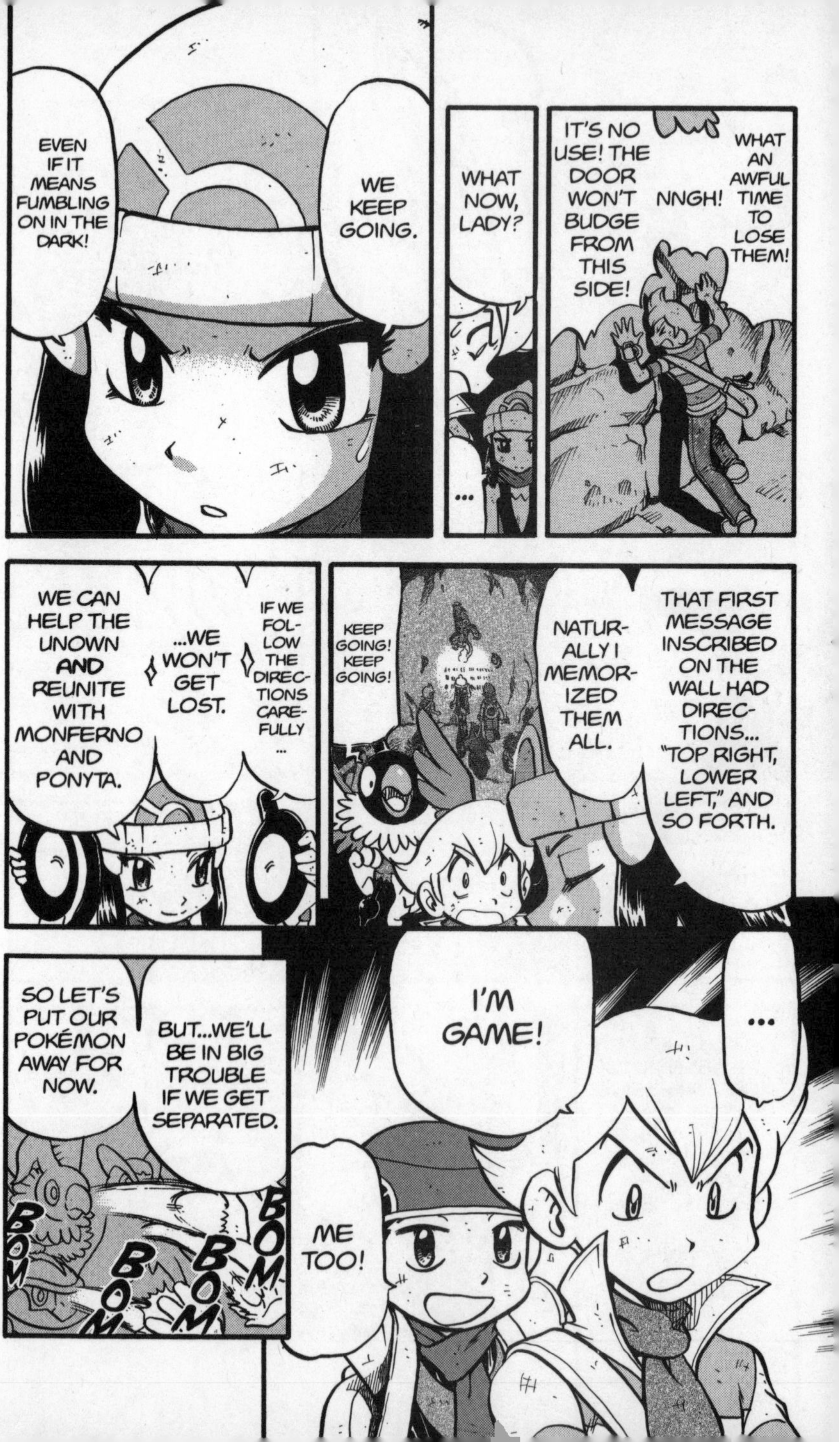
WHAT AN AWFUL TIME TO LOSE THEM!
NNGH!
IT'S NO USE! THE DOOR WON'T BUDGE FROM THIS SIDE!
WHAT NOW, LADY?
...
WE KEEP GOING.
EVEN IF IT MEANS FUMBLING ON IN THE DARK!
THAT FIRST MESSAGE INSCRIBED ON THE WALL HAD DIRECTIONS... "TOP RIGHT, LOWER LEFT," AND SO FORTH.
NATURALLY I MEMORIZED THEM ALL.
KEEP GOING! KEEP GOING!
IF WE FOLLOW THE DIRECTIONS CAREFULLY...
...WE WON'T GET LOST.
WE CAN HELP THE UNOWN **AND** REUNITE WITH MONFERNO AND PONYTA.
...
I'M GAME!
ME TOO!
BUT...WE'LL BE IN BIG TROUBLE IF WE GET SEPARATED.
SO LET'S PUT OUR POKÉMON AWAY FOR NOW.
BOM
BOM
BOM
BOM

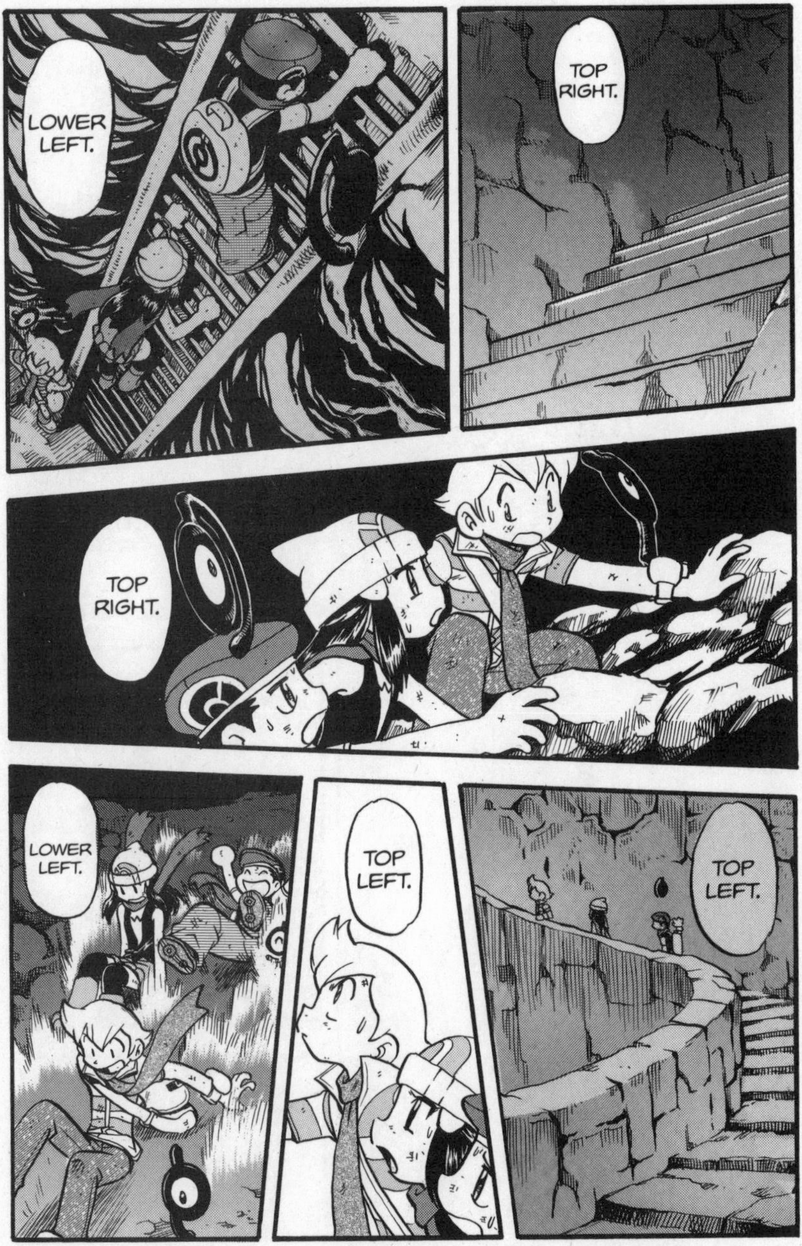
TOP RIGHT.
LOWER LEFT.
TOP RIGHT.
TOP LEFT.
TOP LEFT.
LOWER LEFT.

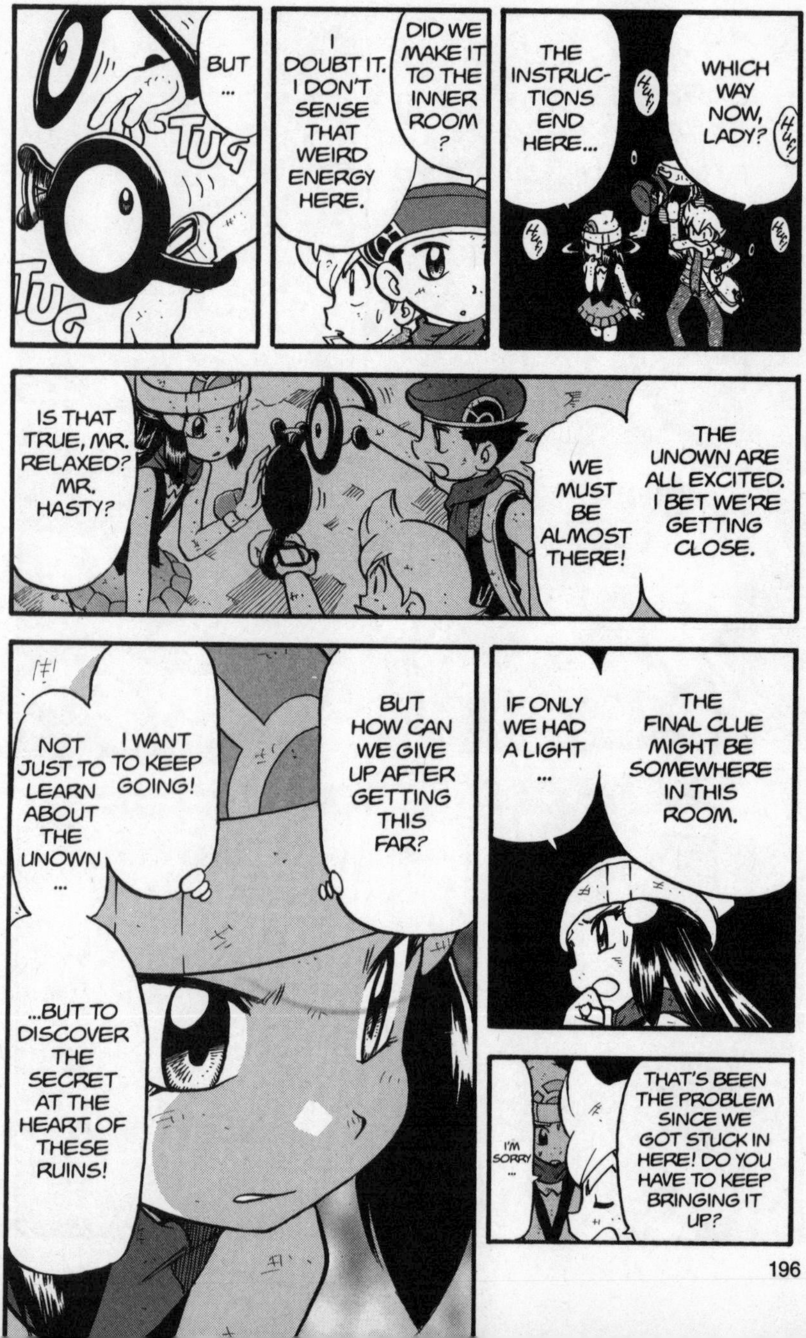
WHICH WAY NOW, LADY?
HUFF!
HUFF!
THE INSTRUCTIONS END HERE...
HUFF!
HUFF!
DID WE MAKE IT TO THE INNER ROOM?
I DOUBT IT. I DON'T SENSE THAT WEIRD ENERGY HERE.
BUT ...
TUG
TUG
THE UNOWN ARE ALL EXCITED. I BET WE'RE GETTING CLOSE.
WE MUST BE ALMOST THERE!
IS THAT TRUE, MR. RELAXED? MR. HASTY?
THE FINAL CLUE MIGHT BE SOMEWHERE IN THIS ROOM.
IF ONLY WE HAD A LIGHT ...
THAT'S BEEN THE PROBLEM SINCE WE GOT STUCK IN HERE! DO YOU HAVE TO KEEP BRINGING IT UP?
I'M SORRY ...
BUT HOW CAN WE GIVE UP AFTER GETTING THIS FAR?
I WANT TO KEEP GOING!
NOT JUST TO LEARN ABOUT THE UNOWN ...
...BUT TO DISCOVER THE SECRET AT THE HEART OF THESE RUINS!

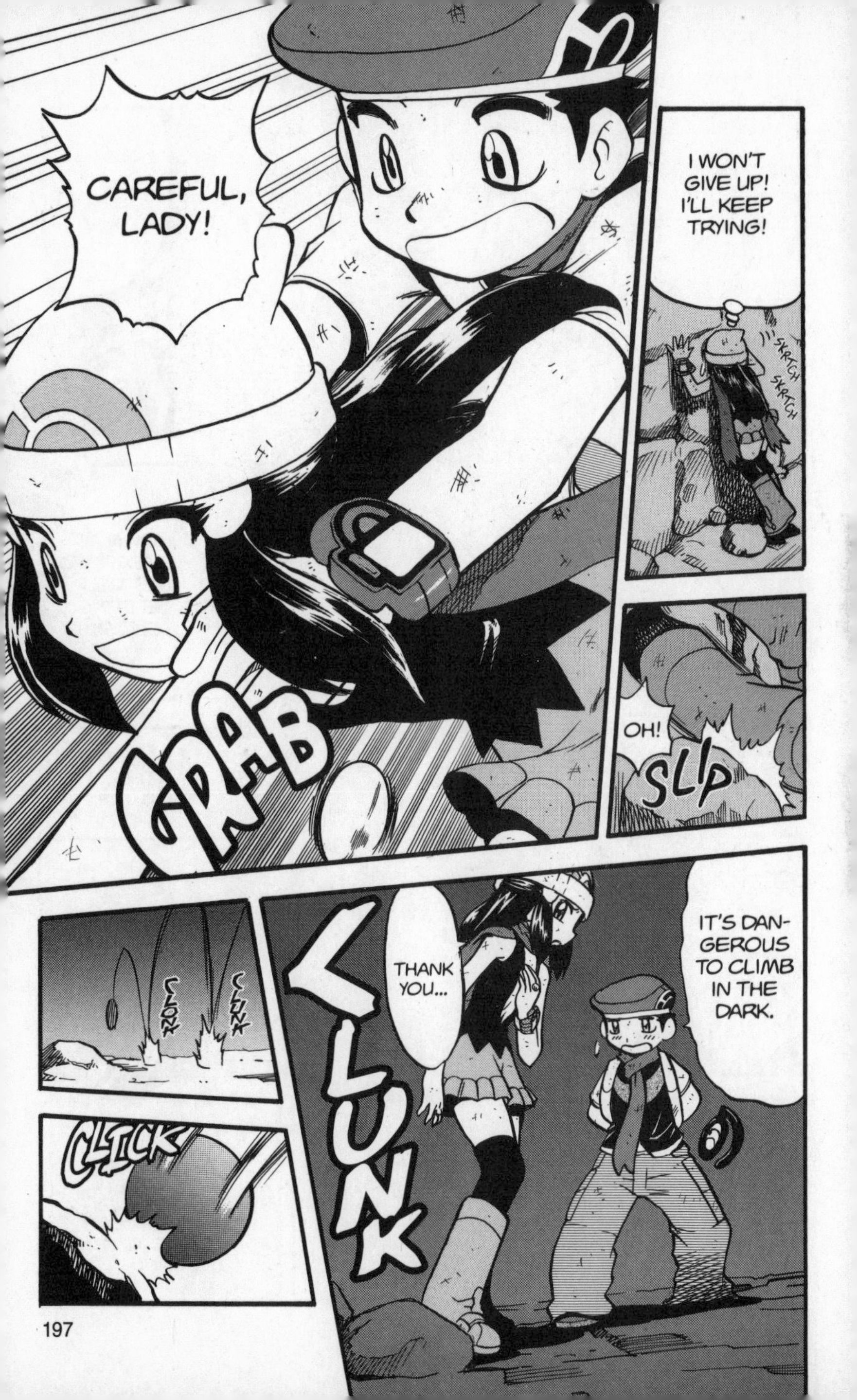
I WON'T GIVE UP! I'LL KEEP TRYING!
SKRTCH SKRTCH
OH!
SLIP
CAREFUL, LADY!
GRAB
IT'S DAN-GEROUS TO CLIMB IN THE DARK.
THANK YOU...
CLUNK
CLUNK CLUNK
CLICK

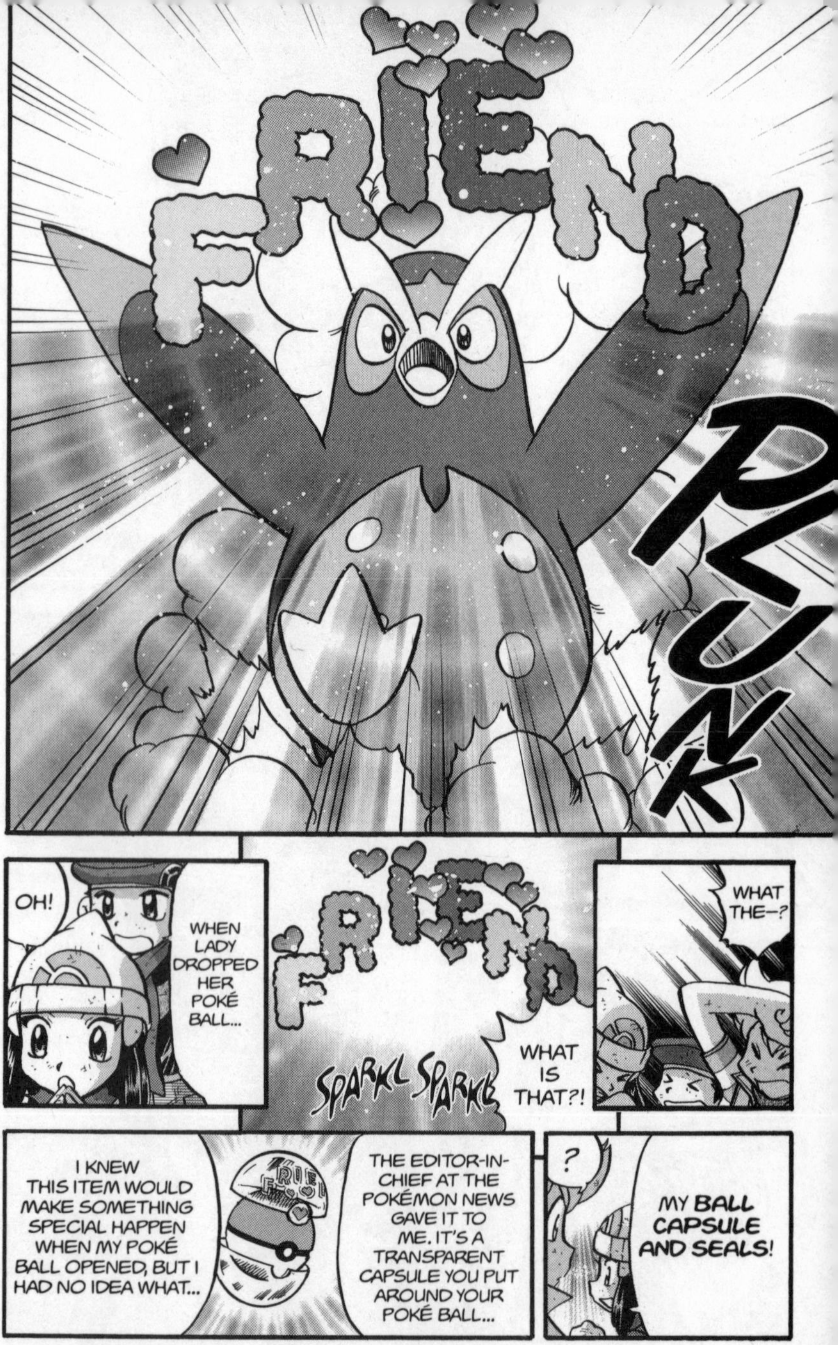
FRIEND
PLUNK
WHAT THE—?
FRIEND
WHAT IS THAT?!
SPARKL SPARKL
OH!
WHEN LADY DROPPED HER POKÉ BALL...
?
MY BALL CAPSULE AND SEALS!
THE EDITOR-IN-CHIEF AT THE POKÉMON NEWS GAVE IT TO ME. IT'S A TRANSPARENT CAPSULE YOU PUT AROUND YOUR POKÉ BALL...
I KNEW THIS ITEM WOULD MAKE SOMETHING SPECIAL HAPPEN WHEN MY POKÉ BALL OPENED, BUT I HAD NO IDEA WHAT...

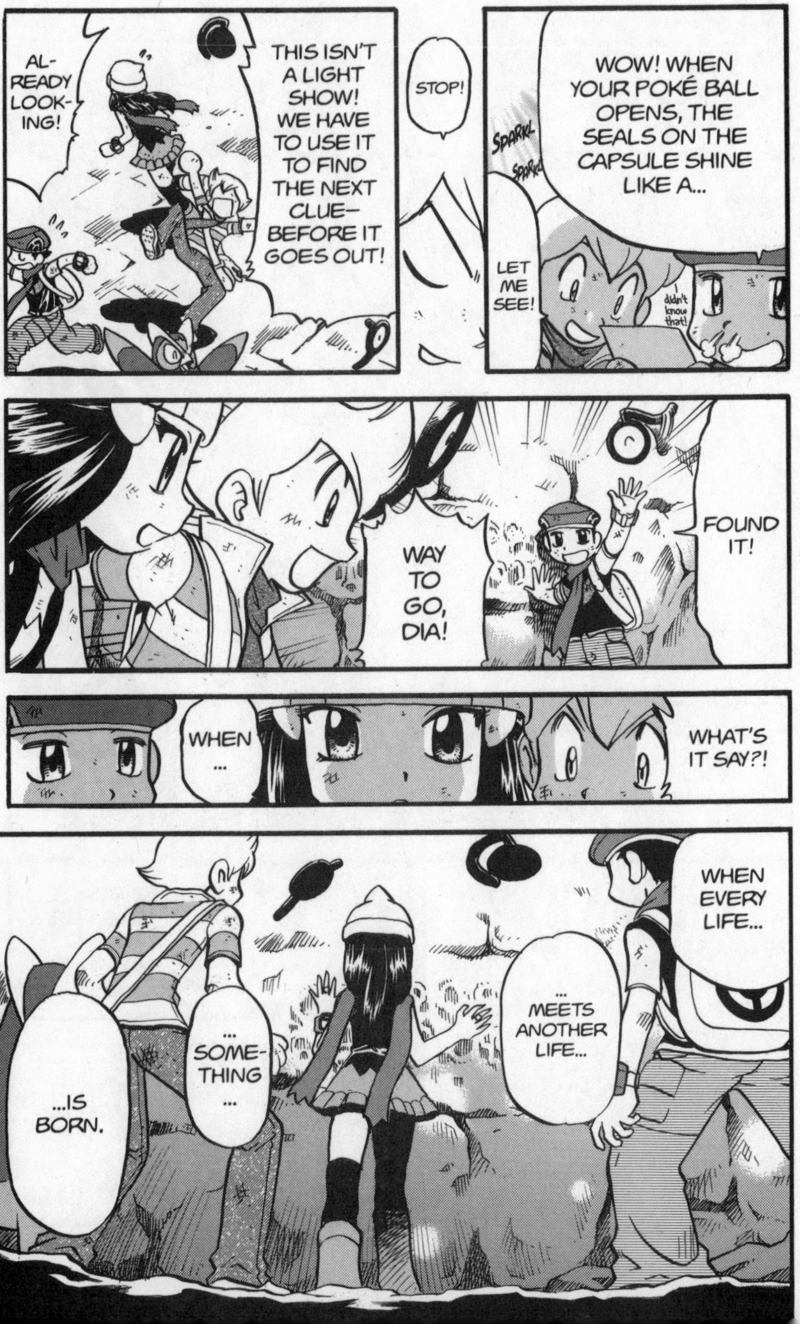
WOW! WHEN YOUR POKÉ BALL OPENS, THE SEALS ON THE CAPSULE SHINE LIKE A...
SPARKL SPARKL
I didn't know that!
LET ME SEE!
STOP!
THIS ISN'T A LIGHT SHOW! WE HAVE TO USE IT TO FIND THE NEXT CLUE— BEFORE IT GOES OUT!
AL-READY LOOK-ING!
FOUND IT!
WAY TO GO, DIA!
WHAT'S IT SAY?!
WHEN ...
WHEN EVERY LIFE...
... MEETS ANOTHER LIFE...
... SOME-THING ...
...IS BORN.

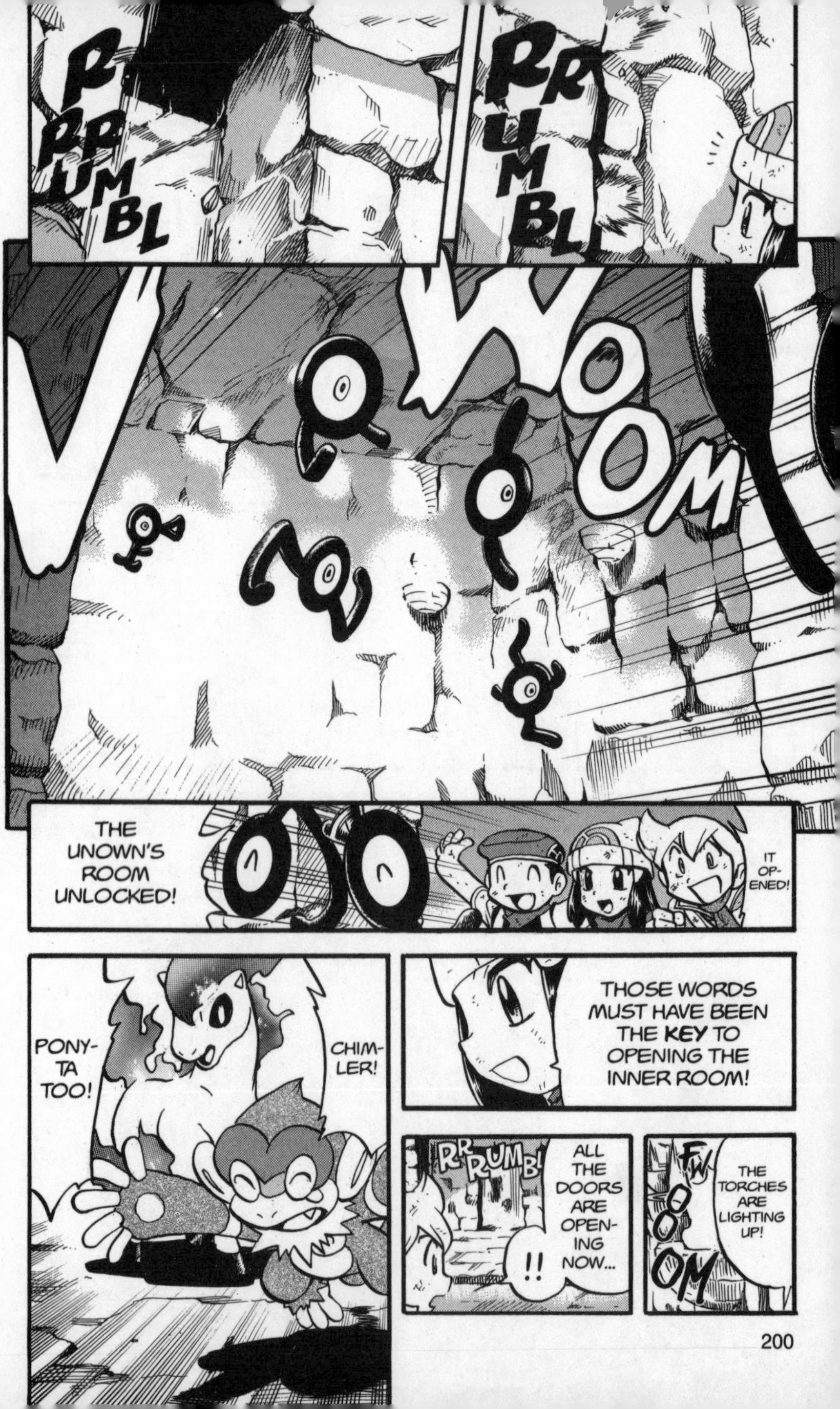
RRUMBL
RRRUMBL
WOOOM
IT OPENED!
THE UNOWN'S ROOM UNLOCKED!
THOSE WORDS MUST HAVE BEEN THE **KEY** TO OPENING THE INNER ROOM!
FWOOOM
THE TORCHES ARE LIGHTING UP!
RRRUMBL
ALL THE DOORS ARE OPENING NOW...
!!
CHIMLER!
PONYTA TOO!

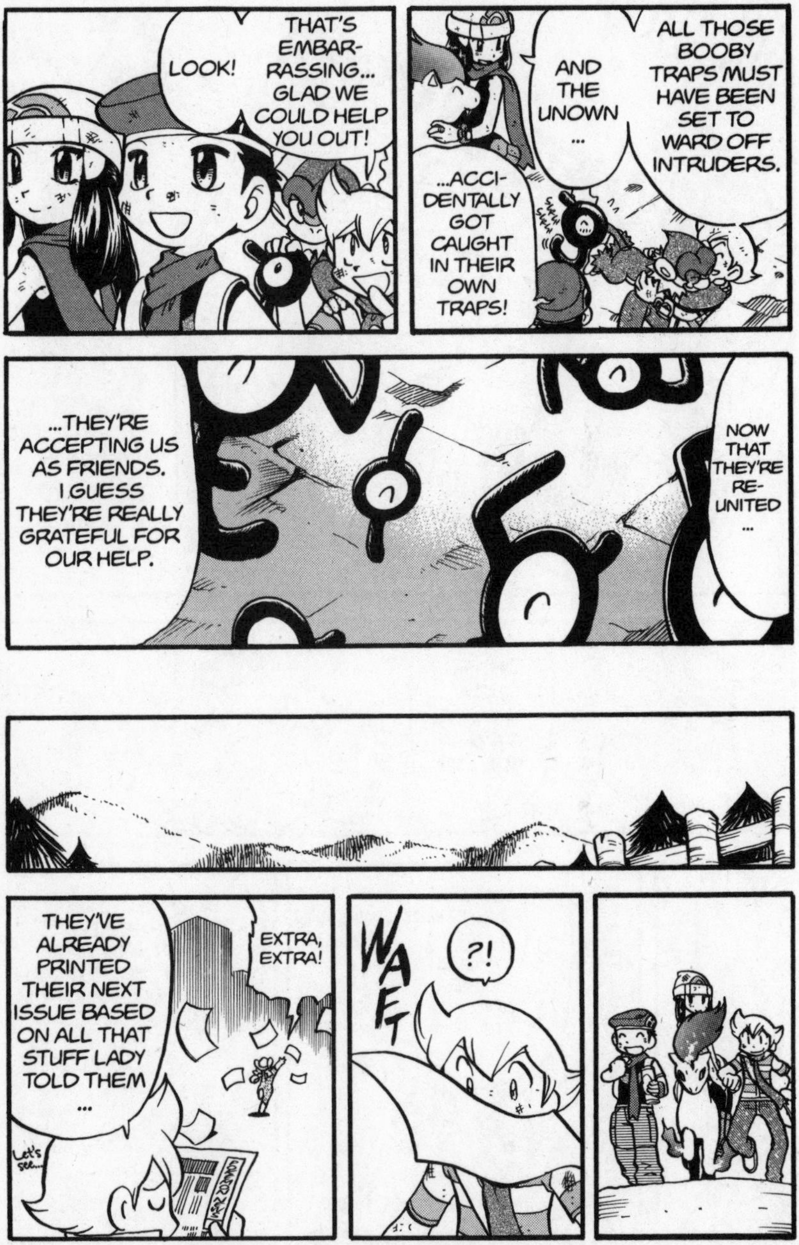
ALL THOSE BOOBY TRAPS MUST HAVE BEEN SET TO WARD OFF INTRUDERS.
AND THE UNOWN ...
...ACCI-DENTALLY GOT CAUGHT IN THEIR OWN TRAPS!
THAT'S EMBAR-RASSING... GLAD WE COULD HELP YOU OUT!
LOOK!
NOW THAT THEY'RE RE-UNITED ...
...THEY'RE ACCEPTING US AS FRIENDS. I GUESS THEY'RE REALLY GRATEFUL FOR OUR HELP.
WAFT
?!
EXTRA, EXTRA!
THEY'VE ALREADY PRINTED THEIR NEXT ISSUE BASED ON ALL THAT STUFF LADY TOLD THEM ...
Let's see...

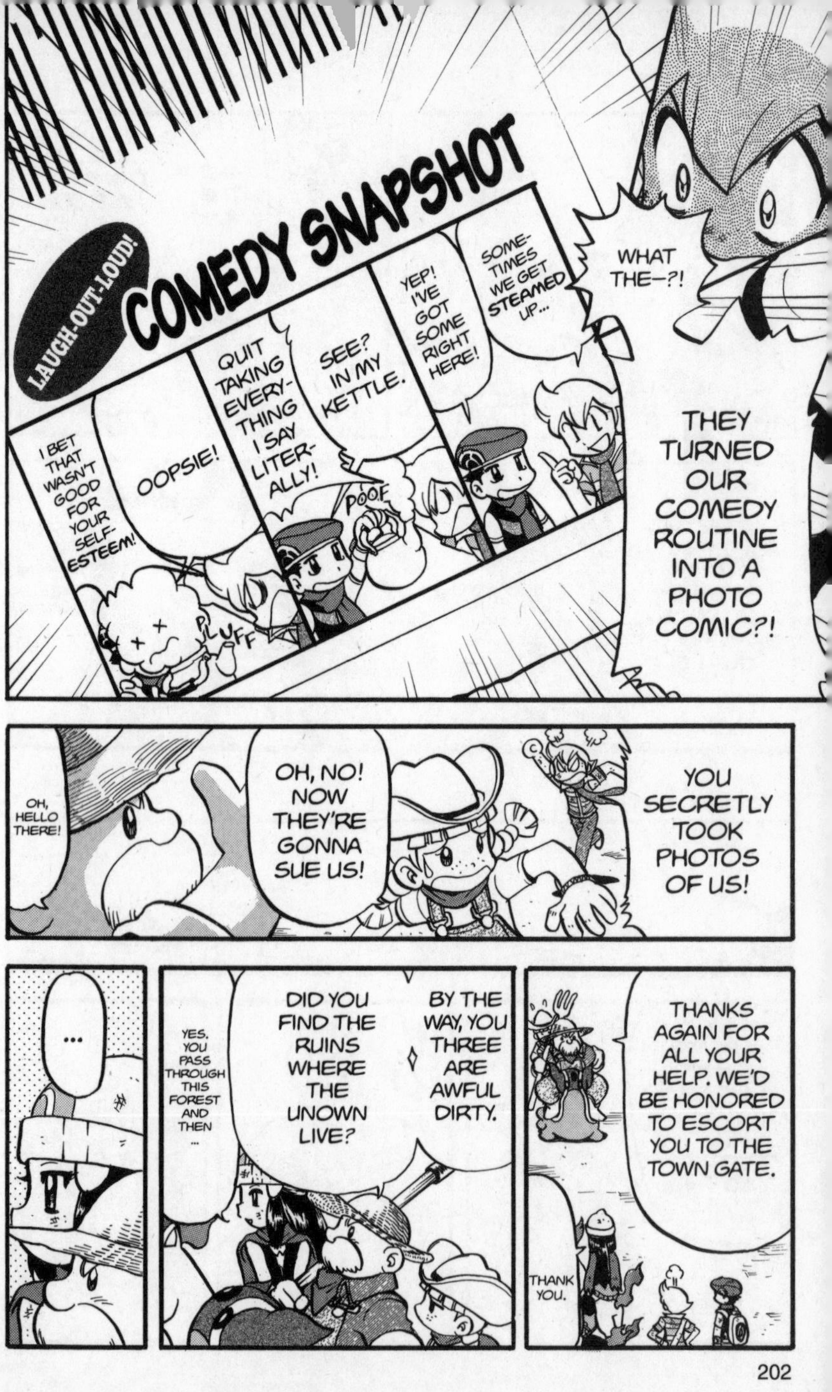
WHAT THE--?!
THEY TURNED OUR COMEDY ROUTINE INTO A PHOTO COMIC?!
LAUGH-OUT-LOUD!
COMEDY SNAPSHOT
SOME-TIMES WE GET STEAMED UP...
YEP! I'VE GOT SOME RIGHT HERE!
SEE? IN MY KETTLE.
POOF
QUIT TAKING EVERY-THING I SAY LITER-ALLY!
OOPSIE!
I BET THAT WASN'T GOOD FOR YOUR SELF-ESTEEM!
PLUFF
YOU SECRETLY TOOK PHOTOS OF US!
OH, NO! NOW THEY'RE GONNA SUE US!
OH, HELLO THERE!
THANKS AGAIN FOR ALL YOUR HELP. WE'D BE HONORED TO ESCORT YOU TO THE TOWN GATE.
THANK YOU.
BY THE WAY, YOU THREE ARE AWFUL DIRTY.
DID YOU FIND THE RUINS WHERE THE UNOWN LIVE?
YES. YOU PASS THROUGH THIS FOREST AND THEN ...
...

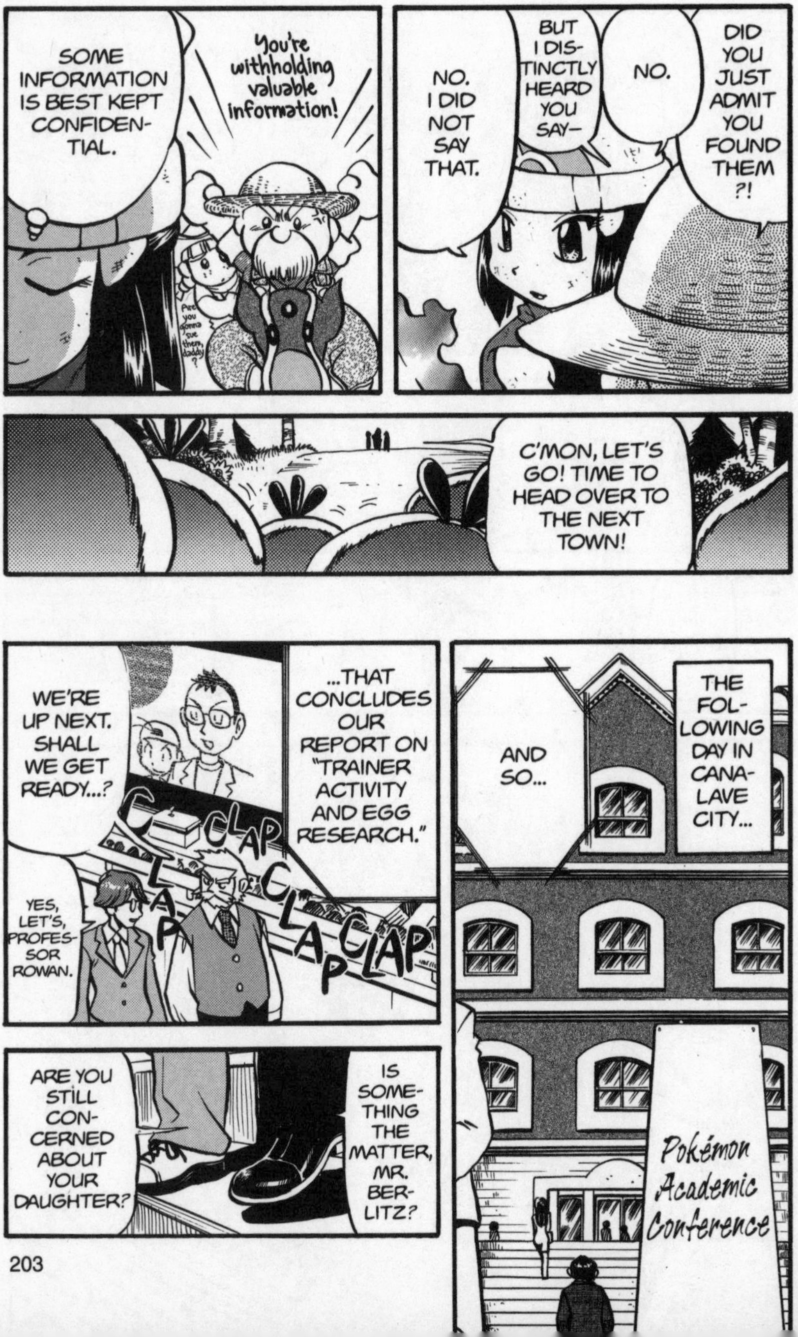
DID YOU JUST ADMIT YOU FOUND THEM?!
NO.
BUT I DISTINCTLY HEARD YOU SAY—
NO. I DID NOT SAY THAT.
You're withholding valuable information!
SOME INFORMATION IS BEST KEPT CONFIDENTIAL.
Are you gonna sue them, daddy?
C'MON, LET'S GO! TIME TO HEAD OVER TO THE NEXT TOWN!
THE FOLLOWING DAY IN CANALAVE CITY...
AND SO...
Pokémon Academic Conference
...THAT CONCLUDES OUR REPORT ON "TRAINER ACTIVITY AND EGG RESEARCH."
WE'RE UP NEXT. SHALL WE GET READY...?
C—CLAP CLAP CLAP CLAP CLAP
YES, LET'S, PROFESSOR ROWAN.
IS SOMETHING THE MATTER, MR. BERLITZ?
ARE YOU STILL CONCERNED ABOUT YOUR DAUGHTER?

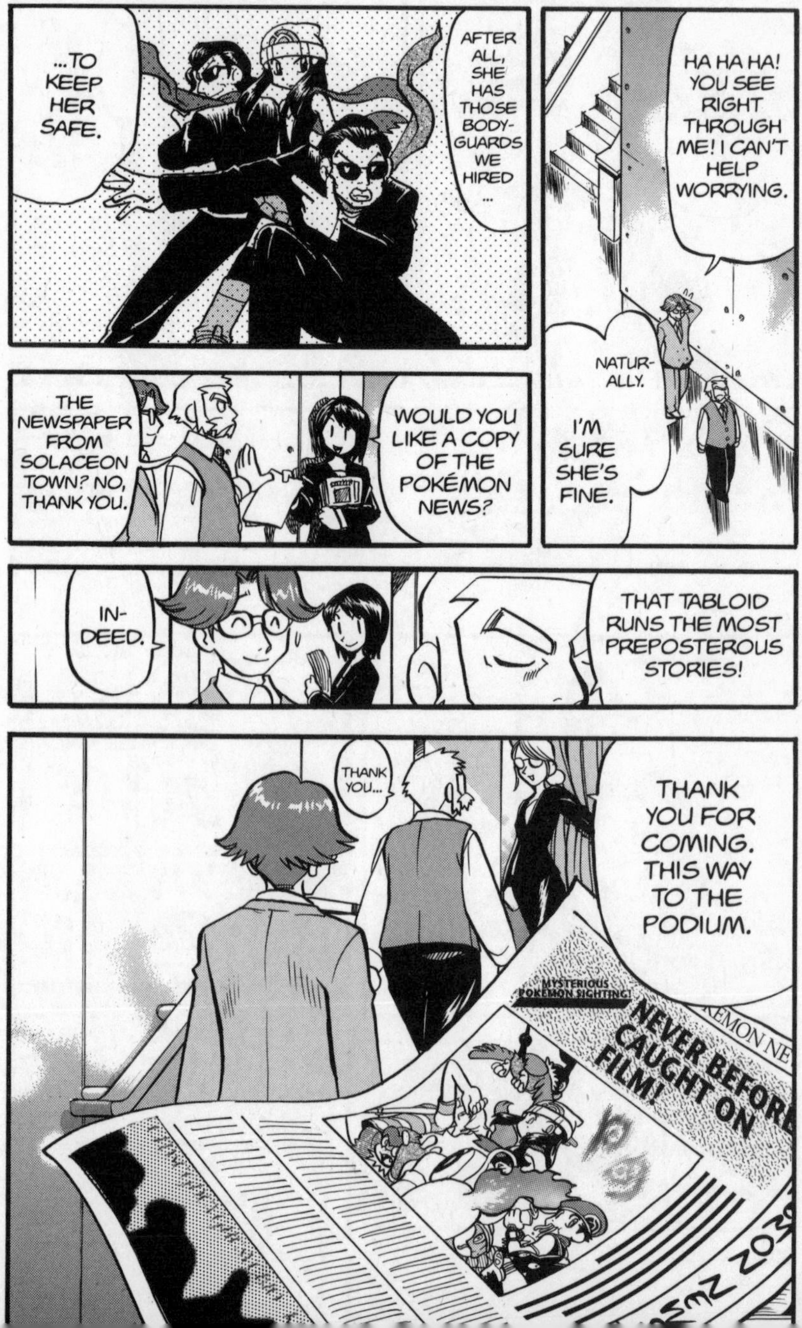
HA HA HA! YOU SEE RIGHT THROUGH ME! I CAN'T HELP WORRYING.
NATURALLY.
I'M SURE SHE'S FINE.
AFTER ALL, SHE HAS THOSE BODYGUARDS WE HIRED...
...TO KEEP HER SAFE.
WOULD YOU LIKE A COPY OF THE POKÉMON NEWS?
THE NEWSPAPER FROM SOLACEON TOWN? NO, THANK YOU.
THAT TABLOID RUNS THE MOST PREPOSTEROUS STORIES!
IN-DEED.
THANK YOU FOR COMING. THIS WAY TO THE PODIUM.
THANK YOU...
MYSTERIOUS POKEMON SIGHTING!
NEVER BEFORE CAUGHT ON FILM!

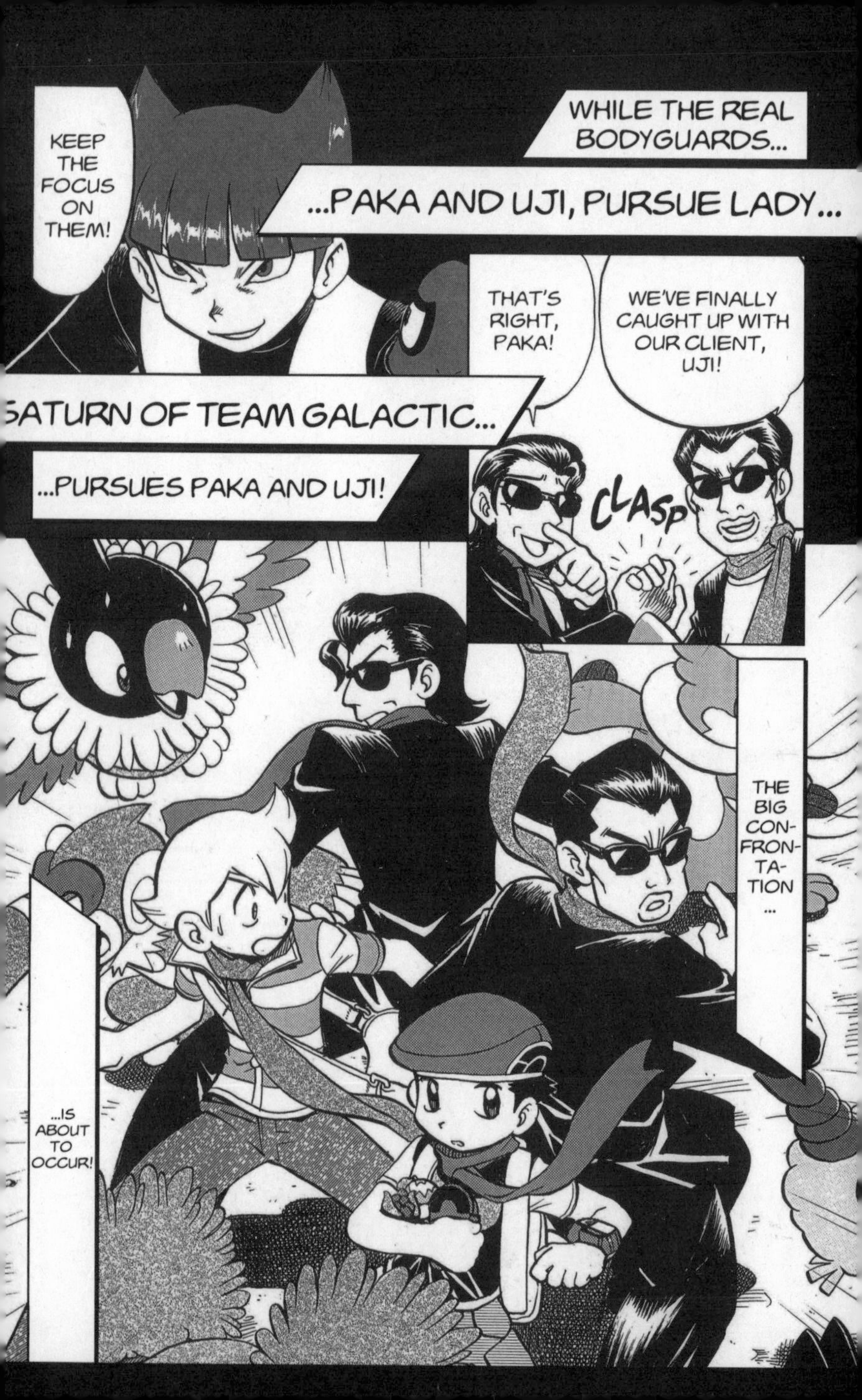
WHILE THE REAL BODYGUARDS...
...PAKA AND UJI, PURSUE LADY...
KEEP THE FOCUS ON THEM!
WE'VE FINALLY CAUGHT UP WITH OUR CLIENT, UJI!
THAT'S RIGHT, PAKA!
CLASP
SATURN OF TEAM GALACTIC...
...PURSUES PAKA AND UJI!
THE BIG CONFRONTATION...
...IS ABOUT TO OCCUR!

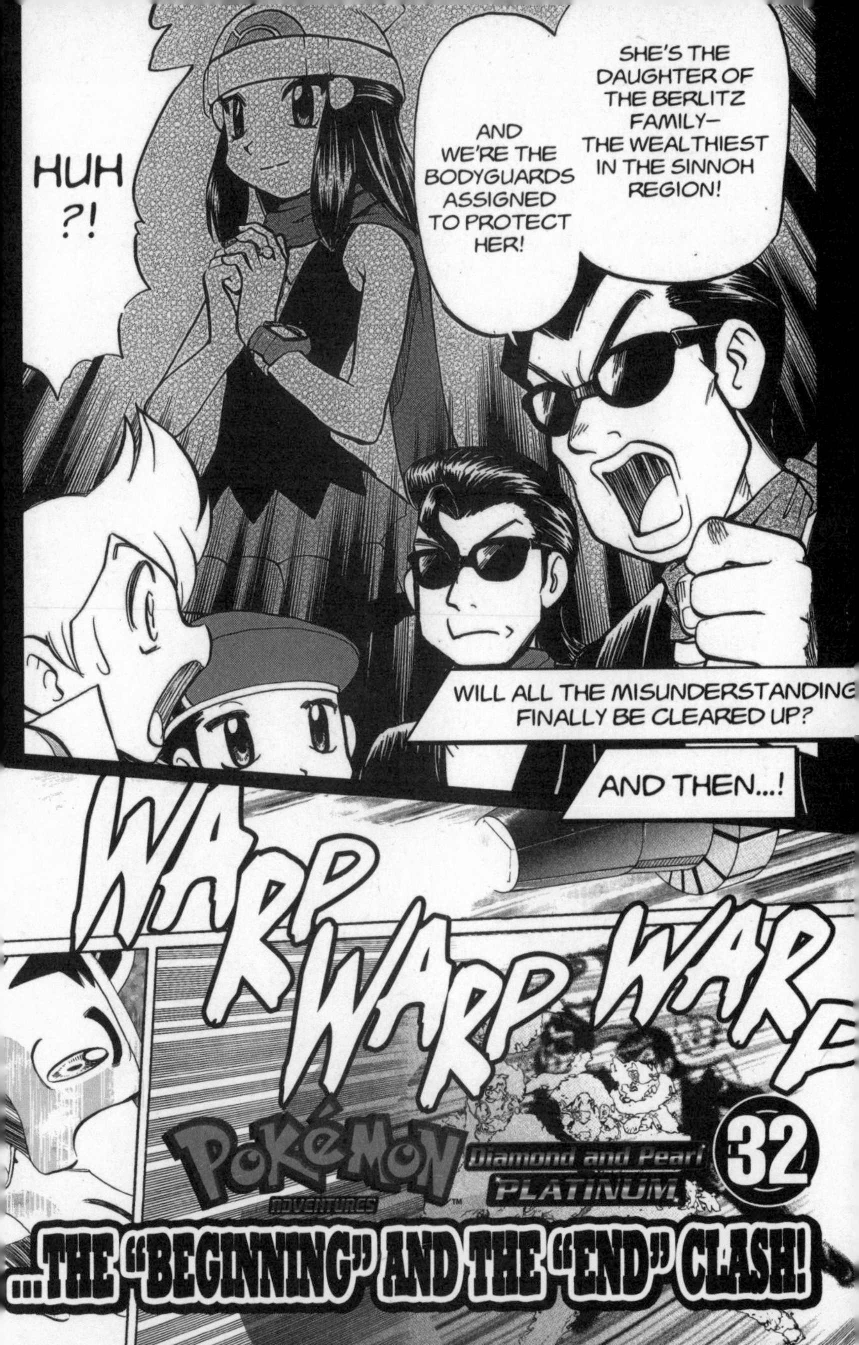
SHE'S THE DAUGHTER OF THE BERLITZ FAMILY— THE WEALTHIEST IN THE SINNOH REGION!
AND WE'RE THE BODYGUARDS ASSIGNED TO PROTECT HER!
HUH ?!
WILL ALL THE MISUNDERSTANDING FINALLY BE CLEARED UP?
AND THEN...!
WARP
WARP
WAR
POKéMON ADVENTURES™ Diamond and Pearl PLATINUM 32
...THE "BEGINNING" AND THE "END" CLASH!

Message from
Hidenori Kusaka

I've given a lot of thought to Dialga and Palkia while working on this volume— the seventh one I've drawn. The Poké- mon who rules time and the Pokémon who rules space... What would it be like to be them? I still can't imagine it. Like me, our heroes will have to be patient in their search for answers. The characters are always growing and changing. Keep reading!

Message from
Satoshi Yamamoto

Volume 1 was full of travel adventure. If you grew fond of our three heroes in the last volume, you'll like them even more this time around! I found the Contest episode in which their friendships evolve quite engaging, if I do say so myself. Of the minor characters, my favorite is the newspa- per editor-in-chief.

More Adventures Coming Soon...

Thieves are afoot. One wants to steal Diamond's Pokédex.
Another wants to steal...Lady! Can Pearl and Diamond protect her...as well as an entire city?! Then join our trio as they follow in the footsteps of a scientist who researches Pokémon footprints.

Meanwhile, what is Team Galactic planning to do with that machine they just invented...?

Plus, meet Riolu, Skuntank, Gible, Hippopotas, Kricketune, Skorupi and many more new Sinnoh Pokémon friends!

POKÉMON ADVENTURES:
DIAMOND AND PEARL/
PLATINUM
Volume 2
VIZ Media Edition

Story by **HIDENORI KUSAKA**
Art by **SATOSHI YAMAMOTO**

© 2011 The Pokémon Company International.
© 1995–2009 Nintendo / Creatures Inc. / GAME FREAK inc.
TM, ®, and character names are trademarks of Nintendo.
POCKET MONSTERS SPECIAL Vol. 2 (31)
by Hidenori KUSAKA, Satoshi YAMAMOTO
© 1997 Hidenori KUSAKA, Satoshi YAMAMOTO
All rights reserved.
Original Japanese edition published by SHOGAKUKAN.
English translation rights in the United States of America, Canada, the United Kingdom,
Ireland, Australia, New Zealand and India arranged with SHOGAKUKAN.

Translation/Katherine Schilling
Touch-up & Lettering/Annaliese Christman
Design/Yukiko Whitley
Editor/Annette Roman

The stories, characters and incidents mentioned
in this publication are entirely fictional.

Printed in the U.S.A.

Published by VIZ Media, LLC
P.O. Box 77010
San Francisco, CA 94107

10 9 8
First printing, June 2011
Eighth printing, June 2019

PARENTAL ADVISORY
POKÉMON ADVENTURES:
DIAMOND AND PEARL/PLATINUM
is rated A and is suitable for readers
of all ages.

VIZ MEDIA
viz.com

POKÉMON ADVENTURES 20TH ANNIVERSARY ILLUSTRATION BOOK

THE ART OF

POKÉMON ADVENTURES

STORY AND ART BY
Satoshi Yamamoto

A collection of beautiful full-color art from the artist of the Pokémon Adventures graphic novel series! In addition to illustrations of your favorite Pokémon, this vibrant volume includes exclusive sketches and storyboards, four pull-out posters, and an exclusive manga side story!

viz.com

Begin your Pokémon Adventure here in the Kanto region!

POKÉMON™
ADVENTURES
RED & BLUE BOX SET

Story by **HIDENORI KUSAKA**   *Art by* **MATO**

Includes **POKÉMON ADVENTURES** Vols. 1-7 and a collectible poster!

All your favorite Pokémon game characters jump out of the screen into the pages of this action-packed manga!

Red doesn't just want to train Pokémon, he wants to be their friend too. Bulbasaur and Poliwhirl seem game. But independent Pikachu won't be so easy to win over!

And watch out for Team Rocket, Red... They only want to be your enemy!

Start the adventure today!

The adventure continues in the Johto region!

POKÉMON™ ADVENTURES

GOLD & SILVER BOX SET

Includes POKÉMON ADVENTURES Vols. 8-14 and a collectible poster!

POKÉMON
ADVENTURES
GOLD & SILVER
Bonus Poster Inside!
GOLD & SILVER BOX SET:
POKÉMON ADVENTURES VOLUMES 8-14

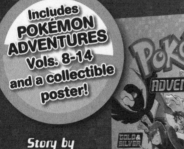

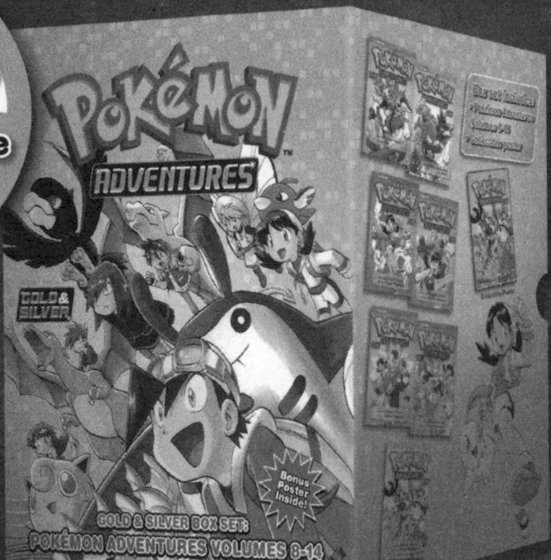

Story by
HIDENORI KUSAKA

Art by
MATO,
SATOSHI YAMAMOTO

More exciting Pokémon adventures starring Gold and his rival Silver! First someone steals Gold's backpack full of Poké Balls (and Pokémon!). Then someone steals Prof. Elm's Totodile. Can Gold catch the thief—or thieves?!

Keep an eye on Team Rocket, Gold... Could they be behind this crime wave?

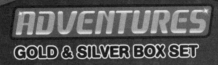

VIZ MEDIA
www.viz.com
PERFECT SQUARE
RATED A FOR ALL AGES
ratings.viz.com

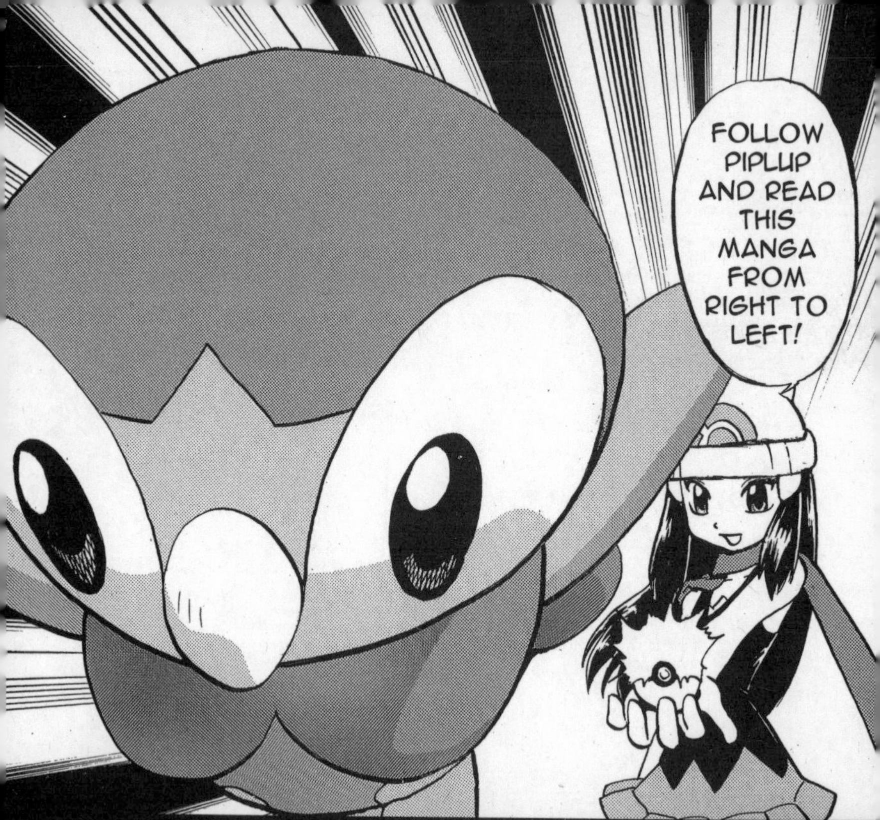
FOLLOW PIPLUP AND READ THIS MANGA FROM RIGHT TO LEFT!

THIS IS THE END OF THIS GRAPHIC NOVEL!

To properly enjoy this VIZ Media graphic novel, please turn it around and begin reading from right to left.

This book has been printed in the original Japanese format in order to preserve the orientation of the original artwork. Have fun with it!

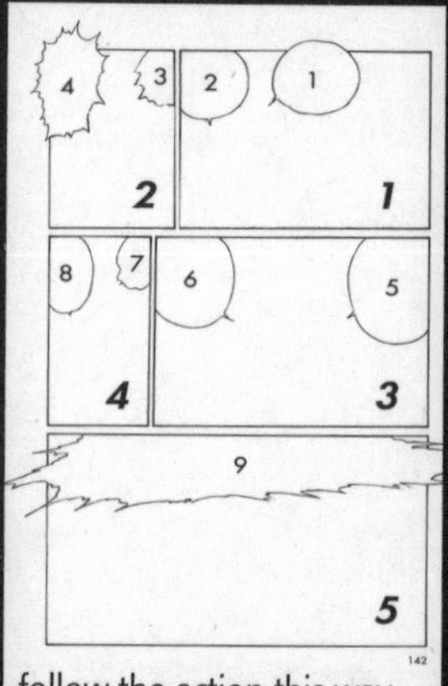
1
2
3
4
1
2
5
6
7
8
3
4
9
5
142
follow the action this way.